I0746361

# J.F.R. COATES

Text copyright 2024

Cover by Chromamancer

Axinstone
978-1-922061-79-9



J.F.R. Coates
Queensland, Australia

# AXINSTONE

## BOOK 1: THE DESTINY OF DRAGONS

### BY J.F.R. COATES

# FOREWORD

As any skilled seer will tell you, visions of the future are difficult to determine. They can appear vague and conflicting, with many branching possibilities. The weaker the seer, the more diverging those possibilities can spread.

When those visions come to pass, the eventual present may feel familiar yet different to those predictions. Enough stays the same, but there's often always that unexpected surprise to keep things interesting.

The fog of time has been lifted at last. Ten years after the first visions of *Axinstone*, the *Destiny of Dragons* trilogy has come from those visions to clear away the uncertainty and inconsistencies that were simply the result of a writer unable to properly express the story it was meant to be.

A decade is a long time as a writer. I have learned so much during that time and recognised that my telling of this trilogy was flawed. What better time to present a more definitive version that the tenth anniversary?

To those who are familiar with the story, there is much here that you will remember. The framework of the trilogy is still intact by design. I did not want to drift too far away from what made this story to begin with. But beyond there, there are plenty of changes.

The world should feel richer and bigger. Characters evolve and grow – or regress – in new ways. Some have changed their fate.

The first version of *Axinstone*, released way back in 2013, was an imperfect vision.

Here, then, is the present revealed. It is the *Destiny of Dragons* as it was meant to be.

Farenar awaits.

# ACKNOWLEDGEMENTS

I don't think I could ever properly thank everyone who has contributed to this series in the ten years since it was first released. So many people have shaped my writing career and skills that I would always risk leaving someone out.

I first have to thank my parents. Not only did they support my choice to become a writer, they also fostered and nurtured my interest in reading as a child. Without that, these stories would almost certainly not exist today.

I also have to thank those other writers who have inspired me over the years. From J.R.R. Tolkien to Philip Pullman, Neil Gaiman to Robin Hobb, my work does not exist in isolation. All of these great writers and more have had some inspiration on the stories I have wanted to tell.

I would also like to thank my husband. His support over the years has provided me with the capability to continue writing these stories.

And then there are my readers. Whether this is your first introduction to the *Destiny of Dragons* series, or you have been with me across the last ten years, thank you all! Without you, the writing process would be a vastly different experience.

And finally, it would be remiss of me not to mention those who supported my Kickstarter campaign to officially launch these 10 Year Anniversary Editions of the trilogy. Your support means the world to me.

Thank you everyone!

# CHAPTER ONE

**Anzig**

A leader of dragons was meant to be brave. To show no fear. To always be wise and calm.

I was none of those things.

My father's advice echoed through my head, adding to the cacophony of noise in my mind that only I could hear. As I looked down at the terrifying sight below me, I could not have felt further from being a leader. I was a scared dragonet, small and insignificant. I knew already that no one would listen to what I had to say, let alone respect me.

Representatives of the forty-two draconic clans packed the massive main chamber of royal Xital almost to capacity. My father, the ddraig of Laxtal, probably the greatest leader our clan had ever had, was busy fighting in the south of our territory, so he required me to take his place. I, as the representative for Clan Laxtal, was to speak to the clans about the war that was devastating our land.

I had witnessed it already. We had been travelling in the western regions of Laxtal's territory; a small group of dragons including my mother, whose adventuring spirit never let her stay in the confines of the central lair. Travelling through the forests there, we hadn't suspected any danger.

Then there was the ambush. My memories became vague after that.

Somehow, I had escaped the carnage, fleeing through the undergrowth on paw. I had thought my mother was following just behind me. It wasn't until silence fell and the threat was gone that I realised I was alone. With great reluctance I had retraced my steps. Nothing could have prepared me for my return to the scene of the ambush. The mutilated bodies of dragons I had known my entire life lay strewn across the small clearing between the trees. With no sign of our attackers, I scampered through the devastation, trying to find some signs of life in my companions.

That was when I had found her. Zhara, my mother, lying in the mud with her wings shattered and blood pooling around her. She still lived – just. The spark in her eyes was already fading as she somehow mustered the strength to look up at me. She whispered my name and then she was gone. I had cried that day. Forbidden tears I could never reveal to another.

I blinked myself back to the present. I stood on a small ledge at the entrance to the great chamber. My wings refused to unfurl, my claws gripping tight on the rigid stone beneath my paws.

"Just take a deep breath, Boss. Everything will be alright."

I turned to my left to face the silver dragon by my side and managed a snarl. Vinzent had no right to judge me like that. It was not his place to guide me, but his words forced me to focus on the noise and movement on the floor of the chamber. We looked to be the last clan to arrive. Even the representatives of Clan Xital were present.

I did my best to ignore Vinzent and put my thoughts to better use. It was no use reliving my mother's last moments. She had been gone a year already. A year of uncomfortable peace had followed the first skirmish of this new war. Humans had moved through the mountains and the foothills, disappearing before our warriors could engage. But there was conflict on our borders again.

"I'm not ready for this," I whispered to Carlee, my aging, brown-scaled mentor. She had protected me for longer than I could remember and had always been there to help me. Though I often resented that she still treated me like a hatchling who needed constant supervision,

I was grateful for her presence, but ashamed that she was necessary. I shouldn't still need her help.

"Anzig, listen to Vinzent. For once, the youngster is actually right," she admonished, just as quietly.

I turned my eyes down at the sight below. I couldn't quite bring myself to believe them. I half-opened my wings and contemplated flying down, but my legs didn't want to kick off from the ground yet.

"Go, Haeraig," Carlee said, seeing my hesitation and stressing on her use of my honorific. "Your father has complete confidence in you. The entire clan has confidence in you, or else you wouldn't be here. Just relax, you're a natural leader, you'll be fine."

A leader showed no fear. I straightened my neck and lifted my head, before fully extending my wings to slowly drift down to the floor. I tried to ignore all the pairs of eyes that turned to look at me. Without exception, they all turned away again as they submitted to me. As the representative of Clan Laxtal, I was one of the most powerful dragons in the chamber, no matter how I felt inside. They recognised me by the azure stone I wore around my neck; the icon of Laxtal. Only Clan Nixa and the Royal Xital Clan were more powerful.

As a result of my clan's standing, the Laxtal representative was reserved a position right at the front of the chamber. To our left was a single red dragon from Clan Nixa, the clan of magic. She was slight in stature, but the way she held herself showed that she was not short on confidence. I tried to straighten my posture to match hers. The reputation of Clan Laxtal depended on a confident and assured display from its representative.

To our right was a large emerald green dragon from Clan Nyri, the most powerful clan from the northern lands. Two smaller dragons, presumably his guards, stood by his side. I didn't know much about Clan Nyri, just that they came from the edge of the inhospitable and cold tundra to the far north.

In all, ten clans sat near the front of the chamber, with thirty-one filling in the space behind us. Clan Xital sat at the front, facing out to all the dragons gathered before them. They were the unquestionable leaders of dragonkind. They would make the final decision on what was going to occur. Forty-two clans in total. Judging by the noise that was quickly building behind me, each and every single one of them had sent a representative.

I tried to block everything out behind me. It was much easier if I just imagined that the only other dragons in the chamber were the five Xitals in front of me. I recognised Ddraig Tsona right away. The large dragon with golden scales was Xital's ddraig, making him the outright leader of dragonkind. He was unusually agitated. Every time I had seen Ddraig Tsona in the past, he had revealed no emotion, not moving at all except to speak. Now though, he was animated. His tail moved in a constant back and forth motion while he looked around the chamber with jerky movements. His wings opened slightly as though ready for flight. That even he showed so much fear did not help my confidence at all, and I sunk just a little lower where I stood.

I waited. Carlee and Vinzent, flanked either side of me, remained in silence. I tried to slow my breathing, but I could feel my heart racing away inside my chest. I began to regret eating before coming here. I should have waited until the feast after the gathering, but Carlee had convinced me that I would need the energy to shake off the lingering night's chill.

When Ddraig Tsona stepped forward from the other members of his clan, everyone fell silent. I could hear a fly buzzing somewhere near the ceiling, high above me. It was as though several hundred pairs of lungs had fallen still.

"Gathered ddraigs and haeraigs," the Xital ddraig said quietly. Because of how the chamber was shaped, I knew that even the dragons at the very back would still be able to hear the royal's words. "We have called you all here at the requests of Clan Nixa and Clan Laxtal. They both have important issues to discuss. I ask that you hear them both out before speaking. Clan Laxtal, if you would like to speak first."

I quailed under the direct gaze of Ddraig Tsona as he turned to look at me. I opened my mouth, but I was unable to speak. My heart felt like it was about to tear out of my chest. I shut my eyes for a moment and took a deep breath. Could I do this, or would I shame my father? I didn't know what I was going to say. Every planned word was gone, chased from my mind by the abject terror inside me.

I slowly released the air from my lungs and opened my eyes again. I stepped forward, my four paws suddenly clumsy and ungainly as I clambered up to the raised podium. I turned around and addressed everyone gathered.

"I am Haeraig Anzig of Clan Laxtal," I announced in a small voice. I doubted the volume carried much farther than the Nixan almost right in front of me. I tried to speak a little louder. "My father, Ddraig Astar, couldn't speak to you directly because bloodshed has broken out on our southern borders."

I paused for a moment to look up at everyone, half expecting someone to speak out, to chase away this pretender who thought he had any influence over them. Against the lightly sanded floor of the chamber, I could feel my paw shaking. I hoped no one else would notice, and I tried to stand a little more upright, desperately craving those extra few inches my diminutive frame lacked.

"We have been attacked without warning, and without provocation. We need the help of all of you to end the fighting, or else I fear we will lose, and many dragons of our clan will die," I pleaded, forcing myself to meet the eye of a dragon close to the back of the chamber. The yellow-eyed dragon turned away and looked to the ground.

"Is this an accusation of any dragon present, Haeraig Anzig?" Ddraig Tsona questioned, meeting my eyes as he looked over to me. I could not keep his powerful gaze for very long. I kept my eyes anywhere but towards him. I realised I had not actually mentioned who it was who had attacked my clan, and I felt foolish for it. A representative from every clan would be here. I was sure many of them – especially those that bordered Laxtal – would be confused or concerned that I was accusing someone of attacking us. But it was no dragon who threatened Laxtal.

"It was humans who attacked us. They have crossed the Gota-Sxinix and have moved into our territory," I explained, ignoring the whispers that began to spread through the chamber. I understood their concerns. The humans beyond the mountains on our western borders had not been in open war with dragonkind for many generations. In combat they were dangerous adversaries with their advantage in size, numbers, and in the weapons that they wielded. Unless all the dragon clans united, we would have difficulty in defeating such a threat.

To my right, Ddraig Tsona let out a quiet hiss and tilted his head to the side. Behind him, the other Xital dragons had remained impassive, barely doing so much as blinking, certainly not reacting with shock or surprise. Their behaviour was disturbing. It was as though they had known exactly what I was going to say and had been prepared for it, and that their ddraig's reactions were just for show.

"You are sure of this, Haeraig?" Ddraig Tsona asked, still holding his head at an angle. I could only nod in response. He hissed again, this time descending into a deep growl. "Thank you then for telling us about this. If Clan Nixa could come and speak now. Let us hear what they have to say."

In gratitude I retreated away from the front of the chamber so I could return to Carlee and Vinzent. As I sat down the Nixan confidently strode up to take her place next to Tsona. Her dark red scales glittered regally in the sunlight streaming in from above. Even next to Ddraig Tsona, the most powerful of all ddraigs, the small Nixan's confidence and poise was remarkable.

"I am Haeraig Zeena of Nixa, and we may actually have an answer for Haeraig Anzig's problem," she said in a loud and powerful voice. My eyes widened. How could she already have a solution to the human invasion?

Haeraig Zeena took a moment to pause and take a deep breath. "The Axinstone was not lost as we told you, we are not that careless, and Ddraig Krateos was rather disappointed that some dragons actually believed this lie. It was stolen from us, and we now know who by. A human called George, who we have learned answers to the ddraig of the Kernow humans, possesses our stone." Zeena stopped speaking again to look around the chamber, her eyes lingering on any dragon who did not drop their gaze.

I had heard of the Axinstone before. There wasn't a dragon who hadn't. It was a large stone, little more than a shard of rock emblazoned with the burning shadow of a dragon's head. It was used to strengthen the magic of all nearby Nixan dragons. Given that only dragons from the Nixan clan could ever wield magic, and the Axinstone held no other use, no ddraig had ever felt the need or the desire to try and take the powerful object from Nixa.

"We believe his human-Nixans are using the Axinstone to increase this human's power over his own kind. If what Haeraig Anzig has said is true, then this has given him the confidence to attack us too." Again, Haeraig Zeena stopped, but this time it was not through her choice. A murmur of disquiet had spread from one of the corners of the chamber and had quickly grown loud enough to distract the Nixan.

Ddraig Tsona hissed quietly and stepped forward. I did not like the look in his eyes. He was furious at the interruption. "Does anyone have something to say about this?" he asked. I thought I could hear a threatening undertone to his voice, as though he was daring anyone to answer and risk his anger.

The murmurs ceased instantly, but then one lone voice emerged from towards the back of the chamber, among the lesser clans. "Human-Nixans? Are they..."

The dragon who had spoken must have realised Ddraig Tsona's anger, or another dragon near him had forced him quiet, as his voice petered out pitifully. Haeraig Zeena understood what the concern was about though. "Humans who can use magic? Yes," she said, finishing the dragon's unfinished question as Ddraig Tsona stepped back again. "We have known of their existence for many years now. But they are irrelevant. All that matters is taking back the Axinstone. Without it, perhaps the humans would have to retreat. We could solve both our problems here."

"Do you know where the human is keeping your Axinstone?" Ddraig Tsona asked, stepping forward so that he was level with the Nixan. He did not look at her though, instead keeping his eyes towards the back of the chamber, unblinking and unmoving. I resisted the urge to turn and see what he was looking at.

Haeraig Zeena turned her head to look at the side of Ddraig Tsona's head as she replied. "We do," she said simply. She paused again, as though waiting for some kind of reaction to come from the Xital ddraig, but he remained completely impassive. It was as if he hadn't even heard her, or was preoccupied with more important thoughts, though I could not think what could be more critical than this. I was not the only one to sense Ddraig Tsona's lack of concern. By my side, Carlee was restless, though her inferior position within the clan meant she was unable to speak her worries.

After a pause of over ten seconds, Ddraig Tsona blinked twice and shook his head. For the first time I noticed a strange blemish on his scales between the ring of horns on his head. A small circle of black that reflected no light was affixed to him. Then he glanced at Haeraig Zeena and tilted his head slightly in request for her to continue, hiding the patch of black from view. As though nothing untoward had happened, the Nixan obliged.

"We understand the Axinstone to be within the human's lair on a small island well beyond the Sxinix, in a territory called Trevena," she said. "It won't be easy to recover, but with Clan Laxtal's news in mind, I believe this to be a very important issue."

Ddraig Tsona looked sharply across at Haeraig Zeena with a quiet growl from the back of his throat. "I decide what is important, Haeraig. Return to your place," he said quietly, only just loud enough for me to hear it.

The Nixan bowed her head in apology, and without once looking up, returned to the space to my left. For just a moment she caught my eye, and I could see how truly scared she was. Then, to my surprise, she looked away before I had chance to do so. I continued to glance in her direction as Ddraig Tsona began speaking again. I heard nothing of what the Xital ddraig said until Carlee nudged me in the ribs.

"Pay attention," she hissed under her breath so that no one else could hear her. No one was permitted to speak when the Xitals were, even if they had something important to add. Rebuked, I turned back to face Ddraig Tsona and try and work out what he was talking about.

"...have any suggestions?" he prompted, practically glaring around the chamber in an oddly venomous fashion, as though he wanted the floor to remain silent, without suggestion or idea.

It was an open forum now. Anyone could speak without first seeking permission from the Xitals. "Why don't we just attack back?" someone called out from near the back of the chamber. "They attacked us, so why don't we gather our full strength and fly on their lands. We've defeated the human armies before. We can do it again."

"Tchaa, no, that would never work," a dragon near the front of the chamber protested. I recognised him as Aranat, the ddraig of Clan Axaatl, the closest clan to Laxtal's eastern borders. I could not see Ddraig Aranat as I was unable to see over the heads of the other dragons around me, but I knew him to be a powerfully built blue dragon. A few years prior I had heard that he had wrested control of his clan from its previous ddraig through a contest of strength. "I believe I know which lair it is that Haeraig Zeena refers to. I have seen this place with my own eyes. Even if every dragon alive were to join this attack, we still would not succeed."

"Then what do you suggest we do?" the first dragon challenged. Given how far back in the chamber he was, I doubted he had much right to speak to Ddraig Aranat like that. The Axaatl drake didn't rebuke the lesser dragon at all, though a few surrounding the two did hiss and growl quietly.

"I don't know," Ddraig Aranat replied calmly. "I wasn't suggesting an idea, just saying that yours can't possibly work. The loss of life would be too great, even in the unlikely event of success."

"You heard what Haeraig Zeena said. We need to get the Axinstone back. Risks must be taken in war," another dragon said in a raised voice, somewhere off to my right, and a little further back.

"A risk must have a chance of a positive outcome. This idea does not," Ddraig Aranat rebuked, turning his anger to the second dragon. "If it's allowed, then it shall be nothing more than a suicide mission. The humans would probably kill us all before we laid a single claw inside their lair."

There were a few seconds of silence as everyone waited for each other to offer further suggestions. What actions could we take? I certainly couldn't think of anything to add, and nor it seemed could anyone else. We seemed to be left with just one option, and like Ddraig Aranat, I believed it would be nothing but suicide to launch a direct attack on the humans.

"If no one has another suggestion, then I have no choice but to authorise an attack on the human lair," Ddraig Tsona declared with a resigned sigh. "Some action must be taken today. Matters are too serious to wait for another council."

I wondered why we had to send the bulk of dragonkind's warriors to retrieve the Axinstone. If just a few survived the attack, even the Axinstone would be unable to help the survivors. The humans would be free to pick off the remaining clans at will. Surely we would be better off sending a couple of dragons to try and claim it. It meant fewer dragons would die, and they probably had the same sort of chance to recover the Axinstone as an entire army would.

"Wait," I said, before I was even aware of what I had done. Every single pair of eyes was on me. I could feel them boring into the back of my head. All five of the Xitals glared at me, and I immediately began to regret speaking up. However, if I said nothing then I would be disgracing Laxtal and my father; he would never trust me with anything again.

"Yes, Haeraig?" Ddraig Tsona said impatiently.

"There is another way. If we send a small group to the human lair, a dozen at most, then if Ddraig Aranat is correct, they will have the same chance of success. If they fail, we lose fewer dragons." I spoke quickly, too quickly, but the pressure of having everyone's attention on me was overwhelming. Ddraig Tsona's eyes widened, but whether in disdain or respect I could not tell.

At least one dragon was not amused by my suggestion though, and she loudly objected. "That is absolutely ridiculous. You would send a dozen dragons against the entire human army? That is nothing short of idiocy."

I felt like curling up and tucking my head under my wing, but some small, vestigial sense of pride kept me standing, though I could not stop my head from sinking down lower.

"No, I don't think it's such a bad idea," Ddraig Aranat commented to my surprise. I noticed it was to Ddraig Tsona's complete shock also. I hadn't expected anyone to agree with my opinion. I barely agreed with it myself. "I doubt Haeraig Anzig was suggesting sending a dozen dragons to fight the humans. We'd send them to steal the Axinstone, just as they stole it from Nixa."

Hardly any dragons sided with the Axaatl ddraig. In fact, the only one I could see was the Nixan haeraig. I hadn't even thought of Ddraig Aranat's suggestion. My only concern had been minimising the number of casualties if the mission failed. Ddraig Aranat could turn my quite ridiculous idea into a true possibility. Though I hadn't really done anything, I still felt a little pride that the older ddraig had been able to build upon my suggestion. It was just enough to inject a little confidence into my posture, with my head rising back up as I stood tall again.

"Where is your sense of honour?" the same dragon said from somewhere near the middle of the chamber. "You would rather steal something than fight for it? I for one refuse to be part of any such tactic, and I hope I do not find myself in the minority, or else dragonkind would be the lesser for it."

"The humans showed us no honour in stealing it from Clan Nixa," Ddraig Aranat said with patience and calmness. "I don't see why we should feel obliged to show them honour when they will not return the favour."

"That is not their way," the ness whined. "Humans are not an honourable species. We should not sink to their level, or we would be no better than them." I had the impression the ness was losing the argument, but I didn't believe she would give in easily, and nor would many of the other dragons in the chamber.

"In a choice between dishonour and death, I would choose dishonour every time," Ddraig Aranat said. A few uneasy mutterings broke out at his words, but the Axaatl ddraig was not perturbed. "I urge the Xital Clan to not disregard Haeraig Anzig's suggestion just because it could be deemed dishonourable. There are times when we must ignore our honour and pride to undertake acts of theft, and other less worthy deeds."

Ddraig Tsona had been intently following the argument of the Axaatl dragon and the other ness from towards the back of the chamber. Now that Ddraig Aranat had turned the talk back to him, he seemed caught unawares. It was a few moments before he even reacted to the sudden silence.

"Yes, we shall take that in mind. If there are no further suggestions, we will keep Haeraig Anzig's plan in consideration," he said, taking a step back towards the other four Xitals. Not a single dragon spoke. After a pause of almost a minute, Ddraig Tsona nodded. "We of Clan Xital shall discuss this in private and will return with our answer shortly." Without a further word, the five Xitals left the chamber through a small opening behind them. The instant Ddraig Tsona's tail vanished into the darkness, everyone started talking at once.

"See, Boss? What did I tell you? Everything went alright," Vinzent said in a low whisper. I chose to ignore his words. I closed my eyes and tried to slow my breathing down to an acceptable pace. I wasn't even aware of the approach of someone else until Carlee hit me with her tail.

I opened my eyes to see the Nixan standing in front of me. She was nervously smiling, and I couldn't help but notice that she never once attempted to meet my eyes. "I understand that honour means nothing in war. Your suggestion will save thousands of lives, and if your actions lead to the recovery of the Axinstone, my father will grant your clan great rewards," she said softly, before placing her head on my shoulder in a sign of affection. I was too surprised to even move, and I let her keep her head there. "You have my thanks, and that of my clan."

I knew I should have responded. My tongue felt glued to the roof of my mouth, and I could only offer a quiet grunt of acknowledgement. I bowed my head as she pulled away.

"We shall speak again soon, Haeraig Anzig, regardless of what Xital decides for us," the Nixan said. With that, she retreated to her place to my left. She shot a shy glance across at me for a moment, before looking away and staring resolutely towards the front, where the Xitals had gone.

"Not bad at all, Boss," Vinzent whispered with a sly look I did not like in the slightest. "She's quite nice, isn't she? Nixan, yes, and a haeraig, but I'm sure her father and Ddraig Astar could arrange something, if you wanted."

I turned and growled at the young dragon, my tongue unsticking as nerves were replaced by irritation. "You keep those thoughts to yourself in future, or you'll find yourself in serious trouble. Do you understand me?" I threatened, keeping my voice to a quiet hiss so that no other but Vinzent and Carlee would be able to hear.

Vinzent nodded, though I doubted he had taken the warning seriously. His pale-blue eyes were showing no sign of apology or regret for his actions. If anything, he was still quite amused. His eyes lingered on Haeraig Zeena until I firmly stood on his paw and butted him on the underside of his jaw with my blunt horns.

"Hey, that hurt," Vinzent complained, trying to pull away from me, but the pressure I was placing on his paw prevented him from going anywhere.

"Good. Now concentrate on where you are. And please, for once, act like a mature dragon," I said, releasing Vinzent's paw and staring him in the eyes as he stepped back from me. I could tell he was fighting the urge to come up with some retort, but fortunately for his sake he was able to restrain himself. Sometimes I forgot that Vinzent wasn't old enough to be considered an adult. He was over two years my junior, and he still lapsed into immaturity.

Only when Vinzent turned and stared at the ground did I look away. There was a good deal of restlessness around us, thankfully none of which was caused by Vinzent's immaturity. Instead, all the talk was on what the Xital dragons would decide, for it could ultimately decide the eventual fate of the species. Or at least, that seemed the opinion of the few clans nearby. The fact that my suggestion could be the one chosen dizzied me. Not that there had been much in the way of alternative proposals.

After an anxious wait that felt much longer than it was, the five Xitals returned to the main chamber. This time it was not Ddraig Tsona who stepped forward to address the gathered dragons, but a slender ness with white scales and green eyes. I believed she was haeraig, but her name escaped my nervous mind. The ddraig of Xital remained with the other three of his clan, his tail twitching in agitation.

"On a count of four to one, we have chosen on Haeraig Anzig's suggestion to retrieve the Axinstone," the Xital haeraig announced. I was so shocked by what she had said that I almost missed the rest. "I ask the ddraigs and haeraigs of the ten ruling clans to meet us here after the sun's peak to discuss who we should send. That will be all."

Leaving it at that, the Xitals turned again and left. I didn't even know why Ddraig Tsona and the other three had felt the need to come back out, so short a time they were there, contributing nothing. Their behaviour in general was most unusual. In my mind, the fact that they preferred my suggestion confirmed something was amiss. I didn't know what, and I didn't know any reason for it to be. I could not understand why so many more experienced ddraigs had been unable to better my hasty and ill-thought-out idea.

Neither Carlee nor Vinzent appeared to share my concerns. Though Vinzent's were a little more muted, both had nothing to say to me but praise. I did not pay attention to either of them. Did I deserve the praise? I couldn't shake the feeling everything that had happened was planned. But planned by whom? For what reason? Again, I could not begin to imagine.

I looked up to the sky, visible through the entry at the top of the cavern, where some dragons were already starting to leave. Why couldn't I be full of pride at what I had done? Why did I have to suspect that another dragon had meant for things to turn out this way?

"Are you alright Anzig?" Carlee asked, breaking into my musings. I looked across at her and sighed.

"Yeah, just a little cold," I lied, turning my head back towards the sky. I couldn't stop my voice sounding as dull as my thoughts. "Let's get back into the sun. I'll feel better out there."

Without waiting for an answer, I spread my wings and flew up towards the fresh air. I could hear the other two following close behind, but I did not slow down for them to catch up, nor did I once look back.

I emerged into the sunlight high above the ground. The Xital lair spread out over a great distance. Many interconnected caves were pocketed in small rocky crags scattered throughout the otherwise flat terrain. The main lair was visible from many miles away, a lone mountain towering up from the flats, marking the central point of draconic society. It was the oldest populated lair, and one of the most visually striking. The entry to the main chamber, situated halfway up the mountain and completely surrounded by sheer cliff walls, was inaccessible to anything without wings.

I had barely left the shadows before I heard someone call my name. It was a voice I could not fail to recognise, and it belonged to a ness who had been my near-constant companion since my hatching day. She was my closest and most trusted friend – Keita. She had waited for me on a small ledge not too far from the entry to the chamber under the watchful eyes of two guardian dragons. I wouldn't have been too surprised if she had eavesdropped on what was being said.

Slowly, Keita flew up to me from where she had been waiting, giving Vinzent and Carlee the chance to catch up. As the masses of dragons began swarming out from the chamber, they buffeted into Keita in complete disregard of her presence, forcing her to dive lower again. I was concerned by their disrespect and swooped down to join her.

"You shouldn't let them bully you like that," I told her once I was by her side. But Keita just looked away with her pale eyes. She had always had difficulty with her sight, having injured her right eye when she was a tiny dragonet. The damage had never fully healed; as a consequence, she had little ability to judge distance. She slowed her flight slightly so that she flew to the right of my tail before she answered.

"They're ddraigs. They have to respect you, but they have no reason to do the same to me," Keita said, staring down to the ground.

I looked up towards Vinzent and Carlee, who had not flown down to join us. Instead, they continued to fly at the same height. "You can be what you want to be," I said, looking back at Keita, as always entranced by the unique beauty of her partially translucent red wings. It was my humble opinion that Keita was the most beautiful ness I had ever laid eyes upon. Though I had rarely given thought to the matter, I knew one day I would ask her to become my mate. I did not know whether Keita felt the same way for me. I knew she loved me as a lifelong friend and companion, but it was impossible to tell if she could love me as a mate too. I had always been too nervous to ask her.

Keita must have been aware of my gaze, for she did not look towards me. Her eyes squinted as she tried to look up at something above us. There was a momentary flash of alarm on her face. Too late did I hear the rush of wind against wings. Too late did I feel the slight shadow against my back. I had no time to move. The next I knew I was falling with a dragon on my back, pinning my wings in place, preventing me from going anywhere. The more I struggled, the tighter my assailant's grip became.

I could not hear any pursuit. No one was chasing to help. I didn't have time to think why. The ground grew closer at an alarming rate. At the last moment, I could hear my attacker flare their wings, slowing us instantly. Then they released me, sending me tumbling down to the ground. I rolled twice and clutched my head in my paws.

"I got you that time, Ziggy!"

I groaned. I knew exactly who it was, and I should have guessed earlier from the manner of the attack. Only one dragon I knew used such tactics when they fought. I looked up to see the distinctive lilac scales of my younger cousin, Ellian. She gently descended, her wings stretched wide to glide down to the ground. She looked rather pleased with herself. I hissed at her, but otherwise ignored her smug look.

In complete disregard to my foul mood, Ellian lay down next to me, her head resting on her paws. "Well, how was it in there?" the lilac dragonet asked, her voice sounding irritatingly like my father's. "Will Ddraig Astar need to send me next time?"

"If you want to, then I'm sure I can arrange something," I replied. I wasn't sure if I was being sarcastic or hopeful. Though my earlier fear had abated, I was really unsettled by what had gone on. I didn't know what to expect from the meeting with the Xitals and the ddraigs of the ruling clans. I hoped it didn't feel like it was all happening according to a plan I was not aware of.

No matter what I thought, Ellian knew what she wanted, and that was most certainly not the opportunity to represent our clan in an official position. "You're being silly," she said with a mischievous smile. "I'm too young to be taken seriously."

She was right of course. She was barely into adulthood, having turned eighteen the previous month. She was only a month older than Vinzent, but while the silver-scaled dragon had shown few signs of maturing, my cousin had already proven herself to be mature beyond her years. Though she may consider it otherwise, I secretly believed she was far better suited to the role as Laxtal haeraig than I was. If she was too young to be taken seriously, then my twenty years were also too young for the machinations of politics.

At that moment, Vinzent and Carlee landed a few feet away, and I gently returned to my paws. Ellian quickly scarpered off to join Vinzent. The two talked together in quiet tones. I watched as Ellian rested her head on Vinzent's shoulder. The silver dragonet looked over at me with a touch of alarm for a moment before returning to their private conversation.

The two had always been close friends. Ellian had known Vinzent for about as long as I had, but I couldn't help feeling surprised at this apparent latest development in their relationship. If their closeness was them moving beyond friendship, I wasn't sure what I really felt. Partly I was worried. Vinzent would be an adult in barely a month, but they were both still so young. However, I knew most Laxtal dragons, and I believed that out of all of them, Vinzent was the one dragon I would be happy for my cousin to become mates with.

I turned from them and looked up at the ness I desired to become my mate. Keita was still descending. A lack of ability to judge distance was not good for aerial creatures, and she had to be a lot more careful when flying near the ground, especially when landing.

Once she was on the ground, she tucked her tail behind her hind legs and sat down, gazing up towards the dragons who still flew overhead. I was about to move across to her, but Carlee stepped in front of me, cutting me off.

"You seem troubled," she said simply, placing her body in the way of where I wanted to go. Her tail wrapped around my foreleg when I tried to back away. "What's the matter?" she asked, seemingly determined to know why I was so distracted, which I knew I was.

I knew I could trust Carlee with any of my worries. My father trusted her with his concerns, though I never heard any of what they were, unless he told me himself, which was rarely. Whatever I would tell her, she would keep to herself until her dying moment, if that were necessary.

"It all seemed planned," I said quietly, so that no one else, not even Keita, would be able to hear me speak. "Everything that happened in there, everything that was said, it sounded like it was organised, and I wasn't told about it. I don't think Ddraig Aranat was either."

Carlee didn't appear all that surprised, but she was unable to give her thoughts about it as Keita had stood up and was walking towards us. Instead, Carlee said, "You did well in there. I think your father will be proud. You saved the lives of many dragons today." She bared her teeth as she smiled, then turned away, allowing Keita to approach me unhindered.

We did not rub heads like Vinzent and Ellian. I kept my affections for Keita hidden from all others. It was expected of me, as the clan haeraig, to mate with a ness who held a higher, more powerful position within the clan. It was only through the strength of Keita's father and her friendship with me that she held any sort of respect. Without those, she would be one of the lesser dragons in Laxtal.

"Azlak wants to speak with you," Keita said softly. She lay down on the grass in front of me, spreading her wings to absorb some heat from the sun. I frowned. Azlak was an enigmatic dragon, greatly scorned and rarely respected. He was a Laxtal with magic, something that was meant to be impossible. Only Nixans were meant to possess magic, and yet Azlak was very much a Laxtal dragon. Marin, Azlak's father, was one of my father's strongest and most powerful supporters. He was proud of being the latest in a long line of pure Laxtal dragons.

I resisted the temptation to lie down next to Keita. Azlak's words were usually too important to ignore. The diminutive gold-scaled dragon had an erratic, but usually correct, ability to see into the future. As a result, his advice was always invaluable.

"Did he say what it was about?" I asked Keita, but she lazily shook her head. Her eyes were closed, and she looked like she was asleep. "Lie closer to the fire tonight," I told her, smiling to myself. She didn't reply. I stood there watching the gentle rise and fall of her chest as she breathed for a few moments, before turning my eyes away with regret.

I turned to Carlee, who was still standing a few feet away, waiting for me. "Watch over her, and bring her back when she's ready," I said, tilting my head down to Keita.

"Of course," Carlee said. She settled down in the soft grass and spread her wings too.

With one last, lingering look back at Keita, half-hidden by the long grass, I left the two nesses alone to doze and absorb the heat of the sun. I ambled towards Vinzent and Ellian, who had their backs turned to me as they sat together, looking out over the Xital lands. Ellian's head rested upon Vinzent's shoulder, and his wing wrapped around her body.

"Vinzent, I want you to come with me," I said, making both dragons jump in fright. Vinzent pulled his wing off Ellian with an embarrassed look on his face. "Ellian, you're to look after Keita with Carlee."

"Must I?" Vinzent grumbled, but quickly changed his mind. "See you later," he muttered sulkily to Ellian. The young silver dragon did not once look up. His eyes were solely on my paws as he bashfully approached. It looked as though he half expected me to attack him for showing affection to my cousin.

"Wait there," I commanded Vinzent, barging by him to approach my cousin. Ellian held her head high and defiant, though she didn't meet my eye to challenge my decision.

"No further," I warned her, keeping my voice quiet so it wouldn't carry back to Vinzent. Certainly not to Carlee. I did not want the veteran ness fretting about Ellian and Vinzent's burgeoning relationship. "You're both too young to consider mates yet. My father would not be happy if I let this grow."

Ellian sniffed softly, keeping her head turned away from me. "You're not my brother, Ziggy. You don't have to act like one," she said bluntly, a touch of annoyance in her voice.

"Since when have you not treated me like one?" I asked gently. Ellian had been orphaned from a very young age, and ever since then she had been placed in the care of my father. Her real brother had been old enough to fend for himself and he had gone out to live with the nomadic dragons, but he had been forbidden from taking his only sister with him. As my father was usually busy, it had fallen to my mother and me to care for my younger cousin. We had grown up as siblings, and it hurt me to hear Ellian throw that away almost casually. I could tell it had hurt her too.

My cousin hung her head. Her eyes fixed onto the soft ground between my forepaws. "I'm sorry. I didn't mean it that way." She took a deep breath and let it back out as a deep and prolonged sigh. "I'll try. I'll tell Vinzent too. We'll wait."

I thought it best not to say anything then, but to silently acknowledge her decision. I simply inclined my head and turned to take to wing. She made no attempt to follow me. From a dozen paces away, Vinzent launched from the ground, his powerful wings allowing him to easily keep pace with my ascent. He maintained his sullen silence.

That gave plenty of opportunity to mull over the worries that gnawed at my gut. I doubted Azlak had anything to share that would improve my mood. The seer only ever had bad news and ill omens to share.

# CHAPTER TWO

**Ellian**

Carlee and Keita didn't need my protection. I knew Anzig simply wanted to separate me from Vinzent. I took to wing almost the moment my cousin disappeared into the pale blue sky. He returned to the cluster of low hills used by Laxtal representatives, so I banked my wings and flew in the opposite direction, towards the great lone mountain that dominated the Xital landscape.

I longed to put some distance between the ground and me. The air in Xital was stuffy and stuck up, much like the dragons who called the mountain home. I longed to return to Laxtal, but duty to my clan came first. For as long as I was needed in Xital, I would remain. Though it felt like my purpose was simply to watch my cousin and learn from him, I had yet to even speak to anyone from outside my clan.

From the air, the Xital lair looked like a series of low hills ringed around the lone mountain. Below ground was a vast network of tunnels and caves, providing the lodgings for hundreds of visiting dragons. A few of those caves were disconnected from the others, reserved for clans of great importance, such as Laxtal. Further separate were the caves beneath the mountain itself, where the dragons of the royal Xital clan resided. Few dragons not of that clan were ever permitted to set paw or wing within those caves.

I lazily scanned the ground as I flew higher towards the light, wispy clouds. The air was thinner and easier to breathe, with less weight of pompous superiority threatening to drown the lungs of all who visited the royal clan's territories.

Thermals lifted me higher still, and I swirled with no destination in mind. Voices from far below fluttered up to my ears, but I ignored them all. It was nice to escape the prideful boasts for a while.

The wind carried me towards the summit of the great peak. Above the wide entrance to the grand chamber were more sheer cliffs, but amongst the clouds were a series of plateaus and ridges with a sparse covering of hardy grasses and bushes. A few birds nested amongst this rough foliage, screeching at me as I swooped down to land nearby.

This high up, I had a fantastic view of the rolling landscape stretching away to the west. I could not see the distant Sxinix Mountains, which had long been the boundary between human and draconic lands. That was the border that had been breached by the invading humans, but here in Xital, that threat seemed distant and small. I could only hope that the ddraigs and haeraigs of the council would take Anzig's warning seriously.

I was not alone.

My tailtip flicked in irritation. Two voices drifted across from the next ridge, the speakers hidden behind the fold in the rock. I wrinkled my muzzle and tried to ignore them, but the whispered voices were annoyingly urgent and insistent, burrowing into my mind. Neither dragon seemed to have heard me approach.

"…need to inform him that there's been a change of plan," one of the speakers said. This one was haughty and a male drake, surely one of the Xital clan. The voice was familiar, but I couldn't be certain who it belonged to.

"You know he won't like this," the second said, this one a female ness. Her distinguished voice also gave her away as a Xital.

"There's nothing we can do about that now," the drake replied, a growl of irritation coming to his voice. A paw or a tail thudded against stone. "We could do no more without arousing suspicion."

Intrigued, I took a couple of cautious steps closer, taking great care of where I put my paws. I didn't want to make a sound.

"If this plan works…"

The male snarled, cutting across the female's protest. "It won't work. I will make sure of it."

"All the same, it makes me uneasy," the ness said. "We're gambling a lot on this."

"It will be worth it, trust me. Not only will it fail, it will also weaken one of the great clans who could oppose us." A moment of silence fell between the two hidden dragons, giving me the opportunity to creep forward a little closer. I wondered what they discussed, if it was anything to do with the meeting in the chamber below. A couple more paces and I would be able to catch a glimpse of the two conspirators.

"Come. Let's go," the male said. Wings flapped and they were gone.

I suppressed a hiss of frustration as I scampered around the corner, into the narrow ravine in which they had been resting. I caught a brief glimpse of scales glinting in the sunlight as the two dragons soared away. One was white, the other gold. I could see nothing more of them to identify who they might have been.

"What was that all about?" I muttered to myself. It stank of Xital plotting and scheming, another one of their plans to cement their power at the top of dragonkind. That came of no surprise. They were always scheming. With no one around to see me, I allowed myself to sneer in their direction, making a rude gesture with my forepaw.

The summit of the mountain had not given me the peace and quiet I had hoped for. Instead, my mind swirled with questions, of which I would not be able to find an answer. I had no idea what had been discussed in the meeting of the ddraigs and haeraigs, so I couldn't be sure what plan the Xitals had in mind. Perhaps Anzig would know more, and I could ask him about it after he finished talking to the seer.

A small patch of grass had been trodden on and crushed where the two Xitals had sat. The scents they left behind were elusive and vague, giving me no hints as to their identities. I sat on my haunches amongst the crushed grass and looked out across the land below, now facing more to the north. Somewhere beyond the horizon was Laxtal and home.

My little corner of peace was breached once again. Wingbeats approached from below as someone flew up from the ground. I let out a little growl of irritation, but quickly snapped my mouth shut as I recognised the red scales of Haeraig Zeena of Nixa. She was alone, and she settled down on the grass in front of me, her hind paws touching down first.

I bowed my head in respect to the Nixan. "Haeraig Zeena. I didn't expect to see you here."

"You are a difficult dragon to find, Ellian of Laxtal," the haeraig replied. A smile touched her short muzzle. Even though I was the taller of the two nesses, the Nixan still found a way to position herself so that she looked down on me.

I blinked in surprise. "You were looking for me, Haeraig?"

Haeraig Zeena nodded. "I have been seeking information from your clan with questions that might be considered rude to ask your haeraig."

I was immediately on my guard. My tail tightened around my hind legs, my wings rustling against my back. Nixa and Laxtal were on friendly terms, but we were still rivals. We were both ruling clans beneath the might of Xital, vying for their favour. "What questions?"

Haeraig Zeena seemed to recognise the awkward situation she had put me in. She inclined her head again and sat down opposite me. "I do not ask for information about your clan. Nothing that Nixa could use against your uncle. It is merely a curiosity on my behalf, and that of my father."

"I will try to indulge your curiosity," I said hesitantly, still unsure just what I was agreeing to.

The haeraig's question surprised me. "Why are you here?"

I twitched my tailtip. "To attend the council and to inform Xital of the human invasion."

Haeraig Zeena hissed softly. "Yes, that is why Laxtal has sent dragons to the council, but why are you here, Ellian? Why has one of dragonkind's most powerful clans sent two dragonets and an inexperienced haeraig?"

My mouth hung open. I hadn't meant to show my teeth, but Haeraig Zeena did not react to the momentary display of aggression. I quickly snapped my mouth shut again and regained my composure. "Haeraig Anzig is here in his father's place. I was chosen to join him as, until my cousin takes a mate, I am expected to represent our clan should I be needed. Vinzent is to be a bodyguard for the ddraig, so he must learn from Carlee. We may be young, but we are capable."

The Nixan kneaded her forepaws into the dry, dusty dirt. "This council is the biggest gathering of dragons for a generation. Ddraig Astar is a dragon respected from the Sxinix to the Snowcaps. With all respect to you and your haeraig, why are you here, and your ddraig is not?"

I tilted my head in confusion. The haeraig's questioning was strange, and I didn't understand her motivations. "Ddraig Astar was meant to be here, but the day before he was to leave Laxtal, we got word of a human raid in our territory. He was forced to leave to lead our army."

Haeraig Zeena's eyes lit up. That had been the answer she had sought. "Curious, isn't it?" she said slowly. "The most important day in dragonkind's history, and one of our most powerful dragons is called away to defend from a human raid. Unfortunate timing, don't you think?"

"You think this might have been planned?" Suddenly the late morning sunlight didn't seem so warm on my scales. I glanced up to make sure no clouds had drifted across the sun, but the sky was still almost pure blue, with only wispy strips of lightest white to blemish it.

"It is something to be wary of," Haeraig Zeena said. She also looked up to the sky, following my gaze. "I do not know what is to come of this meeting, but it would be better if your haeraig was made aware of the possibility. I have no evidence to defend my claim, so I did not bring it up in the council. But if dragons are working with humans, then we fly in turbulent winds. Be careful who you speak around, Ellian."

I bit down on my tongue. The conversation I had overheard could have been related to Haeraig Zeena's theories, but it could also have been unrelated. Like the Nixan, I had no evidence for my concerns. I decided to keep silent about the Xitals. The royal clan was stuffy and proud, but I did not think them capable of conspiring with humans against Laxtal, even in secret.

"What should I do?" I said eventually.

"Keep your eyes open and alert," Haeraig Zeena said. She inclined her head just slightly. "These are dangerous times, Ellian. Our seers warn that dragonkind may turn on itself, rather than facing this threat from across the mountains. If this meeting at noon does not progress well, then our clans should stay in close contact. Your haeraig and ddraig must know of these threats."

"I will tell Haeraig Anzig as soon as I can be alone with him," I said, returning the incline of my head to the Nixan. "I should return, before my cousin wonders where I am."

"And I, too. I must prepare for this meeting," Haeraig Zeena replied. She flared her wings and rose to her paws. "Fly safe, Ellian. I am sure we will cross paths again."

With that, the Nixan took to the sky. She soon faded into the pale blue expanse. I tried to track her movement for as long as I could, but I lost her long before she reached the ground. With a quiet sigh, I spread my wings and kicked off into the vast emptiness. With the wind beneath me, I soared.

# CHAPTER THREE

**Anzig**

I left Vinzent at the surface, giving the silver dragonet strict instructions to stay in the sun by the mouth of the cave. He was not to return to Ellian, and he sullenly agreed. He would not disobey a direct order from his haeraig.

The underground network of caverns was brightly lit with flickering lamps that emitted a discomforting scent, one that made me feel a little nauseous if I stayed close to them for too long. The shadows they cast wavered in the uneven light, lengthening and shortening constantly as I paced deeper below the surface.

Though there was space for two dozen dragons to comfortably rest within the Laxtal caves, Azlak had taken the smallest, dampest, and darkest corner of our network. The little seer was so insecure and bereft of confidence that he refused to take anything closer to the surface. Whenever someone suggested he rest in a warmer cave, he invariably muttered about not deserving any better.

The seer was not surprised to see me when I arrived at his chosen accommodation, with only one hissing lamp to illuminate the chamber. The chill of the air sapped at the heat in my scales. I didn't particularly want to spend more time underground, and I wasn't sure how Azlak was able to put up with it: he was usually only outside to eat.

"I'll be quick, Haeraig, we don't have much time," Azlak said as soon as I came into view. Though the golden-scaled seer was less than an inch shorter than I was, the difference appeared much greater, as he would often press himself down into the ground and he seldom looked up, making him appear smaller than his actual size.

"What do you mean?" I asked, when Azlak had, contrary to his words of being quick, paused.

"I saw how you get the Axinstone, and I know we don't have much time before we lose that chance," Azlak said, looking down into the floor as I stared in shock at the top of his head.

"Me?"

For the first time, Azlak looked up and acknowledged my presence, his golden eyes gazing balefully at my chest. He gave a slow nod. "I have looked for other ways, but I've not found another who can succeed. I didn't see who else you take with us, so you need to use your judgement for that."

"Us?" I was temporarily unable to utter anything longer than a single syllable, and my mind wasn't processing anything at a much faster rate. I couldn't believe I would have to carry out the near suicidal task of breaking into a human lair to steal what I expected to be the most highly guarded object inside.

"I know I go too," Azlak said. He was not enthralled at the prospect of going either. His voice had taken on a dull and sombre tone; one I often heard from him whenever he foresaw danger or death. I only hoped he had seen the former, and not the latter, but I did not have the courage to ask him which it was.

"So when do we leave?" I asked instead, forcing my voice out through my strangled throat.

"Tomorrow. My visions have given us one more night of rest here, but we need to be out of Xital in the morning. I've seen a few safe refuges along the way to the mountains where we can spend the nights, away from any dangers that might threaten us. There is a path we can follow over the mountains. Gather who you think we'll need, inform the Xitals of this, and I'll wait for you outside."

Though it was odd to hear such words coming from Azlak, being almost orders, or at the very least, strong advice, I took heed of them and left at once. I already knew I would have to take Keita and Carlee with me. The two of them would not allow me to leave their side. Ellian would have to remain behind. My cousin would become haeraig in my stead, so it would fall to her to lead the clan and to inform my father of the proceedings, once he returned from the borders.

I did not feel that would be enough though. I had said about a dozen dragons would be suitable, and Ddraig Aranat had said nothing to contradict that estimation. But I could think of no one else I would want with me. That would mean just four of us travelling across the mountains and the entirety of the human lands, and then across the water to the island lair. I could not think who else to ask of this dangerous task, for they would have to be from beyond my clan, but I did not have long to decide.

I resisted the urge to take to wing and ease my anxiety by flying around Xital. Fear bubbled up in my mind from multiple sources. Not only was I terrified of the task Azlak and his visions had given me, but I feared the reaction from the other ddraigs and haeraigs. I also feared the reaction of my father. He would not approve of this, and I knew already he would have refused to listen to Azlak were he here.

Someone else would have been sent on this mission. Someone more experienced. Someone more capable.

But Ddraig Astar was not in Xital. I did not have the spine to tell the seer that I would not go into human lands. The omega of the clan would control my actions.

As the sun reached the highest point in the sky, the representatives of the ruling clans began to arrive. Ten of us in all, plus the one from the royal Xital clan. Flanked by a pair of Xital guards, we were escorted into the great chamber inside the mountain, which now felt so empty and gigantic without the swarm of dragons to fill it.

Ddraig Tsona waited for us on the podium, regal and poised with his head lifted high. One by one, the haeraigs and ddraigs of the ruling clans bowed to the great dragon. My forepaw slipped as I lowered my head, almost striking my muzzle against the stone ground. I retreated quickly, hearing laughter inside my head. None of the dragons behind me broke their decorum to laugh alongside the demons in my mind, but I could sense their scorn nonetheless.

I was the smallest dragon present, a few inches shorter than Haeraig Zeena. Already I struggled not to feel intimidated.

As Haeraig Zeena bowed to the Xital, I chanced a quick glance up to the royal's head. Amongst his crown of horns was that strange square of black against his golden scales, still stuck in place. A strand of strange string looped around one horn. The light didn't reflect off the odd little device, but I was sure it was the same one he had worn to the council. I looked away before Ddraig Tsona could catch my gaze.

Once everyone had given their respect to the Xital, we all sat in a semi-circle around him. No one spoke, waiting for him to break the silence. He made no attempt to meet the gaze of any ddraig or haeraig, instead keeping his eyes fixed on a point somewhere above our heads. Most of those facing him stared at his chest. I struggled to keep my eyes above his paws.

"You know why we are here," Ddraig Tsona said, his low, deep voice sounding almost like a growl. "We are to send a small group of dragons across the Sxinix to reclaim the Axinstone from the humans." He lowered his eyes to glare first at Ddraig Aranat, and then to Haeraig Zeena. The bulky Axaatl dragon didn't flinch, though he never looked Ddraig Tsona in the eye.

The words I knew I must say burned at my throat. Fear kept them inside.

No one else spoke. No dragon was willing to risk their own. Even Ddraig Aranat, who had supported my idea in the council, remained silent.

Ddraig Tsona tilted his head. "We are to send a small group into Kernow, aren't we? Or am I to order the army to launch an invading force?"

I felt like I could sink into the stone. Standing amongst these larger dragons, all older and more experienced than me, I knew I truly did not belong. And yet, I forced my jaw open, forced my tongue to work. "No, Ddraig," I whispered.

All eyes turned to me.

"Speak, Haeraig Anzig," Ddraig Tsona said. I could feel his gaze on the top of my head, almost a physical heat on my scales.

"I must be the one to go," I said, speaking quickly before my courage could fail me. A shocked whisper rippled around the gathered dragons.

"I urge you to reconsider this," Ddraig Tsona said, taking a half step backwards and almost treading on his own tail. His eyes flicked to mine. He was the first to look away, returning his gaze far above me. He shook his head slowly. "As haeraig, you are too important to risk on such a dangerous task. I know you mean too much to Laxtal to be lost."

"I feel it is my duty as a haeraig to do things I would not ask of anyone else to do," I replied quietly, not wanting anyone to think I would deliberately go against the wishes of a Xital dragon. "And I've been told I will succeed. I have the assurance of a seer, whose word I trust."

Haeraig Zeena took a step towards me. "Which seer?" she asked. One of her claws absently scratched at the floor in her confusion. "I brought none with me."

"Azlak. He's not of Clan Nixa. He's of my clan," I replied.

"Ah, him," Zeena said simply. I knew most Nixans refused to accept that Azlak was a Laxtal dragon. They said it was impossible a dragon from outside their clan could ever possess magic. Opinions ranged from Azlak being little more than a lucky fraud – that he only pretended to see into the future – to him actually being a Nixan and lying about his heritage. While I knew these opinions to be wrong, I had never convinced a single Nixan of this.

"I know what he has Seen is true, and I know that if I leave today, I will return with the Axinstone," I said, addressing Ddraig Tsona again. I could still feel the gaze of the other dragons on me.

"You'll need help," the Xital dragon said. I took that as his permission.

"I will. I still need perhaps five dragons, four at the least, ready to leave at the first light of dawn tomorrow," I said, looking around at the other nine dragons, wondering if any of them would be willing to assist me in providing the support I needed. I wasn't disappointed.

"You are risking yourself to retrieve a Nixan artefact. It is only right that I send you some assistance. I have two dragons with me who you may take," Haeraig Zeena said without hesitation. "Isikian is a healer, and his brother, Inilta, is able to control and create fire. Both their talents will come in useful at some point, I am sure. They will accompany you to the human's lair and back without complaint."

No sooner had I nodded my thanks to her, did another dragon speak up. "I can send you Okazuni. He's young, but he's eager to prove himself," the Nyrian ddraig said, whose name I could not recall.

"Nataik is our finest fighter. She accompanied me here, and I'm sure you'll find use of her in this act of espionage. She's chameleonic," said a third. She was Nunahra, the ddraig of Clan Xigax, an eastern clan. Their elongated, almost serpentine bodies leant well to their unique style of fighting. They were heavily influenced by old human teachings of speed and stealth. Their long, whiplash tails were a weapon as deadly as the sharpest tooth or claw. There were also a select few dragons from that clan who could even change the colour of their scales to match their surroundings. It was not magic, but in the right circumstances, it was just as effective. Having such a dragon with us would certainly be a significant boost to our chances.

I glanced to Ddraig Aranat. The Axaatl drake had supported my plan in the council and having a dragon from his clan would be of great help, as they were all powerful fighters, larger than almost any other dragon. The giant ddraig turned his head to the side and said nothing.

I struggled to hide my disappointment.

No one else was willing to offer any dragons to my cause. The other ddraigs and haeraigs looked amongst each other awkwardly, as though waiting for each other to say something. In the end it was Ddraig Tsona who broke the silence. "Four more companions should be suitable, don't you think, Haeraig?" the royal dragon asked me.

"I believe so, yes," I replied. Though it was less than my original estimation, I really had pulled that number out from nothing. I doubted having more companions would make a great deal of difference.

"Then we shall keep you no longer. Go and make whatever preparations you require. If there is anything Clan Xital can do to make your final night here more comfortable, you need only ask. All I will impose on you is that you seek me out tomorrow morning before you leave," Ddraig Tsona said.

I stayed just a few moments longer to organise where and when I wanted to see the dragons that had been volunteered. I offered my final thanks and left the ten dragons to continue their discussions.

# CHAPTER FOUR

**Azlak**

Haeraig Anzig had gathered a wide variety of dragons from several different clans, and they all arrived almost together, just after the dawn's first light. They approached the haeraig to introduce themselves with their respective clan leaders, but they did not share the same courtesy to the rest of us. I knew most of their names. I had Seen them already and learnt a lot about them, some things that they did not yet know about themselves even.

Two of the dragons in particular interested me greatly: the emerald-scaled Isikian and grey-scaled Inilta, the two Nixan dragons. Because of my magic, unique outside of Nixa, I felt a natural affinity to the Nixan dragons. It was not mutual and I was repeatedly shunned by the clan of magic. They wanted nothing to do with me, and Isikian and Inilta gave no early indication they were any different. Yet I remained interested in them and watched them closely.

Haeraig Zeena was the only one of the clan leaders to linger. She mostly stayed with her fellow Nixans, though her eyes kept moving to Haeraig Anzig. She approached him occasionally, only to scarper away again whenever another dragon approached her target. Whatever she had to say to my haeraig remained unsaid.

Before we took to wing, Ddraig Tsona arrived to speak with Haeraig Anzig, resulting in the Nixan haeraig's complete departure. The two moved away to talk privately. A sour expression was on Haeraig Anzig's face as he answered the Xital ddraig's questions. I was intrigued as to what was being said, but I had no intention of moving closer, and I certainly wouldn't be asking Haeraig Anzig what had gone between them. That was absolutely none of my...

*Anzig struggled to rise. His wing was trailed uselessly along the ground and he had a great gash in his right fore-shoulder staining his green scales a deep red. His legs splayed wide, he forced himself up to four paws.*

*"You still haven't given up?" a regal and proud voice said, touched with shock, surprise, and pain. The two had clearly been fighting for some time, and Anzig was almost defeated. "You have courage, I'll give you that. But you are also a fool. I don't want to kill you Anzig, but if you persist in fighting, then I'll have no choice."*

*Anzig's adversary leaped forward, always facing the haeraig's injured side. Fresh wounds were added to Anzig's scales as blood flowed in rivulets, staining the sandy floor.*

*Anzig stumbled on his outstretched wing and collapsed to the ground at the same time his opponent crashed into his side. The two rolled and Anzig found his teeth at the neck of his foe. He bit down hard, choking the life from the gold dragon in his clutches.*

...concern. If Anzig wanted to tell us what had passed between him and Tsona, then he would. I doubted I would ever know. No one confided in me. They were too scared of being close to me. They were fearful of my magic, that I would predict something bad was going to happen. I had Seen the deaths of more dragons than I could care to recall.

I wondered who the haeraig's attacker was. The other dragon had just been a golden blur in my vision, and their voice had been distorted by time. Only Haeraig Anzig, as the subject of the vision, had been clear in my mind. Where and when it occurs, I had no idea, nor did I even know the outcome of the fight. Such was typical of all my visions. Whether that made me more fearful to others because I could See their death, but could not tell them where or when, I did not know. I supposed it did.

I shook my head to clear my mind. Ddraig Tsona had gone. We were ready to leave. Haeraig Anzig was looking expectantly at me.

Everyone was. I took a step back and lowered myself towards the ground a little. I hated it when I was the focus of attention.

"You know the way, Azlak," Haeraig Anzig said, jerking his head up to the sky, indicating that I should take to wing first. The position of power. I had never taken lead during flight before, and my wings shook as I unfurled them.

I glanced back at the haeraig, hoping he'd give some excuse that I wouldn't need to lead, but none came. I kicked off, stronger with my right than my left, and I almost planted myself back into the ground. I corrected myself in time and slowly gained height. I could hear seven pairs of wings just behind me. I resisted the urge to slow down and let them past.

I recalled the route I had Seen we must take. Fragments of visions flashed before my eyes, though I struggled not to focus too much on them, lest I trigger my magic and lose sight of the present again. We would fly west for most of the day, passing over the wild lands of Xital. We would fly directly towards the Sxinix Mountains, which lay well beyond the far-distant horizon. Our first destination was a small system of caves frequented by nomadic dragons, but open to travelling groups too. It was well stocked with wood and food by the nomads. The caves would serve our purposes well.

Until then, I still had to lead a group of seven other dragons. I had never flown lead to a single dragon anywhere before, and every single second was torture. I could feel their eyes burning into my back as well as the morning sunlight. I felt like I was flying too fast. At other times I knew I was flying far too slowly, but I dared not change my pace as that would draw attention to my error.

But for the occasional need to check for landmarks I recalled from my visions, there was little I could do to pass the time. The sun slowly moved higher behind us, until it crested its zenith and began to sink towards the horizon nearly directly ahead. The shadows lengthened as I struggled to keep my wingbeats even and our direction true.

I did my best to ignore the other dragons. If there were any conversations behind me, I did not hear them. I heard nothing but the constant shriek of fear in my mind. There were times I was sure the shriek would free itself from there and escape through my mouth, and at those times I clenched my jaw shut until I felt my teeth biting into my tongue.

The taste of blood was strong by the time I finally caught sight of the caves. I angled down to the ground and slowed down. Immediately, everyone flew past me and landed almost a full minute before my paws touched the ground.

The caves scooped from the side of a small, lone rocky outcrop, which emerged rather obtrusively from the surrounding plains. The top of the outcrop was crowned with a lake of water, gathered by the concave surface and countless years of rainfall. Recent rain trickled down the sides of the outcrop and gathered into a small stream that flowed away to the east.

I washed my mouth out in the stream before entering the caves, spitting out the bloodied water and watching it drift away downstream. The water was cold and stung the cuts on my tongue, but I ignored the pain. I wasn't satisfied until the taste of my blood had gone.

Once inside, I settled down in my own corner well away from everyone else. Our group was the only one present, so we were able to spread out as much as we liked. Someone had already started a fire, which burnt with a pale blue flame. With the exception of Haeraig Anzig, Carlee, and myself, everyone was lying in its heat. The haeraig and Carlee had gone to the opposite corner to me and were discussing something in private. As I watched, Keita moved to join them.

It wasn't long before sunset came, throwing gold and red light against the cave walls. I looked up to the moon as the last of the sun's light faded from the horizon. As I watched, the face of the moon shimmered, changing from the pattern known as the wolf into the lady. No one else watched the coming of the new day as the moon's face changed. They all stayed inside where it was warmer. I turned my attention back to the two Nixan dragons.

The smaller of the two, the emerald-scaled Isikian, already appeared to be asleep. He had curled in a tight ball with a wing over his face. Inilta was still awake though. His red eyes gleamed in the firelight. He caught my gaze. I looked away. In the briefest instant that our eyes had met, his eyes betrayed a multitude of emotions. I saw hostility there, as well as confusion and curiosity. If I had to guess at which the dominant emotion was, then it was Inilta's curiosity.

I knew I would need to speak with him or Isikian at some point. In a group of so few there was no way I could avoid it, no matter how alone I kept myself. I was an enigma to Nixa; that much I knew. As much as I was ignored and shunned by the clan, I was also a mystery that had to be solved. I knew as little as they did why I had magic. There was no logical reason to it. My ancestry was Laxtal, for as far back as anyone cared to remember.

*"I'm a Laxtal, but I have magic too."*

Words. That's all I have. Words from an unknown dragon. And darkness. But in that darkness is my hope of understanding why I am what I am. I don't know who tells me those words, but I have heard them so many times, in so many different voices that they no longer leave my mind. I had long given up half-expecting a Laxtal dragon to utter those words, and I couldn't even begin to guess who they may be. I knew none of the circumstances about when it happens, except that I'm in the darkness somewhere and that I was in pain. I just hoped that when it does happen, that dragon will be able to tell me why we possess magic, and yet are not Nixans.

Until that time came, I knew I would be alone and without support. I could never really connect with another dragon from our clan. This dragon would be my only chance for someone who could properly understand me. A mate. A friend, even. There had been times when I had fantasised about the identity of this stranger and what we might do after this meeting. I did not believe this dragon was ever going to become my mate, even if they were a drake, for I had Seen no such future.

Before I was aware of what I was doing I was standing up and approaching Inilta. He looked sharply at me and narrowed his eyes, judging me, his body tensed, ready to pounce if necessary. I paused, but then he relaxed and allowed me to come closer.

"You're that seer, aren't you?" he asked sleepily, not even looking up at me as he spoke.

"Yes," was all I was able to say in a small voice. I was well used to be called 'that seer', even amongst my own clan. It was no surprise to be addressed thus by Inilta.

"Thought so," he said with a slight sneer in his tone. "You wanted something did you?"

I recoiled at the hostility in Inilta's voice, and I wondered anew why exactly I had approached him. I wasn't even sure what I wanted. An explanation for my magic? I had already asked several Nixans, and always they had given me the same answer. They had told me I must be Nixan. It was my constant denial of that answer that had given me such a bad reputation amongst that clan.

"I just... I wanted..." I stammered, trying to work out what to say.

"Well I'm trying to sleep," Inilta said curtly, drawing his wing over his face. I needed no other sign to know the conversation was over.

I withdrew from the two Nixans and returned to my isolated corner. Inilta's reaction had not been one I was unfamiliar with, but his attitude hurt me still. I had hoped for a better interaction with the Nixan.

Though I was not tired, I covered my face with my wing in a semblance of sleep. I had no desire to be disturbed, even if anyone thought I was worth approaching.

Before long I was the last one left awake. Haeraig Anzig and Keita had come back in and fallen asleep together next to the fire. The others had all clustered in close to share the warmth in the centre of the cave, leaving me alone in the night's chill. Though we needed to keep warm during the cold, dark hours, over the long years I developed my resistance to the chill air, allowing me able to spend a full night away from the heat of a fire.

Though I would not go so far as to say I was comfortable away in the corner, after a long time I was, at last, able to fall into an uneasy sleep.

I was woken by a small, blood red dragon I knew to be called Okazuni, though we had never before met. He did not know me, but he treated me with the same lack of respect I got from all other dragons. His claws were sharp as he cuffed me awake, and I was sure he drew blood.

"Wake up, we're all waiting on you," he said, turning his back on me and impatiently leaving the cave without giving me time to even get to my paws. Okazuni emerged into the sunlight well before me. Though I was more capable than other dragons in staying in the cold, it still did not cease to affect me. My paws were unsteady as my head spun in weakness.

Outside, the light was almost blinding for a few moments and I had to squint to see anything at all. Okazuni had been correct. Everyone else was already out, lying down on the grass with their wings outstretched, soaking up the early morning sun.

Haeraig Anzig glanced over in my direction briefly before returning to his conversation with Carlee. No one else acknowledged my presence as I settled down in an isolated patch of grass a few feet from Isikian. I closed my eyes as I lay. I could feel a headache building at the base of my feeble and blunt horns, a bad thing I knew for so early in the day. Whenever I had a headache I found it much harder to maintain the flimsy control I had on my magic. In addition to the knowledge that I would have to take lead in the flight again, I knew I was in for another bad day.

We had no chance of reaching the mountains this day. They were still not visible from where we had rested. Two more days would still be needed before we had to cross the Sxinix. For the upcoming nights we would rest in nomadic sanctuaries much like the one that had sheltered us overnight. Many caves and burrows littered the large forest that spread right up to the mountains. We would not be short on choice, but I alone knew which ones would give us the best chances of success, and which would keep us from danger. Even on this side of the mountains I knew there were risks; threats in the night that only I was aware of.

Once we left the forest, I would lead the group across the nearest pass through the mountains; a narrow path that clung to the mountainside. It was a dangerous route for the wind there gusted and slammed anything in the air against the rocks. We would have to walk the entire way, but the path itself was thin and crumbling, constantly battered by wind, rain, and snow. If I hadn't already known it was the best place to cross, I would have taken a longer route around to one of the safer passes. Safety was something we would soon be lacking. The mountains were the time-honoured boundary between human and dragon lands. Once we crossed, the danger would truly grow.

"Azlak, a few words?" a voice asked, surprisingly close to me. I opened my eyes in shock. Isikian was standing over me, his yellow eyes looking into mine. I struggled to keep eye contact for a few seconds before looking away. I expected another rude rebuttal from the Nixan like I had received from his brother. Then I realised that this time, the Nixan had approached me.

*Isikian looked around at the six dragons surrounding him. A few paces away was a body, half hidden by the shadows. It appeared dead.*

*"It's too dangerous. He's not Nixan, do you have any idea what could happen to him?" Isikian protested. His tail lashed nervously as he gave another pleading look. The focus of his attention was a ness directly in front of him.*

*"He's dead already," she cried. She was having difficulty standing. Her legs were shaking and she was almost on the verge of tears. Her red scales were bloody and scratched, especially around her face. She had been fighting another dragon. It was hard to tell if she had lost, or whether she had defeated the dragon lying dead on the floor.*

*"Very well, I can try," Isikian said with a sigh. He picked up a jagged shard of rock in his mouth and moved across to the dead dragon. He placed his paw on the body and closed his eyes in concentration. There was a pulse of bright light emanating from the stone and...*

"Are you alright?" Isikian asked, holding his paw out just in front of my forehead.

"You will try to help someone who is already dead. You need to revive them with a stone – the Axinstone I think. I don't know where, I don't know when, but unless something changes it, it's going to happen," I said, batting his paw away from me.

Isikian didn't seem too perturbed by what I had Seen, instead more concerned with the fact I had Seen anything at all. "Have you never been trained to control your magic?" he asked, ignoring my attempts to keep him away and placing his paw on my forehead. His touch was cool, and immediately my headache receded until I could feel no more pain.

"It can be trained?" I asked in surprise. I had always thought magic was something wild and uncontrollable. I hadn't known I could control what I Saw. But then, I already knew why I had never known this. I was Laxtal, and very few Nixans would want to have anything to do with me. Even if they acknowledged my magic was real, they wouldn't be willing to associate themselves with me.

"All Nixans are taught how to control their magic as soon as it surfaces. You should have been offered the same courtesy," Isikian said.

I shook my head and sat up. "I'm not Nixan. I've never even been to Nixa," I said, the same thing I told anyone who believed me to be from the clan of magic. What Isikian said in reply surprised me.

"You look like a Nixan," he said. I was speechless. No one had ever said that before. I was aware I didn't look exactly like the typical Laxtal dragon. But I didn't look Nixan, did I? The most obvious differences between me and other Laxtals were my horns and muzzle. Other Laxtal dragons had long and sharp horns towards the back of their head, which I did not possess. My horns, just above each eye, were short and blunt. My muzzle was quite unlike the long and tapered muzzle typically seen on a Laxtal dragon. Now that Isikian had pointed it out to me, my muzzle was indeed quite Nixan in appearance. My eyes flicked up to inspect Isikian's horns. Short, blunt, and above his eyes.

Coincidence. It had to be coincidence.

"I'm Laxtal," I said to reassure both myself and Isikian. "My parents are both Laxtal. Pure-blooded for many generations. I can't be Nixan."

*"Three eggs left abandoned in the wilderness. Come on, it's not hard to work out." A mysterious black dragon with glowing red eyes spoke out of the darkness to another, smaller dragon, this one a dull green. The smaller dragon said nothing in reply to her.*

I shook my head. I had seen that black ness before, but I had never heard a name for her, nor did I even know where she was. The dragon before her though, it had looked like Haeraig Anzig, but I couldn't be certain.

"Your eyes turn white when using your magic?" Isikian said, looking intently at me. His curiosity unnerved me. I wasn't used to it. Other dragons, especially Nixans, weren't meant to be interested in me at all. Isikian clearly took my silence as an affirmative, as he continued, "What did you see this time?"

"Nothing important," I said, not wanting to explain to Isikian something I didn't even understand myself.

I could tell Isikian didn't believe me, and he seemed to struggle to not question me further. Then he shrugged his wings and stood up. "If you'd like, I can teach you how to control your magic when we get back to Nixa. Or in Laxtal, if you'd prefer. I don't think it is right you should have to struggle with uncontrollable magic, even if you believe you are a Laxtal."

"I am... Thank you, I would like that," I said, interrupting my own protests at his implications that I really wasn't a Laxtal dragon. I didn't think he would much appreciate that, and I didn't want him to withdraw his offer.

We were joined then by Haeraig Anzig, who had broken away from his conversation with Carlee. The old veteran had remained behind and was now sharing a few sharp words with Okazuni. Keita tailed the haeraig over to us. The ness's head bobbed up and down as she looked over Haeraig Anzig's shoulder.

"I think we're all ready to leave," Haeraig Anzig said to the space between Isikian and me. He seemed a little distracted by something as his eyes weren't focussing on anything at all. He stared into the empty space between him and the grass beneath my paws. "We're waiting on you, Azlak."

Behind Haeraig Anzig the others were looking over at us expectantly. Inilta was glaring at me, though I had no idea why. I looked down at the haeraig's paws. He was kneading the dirt as though he was the one who was nervous. He stopped. "How far do we travel today?" he asked.

"It's a long flight today. We cannot rest until we reach the shelter I have Seen. It will be a few nights until we reach the Sxinix, and another day still to cross them. Once we reach the other side of the mountains, I have Seen an abandoned human dwelling to rest our wings in," I said, closing my eyes so I could better See what my visions had told me. "From there, we rest in caves until we come to the shore."

I knew there would be some who would protest at using human buildings to rest, but neither Isikian nor Haeraig Anzig offered any. I guess they knew that because I had Seen it, it was the correct way for us to take. Whether it was the best way, I was not certain. I was sure there had to be a better and quicker way, but I knew our current route would get us to the main human lair safely. From there, things got a lot more difficult to determine. Once we got there, each individual choice would have an impact on whether we succeeded or failed. That I had kept hidden from the haeraig. I hadn't wanted him to know there was a chance of failure.

"We have some way to go then. Lead the way, we'll follow," Haeraig Anzig said, spreading his wings as he glanced behind him at Keita.

I sighed and looked up to the sky. It was cloudless and clear. There was hardly any wind, and what little there was would push us towards the mountains. It was a perfect day for flying, and I knew I would hate every last moment of it.

I took to the air and didn't once look back. I couldn't, or I knew I would falter. The others followed close behind.

# CHAPTER FIVE

**Ellian**

"You don't understand. I could help you lead your clan. I could have you revered as the greatest leader Laxtal has ever seen," Ddraig Tsona said. He looked down on me and I tried my hardest not to turn away. I was representing my clan, and the power of Laxtal meant I did not have to bow to Xital's every whim.

The Xital ddraig had directly summoned me to the audience chamber of the massive lair. I was not the only one present, as several dragons from other clans lingered to the back of the chamber, though none of them were close enough to listen in on our exchanged words. I understood that what he was offering me was rare: Clan Xital preferred not to actively engage with other clans, and they certainly didn't offer aid without expecting something in return.

"I appreciate the offer, Ddraig Tsona, but I must decline. I fear my clan would protest. They would see your actions, no matter how kindly, as an unwanted interference," I replied, risking lifting my gaze to his chin.

A muscle twitched below the Xital ddraig's eye, but otherwise his annoyance was well hidden. It was the first time I had ever stood up to a Xital. I had never before been given the rank or privilege to do so, and it thrilled me to put one of the pompous royals in place. I kept my excitement hidden though, as I doubted Ddraig Tsona would much appreciate it. My claws slowly raked at the ground beneath my paws.

"If that is your desire, then I shall leave you be. Know that you need only ask and I shall assist you," the Xital said with an ever so slight nod of his head. The royal dragon didn't seem too keen to linger on the subject, as he quickly said, "I heard talk that you were returning to Laxtal tomorrow?"

"That is correct, Ddraig Tsona," I said. It had already been a full day since Anzig had left on his rash journey, and there was little point in remaining behind. There was no one of Ddraig Astar's family in Laxtal to rule in his stead, so it would be wise limiting the time away. Though Ddraig Astar was immensely popular and well respected amongst the clan, there was no knowing what idle dragons could do when their leader was absent, especially those wearied by the outbreaks of fighting on Laxtal's borders.

"I hear Haeraig Zeena shall also be leaving come the morning. I imagine you would share much the same journey?" Ddraig Tsona said in a curious tone. His tail twitched ever so slightly in a manner akin to irritation.

I wasn't sure what to say to that. The Xital had posed it as a question, but I didn't know what information he was trying to learn. I said nothing and waited for him to make the next move.

"I doubt this will be the last time we cross wings. Fly safe, Ellian of Clan Laxtal," was all the Xital dragon said, implicitly dismissing me and granting permission to depart. I took to wing immediately, not wanting to test Ddraig Tsona's patience, or to get in the way of the next dragon to step forward: a ness from Clan Xigax.

I flew out the chamber exit towards the top of the lone mountain and into the damp clouds that clung to the tip of the peak. It was a wretched day, and my wings didn't like the moisture dragging them down. Cold drizzle dampened the ground, and even as I descended below the clouds, there was not a single dragon to be seen. Even the cold and dark network of caves was preferable to this weather. I longed for the roaring fire I had left behind in the chambers left for visiting Laxtal dragons.

The entrance to our caves was near the top of a low hill just to the north of the central peak. From the cave mouth barely large enough for two dragons to pass side by side, the tunnel delved down into the heart of the hill, rapidly expanding as it did so until it widened into a large central chamber. Branching out from this chamber were smaller caves used for sleeping in isolation, though Azlak had been the only one using these – the seer had banished himself away in the coldest, darkest, and dampest chamber he could find.

I pushed my way through the ivy that was growing over the small entry and shuddered as their wet strands clung to my scales. I descended into the dark and shook my wings dry as soon as I had space to spread them. The warmth of the fire drew me onwards, and I hurried down to greet Vinzent.

As we were all that was left of the Laxtal delegation, I was surprised to discover that the silver dragon was not alone. At first, I didn't recognise the small red ness sat by Vinzent's side, the two looking into the roaring fire situated in a hollow on one wall, but then I realised I looked upon Haeraig Zeena of Clan Nixa. I had not expected to see her again before leaving Xital, no matter Ddraig Tsona's odd comments.

I froze, standing with one paw raised. I was too surprised to speak, but Vinzent must have heard me as he turned and leapt to his paws. He smiled sheepishly at me, unable to meet my eyes, not even for a moment. He slowly sidled away from the side of the Nixan haeraig.

"To what do I owe the honour, Haeraig Zeena?" I asked the Nixan, finding my tongue at last, remembering to treat the haeraig with the respect her rank deserved. Still on three paws, I stared at the fire just behind the Nixan.

"I wish to give you some advice I wanted to give Haeraig Anzig, had the opportunity presented itself," the Nixan said, looking at me in the eye. I held her gaze for long enough that I didn't appear weak, but looked away before I ceased being respectful.

"What manner of advice?" I asked cautiously, noting as I did so, that Vinzent had taken a long, circuitous route around the chamber to stand by my side.

Haeraig Zeena glanced across to Vinzent. "A warning," she said. "I have sent some messages back to Nixa and sent some scouts around the lair here. My father reports that recent events have caught the attention of some of our seers, and they have become concerned with some isolated human movements around draconic territories, in particular around Clan Xital," She spoke quietly and quickly, as though she was worried about being overheard.

"I still don't understand why this matters to us," Vinzent interjected. Evidently the two had already been discussing this.

Haeraig Zeena growled softly to silence the silver dragon, who bowed his head, chastised for the interruption.

"It matters because the fears I expressed earlier appear to be true. Nixa fears there are dragons within Clan Xital who are assisting the humans. How, why, or who, we do not yet know, but all our seers and telepaths are trying to discover the answers," the Nixan said. That was an audacious allegation, and it didn't surprise me that Haeraig Zeena was so apprehensive about revealing her information.

"Could this be just a few Xitals?" I asked, inwardly cursing my luck that I had not been able to identify the two royal dragons on top of the mountain. I suppressed a shudder and scratched my claws against the stone ground. "Or could this be right from the top? Could this be Ddraig Tsona?"

I got a slight nod of acknowledgement in return.

"That's why I was unable to tell Haeraig Anzig. I didn't want to mention anything in front of the Xitals, and Ddraig Tsona barely left him alone before leaving."

"Do you think the humans will know of Anzig's mission to retrieve the Axinstone?" I asked, a fresh wave of concern for my cousin threatening to overwhelm me. If Anzig was flying into a trap, then I could only fear for his safety. Without any way of contacting him, he would be unaware of the dangers that lay ahead.

Haeraig Zeena did nothing to calm my fears. "I think it would be wise to believe such a thing has happened."

"And you can't send anyone to warn him? You can't send a message at least?" I asked.

"I'm afraid that's unlikely. All our dragons are busy readying the defences of our clan. If humans attack, then we must be ready. We can spare no more, I'm sorry," Haeraig Zeena said. She placed her paw on my shoulder. "He already has two of our number. Isikian and Inilta are two of our finest, and they are both aware of everything I have just told you. They would not let your haeraig fly into harm's way, you have my word."

I found it difficult to put faith in the Nixan's words. Two dragons, no matter how skilled, would not be enough to save Anzig if the humans knew they were coming.

"Don't worry Ellian, I'm sure the Boss'll be fine," Vinzent said quietly.

"But it's not him I'm most worried about," Haeraig Zeena added. "We have sensed movements by Clan Xital against some of the other ruling clans. We believe – and it pains me to even mention this – that Clan Xital may be looking to wrest control of our clans. If a royal dragon is using humans to further their own ambitions, then we could soon be warring amongst ourselves."

"So even if the Boss retrieves the Axinstone, we would be too broken and divided to use it effectively," Vinzent said.

"Precisely," Haeraig Zeena said, nodding her head in agreement.

"So what do we do?" I asked. In Anzig's absence I knew my clan would look to me as the haeraig. They would expect me to formulate some sort of plan against possible human and Xital attacks. I didn't know if I would be capable of stepping up, but at least I would have Ddraig Astar to guide and counsel me.

"It is not my place to tell you how to prepare your clan, but I would advise you to keep this information between yourselves and your ddraig. Rumours that Clan Xital is working with humans must not start spreading," the Nixan said. "Not until we are in a position to move against Xital, should that be necessary."

I understood Haeraig Zeena's response, even though I wished for something different. Just like I had earlier been loath to accept Ddraig Tsona's assistance, the Nixan now didn't want to be seen as interfering in another clan's business. Clan Laxtal would have to work alone to prepare itself, as it had always done.

"Is there anything you can tell me?" I asked in hope for some advice at least.

"Just be on the alert for any suspicious behaviour, especially from any Xitals," Haeraig Zeena said. She paused and looked up to the distant ceiling of the chamber. "I will speak to my father to see if he will provide assistance, but I doubt he will allow any more Nixans to leave our territory until the Axinstone is recovered."

"Anything you can provide would be most appreciated, Haeraig Zeena," I said, bowing my head to her, understanding that nothing would be done. Clan Nixa had a history of denying assistance to their neighbours. Like Clan Xital, the Nixans only offered aid when there was a clear benefit to themselves. Until they retrieved the Axinstone, there was no advantage the clan of magic could gain over their rivals.

Haeraig Zeena excused herself and left, sharing a brief parting glance with Vinzent before the silver dragon looked away. He still couldn't meet my eye, and as soon as the Nixan had left the chamber, I turned on him.

"What was that all about?" I demanded, finally getting the opportunity to get the question off my chest. I hadn't liked the sheepish way he had darted away from Haeraig Zeena, nor her apparent familiarity with Vinzent.

"Nothing. She was just waiting for you. We talked as we waited, but there was nothing to it." Vinzent shrugged. He lay down in front of me, his forepaws resting atop mine. I growled softly but let the matter drop. We had a long flight ahead of us come morning, and I needed the rest. It would not do to have an argument with Vinzent, my oldest and closest friend. He had been my supporter, my champion, for so long, and I knew I was wrong to doubt him. The pressure of replacing Anzig was already getting to me, and we hadn't even returned to Laxtal yet.

I dreaded the reaction of Ddraig Astar. He was going to be furious his only son and heir had gone on a near-suicidal mission to retrieve a Nixan artefact of magic. It sounded crazy. It probably was, but there was nothing I could do to help my cousin.

All I could do was maintain order and control in Laxtal once I returned. I feared the reaction I would receive back home, but I owed it to my cousin to do the best I could.

Laxtal was an undulating land of sparse grassland and clusters of hardy trees that clung to the edges of the few small rivers that ran through the territory. The life-bringing ribbons of water flowed down from the mountains in the west to the far distant shores of the east and south, well beyond the borders of Laxtal. There were no defining landmarks like the lone peak in Xital, or the crystal lakes in Nyri. It was a plain land, but it provided everything a dragon could ever need. There was food for all, enough shelter wherever it was needed, and the sun shone bright and warm in the mornings. But most of all, it was my home, and as such, in my eyes there was nowhere else that was as beautiful as Laxtal.

Vinzent and I had been flying for the last two days. We hadn't stopped at all during the days, only coming to rest at sunset both nights, and taking to wing again as soon as the air had warmed the following morning. Haeraig Zeena had not joined us at any stage, despite the shared route towards Nixa. It had been an arduous journey, and my wings screamed for rest, but I didn't want to delay. Clan Laxtal had been without its leaders for too long.

When I had left with Anzig to attend the council in Xital, we had entrusted three dragons in control of the clan, at the orders of Ddraig Astar before he had left for the borders. It had the potential to become a volatile situation, but Ddraig Astar and Anzig had hoped that the three dragons would be too busy fighting amongst themselves to worry about wresting total control of the clan from the absent ddraig and haeraig.

All three were senior dragons amongst the clan. Marin was one of Ddraig Astar's most loyal and vocal supporters and had been a champion for Clan Laxtal for many years now. His only point of shame was that he was the father of the clan's weakest dragon, the seer Azlak. It was no secret that while Marin was a staunch supporter of the current ddraig, he admired Haeraig Anzig considerably less.

Saya was one of the clan's most respected nesses. She was Vinzent's mother, and I knew she had been grooming her son for leadership since a very young age. It would not surprise me if she was secretly longing for Vinzent to one day become the ddraig of Laxtal, though Vinzent had vehemently denied this when I had once asked.

The third of the temporary leadership group of Laxtal was the albino dragon, Yalle. A close friend of Ddraig Astar since they were both dragonets, Yalle had overcome much adversity in his physical disfigurement to maintain the respect and honour of his clan. His daughter, Keita, looked set to follow in her father's pawprints. Not only did she battle a physical flaw in her near-blindness, but she had also become close friends with Haeraig Anzig, and was reaping the benefits of having such a powerful ally within the clan.

I hoped the three dragons would respect my claim of authority and give control of the clan to me. I glanced across at Vinzent and for just a moment a clawing sense of doubt crossed my mind. If I was right, and Saya wanted Vinzent to become ddraig, then he would never have a better opportunity to take control of Laxtal than now.

Vinzent noticed my glance and seemed to understand the cause of my concern, as he looked away bashfully. "I'm not going to do it," he said quietly.

"I know. It's not you I don't trust," I replied, edging closer to him so our wingtips almost touched as we began to glide down to the ground. A deep gorge was our destination, splitting the hills and winding across the landscape from east to west, until it reached the open plains of Laxtal. Much of the wide mouth of the gorge was scarred by landslides, with massive boulders piled into great mounds no dragon could ever hope to move.

We had passed few dragons even as we travelled through Laxtal territory, and the air around the lair was just as deserted. With rumours of humans pressing further into our land, I was not surprised dragons were being more cautious about when they left the safety of the caves. Even a fair proportion of the nomadic dragons were starting to take up residence in the lair.

Even with the extra population, Laxtal was far from crowded. Beneath the ground was an extensive network of natural caves that had never been fully explored, and it was within these caverns that the clan dwelt. They spread for miles, with some branches rumoured to end deep within the Sxinix Mountains. Only a tiny fraction of these caves were inhabited by the clan. If necessary, they could probably house every single dragon alive, though food and water would rapidly become a concern as Laxtal was not an abundant land blessed with lush fertile plains for grazing animals, or roaring and plentiful rivers. The clan never went hungry, but we often cast an envious eye or two to the surrounding clans. Nixa especially was renowned throughout all draconic lands for being the richest and most succulent prey a dragon could catch. I had only visited the clan of magic once, but the rumours were true: their hunting grounds were legendary.

We had to work harder on our hunts in Laxtal but, as my paws came to rest in the dry and hardy grass on the top of the hill, I felt a profound relief that I was finally home. Vinzent fluttered down by my side, and for a moment we remained motionless and gazed out over the undulating land. Here and there a flicker of movement betrayed the presence of life, but otherwise all was still as the sun began to encroach on the horizon. It was nearing dusk, and there was so much that still needed to be done.

My eyes lingered on a hill directly south, a little taller than any of the others around it. A blocky structure of stone capped the hill. We had flown not far from that hill, but it was only now that I realised there was no light on it. There should have been. The beacons were dark.

"Come on," I said with a little reluctance, forcing myself to drag my eyes away from the vista. Vinzent grumbled, but he followed a short way behind. It was time to confront the clan.

I carefully glided down to the bottom of the gorge that sliced its way through the hill on which I stood. It was a sheer drop of fifty feet, a fall that no creature without wings could survive. Occasionally rabbits and mice would stumble in and present us an easy meal. Sometimes even a deer tumbled down the ravine and provided a veritable feast.

I landed on the gravelled floor next to the small stream that bubbled by – the last remnants of the great river that had once flown through here, cutting away the rock to create the gorge many hundreds of years ago. Scattered boulders littered the ground, scars in the cliffs left behind from when they had fallen.

This far from the mouth of the gorge was barely wide enough for two dragons to stand with their wings outstretched. Partially hidden behind a fold in the cliffs was a large crevasse that led underground. This was the only entrance into the Laxtal lair. Just visible from where I stood was the first of many torches that kept the underground lair well lit.

With Vinzent on my tail, I hurried into the cave through the dark and damp antechamber before plunging into the light. I found myself at the top of a long corridor that gradually descended with a barely discernible curve to the left. Shadows flickered as the torches shone against the rock walls, burning fuel of coal and wood. Smoke drifted towards tiny vents in the ceiling, keeping the air relatively clear throughout the caves.

Oddly, there was no one to greet us. There was always a guard stationed in the first chamber, to make sure no one – dragon or otherwise – could surprise us. No guard at the entrance, no patrols in the sky. The beacons dark. Something was wrong in Laxtal.

Claws scampered from the darkness. A small blue dragon hurried out of the shadows and into the light. Adran, one of the guards tasked with protecting the lair. He bowed his head and tucked his tail between his hindlegs. "Ellian? Vinzent? I wasn't expecting you, I'm sorry."

A growl escaped my mouth before I could stop it. Adran lowered himself further towards the ground. "Why were you not here already? An enemy doesn't come expected."

Adran stared at the floor. "My apologies, Ellian. I was attending to a task for Saya," he said, eyes flicking towards Vinzent for a brief moment.

Vinzent's wings fluttered. "What was my mother wanting this time?" he groaned.

I didn't give Adran time to answer. "You are to remain here until relieved of duty," I snarled. My claws scratched at the stone. Anger flared hot within me. How could dragons here be so lax, while our ddraig was at the borders, fighting against this human threat? We could not afford to leave our lair unguarded.

I barged past the flustered dragon, pushing him aside with my shoulder and stalking deeper into the cave. Adran's spluttered apologies followed me for a short distance, but he did not follow us. He was willing to consider me a figure of authority, obeying my commands.

I had passed the first test. One dragon had listened to me. I knew Yalle, Marin, and Saya would prove a tougher opposition than a lowly guard.

I did not get far through the narrow, winding tunnel before Vinzent caught up to me.

"Ellian, stop," he said, treading on my tail to force me into a reluctant halt.

I turned quickly, baring my teeth. "Why? What are you stopping me for? Some plan of your mother's?"

Vinzent stepped back as though burned by my words. His eyes widened and lowered. His neck trembled as he struggled not to look away. "I told you I wasn't going to do anything like that. Whatever my mother has planned, those are her plans, not mine. I have no intention of being ddraig or haeraig, especially if it means cutting into your air."

I could see the hurt in his eyes. I sighed and softened my posture, relaxing my wings and paws. "I'm sorry, I know that's true. But Anzig asked me to be haeraig in his absence. Will you really stand against your mother if she asks you to take control of the clan over me? Will you really support me until Ddraig Astar returns?"

"I will always be behind you, Ellian. I will always be there to guide and support you, and I will speak out against my mother if I must," the silver dragon said. He slowly approached and rested his head against my shoulder. "Now come on, let's show these older dragons how to really run the clan."

Vinzent's cheeky grin was infectious. I felt a few of my worries ease. If Saya, Yalle, or Marin had any ideas of taking command of Laxtal, then I would have one ally at least. Anzig had tasked me with leading our clan until his father returned. He trusted me, and I would not dishonour him by losing control before I had even begun. I had to repay that faith, or else the stigma of my failure would stick with me for the rest of my life.

We made our way down through the slightly winding passage until it opened into the massive central chamber of Clan Laxtal. The roughly hewn walls glimmered in the flickering torchlight as a hundred dragons lay together on the distant floor, huddled by a large fire that almost constantly burned, kept alive by the massive stockpiles of coal stored deep within the caves.

A ripple of intrigue passed through the dragons as they noticed my presence, and it wasn't long before the clan leaders were summoned. Saya was the first to come, and she warmly greeted her son as she landed near the fire. The ness barely even gave me a second glance as she took Vinzent away.

"Where is father?" I heard Vinzent ask his mother.

"Out hunting," was the red dragon's reply, but I could hear no more of their exchange, so I chose to focus instead on Marin and Yalle as they approached the fire.

"News from Haeraig Anzig, Ellian? Will Clan Xital be helping us face the humans?" Marin asked from behind the cloud of dust his wings kicked up as he fluttered to the ground. The green-scaled dragon kept his head raised and did not bow to me.

I glanced back at Vinzent, but his attention was solely dedicated to his mother, and he appeared not to have even heard Marin's question. Despite his promises, he had already left me to face Marin and Yalle alone.

"As such. Haeraig Anzig has flown into human lands to retrieve the Axinstone for Clan Nixa," I said quietly.

"He's done what?" Yalle exclaimed, almost missing his grounding as he landed.

"Haeraig Zeena of Nixa suggested the course of action, as she felt it would benefit the western clans and aid our defence against humans," I explained, slightly amused by the look of abject shock and horror that defined every movement of the two veteran dragons.

"What madness led him to take on such a task by himself?" Marin said.

"He took the advice of your son, Marin. It was Azlak who suggested that the haeraig go. He took with him a few dragons from other clans, but their number also includes Carlee and Keita," I said, nodding my head towards the albino, Yalle, acknowledging the involvement of his daughter.

"Azlak," Marin hissed, taking a few steps back and looking up to the far-distant ceiling. "I'll have a few words with him when he returns."

"If they return," Yalle said mournfully. He sat back on his haunches and pawed at the rocky ground.

"Haeraig Anzig was convinced that Azlak spoke the truth to him, and that he will return safely with the Axinstone," I said, trying to inject confidence into my voice. I did not like the look of utter hopelessness that had crossed the face of Yalle. In the brief moments I was able to look into the albino's pale pink eyes, they were forlorn and full of loss, as though his daughter had already passed.

"I fear the haeraig's trust in my son is severely displaced. Nothing he has ever contributed to this clan has been for the better. Sometimes I wish his egg..." Marin said bitterly, before he was interrupted by a low growl from Yalle.

"Better not to speak of such things," Yalle warned.

Marin growled, but went no further with that line of thought. Had he been about to suggest that he would rather Azlak had never hatched? The seer may not be a popular figure amongst our clan, but I had never known a dragon to disown their young before. If that were the case, then Yalle had been right to intervene. If word of that broke out, then Marin would have been shunned by the clan, not out of respect for Azlak, the seer had none of that, but because such thoughts went against the draconic way. A dragon deserved the respect of their parents, if no one else.

"But enough of this matter, who will lead the clan in the haeraig's absence? Does he intend for the current situation to persevere until he or Ddraig Astar returns?" Yalle asked with a sharp glance in my direction.

"It is... It is Haeraig Anzig's wish that I take control of the clan in his absence," I said. I quailed under the cold glare Marin gave me, but this time I held my ground, and he looked away first. This small victory was short lived as Saya and Vinzent returned, and the older dragon was looking particularly furious.

"Put Laxtal in the paws of an inexperienced dragonet like yourself?" Saya said, advancing on me. It did not escape my attention that she called me a dragonet, despite becoming an adult dragon already. I doubted she would call her son a dragonet, even though he had yet to come of age. He would not be a full adult for another month.

"Those were Haeraig Anzig's wishes," I replied, placing a hindpaw back but otherwise remaining where I stood.

"And I reject Haeraig Anzig's wishes," Saya said, halting less than a pace in front of me, the tip of her muzzle practically touching mine. I somehow kept her gaze, ignoring the flames of hatred I saw there, or was it just a reflection of the fire behind me? I couldn't be sure.

"In times like these we need experienced dragons to lead us. Clan Laxtal needs strong leadership, and you are not the one to provide it, Ellian, no matter what the haeraig thinks," she finished.

This time I couldn't help it. I took a full step back and looked away from Saya. The ness knew she had won. A flash of silver crossed my vision.

"Know your place, mother," Vinzent growled. He stood between me and Saya, and not once did he drop his eyes.

Her son's dissent threw the wind out of Saya's wings, and she immediately backed away. "My son?" she whispered. "You betray me?"

"No mother, you betray yourself. You are not ddraig of this clan. You are not haeraig. Ellian is their chosen representative. If you challenge her authority, then you challenge them. Are you challenging Ddraig Astar, mother?" Vinzent said, a sharp tone to his voice I had never heard before. I could see why his mother hoped he would someday have the chance to be ddraig. He was a powerful leader, one worthy to rule Clan Laxtal. I pushed those thoughts down. He was right. Haeraig Anzig had chosen me, and none other. Without an official challenge placed, I was the rightful leader of Laxtal.

Saya also understood this, and she bowed her head in submission. "I apologise Ellian. I submit to you, and relinquish my share of power. If Marin and Yalle agree, then we shall look upon you as our leader in the absence of Haeraig Anzig, but I do not feel you should take the rank of haeraig, not without any formal ceremony with the consent of the ddraig," she said, looking down at my paws.

"I agree," Yalle said immediately.

"As do I," Marin said with a little more reluctance, but still bowed his head towards Vinzent and me.

"So what do we do, Ellian? Human movement has been increasing on our borders, but we were waiting for the haeraig's return to take action. Now we know he won't be flying home soon, I do not believe we should be idle until Ddraig Astar returns," Yalle said. It felt strange for such senior dragons to ask me for advice, and it was a few moments before I even realised I had been asked a question.

I looked towards Vinzent, but I noticed an almost imperceptible shake of his head. This had to be something I answered, and I had no time to think it through. Saya, Yalle, and Marin would not accept hesitation, for they would see it as incompetence. They had been cowed by Vinzent's show of support, but that would not last if they saw weakness in my leadership.

"We double the protection on our borders. Have daily patrols throughout the clan territory, and ensure the beacon-keepers are alert. I want to know if any human or dragon is passing through our lands when they should not. You weren't expecting our arrival and we surprised even the guard on duty. An enemy force could have flown straight into our lair, and you'd have been none the wiser. That must change," I said slowly. If these rumours of Xital treachery were true, then I knew the clan had to be better protected away from our central lair. Of course, I could not tell my clan that. The protection had to be against the humans, at least at first glance. Then there was the matter of security within the lair itself. We had already passed through the entry chamber before the guard stationed to that post even knew we were there. That would not do, and I told the three older dragons as much. Saya looked embarrassed by the matter.

I began to grow in confidence as I further discussed how I felt the lair should be protected. Once or twice Yalle and Marin looked impressed with what I said, though Saya never wavered from her expression of forlorn reluctance. The whole time, Vinzent stood by my side. He was silent, but the tip of his tail touched mine, and that gave me all the support I could ever need.

I knew the beacons would be crucial to maintaining the clan's safety. They were a network of towers throughout the clan's territory that spread out like a great web. They were lit with fires once an enemy was sighted. The dragons that occupied the beacons could use different powders to alter the colour of the flame, warning the other beacons of the nature of the threat that approached. It was said that once a beacon was lit, wherever in Laxtal it was, no more than two hours would pass until the central lair was notified of any danger.

"A good plan, Ellian. I shall see it done," Yalle said once I had finished. He ducked his head and backed away a couple of paces. Marin followed suit before flying away with the albino.

Saya lingered a few moments longer, but only remained to speak to her son. "I'm glad you're home," she said stiffly before she, too, had launched herself into the air. She soon disappeared out of sight as she fled the chamber, towards the passages the led to the surface.

Vinzent was smiling again. "How do you feel, Boss?" he asked, mimicking the tone he usually only reserved for Anzig.

"Oh please don't start calling me that," I said, in turn mimicking my cousin's usual response to the silver dragon. He didn't seem perturbed in the slightest, and I knew that I would have to endure that nickname for some time to come – probably until Anzig returned.

"Why not? You totally were the boss back there. I think you caught them unawares at just how good you were," Vinzent said. His tail twitched and he absently pawed at the ground as he turned to face me. His smirk turned nervous. "I knew you had it in you. I know what you're capable of, Ellian. And..." He paused.

"And what?" I asked, when it seemed like he was unable to continue.

"Haeraig Anzig told me not to. He said he wouldn't allow it." Vinzent whined, shaking his head vigorously.

"Haeraig Anzig isn't here though," I said pointedly. My head was a whirl of thoughts. I thought I knew where Vinzent was going, and the prospect thrilled me. Before leaving for Xital, it was something that had dominated my mind, and it was only a question of when, not if.

A wicked grin spread across the silver dragon's face as he contemplated this fact. "There's nothing he can do to stop me," he said. His twitching tail found mine and settled, its length wrapping around mine in a tight embrace. "You see, I know that you could be the most powerful dragon this clan has ever seen, and El... Ellian, if you'll let me, I want to be the dragon by your side.

"I know we're young, but, well, it won't be long before I'm old enough to be a dragon, not a dragonet. I am old enough to make my own decisions, to forge my own flight. Would you be my mate?"

I didn't hesitate. "Vinzent, of course I accept." I looked across at him and smiled, and he glanced back at me with those beautiful blue eyes and started laughing.

"Come on then, there's somewhere I want to show you," he said, suddenly leaping to his paws. Full of energy once more.

I hesitated, glancing to the other dragons gathered around the chamber. My eyes lingered on Yalle and Marin, barely visible on the other side of the cave. I curled the tip of my tail. "I shouldn't."

Vinzent scoffed, lightly batting me with his paw. "Why not?"

I spread a wing, gesturing broadly at the cave. "Because I have to act like their leader, at least until Ddraig Astar returns," I said. I nudged my muzzle against his paw, which was still outstretched. "There will be plenty of time when he's back."

The silver dragon rolled his eyes. "Ellian, you're basically the ddraig at the moment. You can do what you want and no one can challenge you." He flared his wings and crouched, bracing to lift into the air. "Come on. Follow me."

Without waiting to see if I would follow, Vinzent launched into the air. His wings beat up clouds of dust, which swirled around me. I remained firmly on the ground, unmoving but to turn my head as my eyes tracked him. "That's not how it works," I said quietly, too softly for anyone to hear me. Though my heart wanted to follow him, I did not allow myself that luxury. Intended mate or not, I had my duties in the lair.

Perhaps I had been wrong about Vinzent. Perhaps he wouldn't be such a good leader after all.

# CHAPTER SIX

**Anzig**

It was our third morning since leaving Xital, and the knowledge that we would reach the Sxinix Mountains that day gave energy to our wings, like a strong tailwind pushing us along. Whether by fortune or design by the seer, we had come across an empty nomad cave at the end of each day, just before the sun set and took the last of the light. Though there had been fresh scents in the shelters, we had not seen any dragon, or indeed a human, since departing Xital. The land was ours and ours alone.

After seeking my permission, Isikian moved forward to fly with Azlak. I had never known of any dragon who had chosen to fly alongside the seer, or even willingly sought out a conversation with him. For a conversation is what they shared. I was too far behind them to hear what they had to discuss, but Azlak especially was often quite animated.

Beyond my occasional glances forward, my attention was largely devoted to Carlee. The old veteran had been trying all morning to make me reconsider the entire mission. She had not taken well to us going when I had first informed her of the plan, and it was only through my authority that she was actually present. Even though we were now all committed to the task ahead, she was still trying to find some way to make me stop. I knew her motives weren't through cowardice, but partly because she didn't trust Azlak's word, and also because she didn't see how recovering the Axinstone would benefit all of dragonkind.

I did trust Azlak's word. And though I did not understand how the recovery of the Axinstone would benefit any clan but Nixa, I trusted Haeraig Zeena enough to know that she had spoken the truth too. Nixa would find a way to help us all. I could see no other way to defeat the humans.

The mountains began to rise from the horizon shortly after midday, slowly at first, but soon growing into the monstrous peaks that divided dragon lands from human. Except for a few areas, they rose to pierce the clouds; too high for any dragon to fly over. I only knew of two passes across the mountains, neither of which was near us. One was the Gota-Sxinix, a large plateau to the north, the highest point of which brushed the bottom of the clouds. It was from there that the humans had crossed the mountains and into my clan's territory.

The second pass I knew of was a small unnamed one about a day's flight from the northern-most border of Clan Nixa. I had crossed it once before, in my only other foray into human territory. It was little more than a dark and winding crevasse that passed right through the mountain. I had found it treacherous, but at the time I had been nowhere near the Gota-Sxinix. I was glad we wouldn't be taking it this time.

As the distance to the mountains reduced, so did the chatter. No one spoke a word after mid-afternoon. Even Carlee's protests had ceased. The Sxinix were a physical reminder that we would soon be leaving the safety of dragon territory and throwing ourselves into the unknown of human lands. I didn't want to admit it to anyone, but I was terrified.

I could only hope that terror stayed out of my wings.

Azlak was beginning to falter.

Evening closed in around us. The sun, low in the sky behind us, was casting orange and red hues across the trees below. We had maybe an hour of light left before night set in.

I knew the seer was struggling. His wingbeats were becoming irregular, and he no longer maintained a level flight. He was tiring badly, but he was by no means in the worst condition. Carlee no longer possessed the stamina she used to have in her prime, and she was starting to lag behind the rest of the group. The little red, Okazuni, was also having difficulty maintaining pace. We would all deserve a hunt in the morning, should any of us be alert enough to catch anything.

"Is it much further?" I asked the seer as I moved up beside him and Isikian.

"Not far," Azlak replied breathlessly. Even as he spoke he nodded down to the ground and added, "Just there, by the tall oak. There's a burrow system. Below the roots. There will be food. And water."

I looked down to where Azlak indicated, and easily spotted the tree he meant. It towered over the trees around it, a lone beacon in a sea of green. It was less than a mile distant. True to Azlak's word, I could hear a river nearby too, forging its path below the thick canopy of leaves.

Azlak started to descend to the trees, but then pulled back up again with a strained stretch of his weary wings. It was only when he looked up at me when I realised he was waiting for me to move past him and reclaim my position at the head of the group, which I immediately did. I couldn't explain why I had almost allowed Azlak to continue in the lead position even after he had told me our exact destination, but the thing that confused me even more was how close Azlak had been to continuing to lead.

I shook my head and blamed it on a lapse of concentration. Maybe I'd just allowed myself to grow used to having to follow Azlak over the course of the previous few days. It was likely nothing I would have to worry about. The seer was no leader, after all.

"Finally," I heard Okazuni say from above me. Azlak wasn't the only one in desperate need of rest. All of us deserved it, but we smaller dragons were not built for these long flights of stamina and endurance. It would take every bit of my strength to keep the worst of my exhaustion hidden from the group, for I did not want to show weakness to them. Not so soon after meeting them all. It would leave a poor impression on me and on Laxtal.

The canopy of leaves was thick and complete. There wasn't a single break in its coverage except for the ones we made as we forced our way through. The branches tried to tear at us as we dived but could not break through our tough scales.

The ground came at us suddenly. The bottommost leaves were so close to the ground that it nearly didn't give me enough time to slow down my descent and land in a dignified manner. The ground was damp underpaw, and half-rotted brown leaves littered the forest floor. There was the sound of feathered wings fluttering as an unseen bird fled from the vicinity.

As Azlak had said, there was a burrow entrance below the roots of the great oak tree. It was dug right out of the soft soil, and to all appearances it was made by a nomadic group of dragons and then abandoned. It was not the greatest of places to rest, but no one was willing to complain.

Everyone landed around me, and a few simply collapsed to the ground, Azlak included. It took a great effort to remain on my paws.

"There must be a reason why this was dug here," Keita said as she landed by my side, her wings brushing against my body as she folded them.

"Feel the ground, it's warm," Azlak said suddenly from where he lay. As Keita and I looked down at Azlak he turned away, staring at something in the distance. He was right though. I could feel an unexpected warmth emanating up from below the layer of leaves.

"But then why was it abandoned?" Okazuni added. He had been listening in to what we had been saying and expressed what I believed to be the hidden concern of everyone. Again, we turned to Azlak, but he wasn't offering any reply. Whether that was because he didn't know or didn't want to say I could not be sure.

"Could have been anything," I said evasively. I was weary, and just wanted to rest. I didn't want to worry about why the burrow had been abandoned when it seemed quite ideal, if a little unspectacular. "It will be safe for the night. Let's all get some rest."

Okazuni did not appear convinced, but he followed me inside the burrow anyway. The red dragon barged his way in before Keita and Carlee, who had tried to follow directly behind me.

The burrow was deep and long, twisting its way around the roots of the oak above our heads. The walls were bare earth, drier inside than the surface, but still slightly warm to the touch. There was also an eerie red glow coming from somewhere, lighting our way and revealing many small chambers to either side of the main passage. Each chamber was large enough for a couple of dragons to comfortably sleep in.

One by one, everyone claimed a chamber for their own, until it was just me, Keita, and Isikian left. The largest and warmest chamber was left empty, no one daring to claim it ahead of me.

The Nixan healer ignored the requests of his brother to join him to remain at my side. Keita slowly peered into the final chamber, before settling down on the warmed ground. She waited quietly for me as I turned to Isikian, who was gently clawing at the walls. I could tell he wanted to say something. The tip of his tail twitched so quickly it was almost a vibration.

"Look at this," he said after a brief period of silence. He stopped clawing as something fell from the wall. Isikian gently picked it up in his claws and held it up. It was a tiny, blood-red crystal, barely big enough for the eye to see.

"This is what is giving off the light and heat. There must be hundreds of them in the soil here, thousands maybe. I've never known of such a high concentration before," he said, rolling the crystal over in his claws.

"What are they though?"

Isikian paused, lowering his head so he was looking up at me, despite his superior height. "This place is charged with raw magic. I've never seen anything like it. These crystals have absorbed the magic from the ground and are radiating it as heat and light," he said, passing the tiny crystal to me.

The moment the crystal touched my scales I felt a sudden rush of heat pass through my body, causing me to shiver involuntary as...

*If we get enough of these*

...I dropped the crystal in shock.

"Anzig? Are you alright?" Isikian asked in concern.

I shook my head and stared down at the crystal, gleaming in the red glow it was giving off. I could not even begin to explain what had just happened there. The heat hadn't burnt at all, it was more like a surge of energy, or static, but I had not noticed Isikian feeling the same sort of effects from it. And then there was the voice I had heard that was definitely not my own. If anything, it had sounded like the healer's voice, but he had not said anything. I shook my head again, more vigorously than before and looked up at Isikian, who had taken a few tentative steps towards me. His right paw was raised from the ground slightly.

"I... I'm just tired, I think. Get some rest, I'll be fine in the morning," I said, backing away from Isikian and the crystal lying on the ground. Isikian lowered his paw, but he made no attempt to leave. His eyes never left me, his gaze high enough to cause disrespect.

"Haeraig, your horns," the healer said slowly.

"What about them? I snapped. It was all I could do not to reach up and cover a horn with my paw. I had never liked how they looked, so pitiful and weak compared to others in my clan. To control myself, I dug my claws into the soft soil, feeling the heat of the strange red crystals against my scales.

"I just… never mind," Isikian said, dropping his gaze as though he realised the insult he was causing. The Nixan healer backed away, lowering his head. "A trick of the light. Think nothing of it, Haeraig."

I said nothing as the Nixan continued to back away, before he turned and disappeared through the red haze and into the darkness of the warren. I remained still for a few moments longer. I did not like the idea of the healer keeping secrets and speaking in vague notions. I may not be the haeraig of his clan, but I was still a haeraig. I should have spoken against his evasive words and demanded he tell me what had been on his mind, but that chance had long gone.

Keita raised a tired wing as I crawled into the tight, dark chamber. The red glow of the crystals gave her crimson scales a bloody appearance.

"What was that about?" Keita murmured as I settled down near her. We were the only ones in this small chamber, though the muffled conversation of others reached my ears from different parts of the warren.

I turned my head away from Keita and stared towards the darkness of the warren. Slowly, my paw moved up to feel the blunted horns over my brow. The horns that had never developed as much as those sported by other Laxtals, whose long horns were a source of great pride.

"Nothing," I said, hoping Keita would not question any further. She would not understand.

The ness sighed softly. "It doesn't sound like nothing."

"Can we please not talk about it?" I demanded, my words a little more forceful than I intended.

A moment of silence. "Yes, Haeraig," Keita said, slipping back into formality after my rebuke. She gave me no chance to apologise before she drew her wing across her face and curled up to sleep. Her hind legs twitched as she got comfortable.

I held my head in my paws. I didn't think I could have handled that worse if I tried, but I did not dare break the silence again. Keita had already made it clear she wanted to say nothing else.

Isikian had unnerved me in a way I could not explain. An uneasy sensation had settled deep within my gut, but I had destroyed my chance to talk it through with the dragon I trusted most. Perhaps if I got the chance to get some time alone with Carlee, then I could share my worries with the veteran, but she would inevitably share my concerns with my father. Ddraig Astar could not know about my doubts.

All I could do was hold them inside, as I had always done.

With so many worries and questions buzzing through my mind, it promised to be a long, lonely night.

It was hard to tell whether it was night or day when I woke. The walls still glowed with the same crimson intensity, but I believed it to still be before sunrise. For a few minutes I was not sure what had woken me, but then I heard a noise from the surface. Something large was crunching on leaves and snapping branches underpaw. Whatever was up there, it was not far away from the entrance to the burrow.

I slowly stood up, taking care not to make a noise myself so I didn't wake Keita. She was still in a deep sleep by my side, comfortable and oblivious to the disturbances above. I did not want to go out and find out what was there. It sounded large and heavy, much bigger than any dragon. I could tell that much without needing to see it. But I also knew that I needed to find out what it was in case it was a threat. Bears weren't unheard of in these parts. Other dangers flashed through my mind. Human or otherwise.

I was haeraig. It was my duty to ensure the safety of my companions, no matter my fear. I forced myself to walk forward.

Wary of what had happened earlier, I kept a cautious eye on the walls and floor for any loose crystals. My long musings had not given me any answers as to what had happened, and I certainly did not want a repeat experience. I did not have to worry. There were none visible, though their red glow still permeated the tunnel going towards the surface.

As I had expected, dawn was still yet to come, though the night was not pitch dark as the near-full moon was still high in the sky. I ducked my head out from the burrow slightly, crouching low to the ground and shivering in the cold night air.

At first I could see nothing, but then a shadow moved just a few feet in front of me. I pulled back into the burrow, recoiling in fear, trying to make out the silhouette of the intruder. Very slowly I crawled forward again, taking care not to stand on a leaf or a twig.

Something rustled softly behind me, and I had to resist the urge to spin around to face it; instead just turning my head to look back. There was nothing there. I took another few paces forward without paying attention to where I was going and bumped muzzle-first into something hard, unyielding, and definitely not a tree. It was something living.

"What the hell?" the thing said from high above me, and I instantly recognised the voice as human. There was sudden pressure on my back as the human dived on top of me, pressing me into the ground.

"A dragon?" the human hissed. The full weight of his body down pushed on mine. Panicked, I thrashed and squirmed, trying to free myself of his weight, but his strength was too great. I tried to twist around to bite the human's soft skin, but I couldn't reach. My claws, pinned uselessly beneath my body, could not find vulnerable skin either. Even my wings were immobile, trapped beneath the human's hefty torso.

I changed tactic as the human clambered to his knees and tried to lift me up. I dug my claws into the ground, taking advantage of every root and stick I could find to keep myself as low as possible, desperate not to allow the human to lift me into a more vulnerable position to what I was already in. I kicked out with my hindpaws, catching the human on the face and drawing another agonised grunt.

Then the human moved, his legs shifting slightly to better lift me from the ground and placing them within striking range of my teeth. I did not waste the chance, snapping out at the weak flesh of his leg, just above the knee. The human cursed loudly, and for just a moment lessened his grip on my body. A moment was all I needed as I squirmed free, unfurling my wings to prevent him regaining his grip again.

A flash of fire burst into existence a few feet into the air, illuminating the human briefly, before the fire vanished again. The human looked alarmed. Then a second flash of fire, followed by a third, quicker this time.

Both the human and I took a step back, not quite sure what was going on as fire continued to flash all around the human's head and body. The individual flames were lasting longer now, and starting to merge with each other, morphing and twisting into some new form. A dragon's head. Its jaw gaped wide, revealing the fiery teeth within. The eyes were empty, made blacker by the fire surrounding them. Slowly it advanced on the human, who continued to step back. I could see fear in his eyes now in the instant before he turned and fled. The fiery dragon collapsed in on itself before vanishing with a quiet crackle.

"I'd mind yourself a bit more next time, Haeraig. I may not be around next time to help you," a voice said from behind me. I whipped around, a snarl ready in my throat, which I released in an inaudible hiss when I recognised the identity of the dragon. It was the grey-scaled Nixan, Inilta. Fire still flickered around his paws. Thin tendrils of smoke rose from fallen leaves around him as they curled up in the heat.

I growled. "I didn't need your help. I had it all under control."

Inilta sniffed, a smoke ring coming from his mouth as he did so. "Of course you did," he replied with an air of arrogance around him, but not enough to show disrespect. Then a touch of concern entered his voice. "I've never heard of a human in this area before, even since they started to come across the mountains," he said.

"Nor have I," I said. We were a long way south of the Gota-Sxinix, where the humans were gathering on Laxtal's borders. I could think of no reason why a human should be here, and I highly doubted he would be alone. Humans, like dragons, rarely travelled without company. As I thought that, I began to feel afraid for our safety. If the human that Inilta had chased away warned others of our presence, then we did not want to be caught out in the open.

"It's hard to say if the human was here by chance, or…" Inilta said quietly, falling into a hasty silence. He didn't meet my eye, instead looking up towards the moon. Strange patterns, almost like twisting shadows, danced across the moon's pale face.

"Or, what?" I pressed. My ears strained for any sounds in the woods, but the lone human had quickly vanished from my senses.

Inilta flicked the tip of his tail. "Nothing. Forget I said anything, Haeraig. We should not linger outside."

Another Nixan holding secrets. I opened my mouth to protest, but before I could speak, bats shrieked to each other about a hundred feet away. Something had disturbed them. I snapped my mouth shut again.

Inilta seemed to be well aware of the danger too. "After you, Haeraig," he said, gesturing his head to the burrow entrance, waiting for me to enter and follow in behind. I sniffed the cold air, trying to find the scent of human on the gentle wind. There was just the receding smell of the one Inilta had scared off. Even so, I had no desire to be caught unawares again. I led Inilta inside, but before I could question the Nixan some more, he melted away into the darkness and lay with his wing over his head at his brother's side. I would get nothing more from him.

I didn't speak of the incident with the human the next day. There was no point in concerning the others with what I hoped would turn out to be just an isolated event. I had thought much about it during the night, and I had been able to convince myself that there wouldn't be any other humans in the area. After all, what reason could they have of being so deep into our territories? Their conflict was on the borders.

As we flew I looked for any traces of humans, but I could see nothing. But then, the forest would be hiding any traces of the humans, unless they were foolish enough to utilise one of the few open spaces, or to make themselves visible above the trees. The land was peaceful and quiet. It reminded me of the day my mother died, of the moments before that ambush.

Shadows crawled at the back of my mind. Lost thoughts burrowed their way into my fears. Words of doubt and of fear. I didn't know how long I could ignore them, for they were relentless. All I could do was focus on the regular rhythm of my wings.

Azlak led the way again. Once more Isikian flew by his side. I was at a loss to explain why the two seemed to have developed such a strong friendship over so short a time, especially given Nixa's usual attitude to the diminutive seer. Inilta's reaction to Azlak was certainly more like the norm. But then, the grey dragon had been quite cold to everyone this morning. Something was bothering him, everyone could tell that, but for once Isikian didn't seem concerned about his brother's worries.

Unlike what she had done the previous few days, Carlee did not trouble me with her concerns about the folly of the mission. Instead, she hung back towards the rear of the group without speaking to anyone. Her face was sullen, but her wing beats were faltering and tired, even in this early stage of the day's flight. Her exhaustion did not bode well for her ability to remain with the group. Perhaps that was the true reason behind her wanting to turn back; she knew she lacked the stamina to stay with us.

Until Carlee raised the issue first I would do nothing about it, unless I could tell she was really starting to have difficulty. It was not up to me to embarrass her by turning her back. Besides, her advice and experience would be invaluable. If there was any chance of her staying, I would make certain she did.

"Haeraig, if I may?"

I looked back at the voice to find the Xigax dragon, Nataik, trailing my wing. Her scales were the colour of muddy leaves, though I was sure they had been pale blue the previous day. In the scant few days since we had first met, I had barely spoken with the slender ness. In fact, I couldn't recall a time ever since she had been formally introduced by her ddraig.

I slowed down a fraction to allow her to come up beside my wing.

"Forgive me for sounding presumptuous, Haeraig, but it seems to me that we're proceeding without much of a plan in mind," she said, not meeting my eye.

I clicked my tongue and hissed quietly. If I were to be honest, I would be inclined to agree with Nataik, but I knew that I couldn't admit such a thing, or else I would lose the tenuous trust and faith they had in me. We were flying blindly into danger, relying solely on Azlak's notoriously unreliable magic to guide us. The plan would have to be formed once we got to the human's lair, and even then we still had to rely on Azlak to See the way.

"I know what I'm doing," I said. "I trust Azlak's guidance. I trust that he will get us to the human's lair and find a way for us to recover the Axinstone. You should put some faith in him too."

"I find it hard to put trust in the runt," Nataik said bluntly. I growled at her, but she did not apologise for her harsh words. "I don't question your ability to lead us, Haeraig, but the runt is no leader. I don't believe he is capable of guiding us to our goal safely."

I growled again and put on a burst of speed to leave Nataik behind me. She did question my leadership, I could tell. She believed my trust in Azlak to be misplaced, and that told me she didn't trust me either. I wasn't obligated to win her respect, but it would certainly be beneficial to do so, and that meant finding a way to put her trust in Azlak.

Nataik didn't approach me for the rest of the day's flight, which ended shortly after noon. Azlak led us to the base of a sheer cliff on the easternmost mountain in this part of the Sxinix, and then took me to the side to speak privately with me.

"We must wait an hour here. I can't see a chance to hunt again for two more days. We may want to use this last chance to do so," he said. Was it my imagination, or was he holding himself just a little taller than he usually did? His belly wasn't so low that it was practically dragging through the grass stems.

"Why must we wait?" I asked.

"I don't know." Azlak scratched at the dirt beneath his paws. "I just know it's dangerous to attempt the cross now."

I couldn't help but notice that he looked across at Carlee as he said that. Was it dangerous in general to cross the mountains now, or just dangerous for the veteran? She was certainly the only one of our small group not to remain standing, as she had immediately slumped to the ground with her wings outstretched.

"Okazuni, Nataik," I called across to the group. I waited for the two dragons to acknowledge my call, which they both did with a little hesitation, as though they expected something bad. I didn't have anything too arduous for them. "I want you both to hunt for the group. We're resting here for an hour before crossing the Sxinix."

Okazuni and Nataik didn't need a second excuse to launch themselves back into the air. None of us had eaten for a couple of days. That was not a particularly long time for a dragon; even back at Laxtal I usually only hunted once every other day anyway, but I never flew without rest for so long either. I had no doubts that all the others would be feeling the same stabbing hunger pangs that I felt. As the two hunters, Okazuni and Nataik would have first picks of their kills, even ahead of me. Clan rank counted for nothing for those not involved in the hunt.

While Okazuni and Nataik were away, the rest of us used the opportunity to rest our aching wings and take in as much of the midday sun as we could. Carlee had covered her face with her wing, an obvious sign that she did not want to be disturbed. I respected that wish and left her alone.

Any expectations I had of waiting in silence was shattered by the approach of Keita. She looked very much like a dragon with something on her mind, a look that she seemed to have borrowed from Carlee. For once I wasn't thrilled by Keita's approach.

"What is it, Keita?" I asked her as she drew near. She had mentioned nothing of my irritation the previous night, but I was still wary that she might bring it up again. I still didn't know what I could say to her, and my eyes were drawn towards the curve of her long horns. I had always found them beautiful, but Isikian's words had roused an old jealousy within my heart.

"Do you trust Azlak with your life?" she said, staring with particular intent at a broken twig by her paws.

I hissed quietly before answering. I thought that Keita at least wouldn't feel the need to question who I placed my faith in. "Of course I trust him. I wouldn't have come if I didn't believe he can See the safest way for us to go. If he says we can come away with the Axinstone, then I trust him. With my life if necessary."

Keita now seemed entranced by a leaf that was rolling over the grass, the wind just strong enough to turn it over and over. "He's been wrong before..." she said uncertainly.

"Only because something happened to change it, and never for something this big," I replied. It was true that Azlak's prophecies turned out false quite frequently, but only because he had actively sought to change the future he had Seen. I knew that this time he was making sure nothing changed. He was following his visions exactly. If anything altered, I would be the first dragon he told.

"If you're sure..."

"I am sure. I know that this is going to work, Keita. I wouldn't have brought you or Carlee if I thought you'd be in danger."

"We are going to be in danger, Anzig," Keita pointed out.

It was my turn now to look at the ground. She was right of course. There was no conceivable way we couldn't be in danger. But Azlak could See a safe route for us. He could navigate us to the human's lair, take us to the Axinstone, and get us out safely.

"You know what I mean," I said, the words weak even to my own ears.

"If you're sure, Anzig. I'll follow you no matter what, you know that. But... you may need to convince some of the others that Azlak is someone who can be trusted. The Nixans especially. I don't think the grey one has taken to Azlak as well as his brother."

"Inilta? I'll do my best to keep my eye on him then, thank you," I said, looking over at the grey dragon. He was lying with his brother a little way from everyone else. Like typical Nixans, they were quite solitary in the presence of other clans. I supposed though that I was being a little unfair on the Nixans. All dragons preferred the company of their own clan, Laxtals were certainly guilty of that too. It was simply part of our nature, though in times like these I did question the folly of such behaviour. Working together was the only way we could defeat this human threat.

Okazuni and Nataik returned not long afterwards, each carrying two dead pheasants. As soon as they deposited the carcasses they returned to the air to collect the rest of their hunt. They had managed to kill eight pheasants – one for each of us, so even the submissive Azlak, who usually ate long after everyone else had finished, was able to eat his fill.

As much as we wanted to lie down and rest after eating, Azlak quietly informed me that we couldn't allow ourselves such a luxury. We had to keep moving.

Though there were some protests, no one dared contradict a direct order from me when I demanded we take to wing again. Azlak again led the way, taking us almost vertical up the cliff face. I was not familiar with this area, so I had no idea where the seer was leading us. I doubted even he truly knew. He was simply following where his visions told him to go.

The seer led us over the top of the cliff and up a steady slope. The mountain we climbed appeared to be one of the tallest in sight, though I knew Azlak would have no intention of flying us all the way over the top; dragons simply couldn't ascend that high. However, I couldn't see any pass between the mountains anywhere near where Azlak was guiding us, a fact a few of the others behind me had noticed too. Still Azlak flew on though. I wasn't sure he heard the mutterings of discontent that were starting to form behind him. Finally, I saw where we were going, but it didn't fill me with too much optimism.

Clinging to the side of the mountain was a narrow path that snaked its way ever higher, much higher than we could safely fly. That was our passage across the mountains; we were to walk the entire way.

# CHAPTER SEVEN

**Azlak**

The frigid evening air was as cold as the rock and ice beneath our paws. But that was nothing compared to the frostiness I could feel emanating from the dragons behind me. Already they were starting to doubt me. They spoke about me as though I could not hear them, but their words echoed against the cliff to our left. I could hear every whispered syllable. I tried not to let it get to me and just focussed on the ground before my paws as we sought out shelter from the oncoming darkness. This was a treacherous path. It would not do to lose grip and fall. Our wings could not save us. We would still be dashed against the cliffs if we tumbled. No. It was better to remain on four paws at all times.

Recognition flashed through my mind as familiar shapes in the rock loomed from the darkness. We walked the right path, no matter what mutters reached my ears. I understood their concerns. Without shelter, I doubted we would survive the oncoming night, but the slopes of the mountain were barren and bare, with not even a tree to break the force of the strong wind blowing down from the distant peaks.

I didn't keep track of time as we walked. My only focus was putting one paw in front of the other and keeping a speed great enough that I didn't hold up the seven dragons on my tail. Then, just as the sun was beginning to set and bring complete darkness, I caught sight of a familiar formation in the bare rock, a column rising like a beacon in the gloom. At the base was a deep crack that would provide shelter from the wind. We would have no fuel for a fire, but with Inilta's magic there would be no need.

With a weary wing, I pointed towards the opening of the cave. Almost immediately, the seven dragons pushed past me, bounding up the steep incline with an energy I no longer possessed. Instead, I trudged up the narrow path, one wary eye on the sheer drop to my right. I was so slow that Inilta already had a fire blazing by the time I reached the cave, his magical flames burning blissfully on bare and dusty bedrock.

I waited outside just long enough to look to the moon as its face changed. Farmer shimmered into thief. I shivered. Perhaps we could reach George's castle when the thief showed once more. It might give us the fortune we needed.

My eyes lingered on the distant, near-full moon a few moments longer, before I returned my gaze to closer matters. I knew there were some who put belief into the power of the moon. Dirus was an ancient goddess. According to the old stories rarely told anymore, she had been worshipped long before dragons and humans had ever come into conflict. I doubted she would care about our plight.

Isikian cast a quick glance in my direction as I slumped to the ground, as close to the mouth of the cave as I could without still being in the wind, but the Nixan quickly looked away again. The healer huddled next to his brother, with only the haeraig closer to the fire than them. Keita had not taken her usual customary place by the haeraig's side, instead sharing a quiet word with Okazuni in the dark shadows beyond the fire. As I watched, Haeraig Anzig lifted his head as though to search for Keita, but he was intercepted by Carlee before he could find his ever-present companion.

I stared into the fire, watching the flickering tongues of magical light twist around each other. Shadows danced, casting patterns onto the cave walls...

*Anzig stood proudly before his clan, dappled in ceremonial paint from muzzle to the tip of his tail. He spread his wings as a joyous Carlee stood before him, letting the blood of a fox drip from her paw onto his forehead. "Blood of the ddraig who came before!"*

…twisting into shapes of dragons. Shadow and vision became one and the same.

*"May the spirit and wisdom of your predecessor guide you." Yalle put his bloody paw onto Anzig's forehead. The albino glanced down to the carcass of a hare, prone on the altar between the two dragons. Anzig's wings twitched as he struggled to keep them tight to his sides.*

I recognised the vision. Though I had never been witness to the ceremony in the present, I was aware of the wylax, the traditional ritual that honoured a dragon as they became ddraig of their clan. I had seen Anzig's ascension to ddraig many times now, though I had never seen him clear enough to recognise how old he was. The wylax could be this year, or it could be a decade or more to come. The future was intangible in so many ways.

Two different futures danced in front of me, both with Anzig becoming the ddraig of Laxtal, but it was the variances that intrigued me. Carlee was present in one, with Anzig strong and proud. But when Yalle placed the blood on the new ddraig's forehead, Anzig was uncertain and insecure.

I looked to Carlee, deep in conversation with the future ddraig. She was crucial to Anzig's success. I knew that much. I was glad she was here, but also worried. Her health was not what it once was. She was the crucial factor in the success of this mad mission. She would bring us success, but it could also be her weakness that causes us to fail. The old veteran would need protection, but I didn't know how to provide that. She would not accept my help.

I sighed and closed my eyes. The fire did little to warm my scales, but I was outside of the wind. That would be enough for the night. It did not take long before my exhaustion claimed me, and I drifted off to sleep.

*The moon shone brightly in the clear sky, several days out from full. The face of the mystic glowed with divine radiance, bathing the land with the magic and light of Dirus.*

*I soared far above the land. Pinpricks of light gave away the presence of human settlements far below, but I did not fear them. I was so high that they would never see me, even during the day. At night, I was utterly invisible.*

*In the darkness of the night, the mountains were little more than an inky void that reached up to the starry sky. I banked towards the great heights, my destination a small hamlet nestled in the foothills of the Dragon Teeth Mountains.*

*Anticipation welled in my chest as I began to descend. My nostrils flared, picking up the scent of humans mingled with their machines and technology. By the time I came to land, I could sense something else in the air. Fear. I revelled in it, drinking in that terror. It was better than any thermal or even the most satisfying of meals.*

*I thundered to the ground, landing in the middle of the main street that wound between the houses. A few human faces peered out from behind windows, eyes wide and full of rightful terror. Whispers of my name followed my progress.*

*Breathing in that fear, I gracefully made my way through the small village. The tarmac was rough beneath me, and I bumped my way through some of the vehicles that lined the narrow street. I knew what I sought was not here. Not yet, at least. But they were coming. It wouldn't be long now.*

*I paused at a fountain in the middle of the village. I went to take a drink and caught sight of my rippled reflection. I saw nothing but a shadow and eyes that burned red with smouldering fury.*

I jerked awake, heart racing. The night was dark still, the wind howling through the mountains. Slowly, silently, I rose to my paws to creep out of the cave. No one stirred, slumbering around Inilta's fire, tails entwined and bodies draped over each other.

The moon showed the face of the thief still. It hadn't changed unexpectedly. The mystic was three days away, or two days past. Had that been a dream or a vision? I couldn't quite be sure, but the terror lingered with me, as did the name I had heard.

Nightwings.

A spectre to make even humans afraid.

Just what terror haunted the far side of the mountains?

Our trek through the mountains continued almost as soon as the sun rose, chasing away the last of the nightly terrors. I spoke nothing of my worrying dream or vision, not wanting to raise any alarms should it merely have been a dream and nothing more.

The mutters and snide comments didn't take long to start again. There was seemingly no end to the ever-increasing incline as we climbed higher and higher. The air was cold and thin, making each breath sear at my lungs. I knew the others struggled for air as well, because it was not long before those muttered complaints fell into silence again.

Each step was a chore. My wings fluttered in the strong wind. It would be so easy to let them open and for the thin air to take me wherever it willed. My head dipped. I didn't know how much further we could go. I knew this was the best way. I didn't know why it was, I just knew, without a shadow of a doubt, this path meant we had the greatest chance of ultimately succeeding.

One paw in front of the other. That was all that mattered.

"Azlak, stop."

I ignored the voice. It might have been the haeraig. It could have been any of the others. In my haze it could even have been my father. All I knew was that I had to keep going.

Almost imperceptibly, the ground shifted beneath me. I began to creep downhill. We were on the other side of the mountains. In the human lands.

A series of ridges and peaks still lay ahead of us, but the narrow path wound its way around the worst of them, keeping us on a consistent downhill slope. The wind wasn't as strong on this side of the mountains, and the air was a little warmer against my scales. Each step felt that little bit easier than the last.

Then, after an exhausting few hours, we cleared the last of the ridges and we stood at the top of a towering cliff to overlook the human land of Kernow.

At first glance, the other side of the Sxinix was very much like the draconic territories; open green fields as far as the eye could see with the occasional dark patch of forested land. A river burst forth from the mountains about ten miles south of us and meandered around the natural contours of the land. But after careful observation, even from a height as great as ours, the signs of human settlement came to prominence. There were features that would never be seen anywhere near a draconic lair. Dark twisting lines cut across the grasslands. They were what humans travelled along, for some reason preferring not to dirty their paws by taking the often straighter path through the grass. At the ends of these travelling lines were the many lairs. They were nothing like the lairs we dwelt in; for one they were all built above the ground. Whereas we went underground for protection, humans built ever higher and taller, seemingly disregarding self-preservation entirely. It was a curious habit of humans, one I had never been able to understand. Perhaps they reached for the sky that was denied them for their lack of wings.

Closer to the Sxinix, far below but almost directly in front of us, was a barely-visible cluster of human dwellings. Though we would not usually pass anywhere near to such a place, this was in fact our destination. I knew the place to be empty. I didn't know how long for, the past was not what I saw. I just knew that for the purposes of this coming night, we would be able to safely rest.

Once I had pointed the place out to Haeraig Anzig, he retook his customary position at the front of the column, and I was quickly shunted back to the rear. To my surprise it was Carlee right in front of me now, and not the healer Isikian, who had often walked or flown with me, whether by passive nature or a bizarre need to befriend me, I could never be sure.

I focused on Carlee. I did not need to wonder about her. She looked…

*Carlee was lying in the grass, her chest heaving. A green dragon stood over her, trying to coax her onwards, but it was already too late.*

*Her teeth were stained red: her own blood. Four others looked on, sadly, from a distance.*

*"No, no, you can't die," the green dragon said, pleading with the veteran.*

*Carlee moved her head, revealing a terrible wound that had rendered her right eye blind. "No, it's my time," she said, her voice pitifully weak. With a great effort she leaned forward to whisper something to the green dragon.*

*"No..." the green dragon said as Carlee's last breath escaped in a long, drawn-out sigh and her head fell back limply. She was dead.*

...so tired already. She was struggling the most out of all of us, and this was only our fifth day of travel. I looked at the back of her bobbing head with sorrow. Though I had never been close to her, I had been told stories of her incredible acts of heroism in the years long before my hatching. She was a living Laxtal legend, and to know that this expedition could well be her last filled me with grief. I mourned her death, even though she walked before me still. That was one of the pains of being a seer. I grieved for those who hadn't yet passed. I had seen a death for three of the dragons who travelled with me now.

We took to wing about halfway down the mountain, which vastly increased our pace. We plummeted in a controlled fall, all of us eager to land and rest where the air didn't hurt our lungs.

The human dwellings were mostly made of some sort of red, stone-like material. In all, there were four of the houses, all centred on a small courtyard of stone. All four of the houses were identical except for the vines of ivy that grew up the walls. A collection of smaller structures, made of wood and metal, were situated behind the larger buildings. I couldn't be sure what the humans used them for. They didn't seem large enough for living in.

In the centre of the small lair grew a large oak tree and a fountain of bubbling water, which we found to be drinkable. Other than the rustling of the great oak's leaves and the running water, we were the only things moving; everything else was completely still and silent. Though there was no prey to hunt, and though the air still stank of humans, the strange human lair would suit us well for the night.

It took a few minutes of rest to realise there was another scent in the air. It took me even longer to recognise it as wolf – a creature that only rarely patrolled Laxtal territories. It was softer than the human smell, but fresher. I shook my head and tried to ignore it all. Nothing had yet contradicted my visions. Though I was uneasily reminded of my dream, this place was safe.

We had timed the trek across the mountains well; sunset was almost upon us. Haeraig Anzig led the dragons in through the open window of one of the structures, but I remained outside, perched on the stone wall of the fountain. I looked across at the sun, and then a little further around to where I knew the human George's lair was, some distance to the west and north. Then I looked back at the structure my companions had entered. Were they right to doubt me?

I covered my head with my paws, and it was a long time before I realised I wasn't alone.

The other dragon shuffled their wings. I was so tuned to the silence that the sudden noise made me shriek and fall off the stone wall in shock, landing on my back on the hard cobblestones.

"Sorry, I didn't mean to scare you," Isikian said. His head emerged from beyond the stone wall; his emerald scales almost perfectly matching leaves of the tree behind him. "I just saw you out here and thought you may want to talk about something."

I rolled off my back and tucked my tail beneath my body, keeping myself as small as possible. "You're the only Nixan to ever take an interest in me," I said quietly. I couldn't bring myself to look at Isikian. I was too afraid I'd see that his concern for me was not sincere.

Isikian jumped down from the fountain and stood in front of me. "You're the first Nixan not to hatch in Nixa. Others in my clan see you as a fraud. I see you as a mystery. There's an explanation for this that's greater than we can imagine at the moment.

"You say your lineage is Laxtal, then I'm willing to believe you. But somewhere Nixan blood has entered your veins. I know you want the truth. I want to help you find it, for unlike the rest of my clan, my brother sadly included, I care about those who share our gifts, even if they were not raised a Nixan."

"But what have I done to deserve your attention?"

Isikian laughed. "You haven't needed to do anything. That's what I've been trying to say. You are who you are, and to me that's enough to make you one of the most intriguing dragons there has ever been. You are an impossibility. You are unique."

"No, I'm not." I don't know why I chose to divulge my most hidden secret to this dragon I had known for scant days. While it was true he had become the only dragon I could consider a friend, he was still a near-stranger to me. Without even making a conscious decision to do so, I was telling Isikian about my most regular vision, where the unknown Laxtal dragon tells me of his magic. I watched the Nixan's expression out of the corner of my eye. Though he hid it well, there was a moment where I could see scepticism clearly on his face.

"I... well, I must say that's completely unexpected," the Nixan said. He seemed quite flustered. "One dragon we were willing to put up with... but... well... we can't have Clan Laxtal challenging us by having better magic than us, can we?" Though he forced a smile, I could tell that he was greatly disturbed by my news that there could be a second Laxtal dragon possessing magic. I didn't know why that was so disturbing, but Isikian was alternating between shaking his head and pawing at the bumpy stonework ground.

"Are you sure they're Laxtal?"

"Yes. He tells me that he is."

"But is he telling the truth. Did you recognise the dragon? Do you know beyond any doubt he's Laxtal?"

"No. I told you, I never see his face and the voice is distorted. I don't know what he looks like or who he is. I just know that he's telling the truth. He has to be." The last part came out as a pathetic whimper. I was admitting my weakness, but I knew that this mysterious dragon had to be telling the truth. I couldn't bear being the only one.

Isikian didn't reply for a few minutes, letting the silence drag on awkwardly. I tried to work out his mind, but my magic was no help there: it didn't help me interpret the present, only the future. I sat without moving and kept the silence going. I didn't dare break Isikian's thoughts and ask what he was thinking. I didn't like the look on his face nor the steady, thrashing movements of his tail.

Finally, Isikian spoke. "Excuse me. I need to speak with my brother about this." He made to move away.

"Please. Don't." The words were out of my mouth before I could stop them. Isikian turned back to me. His eyes blazed. I looked away. I knew what I had asked him to do: keep a massive secret from his own brother. But I had to ask him. "Please. I've never told anyone about this before."

The fires in Isikian's eyes faded slightly. He relented. "Very well. This time I won't tell anyone. But if you See anything else of that dragon, you tell me immediately."

"I shall," I said quietly. I had no expectation of ever having to tell Isikian anything more. The vision hadn't changed since I had first Seen it over seven years ago.

"Come on in. It'll do you no good to stay out. It'll be cold soon."

Isikian waited until I stood up before he took to wing. He hastened ahead of me up to the window the others had flown through earlier. With a resigned sigh I followed him. He was right. There was no point in staying alone out in the cold. With one last glance to the moon, just as it shimmered to the face of the wolf, I slipped inside.

The room appeared to be where the humans slept. It was the exact same room I had first seen in my visions. That was good. Nothing had changed so far. Haeraig Anzig and Keita had taken the raised bedding, where they were lazily sprawled. Most of the others were resting on the floor, though Okazuni had perched himself at the top of one of the wooden furnishings. Thankfully there was a place to light a fire. Judging by the pale blue flames, Inilta had used his magic to light that. It was warm inside, even more so when Nataik managed to shut the window.

I settled down out of sight, beneath the bedding Haeraig Anzig and Keita were lying on. I could see the haeraig's tail drift from side-to-side just inches away from my muzzle. There was a moment when I felt a playful urge to swat at it, but I resisted. I wasn't a hatchling after all.

Conversation was muted as everyone drifted off to sleep. Despite my assurances that this place had been abandoned, the stink of humans still permeated everything here. It made the others nervous, I could tell, but not concerned enough to remain alert. Before long I was the only one left awake. I couldn't sleep, and I lay restless for quite some time, with just my thoughts to occupy me. I wasn't fully at ease, but I had the advantage of the visions to assure me that we would not be disturbed by humans during the night.

*Pawsteps. Pawsteps in the hallway. It was pitch black in the room, but through the crack beneath the door there was a clearly visible beam of light. The beam was moving slowly, sometimes vanishing from view, but never for long. It was steadily coming closer. Then it stopped and I knew it was right outside our room.*

*The door opened and the beam swept across the empty floor.*

*Behind the light stood three humans.*

This was not good.

I tugged on Haeraig Anzig's tail. I heard him moan softly in his sleep, but otherwise got no response. I quickly slipped out and leapt onto the soft bedding.

"Haeraig Anzig," I hissed, shaking his shoulder.

"What?" he said as his eyes opened. Though he kept his voice quiet, I could tell he was annoyed I had woken him.

"They're coming, Haeraig."

"Who?"

"Humans. They're coming here. This room."

"But... you said... you said we were safe here." It hurt me to hear the accusation in Haeraig Anzig's voice, but I also knew he had every right. I had said we would be safe here.

"I did, but something's changed. I don't know what. But humans are coming..." I broke off as I looked around the room. Something had to have changed to make the humans come. I tried to remember my first vision of the room. It was all the same... but for the fire. In my visions the fire hadn't been lit. That was the difference.

Haeraig Anzig had followed my gaze, and he too, realised too late the dangers of the fire. He hissed a curse under his breath. "The smoke. The smoke will draw them here." He leapt off the bed, narrowly avoiding the sleeping Carlee as he landed. By my side Keita stirred but did not wake.

After nosing around the fireplace for a few moments, the haeraig turned back to me. "Is it too late? Have the humans already seen the smoke?"

"I don't know. I don't know when they come. I just know that, unless we change something they will come, and they will find us..." Again I trailed off. I hadn't realised before: I was more concerned with the fact that humans were coming, I'd missed the fact that I didn't See them finding us. The floor was empty when the humans arrive.

Haeraig Anzig gasped in pain. He had tried to swat the fire, probably attempting to extinguish it. He turned to me and grimaced. "Wake Inilta. We need to get this out, just in case."

I nodded, feeling a little nervous. I hadn't spoken with Inilta since the first night, when he had so bluntly refused to have anything to do with me. I had to suppress that thought though. This was crucially important. I glanced back at Haeraig Anzig. "Try and wake everyone. We need to clear the floor. If the humans do come, we can't be seen at any costs."

Haeraig Anzig set off first to wake Keita on the bedding, while I tentatively approached Inilta, curled up in the corner of the room. I tried the same tactics I had with Haeraig Anzig, just gently nudging Inilta on the shoulder. The Nixan growled in his sleep but did not wake.

"Inilta, wake up," I hissed, cuffing him around the muzzle.

This time he woke, and without any trace of sluggishness, he was on his feet and savagely snarling. "What?"

I took a few steps back, my tail tucked under my legs, my head held as low as I could manage. "The fire needs to go out."

Inilta lifted his paw in front of his face and inspected his claws for a moment before saying, "No, I don't think it does."

"Haeraig Anzig's orders."

Inilta glared down at me. Without meeting his gaze, I could almost feel his eyes boring against to the back of my neck. Then his attention flicked over to Haeraig Anzig, who was trying to rouse Okazuni by dragging him down from his raised position on top of the furnishings. Inilta wasn't quite so keen to break one of the haeraig's orders, clearly.

"Why?" he asked, suspicion and curiosity etched into his tone.

"I have Seen humans. They'll see the smoke. We need to put the fire out now, if it's not already too late."

"We'll freeze in here without it."

"We'll be dead in here with it." I flinched at my own response. I almost cowered from the fire in the Nixan's eyes, but I held my ground.

"Fine, I'll get rid of it," Inilta snapped. He raised his paw in the direction of the fireplace, and a few moments later the room plunged into darkness. The cold chill, no longer held at bay by the fire's warmth, soon rose, seemingly right through small cracks in the floor, and the gaps around the door and window.

Everyone was soon awake, and gathered at the end of the bed, while Haeraig Anzig addressed us from above. He wasted no time in informing everyone why we were all standing around in the dark and cold.

"We're not safe here. Humans may be coming. We think they may have seen the smoke from the fire."

"Humans? How? You told us it was safe here, Haeraig," Okazuni said with ill-concealed disdain.

"No. I said that it was safe," I said quietly. Laxtal's haeraig wasn't going to take the blame for my mistakes. All eyes turned on me. Great. I wished I hadn't spoken. I hated it when I was the centre of attention. I shrank in on myself. "It was safe but something changed. The fire. We weren't meant to change that. I think lighting the fire has attracted attention."

"So now you're blaming me are you?" Inilta snarled. He had been the one to light the fire, I remembered too late. Of course he was going to think I was blaming him.

"No... I..."

"Shut up, all of you." Carlee had been looking out the window. She didn't need to tell us what she'd seen. We all heard it. The sound of something heavy walking across the stones outside. Something about as heavy as a human. As heavy as three even. Then we heard their voices. We were too late. They were here.

Under the orders of Haeraig Anzig, everyone sought a hiding place. All except Nataik and myself. I watched the Xigax dragon leap over to the door, where she raised up onto her hind legs and, with surprising ease, moved a small strip of metal to the side.

I alone had remained stationary as I watched Nataik. She had clearly seen my curious stare, for though she never once turned to face me, she said, "It locks the door so they can't open it. Seals it shut. It should hold them back, if we're lucky."

"It seals it? Something that small? That changes everything," I said, struggling in my enthusiasm to keep my voice down. In my vision the humans had not been bothered by a sealed entrance. They had just walked through. Even the unknown I was now in was much better than the certainty that the humans would come in – they may be content that the entrance was sealed and the dwelling empty. If they were able to break Nataik's lock and pass through the entrance then I was afraid they would still find us, though I had not actually Seen that eventuality.

Turning around, I saw that all the others were already hidden so thoroughly that I couldn't see any of them. I suddenly felt very exposed, seemingly all alone with Nataik and the approaching humans for company. We needed to get into hiding quickly, but I couldn't think where to go. The room didn't offer itself any obvious hiding places, although my companions had already proven me wrong.

The Xigax ness was obviously more knowledgeable about humans though, as she had pawed open the front panel of the furnishings that Okazuni had been sleeping on. I hadn't even known it could open, yet Nataik had been unerring.

Again, Nataik had seen my surprise and she paused to explain. "I've been around humans enough to know how their technology works. They call this a wardrobe. They keep their clothes in here, so it should be big enough for both of us." Sure enough, hung inside were the bits of fabric that humans used to cover their naked, vulnerable flesh. I brushed up against them as I cautiously stepped inside. They were soft; no real replacement for our tough scales, but it was all the humans had.

Nataik shut the entrance behind us, plunging us into complete darkness. There was barely enough room for the two of us, and her elongated body wrapped around mine. I closed my eyes to no discernible difference. I had never known a blackness so absolute, so perfect. I was not afraid, not of the darkness at least. Out of all the dragons I knew, I had spent the most in the dark and cold. I could withstand the night better than any other. I could feel Nataik shaking beside me. I placed my paw on hers, finding it after a moment's search.

"Everything's going to be fine," I whispered, wishing I could really mean that. We had escaped the certainty of capture but we were far from safe.

Nataik seemed more comforted by my words than I could have ever imagined. "You've Seen this?" she asked.

She was hopeful. My words had never inspired hope before; only despair, anger, hatred, or outright ignorance. It was quite a shame that I had to rupture Nataik's hope.

"No, I haven't Seen it," I said. I could feel a tingle of disappointment pass through our connected paws. "But sometimes that's for the best. I mean, I haven't Seen that we get caught in here. I usually See danger more anyway." I didn't know why I felt the need to say that. Perhaps it was some sense of pride I didn't know I possessed, unearthed when I had, for the first time, said something to make someone feel better.

"Hush now," Nataik said. She pressed against me. "Hush now and stay quiet."

The reason for Nataik's warning became apparent as something slammed loudly below us. That was soon followed by the sound of heavy pawsteps gradually coming closer. The humans were inside the building.

Sure enough, through a tiny crack in the wardrobe, I could periodically see their beam of light as they spoke indistinctly amongst themselves. Though I strained to hear, I couldn't make out what they were saying.

Then they approached the entrance of our room.

Nataik's paw trembled and I gripped it even tighter, hiding the trembling of my own.

I heard them trying to open the entrance, but whatever Nataik had done to it worked. It stayed closed. No light swept across the floor.

"Can't be anything in here. The door's locked," said one of the humans in a deep, gruff voice.

"Doesn't it lock from the inside?" said a second.

There was a short silence.

"Break it down." A third. There were three of them out there. That was too many for the eight of us to tackle, should they find any of us. Nataik huddled close to me, whether for support or to offer me protection, I was unsure.

With a loud bang, light flooded into the room.

Though my sight was limited to a tiny crack, I could see that the humans' beam of light swept back and forth across the room, finding nothing.

"Empty."

The beam disappeared from my sight and the light from the room outside started to lessen. They hadn't seen us.

"Wait."

Pawsteps thudded across the room. A shriek – a draconic scream of terror. There was an all-too-brief struggle and through the crack I could see a human clutching a squirming form in his arms. As the other two humans came forward to help the beam of light fell upon the struggle.

A flash of red scales and they were gone.

They had Keita.

# CHAPTER EIGHT

**Anzig**

I was numb. I simply couldn't believe they had taken Keita, but the three searing lines of pain across my face told me it hadn't all been a dream. The three humans had dragged Keita away. It had taken Carlee desperately clawing at my face to stop me from chasing after them. Though her attack had worked for the time being, I was restlessly pacing the room in defiance of the cold night air. All around me the others had collapsed to the ground, with the exception of Azlak, who stood on his own a little distance away. His eyes were milky white, as they had been since he had stepped out of the massive wooden construct behind him, with Nataik by his side.

There was utter silence. No one had dared speak. I knew they were all looking to me to think of a plan to rescue Keita, but my mind was blank. There was nothing I could think of. No plan that could see seven dragons rescue another from three humans; location unknown. Logic was screaming impossibility at me, but I refused to listen. I was not about to abandon my oldest companion and dearest friend.

"Haeraig?" Azlak's shaky voice broke the silence. I snarled in response but didn't look at the little seer. "I think I may have Seen a way. We have no choice but to follow it."

"Why?" Inilta said lazily, before I could respond.

"Because otherwise we all die."

A short silence followed Azlak's revelation. There was very little movement around the room, more likely because of the cold, rather than the sudden dread chill that had descended over me. Succeed or die was not an attractive proposition, and nor had it been what I had thought I was getting myself in to.

It was Inilta who spoke again. "So what? We go and rescue Keita and we all get killed? I don't think there's much to decide here," he said.

"I am not leaving Keita behind," I snarled, turning on Inilta immediately. The Nixan dragon didn't raise his eyes to meet mine.

"No, you don't understand," Azlak said, sending everyone's attention the way of the seer again, who squirmed under the expectation in everyone's eyes. "We die if we don't rescue Keita. If she doesn't come with us, we can't succeed in the human's lair."

Inilta wasn't convinced. "Weren't you the one who said we'd be safe from humans in this room?"

"I told you. Something changed. The humans were attracted by the fire. We weren't meant to light it."

"You're still blaming me for this?" Inilta said, his voice rising in anger.

"No... I..." Azlak stumbled over his words as he shrunk within himself, but then support came to him from a very unlikely source.

"I'd listen to the seer," Nataik said. Her scales shimmered in the shadows, blurring her outline and making it hard to properly see her. "He may have made a mistake, but there's no doubting he still saved us then. If the humans had come in while we were sleeping..." The Xigax ness left her sentence dangling. We all knew what would have happened had Azlak not warned us that the humans were coming.

Inilta didn't seem quite so eager to argue with Nataik, for he offered no response to her. Instead, he simply muttered darkly to himself and pulled his wing over his face.

"We listen to Azlak. We follow the humans and rescue Keita," I said. I just didn't know how. And nor, it seemed, did anyone else. Despite the urgency, no one seemed to possess the energy to do anything either. Now that direct danger had passed, we were quickly falling into sluggishness that only basking in the sunlight could cure. Dawn hadn't even begun to touch the eastern horizon yet.

"We're tired, Haeraig. We can't do anything tonight. We need to wait for the sun," Isikian said quietly. He didn't meet my eye either, as though he feared my retribution for speaking against chasing after Keita. He spoke truthfully though. We wouldn't make ten feet in the air in our current condition. The air was too cold, sapping our strength and keeping us sluggish and slow.

Unless... "Couldn't you do something Inilta?"

The grey-scaled Nixan raised his wing and looked at me, his mouth agape. "Huh?"

"You can control fire. We need warmth in our bodies before the sun rises. Is there nothing you can do to help us?"

"Perhaps. But anything I do will leave me far too tired to follow you, and I'm not remaining behind on my own," Inilta said uncertainly. He glanced across at his brother, who simply returned the gaze, unblinking.

"If I leave someone behind to watch over you, will you at least try?"

Inilta sighed. I hadn't given him much option but to agree. Even though I wasn't of Clan Nixa, I was still a haeraig; he still had to follow my commands. "I shall try," he said.

"I'll stay back," Isikian predictably offered, but I shook my head. We could need his skills once we caught up to Keita.

I turned to Carlee, who had been watching us in silence as she huddled with Okazuni for warmth. Okazuni and the Laxtal veteran were both keeping track of the discussion with interest, with the little red seeming keen to get involved. Carlee already knew who I had chosen to remain behind. I could see it in her eyes; she was dismayed that she was being left out of Keita's rescue, but also a weary resignation to the fact that she would be better served remaining back. I knew I wasn't the only one doubting whether she was strong enough to complete the mission of recovering the Axinstone. I could hardly bear to look at Carlee appearing so dejected. I was glad when she looked away.

Looking back to Inilta, I said, "Carlee will stay back and watch over you while you recover."

"Very well. Please try not to move too much. I've never done this before, and I'm not even sure it will work," Inilta said, closing his eyes.

I could feel the effects of Inilta's magic almost immediately. Warmth tingled through my veins; more intense than basking in the sunlight but not hot enough to become uncomfortable. In front of me, Isikian appeared to be glowing. Then I noticed that the light wasn't emanating from the Nixan, but from a film of blue flames that surrounded him completely, just a fraction of an inch above his scales. I knew then that Inilta would be coating us all in the same fiery film, his magic controlled perfectly to heat us all enough to last until sunrise.

Even after the flames vanished from our bodies, the heat still lingered on. As Inilta slumped to the ground, exhausted, the four dragons who would be accompanying me rose to their paws. Carlee alone remained on the floor, staring forlornly at the floorboards.

"We'll be back as soon as we can. Stay in here or on the roof once the sun rises. Keep out of sight," I said to the two weary dragons. Neither responded. I wasn't sure they had even heard me at all. I turned to the four behind me. Okazuni, Isikian, and Nataik already had their wings unfurled, ready for my command to fly. Azlak, just behind them, was holding himself taller than I had ever seen. Inilta's fire still seemed to be blazing in his eyes. I deliberately avoided making eye contact with him. I doubted he would look away first if I did.

Shaking my head to remove such unsettling thoughts, I launched myself into the air, scrambled at the window to force it open, then darted outside before I could reconsider the foolishness of what we were about to do. Five dragons against three humans. It was insane. But, if Azlak was to be believed, we had no choice.

Flying at night was a completely new experience for me. It was drastically different to flying during the day, mainly because I could barely see a thing, even with the full moon to light the way. Our eyes were not suited to low light conditions. Of course, seeing was not our biggest problem at the moment. That lay in simply knowing where to find the humans who had taken Keita.

I heard someone flying just behind my wings. Expecting it to be Nataik, who seemed fairly knowledgeable on humans, I called out, "Where do you think they've gone?"

I almost fell out of the air when I heard Azlak reply. "Head east. There's a small lair that way. I'm pretty sure the humans are going there," he said. I had to look back to make sure it was indeed Azlak who had come up to my wing. Since when had he ever voluntarily come up towards the front of a travelling group? I was so shocked that I couldn't even remember what Azlak had told me until the seer said, "Haeraig? We need to fly east."

"Right, yes," I said, trimming my wings and banking to the right. We were flying back towards the Sxinix. They were not very far distant but, true to Azlak's word, I could see a few pinpricks of light at their base. There was a human dwelling up ahead. Then I saw something else. There was another light source about halfway between us and the human dwellings, but this one was slowly moving towards the Sxinix and the lair that was also our destination. That had to be the humans and Keita. I shared that with Azlak, but he just offered a non-committal grunt in reply.

The path of the lights below was not straight and so we were gradually able to catch up. In fact, so winding was their path that we were able to get to the small cluster of human dwellings before the moving lights. We landed in a field just before the lair and waited. I found it hard to keep still with so much energy warming my blood. I could tell Azlak and Isikian were having the same difficulty.

The humans were in some sort of metallic beast that rumbled and roared as it passed us by. Two lights shone brightly from its front. I could just about catch sight of the three humans inside, though there was no sign of Keita.

Eager to have the chance to move again, I leapt back into the air, the others close on my tail. All we had to do was follow the roaring beast the humans were controlling. Keita had to still be with them.

It was another small lair we soon found ourselves in; a cluster of eight human structures, again built around a stone courtyard with a fountain bubbling in the very centre. Though slightly larger than the one we had rested in, it was otherwise virtually identical. Even the vines of ivy that grew up the walls of the structures were almost the same pattern. Humans weren't exactly renowned for their imagination in their buildings. Whereas no two dragon lairs were the same, humans preferred conformity and regularity. I called it boring.

The beast stopped in front of one of their dwellings, and the humans appeared from wing-like openings on either side. Keeping low to the ground, I took a few steps forward so I could see what was going on. All three of them were there. Though I had difficulty differentiating between humans, and I hadn't got a good view of them in the first place, I was still reasonably sure these were the same ones that had taken Keita. Then I saw her. She was gagged and her wings were bound, but otherwise I couldn't see that she had come to any harm. She didn't struggle as one of the humans carried her into their dwelling. The other two humans soon followed.

I took a few steps back and returned to the others. "Well. We know where she is now," I said. We had achieved the most important task. Finding Keita was relatively simple compared to getting her out of this lair. There didn't seem to be any other humans awake, other than the three kidnappers, but that was little comfort. I was sure they were still there, sleeping for now.

"So how do we get her out?" Isikian asked.

I turned to Azlak, hoping that he had Seen something, but he shook his head. We couldn't rely on the seer's magic to help us now; we simply had to react to whatever opportunities arose.

"Right. First, we need to find out where she's being held in there. We can worry about how to get her out afterwards," I said, turning back to face the human structure. Though it looked quite impenetrable, I knew that there were ways in: the windows. We could also use them to check each room. Once we had a good idea of what exactly was inside, then we could develop some form of plan.

"Okazuni, you take Isikian and search the lower windows. See if you can find a way in," I said, my eyes sweeping over the two dragons. I then glanced up, towards the upper level. "Azlak and Nataik, you'll come with me."

"Do we come back here, Haeraig?" Okazuni asked. He scratched at the soft dirt, his wingtips drooping slightly.

"If I may, Haeraig," Nataik said, interjecting before I could answer. She didn't continue until I nodded, giving her the permission to continue speaking. "Humans often keep trees and bushes at the back of their homes. Perfect places to hide in and discuss what to do next."

I flicked my tail and bared my teeth in a smile. "Good. We'll meet there. Be careful and don't split up. I don't want anyone else getting caught unawares."

Okazuni and Isikian hurried away, keeping their wings furled. They did not need to take to the air to do their job. The rest of us would be at greater risk, more exposed away from the ground.

I counted seven windows on the upper level, with a further six below. It would only take a few minutes to look through them all and hopefully find Keita. Getting in though would be tougher than I would like, for none of the windows appeared to be open. We didn't have much chance opening them from the outside.

The first two windows yielded nothing; there was no light within and we could see very little. We could see clearly into the third window, but it was obvious the room was empty, with no trace of either human or dragon. The fourth window was distorted so none of us could see through it, though there was a light on beyond it.

At the next window I had to duck back quickly. All three humans were there. Thankfully none of them had been looking out the window at the time, or else I was sure they would have seen me. They were clearly discussing something, but no sound came through the window.

And there she was. I hadn't seen her initially as she lay on the floor by the humans' feet. She was still gagged and bound; her eyes were closed, probably trying to ignore her surroundings. Unless the humans left, there was no way we would be able to get her out.

I reluctantly called for a withdrawal to regroup with the others. I hoped they had at least been able to find a way into the house. Nataik took over from Azlak at the position by my wing.

"We could break the windows, Haeraig," the Xigax dragon mused. Our paws touched the ground, and we quickly hurried towards one of the bushes Nataik had promised would be there. She leaned in close, whispering to me. "The glass will shatter, but it will attract the humans' attention. We should only do so if we have no other option."

No sooner had we crawled beneath a large, thorny rose bush, I saw Okazuni and Isikian approach. Whilst Okazuni already seemed to be wearying, Isikian was full of energy as he bounded up to me. He ducked his head reverently.

"She's not downstairs, but I think we've found a way to get in," the Nixan said without any preamble.

"I'm sure we could find another way," Okazuni whined, but I shook my head. We didn't have time to search for something new, and the option of shattering the windows did not appeal to me. We had to take every opportunity that was given to us.

"Lead us there, Isikian," I said. A combination of the heat that coursed through my body and this early success had me feeling giddy with confidence. We couldn't fail. We would soon have Keita with us once more.

Isikian led us along the ground to a box-like structure built out of the stone wall at the side of the house. A hatch was open on the top, and from within came a very familiar smell. Okazuni's reluctance was obvious, and he wasn't the only one less than impressed with Isikian's find.

"You want us to go through the coal cellar?" Nataik said with an air of disgust.

I put my paws up on the open hatch to look into the cellar. It was a void of black, but Isikian seemed confident it would cut through to the inside of the house somewhere. The unmistakeable smell of coal pervaded the air, though the cellar was mostly empty.

Okazuni and Nataik's hesitance were perhaps understandable; the cellar was filthy and the smell was quite choking. I had no real desire to go in either, but did we really have much choice? I looked towards the Sxinix in the east. I wasn't sure if it was my imagination or not, but the sky looked like it was ever so slightly lighter. If dawn came and the other humans woke while we were still here then we would not get away. We didn't have time to try and find another way in.

I knew that if I led then the others would have no choice but to follow. Taking one last look at the slight pink tinge in the sky to the east, I plunged forwards into the utter darkness before me. I could hear the grumblings of the others as they knew they now had to enter the coal cellar. Almost immediately I wished that I could have Inilta's magic to light our way, but we could be afforded no such luxury. The best that could be said about stumbling forward in the pitch black was that it was short, no more than six feet or so in length. At the very end was a small pile of coal that almost completely obstructed the narrow opening into the house beyond, but it didn't take long to dig through. The chute was so narrow that Nataik, the largest of our group, had some difficulty in squeezing through, but before long all of us were standing in another dark room. Years of living in Laxtal had made me very aware of the strange feeling of suppression I now felt; we were definitely underground.

Aware that the others, visible only as indistinct silhouettes in the gloom, were waiting on me to make a move I took in what little of our surroundings I could see. We appeared to be in some sort of storage room for there were boxes and assorted human junk strewn around the firm, cold floor with no real order or design. Above us, what must have been fairly close to the ceiling, were a couple of cracks of light squeezing beneath the bottom of the doorway. That looked to be the only way out of the room.

Even as I watched, shadows moved across the thin beams of light, briefly hiding the swirling clouds of coal dust we were all breathing. I could hear a low murmur of voices; the humans were just outside.

I took a few steps forward then froze. The click of my claws against the hard floor echoed loudly. There was no sudden movement from the light; in fact I couldn't even hear the humans any more. Cautiously I moved forward again, keeping my claws off the ground as much as possible, just in case the humans were still there.

Slowly, I clambered up a series of raised platforms that took me closer to the doorway above. Behind me I could hear the others do the same with a little less grace and a lot more noise than I could care for. Only Nataik seemed capable of moving silently.

The door was a typical human design; a simple plank of wood attached to the wall and locked into place with a complicated mechanism that was very difficult to operate without dextrous human paws. Nataik was the only dragon I knew who was able to operate the things. Why humans even had to bother with such nuisances was beyond me. A dragon was perfectly happy with an open archway. If privacy was really needed, a simple veil could be drawn across the entrance of most dens. At least, that was the way things were done in Laxtal. I knew other clans had different ways of maintaining privacy, but none as awkward or complicated as the human method.

I was about to turn to Nataik to get her to open the door when I heard the heavy, thumping pawsteps of a human. We all froze. I stopped breathing.

The human was talking to someone, though I could only hear one voice, one set of pawsteps. I thought of the rumour that had circulated the draconic clans; that humans had developed some way of speaking to those who weren't present and without the aid of magic.

"They'll be here soon with Nightwings," the human was saying. He paused as some silent response was made. "Yeah, we caught a dragon over at Gary's farm... No, of course he wasn't there. It's wyrsday and Dirus is full. He won't be anywhere near here tonight... Yes, just the one... Of course, we're quite sure... Alright, if you insist. We'll check back once we've secured this one..." The human's voice faded as he walked away.

"Haeraig..." Azlak's voice quavered through the darkness. I looked back but couldn't make out which of the indistinct figures he was.

"What is it?"

Azlak's voice was pitifully quiet as he struggled to contain his fears; gone was the confident Azlak I had witnessed just outside. "I know Nightwings. I've Seen it," the seer was saying. "We can't be here when the humans come with it."

"Why? What is Nightwings?" I asked.

"All I've Seen is shadow. A terrifying shadow with red eyes. Nightwings is terror and death."

Death again. I was beginning to doubt Azlak's assurance that we would all return to Laxtal unscathed. We had barely entered human territory and he had threatened us with certain death twice already. I kept this accusation out of my voice.

"We'd better hurry then." I paused for a moment as I considered the best course of action. We had to get up another level, find and break into the room Keita was being held in, and then escape; without being seen or detected by any of the three humans in the house with us. And all before a fourth human arrived with the spectre of death Azlak had Seen.

There was only one amongst us I would trust to send out of the door first. "Nataik, can you go out and make sure the way is clear. Find a way up if you can," I said, turning to the chameleonic Xigax ness.

Nataik offered no complaints to my request. Instead, she simply reached up and fumbled with the door's opening mechanism. She opened the door just slightly and slipped out. The rest of us crowded in the shade behind the door panel, trying to avoid being seen by anything that may pass by in the bright corridor.

There was very little space, and we huddled close together, shaking in ill-suppressed fear. I hoped that the others couldn't discern my scared movements from their own. I was supposed to be inspiring hope in the others, but I felt a coward, a fraud. I looked back at the others. Okazuni attracted my attention. Through the gloom I could see fear in the little red's eyes, but courage also. There was a determination in his eyes that shamed me.

I heard movement approaching and for a moment I thought we had been discovered, but it was Nataik who ducked her head around the door, allaying my concerns. "Let's go. Hurry," she whispered.

We all scampered after Nataik as she crept away. I had to keep my eyes on the Xigax dragon as, even though I was scant inches away from her, I found it difficult to see exactly where she was. Her chameleonic scales blended her in with the background. She was almost indistinguishable from the lurid green wall behind her.

The floor was soft and fuzzy beneath our paws, shielding the sounds of our claws. I could hear the humans in some other part of the house, but their sounds didn't seem urgent and they certainly weren't approaching us. I barely dared believe that we may be able to get through the house unnoticed.

Without once erring in her step, Nataik led us to another series of raised platforms. Enclosed on both sides by the green walls there was little chance of being seen except from either end. It would also be easy to trap us in, unless all the humans were on the lower level of the house. I hadn't heard any noises coming from above us, but I couldn't shake the feeling of unease that we were walking into a trap.

"Alright, where now?" Nataik whispered softly.

We were in another brightly lit corridor with five closed doorways leading off it. Fully aware how exposed we were, I closed my eyes and tried to remember which side of the house I had seen Keita. Any hope I had in catching her scent quickly vanished as that sense was overpowered by the choking smell of humans and the lingering scent of coal that clung to our scales. Even so, I had confidence in my sense of direction and was able to narrow it down to one of the two doors to our right.

"Nataik?" I said quietly, looking at the door on the left. The ness knew what to do. With more than a hint of fear, she approached the nearest of the doors. I knew why she was so scared; we all probably had the same thought running through our heads. What if there was a human just the other side of that door?

The door eased open, thankfully without a sound. Beyond it was darkness. Unlike the rest of the house, this room was not floored with the soft surface, but a hard one that gleamed in the light that had rushed in from the corridor. There were several strange, white devices throughout the room, but no sign of Keita. I could just see the window; it was the frosted and opaque one. Keita would be in the next room.

Nataik was just reaching up to open the door when we all heard it: thudding pawsteps from the level below us. They were starting to climb.

I frantically looked around but the only door that was open was the one that led into the opaque-windowed room. That was almost directly in front of where the human was coming from. There was no possible way we could hide in time.

I backed away, only realising what I was doing when my tail hit the door behind me. Glancing back at the others, I saw that they were all looking at me; waiting for me to give a command. I had nothing. No plan. No solution.

The human came into view, mercifully looking the other way. For the moment. There was nowhere to hide; I knew we couldn't escape detection.

Two shadows slipped past me.

Okazuni lunged for the human's legs, knocking his large prey back into the wall.

Before the human could even cry out, Nataik had entwined herself around its upper body and plunged her teeth into the soft, vulnerable flesh of the human's neck. With a quiet grunt, the human slipped to its knees.

Okazuni reacted in time to avoid being crushed by the human as it fell, but the little red dragon darted back in to nip the human on the arm as it tried to swat Nataik away. Isikian then dived forward to restrain the human's other arm, while Nataik remained latched on to the human's throat, her death grip squeezing the life out of her adversary.

The human paled as it struggled to free itself from the grip of the three dragons, but it was weakening. With a final, strained gasp, it keeled over and thudded to the floor, where it remained motionless. Nataik hesitated before unclenching her jaws. She spat out a mouthful of crimson. "Human blood is foul," she muttered as she wiped her muzzle clean.

"You... You killed it," I said, finding my voice for the first time since the human had approached. I was only dimly aware of the sounds coming from the other two humans below us.

"I didn't exactly have much choice, Haeraig," Nataik said, not entirely succeeding in her attempt to sound respectful. I knew my authority had taken quite a knock thanks to my inability to lead in a crisis. I had frozen when I had needed to be at my strongest.

I resisted the urge to duck my head. "Let's just find Keita and get out of here."

It didn't take much effort to force open the door, though I cringed at the sound of splintering wood as Nataik bashed the locking mechanism a few times. Thankfully there was no sound from the humans downstairs. They were still unaware of our presence.

I didn't take in any of the room that was revealed once the door opened. All I saw was Keita lying in the centre of the room with her legs and wings bound, her mouth sealed shut with a dull grey strip. Her back was faced towards us, and she struggled to move as the light from the corridor shone on her, no doubt scared the humans had returned.

I quickly sliced through her bonds, before putting a paw over her mouth to suppress her squeak of joy. The moment Keita was free she buried her head in my shoulder as I wrapped a protective wing around her body.

"Oh Anzig, I didn't think you were going to come," she said, her voice quavering as she fought to stay quiet.

"Of course I'd come. I wouldn't even think of leaving you behind," I said. Nothing would have kept me away. Keeping my wing over the distraught ness I turned to face the others, clustered together a few feet away. Okazuni was keeping a wary eye on the corridor where the dead human was lying. I silently lauded his intuition at taking watch, while berating myself for not having thought of it. I did not want a confrontation with another human. We had been lucky the first time; the human hadn't been aware of our presence, but it could not be long before the two remaining humans realised something was amiss. We had to leave.

"Nataik. Those windows can open from the inside, right?" I asked, turning to face the Xigax dragon. "You can open them, yes?"

"I can open them," she replied with a haughty sniff. Without so much as a second glance in my direction, she leapt up to the ledge below the clear pane and set to work on the little locking mechanism. "There hasn't been a single human device that I haven't been able to work, given a little time," she continued to mutter.

I had no intention of risking running into the humans below us. We would escape by the window and be gone before they even knew we were here. With a glance into the room, Okazuni silently pushed the door closed. For a brief moment it seemed like we would actually get away with it too, but then two things happened in very quick succession.

Nataik succeeded in unlocking the window, which yielded when she put pressure on it, slowly opening with a rusty screech. That did not fail to hide the more chilling noise that emanated from somewhere below us. A human voice called up. "Hey Tim, is everything alright up there?"

There was a long pause when none of us dared move, hoping against hope that the humans wouldn't come up and discover the fate of their companion. We weren't so lucky. I could hear their pawsteps slowly come closer. They were coming.

Our cold bodies sprung into life as adrenaline replaced warmth in our veins. My wings unfurled and I was in the air before my mind had chance to catch up. "Fly!" I yelled, quite redundantly, for I was the last to take flight.

Behind us the pawsteps faltered, and a cry of horror followed us into the rapidly lightening pre-dawn sky. The door almost crashed off its hinges, but the humans were too far behind. Too far away to do anything about our escape. So I thought.

A loud blast rang through the air. A flare of pain punched into my left wing and I cried out as it collapsed under my weight, no longer able to support me. I plummeted from the sky, past the reach of Isikian and Keita, who lunged out and tried to position themselves between me and the ground.

Another blast penetrated the air. There was no cry from any of my companions. No one else was struck down by whatever weapon the humans were using. I had heard about these things before, though never encountered any; these weapons that could inflict pain and death from a great distance.

I cringed and closed my eyes as the ground raced towards me.

With a sickening crunch I landed on my outstretched wing and slid into the middle of a clump of heather. The fragile wingbones smashed, fractured beyond any hope of use. Pain seared through my left side, rendering myself unable to even roll off my back without almost fainting from the agony.

Keita took to the ground by my side and gently placed her paw on my chest. I kept my eyes closed rather than see her horrified gaze.

"Anzig, can you move?" she whimpered, glancing back over her shoulder. I could hear the humans starting to pursue us; we didn't have much time.

"Fly, Keita. Go," I demanded between sharp, pained breaths. She tried to argue, but I cut across her before she could properly vocalise her protestations. "Fly. You don't have time to wait for me. I just need Isikian."

"Already here, Haeraig," I heard the healer say from somewhere just behind my head. I heard Keita take to wing as the cool touch of Isikian's paws rested on my scales. A soft blue glow shone through my closed eyes, and almost at once the pain disappeared. I could feel none of the healing but I could hear the shattered bones reconnect and pop back into place.

"Haeraig..." Isikian said uncertainly.

I opened my eyes to see the Nixan looking back at me, an expression of concern etched in his face.

"What's wrong?" I asked, not daring to move for fear his healing had somehow gone awry.

"Nothing," he said before pausing. He looked back down at my wing. "It's all fixed."

He still didn't sound certain about something, but as he stepped away I tentatively rolled over and regained my paws. I flexed my wings. No pain at all.

A human shout from not far away brought us back to our senses. I glanced across at Isikian. "Let's catch up with the others."

"Waiting on you, Haeraig," the Nixan replied.

We took to wing, staying close to the ground to try and avoid the humans' searches. It would not be long before they recovered our trail and gave chase. We had to get back in time to warn Inilta and Carlee. If we were able to escape from there undetected then the humans would never find us again. We would be able to leave this place behind and move on to Azlak's next destination.

I should have been happy. We had rescued Keita. We had escaped the humans. But I had proven I was not a leader. We may have succeeded, but I had failed.

That failure would be a shame that would be very difficult to escape.

# chapter nine

**Ellian**

"Ddraig Astar returns. He is perhaps four hours behind me," the messenger dragon said. Though he had landed some five minutes ago, his chest was still heaving as he spluttered for breath, so furiously had he pushed himself to get here. He had arrived so quickly that we had not even received warning from the beacons. "He says he looks forward to seeing his son again."

I shared a worried glance with Vinzent. He knew as well as I did that the ddraig was not going to be happy to learn that his son was not in Laxtal. We hoped he would be placated by the Nixan messenger who had arrived the previous day, announcing that Ddraig Krateos was planning a rare visit to Laxtal to arrange the details of the potential treaty, should Anzig be successful. He was to be expected within three days.

I dismissed the messenger and summoned Marin and Yalle. The two senior dragons had shown a strong willingness to assist me over the past few days, though the same could not be said for Saya, who had made herself scarce. We all agreed that the ddraig would be less than impressed at the news, but of course there was nothing any of us could do to change what had already occurred.

To distract my mind for a few moments, I arranged for a large hunting party to go out onto the plains and gather fresh meat. We had been advised that Ddraig Astar returned with a force of nearly one thousand dragons, and that they would require food after their long flight. Some one hundred hunters had gone to scour the plains for deer, cattle, and wild birds. There would be a feast tonight to celebrate the return of our clan's great leader. I could only hope that Ddraig Astar would be in a mood for frivolity.

Under my supervision, the feast began to grow. A steady supply of meat returned from the plains, brought through the narrow tunnels by the hunters. The dragons then flew out again, gathering more and more prey. Others remained to prepare the meat, skinning and seasoning the corpses, then cutting them into manageable sizes and cooking them on the main fire. It was not long before the entire lair smelled of cooked meat. Already, many dragons looked towards the growing feast with watering mouths, but there was still work to be done.

Excitement bubbled through the clan when the beacons warned us that we had barely an hour before Ddraig Astar's arrival. I took a moment to look around the great chamber. Platters of cooked meat were presented on carved wooden boards, imported from across the mountains in times of greater peace. Several dragons carefully hauled heavy stone flagons, each filled with spirits traded from the smaller clans on our northern borders.

Other dragons still were tasked with cleaning the lair, ensuring the dust and dirt trampled in from outside was cleared away. I couldn't help but smile as I watched it all, the activity through the lair happening to my orders.

Yalle came to stand by my side. The albino dragon dipped his head respectfully towards me. "Do you hope to placate Ddraig Astar's anger with this feast?"

I scoffed and shook my head. "No. His anger can't be avoided. He will be angry that Haeraig Anzig is not here. There is nothing we can do to avoid that," I said. My gaze slowly moved from the activity through the chamber, towards the pale albino. "This is because our clan will want to celebrate the success of our warriors."

"And should they not have been successful?" Yalle asked, his voice dropping to a whisper.

I clenched my forepaw, lifting it slowly from the ground. My wings fluttered against my back. "No," I said with a growl. "Ddraig

Astar would not have lost. He never has before. I don't think he would start now."

"Perhaps you are right," Yalle said. He turned his head to look towards the entrance chamber, high above our heads. "But I worry about all of this. Our clan cannot survive these raids for long. Our luck will run out eventually, if we do not get help from our allies. That was what Haeraig Anzig was meant to achieve. Not this foolish mission he has fled on."

I stamped my paw down. "It was not foolish. He did not flee," I said, barely managing to keep my voice quiet. I did not want to be heard shouting at Yalle. I would appear juvenile and immature, unfit for leading a clan. All the work of the last few days would have been for nothing.

Yalle did not look towards me, keeping his eyes raised towards the distant ceiling. "I was not in Xital. I can only take your word, Ellian. But just know I have my doubts that the haeraig's quest will help us."

I growled quietly, glaring at the back of Yalle's white-scaled head. He showed no concern, his poise still strong and confident.

The albino sighed. "I fear we might soon have to fight for our survival. Not just Laxtal, but all of dragonkind. The humans across the mountains are merciless. Once they get a taste of our blood they will not be sated."

"We're strong enough," I replied. My claws lightly scratched against the rock. I gazed towards the bonfire. Dark smoke billowed from the coal and kindling, drifting towards the ceiling where it vented out through small cracks in the overhanging stone. Amongst the bright orange flames were dark shadows, constantly moving and changing. The longer I stared, the more shapes I could see in them. One moment they looked like a dragon dancing, the next a human attacking. The shadows warred with each other, until suddenly I blinked and the mirage was gone. The fire was just fire again.

"I must make final preparations," Yalle said, drawing my mind away from the flames. The albino spread his wings, but he did not take off just yet. He glanced back at me, eyes down. "Victorious or not, our warriors will want more than just food and drink and a warm place to lie."

I inclined my head. There were other preparations I could make, and I had not seen Vinzent all day. I would need to find him, to make sure he was ready for the ddraig's return. Despite all his promises, I had barely seen him since we had returned to Laxtal. He had spent a lot of time with his mother.

Putting aside my worries, I managed a smile. "Food, drink, and warmth will be exactly what many of them want," I said, before turning to look up towards the entrance. "But we shall have music to honour them, and healers ready to tend to any wounds. They will be welcomed home."

Yalle nodded, but he said nothing more. He took to wing and quickly flew away, soaring towards the far end of the great chamber, behind the fire. I watched him all the way, before turning and tensing a forepaw, dragging my claws against the ground.

The main chamber was large enough to fit the entire clan and then some more. We would not worry about running out of room, even with the influx of Ddraig Astar's warriors. Space around the fire was a luxury, but that was far from the only place where the returning warriors could find warmth. My eyes found one of the many small alcoves around the edge of the chamber, some at the floor level, but others higher up on the wall. Some had already been lined with thick rugs, small lamps hooked up to metal bars chiselled into the rock walls.

Feeling the need to do something to occupy my paws, I leaped forward. Piles of rugs needed distributing through empty chambers. Dozens of disconnected wires still had to be plugged in so the darker recesses of the caves could be illuminated. Human technology in a draconic lair. I was sure there were some dragons who hated that we were so reliant on the enemy across the mountains for the comforts we enjoyed. I just saw it as another reason why my cousin needed to succeed. Only Anzig could help us avoid a costly war with the humans.

I just needed to convince Ddraig Astar that was true.

The returning troop could be heard before word of their arrival filtered down from the guards stationed at the entry chamber. The deafening thunder of a thousand pairs of wings rumbled through the rock, an airborne stampede.

The lair waited for their arrival into the great chamber. The feast was prepared. Hares and pheasant provided mouth-watering morsels as appetisers, before the temptation of deer and beef filled the belly. Spices gathered from Laxtal or imported from afar added to the delicious scents that wafted through the caves. A band sat to one side of the chamber with their instruments. Most had drums and bells, which they would play with their paws and tails. Once the returning army settled in, the musicians would provide most of the noise as the clan enjoyed the celebratory feast.

Every dragon who had been within a day's flight of the lair had come to honour the return of the ddraig. I stood amongst them, close to the fire. The three dragons who had taken over leadership sat around me: Yalle to one side and Marin to the other. Saya sat a wingspan behind me, with Vinzent by her side.

"I could inform the ddraig of his son, if you wish," Marin said, taking advantage of a small lull in the noise.

"No, Marin. It is my duty and I would have no other face the ddraig with this news," I replied, but thankful for the older dragon's offer. Already Marin was warming up to my leadership, though its temporary nature was about to come to an abrupt end.

Just a few minutes later the first dragons came from the tunnels and into the main chamber. At the head of the column was a massive red-scaled dragon, Ddraig Astar. He still wore the ceremonial chalk that was rubbed on to every dragon's scales during battle. Each clan had their own colours, and clan Laxtal traditionally wore a deep blue.

The ddraig landed by the fire, making eye contact with each gathered dragon in a slow, steady sweep of his impressive head. Without exception, everyone dropped their heads to avoid the burning contact of his smouldering amber eyes.

His gaze finally reached me.

"Ellian, where is my son? Where is Anzig?"

"Ddraig Astar, your son was a credit to the clan and upheld your honour in the council. Haeraig Zeena of Nixa spoke most highly of him, however..." I said quietly, looking down at Ddraig Astar's tense paws as they clawed at the sooty rock.

"Where is my son?" Ddraig Astar repeated with a small snarl.

I chanced a glance up at the ddraig, but seeing the hostility in his eyes caused my courage to flee, rendering myself mute. I couldn't speak a single word, but Vinzent's gentle tail-touch gave me the courage to explain what had happened to the mighty ddraig.

"The council decided that the Axinstone was to be reclaimed from the humans who stole it. Haeraig Anzig took it upon himself to carry out this charge with the promise of an alliance from Clan Nixa should he succeed. We have received word that Ddraig Krateos is on his way here as we speak to discuss this matter," I said quickly, before cringing back, expecting to receive the full brunt of the ddraig's ire, but it never came. Ddraig Astar had frozen, as though turned to stone; his tail had stopped moving mid swing, and his eyes had widened to contain the horror they betrayed. I couldn't look at the ddraig any longer, and lowered my gaze to his paws. I couldn't see my ddraig looking so vulnerable.

A period of uneasy silence passed before he was able to speak again. "Why? Why would he do this?"

"I'm sorry Ddraig Astar," Marin said as he came forward. He bowed his green-scaled head before the ddraig. "Haeraig Anzig appears to have been following the advice of my son. I was told Azlak informed the haeraig that he could not fail in retrieving the Axinstone."

"I see. My son has placed his trust in Azlak before and come to no ill. We can only hope that nothing happens this time," Ddraig Astar growled. His eyes clouded as he glared Marin. Two maelstroms of growing rage bored into the older drake. No dragon present was left in any doubt who would be blamed should Anzig perish. Azlak's actions would reflect very poorly on his father. Still none met his seething, withering gaze. "Who went with him?"

"Azlak went, as did Keita and Carlee. With them went two from Nixa, a ness from Xigax, and a Nyrian drake," I said quickly, trying to remember the group of dragons my cousin had gathered, having seen them only once.

"At least he took Carlee. Hopefully she can talk some sense into him," Ddraig Astar muttered. It seemed I had been spared the intimidating glare he had given Marin.

As the last of the returning dragons fluttered into the chamber, almost filling it to capacity, Ddraig Astar turned to face them. Though I could tell he was disappointed that his son wasn't present – his tail was completely motionless – outwardly the ddraig was confident and powerful as he addressed his clan.

"Our lands are safe once more," he roared, loud enough so the dragons in the farthest reaches of the chamber could hear. "Three hundred humans have been forced beyond the Gota-Sxinix and back into the western lands where they belong."

A cacophony of noise greeted Ddraig Astar's words, and he waited for the commotion to die down before speaking again. "We stand united with the Sxinix clans. Clan Nixa is closer to us than ever before, and the Axaatls will pledge allegiance to us should the humans invade in force. Clan Xital will unite the draconic armies on our call. We will not be cowed by this human threat. We will not let them take what is rightfully ours. This victory is Laxtal's first in the war. As surely as I breathe, it will not be our last!"

The ddraig paused then, his wings flared wide as he took in the roared adoration of the clan. I could never have hoped to get such a response from them. The air felt electric, and my breath was taken away from the force of emotion.

When the cacophony finally died, the ddraig spoke once more, his voice ringing out loudly. "A feast has been prepared to honour our victory. Drink heartily and eat your fill. Remember those who fell in defence of their clan. Honour them and celebrate this evening, for we are safe once more!"

As the clan made known their delight, Ddraig Astar turned to me and met my eyes. I held his stare for as long as I could. After only a few heartbeats I had to turn away. The ddraig grunted in approval. "If it was Anzig's desire for you to become haeraig in his stead, then I shall honour that wish, though I will not hide the fact that I would prefer my son. Follow me and come to my chambers and let us see what you've done, and let me find out how good you really are."

Ignoring the feast we had prepared, he took to wing and soared through the chamber. Though the scent of meat allured me, I obeyed my ddraig's command. I stayed as close to his tail as I could, though he was a fast flyer even after such a long flight. Another set of wingbeats and a quick glance back told me that Vinzent had come too, even though Ddraig Astar had not directly addressed him. We flew out the back of the giant cave, and away from the catacombs where the rest of the clan dwelt. There was a tiny network of caves behind the great fire pit that were warmer and drier than anywhere else in the lair. It was here that the leading dragons of the clan took up home. Visiting ddraigs and haeraigs were also afforded lodging here. I was one of the few dragons of low standing permitted regular access to these tunnels.

It had been many years since I had last been in Ddraig Astar's chambers, though. Even Anzig was rarely permitted access.

My last memory of his chambers had been just after my mother had died, leaving me an orphan. My brother had also been there, but I had never seen him again since. The ddraig had taken us in to explain what had happened, and that he would be looking after me. Being just a young dragonet at the time, I hadn't fully comprehended what he was talking about. I had been far more fascinated by the silver statue which adorned his chamber; a wingless creature shaped more like a four-legged serpent than any dragon that truly existed. I had been convinced that the statue had winked at me, but for months after, whenever I mentioned this to Ddraig Astar, he simply smiled and said nothing.

The silver statue was still there, and despite a strange urge to bow my head towards it, the statue did as a statue should. It remained perfectly still, and certainly did not wink at me.

Ddraig Astar growled as Vinzent sidled into his chambers, but he allowed the younger dragon to stay. Vinzent quickly sat by my side as the ddraig settled down by the small fire pit, set into a small alcove in the wall. The fire had not yet been lit, but the air was warm enough without the fire, thanks in part to the thick fur rugs that covered the floor. No dragon in Laxtal had such soft and comfortable rugs as Ddraig Astar, though I had been told such things were common in the northern clans. The rest of the clan had to make do with rugs that were thinner and trapped less heat.

For a while nothing was said, as Ddraig Astar glanced lazily between the two young, nervous dragons before him, neither of us able to keep the gaze of the older dragon. He seemed to be evaluating us, testing our mental fortitude. I tried my hardest to keep my head high and show strength I wasn't convinced I possessed. After a while, he snorted and rose to his paws.

"You wish to become the haeraig of Laxtal in my son's absence? It is a position of power and of honour. I will not allow a dragon to take my son's place if they are not strong enough to lead, for any error, any failure, becomes a slight against me," he said, pacing back and forth in front of the fire pit.

"I understand, Ddraig Astar," I replied, bowing my head to my paws in front of him. "I will not fail you."

"No, you must not, for I will not allow any dragon to threaten me, directly, or indirectly. Should you show weakness, then you indirectly threaten me. Your only blood bond to me is through my dead sister. Vasti's blood is not enough for me to overlook any failures, Ellian. I will cast you aside without a second thought if I must," the ddraig said, his clenched paw thudding against the rock as he spoke.

The ferocity of Ddraig Astar's words startled me, but I knew why they had to be spoken. Any dragon within Laxtal could become ddraig, should they successfully challenge and defeat the incumbent's authority. A weak haeraig was a potential flashpoint to a rebellion.

"She is not weak," Vinzent growled, showing a great courage to stand up to his ddraig. The young dragon's tail thrashed back and forth and even managed to hold the surprised stare Ddraig Astar gave him.

"And you have Saya's strength of mind, young Vinzent," he said, clearly quite impressed. He looked between the two of us and hissed quietly in thought. For a moment all his teeth were bared, and I felt myself shrink back. I forced myself to suppress my fear and hold my ground. I could not show weakness now, not when Ddraig Astar judged me for my strength.

I looked the ddraig in the eye. "I will not fail you, I swear this."

For a few seconds I was able to maintain eye contact before I had to relent. I looked down at my paws, hoping I had done enough to convince the ddraig.

"I hope that will be the case. I must admit, already I have been impressed with what you have achieved. Our borders are secure against human attack. I also saw the beacon garrisons were reinforced, another good initiative, and one that will protect us from ambushes. Even the feast is appreciated. My warriors are weary and hungry. They are eager to gorge themselves on meat, and you have done well to provide that to them. Continue this fine decision making, and Clan Laxtal could have another great leader," the ddraig said.

"You flatter me, Ddraig Astar, but I am not even half the haeraig that Anzig is," I said, glancing down at the ddraig's restless paws.

The smallest of growls escaped the ddraig's mouth. "Haeraig Anzig is not yet the leader he is capable of becoming. He has no confidence in himself, a problem I do not see in you. If my son can return with the Axinstone, then maybe he shall prove himself, but until then, I can only wait and hope," he said quietly.

I exchanged a startled glance with Vinzent. I could tell by his stunned look that he had never known that Ddraig Astar was disappointed in his son. It was a monumental truth, and one I felt I had no right in knowing. I didn't know what the right thing to say was, so I remained silent, and Vinzent did the same.

"You're right, I shouldn't have said that," Ddraig Astar said, responding to the unspoken awkwardness that had filled the chamber. Evidently he had caught our stunned looks and realised he had erred. I bashfully looked away, silently vowing that I would not discuss the ddraig's words to another dragon, other than with Vinzent.

The Laxtal leader had turned away from us again. He stood facing the silver statue, lost in thought.

"Leave us now. Go and enjoy the feast. I will eat later, when I have rested," he said after a while. "We shall soon need to prepare the clan for the arrival of Ddraig Krateos. If he is coming to propose an alliance then we must impress him. Even Clan Xital would fear a union between our great clans."

I hesitated for a moment, considering whether I should inform the ddraig of Haeraig Zeena's warnings of a potential Xital betrayal, but I held my tongue. He had already turned away and was gazing inwards; I doubted he would have heard had I spoken. Instead, I turned tail and fled the brooding dragon, with Vinzent scurrying to be at my side. We would return to the feast and enjoy the food and music, before setting into preparations for the Nixan ddraig's arrival.

I felt absurdly pleased with myself, yet completely afraid at the same time. Ddraig Astar had taken surprisingly well to his son's absence and had been full of praise for my leadership. On the other paw, even the slightest mistake and Ddraig Astar could well see me expelled from the clan, lest he face the repercussions of my weakness. I had no choice but to excel at everything I did and remain in the ddraig's favour. A tiny thought entered my mind. If I did well enough, maybe I would become haeraig permanently, even after Anzig's return.

I suppressed it with a shudder. Anzig was the true haeraig. I would not challenge him the right of rule he had hatched into. He was the only hatchling of Ddraig Astar, and uncontested haeraig. That would never change.

Ddraig Krateos arrived three days later to much advance fanfare. His presence had been detected from the Laxtal borders. The beacon fires had been lit, and Ddraig Astar was already waiting when the messenger arrived to alert the clan of the Nixan's approach. With him came nearly a dozen other dragons, including Haeraig Zeena.

Ddraig Krateos was not the largest of dragons. In fact, the bronze-scaled leader of Clan Nixa was quite physically stunted for a ddraig. I had been told though, that this did not diminish his power amongst his fellow Nixans. His strength lay in the power of his magic, and those few who had dared to challenge Ddraig Krateos had been swept aside by the force of his mind alone. He would make a terrifying enemy, and a fearsome ally.

I heard whispers amongst the gathered Laxtal dragons of the hopes for a display of magic from the visiting Nixans, like they were a travelling act set to perform at the feast prepared for their arrival. Those dragons were left disappointed. Ddraig Krateos spoke to no one but Ddraig Astar, and the two powerful dragons quickly retired to the private chambers behind the great firepit. The remaining Nixans, eleven in all, lay by the fire and communed amongst themselves, by and large ignoring the curious Laxtal dragons around them. They enjoyed the food and drink we had prepared for them. They listened to the musicians who played on a raised dais towards one end of the chamber and watched the dancers around them, but otherwise they had little to do with us.

I recognised Haeraig Zeena amongst their ranks. The red-scaled ness was keeping quiet, only occasionally interacting with her clanmates. As though sensing my gaze, she looked up and caught my eye. She smiled and bowed her head, submitting to me before I had the chance to submit to her.

The Nixan haeraig excused herself from her companions and made her way over to me. Once again, she bowed her head in my direction, but she met Vinzent's gaze without flinching, and the young silver dragon twitched involuntarily and soon looked away.

Another dragon followed Zeena across to us; a bright blue dragon whose scales gleamed in pristine beauty. "Haeraig Zeena, please don't stray from safety," he said, turning to face Zeena after giving me the slightest of nods.

"What danger could I be in, Kaz? You fret too much," Zeena replied in a weary tone.

With a loud crack that almost made me leap back and shriek in fright, a second drake, identical to the other, materialised by my side. "All the same," this newcomer said, "We would rather keep you close by, Haeraig."

"If you insist, Airil, then you may stay," Zeena growled.

The two azure dragons smugly took their places either side of their haeraig, who swung her head to each as she introduced the two dragons. "This is Airil and his twin, Kaz. They're my self-appointed protectors," she said, sticking her tongue out slightly.

"Hardly self-appointed, Haeraig. Ddraig Krateos himself asked us to make sure you came to no harm," Kaz said, the slight flaring of his wings suggesting that he was enjoying himself more than he perhaps should.

Zeena responded by lightly cuffing the dragon across the muzzle, but the sparkle in Kaz's eyes was not diminished. I suppressed a snicker as I watched the Nixans scuffle.

Airil, ignoring his brother and haeraig, ducked his head towards me. "I apologise if I startled you, Haeraig Ellian. I sometimes forget that my magic can alarm those not expecting my arrival," he said.

"Think nothing of it. I'm sure it was not your intention. And please, I am not the haeraig of Laxtal. That falls to my cousin, Anzig. I only fill in during his absence," I replied. I was surprised by the Nixan's apology. Normally they weren't overly concerned about whether their magic unnerved dragons from other clans; in fact they usually tended to go out of their way to ensure it did. But Airil, he seemed different somehow.

"I must admit, I've not really been able to perfect my aim. Sometimes I end up quite some distance away from my target," the Nixan said bashfully. He smiled nervously. "I once managed to appear on top of a ness who did not take too kindly to my sudden intrusion."

I couldn't help but laugh, and for a moment I feared the Nixan would think I was mocking him, but I was relieved when he joined me. "I could barely show my face for weeks after that. Almost got myself trapped inside a rock once before too. Lost a claw to that experience," he said, showing me his right forepaw, which was indeed missing a toe. He nosed his brother's flank, who was keeping silent as Zeena and Vinzent talked. "We use that as the only way to tell us apart."

"Zeena said you were twins?" I asked.

"Yes. Two dragonets from just the one egg. Our parents were a little shocked," Airil said proudly. Twins were a rarity amongst dragons. Clutches of up to three eggs were common enough, but very rarely would two dragonets form inside the same egg. There weren't any living dragons in Laxtal that had hatched in this manner.

"And Kaz shares your magic?"

"No. He's a healer, one of the best in the clan actually," Airil said. Kaz had turned at the sound of his name, and Airil gently flicked his tail at his twin. "Just talking about you, no need to worry."

Kaz groaned. "Has he told you about that time he appeared into a rock yet? Every time he meets a pretty ness he hasn't spoken to before, that's the first story he tells," he said in exasperated tones.

"Oh, be quiet you," Airil said, hitting his brother with significantly more force this time.

Feeling a little giddy from Kaz's comment, I glanced across at Vinzent to see if he had heard, but he had actually moved away a few paces to talk more privately with the Nixan haeraig. He seemed oblivious to anything else but the other ness. My heart felt like it skipped a couple of beats as conflicted emotions warred within me. I was both flattered by the attention from the two Nixan dragons, but I had experienced a sudden rush of jealousy towards Zeena as she held the total attention of the dragon who would become my mate.

Agreed to, at least.

That was the extent of my relationship with Vinzent. Though he given me his promise, we were not yet formally mates. We had spoken of intentions and plans, but he was still worried about Haeraig Anzig's disapproval, and that of Ddraig Astar. I feared another ness may turn his eye. The Nixan haeraig would make a powerful mate, and Vinzent would be likewise for her. I had to hold myself back from snarling at the Nixan haeraig and chasing her away from Vinzent. I tried to convince myself that I was simply being paranoid.

"Ellian, are you alright?" Airil asked, cutting into my black thoughts.

I forced a smile, which quickly turned sour as Zeena and Vinzent came back towards us, both laughing at something. "I'm fine. Nothing to worry about," I said bitterly. I just couldn't suppress the anxiety that was welling up in my chest.

"Vinzent was saying how strange it was that we hadn't been asked to join the ddraigs," Zeena said sulkily as she sat down by my side. Vinzent remained standing by the Nixan twins, who both looked particularly troubled. I marvelled at the open petulance of the haeraig; this was a side to the Nixan that had been kept hidden in Xital. I knew she was quite a few years my senior, so it could not be simple immaturity.

"I suppose this is a matter too important to risk having inexperienced haeraigs mess up," I ventured. My intention had been to try and put down the Nixan, but I also felt a little disgruntled that Ddraig Astar hadn't requested my presence in his chambers again. The Nixan growled but didn't argue with my suggestion. All things considered, I could hardly blame Ddraig Astar for not wanting me present. Anzig would be the dragon he would want by his side, but my cousin was far away, surely on the other side of the Sxinix Mountains by now.

I sighed and rested my head on my forepaws, looking up longingly at the chambers beyond the fire. I tried to ignore the general commotion of the clan, whose fascination with the Nixan dragons had dwindled somewhat. Zeena resumed her conversation with Vinzent again, but I tried to ignore them both, and tried to force my concerns from my mind. I concentrated on Anzig and his small group. Carlee's experience would probably be much missed here, but hopefully she would be able to guide the haeraig safely home.

"Ellian?" Vinzent said haltingly, pulling me away from my contemplations. I could immediately tell something was different. There was a cold chill in the air that was not tempered by the fire. At first I suspected Nixan magic, but then I realised it was no physical chill I felt, but a drastic change in mood that had been heralded by a second fire, high up near the ceiling of the great cave.

The Laxtal Beacon.

The beacons had been lit. The enemy was within our borders.

I didn't even think twice. I took to wing and launched myself into the air, heading directly for the ddraig's chambers. Whether this threat was human or draconic, Ddraig Astar would want to know immediately, even though he was probably still weary from his last victorious campaign. Again, this was a situation when Anzig's presence would be beneficial; I had no experience in war and had never fought outside of Carlee's ferocious training.

Another dragon was right on my tail. I glanced back, expecting to see the silver shine of Vinzent, but was surprised to see the Nixan haeraig there instead. She probably didn't know the significance of the beacon flame, but saw my urgency as a sign that she wanted to be wherever I went.

I took to my paws as soon as I dived into the narrow passages that linked the ddraig's chambers and the central cave. Still the Nixan sprinted by my tail, but her pawsteps were the only ones I heard – Vinzent had not followed us.

A thin veil of cloth had been drawn across Ddraig Astar's personal chambers, beyond which the muffled voices of the two dragons could be heard. I paused just outside, suddenly nervous about interrupting the two ddraigs, but I knew this was a matter that required his immediate knowledge.

Zeena nosed my flank to hurry me along, and I obliged by pushing through the veil and into Ddraig Astar's chamber. Immediately the two dragons ceased their conversation and turned to look at me. I averted my eyes instantly and waited for them to address me.

"Haeraig Zeena? Ellian?" Ddraig Astar rumbled.

"We're sorry to interrupt, but the beacon has been lit. I fear the enemy approaches again," I said.

Ddraig Astar was on his paws in moments. "Tell me everything, Ellian. Where from? Who is the foe?"

"I do not know, Ddraig Astar. I came here as soon as I knew the beacon was alight. I expect a messenger will come soon to warn us of the exact danger," I said, realising that I hadn't even lingered to note the colour of the flame. In hindsight, I realised I should have at least sent a dragon out to confirm the threat, but there was nothing to be done now.

"I have a dragon with the gift of farsight amongst my number here. Once I return to the rest of my clan I shall ask Muwele to determine the source of this threat. My clan shall aid yours in this manner without anticipation of compensation," Ddraig Krateos said.

"Your assistance is most welcome. Though you do not seek a reward now, I shall ensure that one day Clan Laxtal's debt to you shall be repaid," Ddraig Astar said. He dipped his head in the direction of the Nixan ddraig, enough to show respect, but not enough to indicate submission.

Ddraig Krateos twitched his wings in acknowledgement of this. "I am sorry my friend, but it seems like our negotiations must conclude here. I cannot risk being caught up in Laxtal's battles, not until your son returns with the Axinstone," the Nixan said. Even though he was the shorter of the two, he still managed to look down on Ddraig Astar. It was clear where the power truly lay.

"I understand, of course. This is Laxtal's war, though we hope to fight with you by our side in the near future. For now, any help is much appreciated, and if you can identify this enemy for us, then we will be grateful," Ddraig Astar said. This time, he kept his head raised high.

"We're leaving already?" Haeraig Zeena asked quietly, addressing her father. "I was hoping for more time to..."

"We cannot get caught up in another clan's war, my daughter," Ddraig Krateos said. I immediately picked up on the Nixan haeraig's words. What had been her intention for coming to Laxtal, for surely it was odd that both haeraig and ddraig had made the journey to Laxtal? Only one was needed, unless they both had reasons for being here: Ddraig Krateos to negotiate the treaty, and Haeraig Zeena... for what? To find a mate? Did she really seek Vinzent as a mate?

"I hope that next time I fly to Laxtal I will be able to stay longer," Ddraig Krateos continued, with the merest hint of accusation in his voice, as though blaming us for the lack of security on our borders. I bit down on the retort that threatened to escape my throat. It was not my place to confront the ddraig of Nixa, no matter how badly I disagreed with him.

Ddraig Astar did not seem to hold my reservation, as he was a bastion of understanding as he answered, "Of course. I hope you have the Axinstone in your possession when you next come to Laxtal. My son and I would be honoured to accommodate you then."

I noted that Ddraig Astar did not include me in that statement, and again I was forced to bite my tongue and keep my silence. I understood why the ddraig would be anticipating his son's return, but for the moment I was the haeraig of the clan. As I sat and watched the retreating backs of the two ddraigs and the Nixan haeraig, I felt a pang of jealousy at my absent cousin. I had impressed my uncle, he had told me so, and yet he still treated me with no respect or honour. He hadn't even thanked me for the work I had done.

I allowed myself to growl at the empty room and vent some of my frustrations.

"Be calm. Your time will come."

I shrieked in fright, desperately spinning around to find the source of the voice, but the chamber was empty. I was completely alone, and yet, someone had spoken, a ness, I was sure.

I glared at the silver statue, perched high on its ridge. I was sure it was my imagination, but it looked a lot more smug than usual, like it enjoyed my fright. I shook my head to clear my mind and hurried after the two ddraigs.

The music had stopped, a hushed silence falling over the chamber. The fire still crackled and burned, but I could hear nothing else. Even breathing seemed to be stilled.

Ddraig Krateos's wings rustled as he soared down to the rest of his clan, but Ddraig Astar did not follow the Nixan. Instead, he banked left and ascended further, towards the beacon fire set into a great alcove at the ceiling. The flames burned vivid red, a far deeper and richer flame than the fire that warmed the chamber.

I hesitated at the crest, the steep drop to the floor below me. Haeraig Zeena stood by my side, having not followed her father down to her clan so quickly. She flicked her tail in obvious irritation as a brown-scaled dragon took flight from the Nixans, quickly departing the chamber towards the surface.

"Another unhappy coincidence," the Nixan muttered. She spoke so quietly I almost didn't hear her.

My head snapped to the side. I stared at her, forgetting all pretence of decorum and respect. The haeraig didn't seem concerned that I met her eye for longer than was proper. In fact, she was the one who looked away first.

When I finally found my voice, it came out as a hoarse croak. "You think this was planned as well?"

Haeraig Zeena did not look towards me. Her gaze fell to the firepit, around which was gathered the other representatives of her clan. The two blue-scaled twins were easily visible amongst them. "It is a curious thing," the haeraig said quietly, "that a meeting to determine an alliance between two powerful clans is interrupted by another human incursion. Almost like someone doesn't want our clans to find common ground."

My throat was dry. My wings fluttered as I pawed at the ground, my claws scraping against the edge. "It would appear fortunate for our enemies," I admitted.

"Be alert for any strange behaviour from Xital," Haeraig Zeena warned. She still did not look at me. "They will try to break our alliance before it can be formalised."

"My cousin will recover the Axinstone for your clan," I said, hoping that the Nixan wasn't suggesting that her clan would go back on the agreement made in Xital.

This time, Haeraig Zeena did turn her head. Her eyes met mine for a second, and we both looked away at the same time. I stared at her shoulder, while her eyes slipped back to the chamber. "Haeraig Anzig is our best hope. He simply can't fail."

The Nixan gave me no chance to answer. She spread her wings and kicked off into the air, dropping a few feet before stabilising her flight. I tracked her movement until she landed with her kin. One of the twins hurried over to her. They exchanged quick words, but neither of them looked back up towards me. Her warnings had come without any advice, no suggestions on what to do now. How typically Nixan.

Even so, I was grateful for the warning. I suppressed a shiver of worry. If Xital was siding with the humans, then of course they would want to position themselves between Nixa and Laxtal. It was the only move that made sense. Two of the ruling clans allying together would draw ever more clans to us. If Xital wanted to win, they would have to prevent us from unifying.

Ddraig Astar was still at the beacon fire. I didn't dare disturb him, so I turned my eyes instead to the ground. I found Vinzent down there, nervously loitering around his mother. Yalle and Marin were with them, their gaze seemingly fixed on the ddraig.

If I was to be the haeraig in Anzig's absence, then my place would be amongst them. It would not do the clan any good if I stayed by myself, especially when the clan would be worried about the threats the beacon warned us of. I took to wing and soared towards the ground, ignoring the Nixans as I aimed directly for Vinzent.

Already the calls for warriors spread. They did not need to wait for the ddraig's command to gather. While normally this would be a time of excitement and displays of strength, the dragons who gathered looked weary and nervous. Wings drooped, tails held low. This was not a force confident of their chances.

As I landed, Saya bumped her muzzle against Vinzent's side, prodding the young silver dragon towards me. I tilted my head, but the ness said nothing. She met my eyes and then submitted with an exaggerated bow of her head.

"I didn't think they'd be back so soon," Vinzent said quietly, stepping away from his mother. He kept his eyes on the beacon. His wings weren't tight against his back, as though he prepared to take to flight at a moment's notice.

"This is how they win," I said, just as quietly. I didn't want any other dragons to hear me and spread discontent. "They wear us down and defeat us, and then move on to the next clan. That's what the council was meant to do, but Anzig didn't have enough time."

Vinzent twisted his head to look behind him for a moment. Then he reached out to place his paw against mine. He shook a little. "I don't think the ddraig should go," he whispered, pressing his head so close to mine that our horns touched. "He's tired. He hasn't recovered from the last battle. And you know what my mother's like. She might not be able to resist with him gone again."

"What are you saying?" The fire no longer felt warm against my scales. I struggled to resist the urge to spin around and confront Saya, to bring the accusations Vinzent suggested into a place where Ddraig Astar could hear.

"I'm saying that you have a chance to prove yourself," Vinzent hissed. He paced in front of me, his tail flicking around. Each time he met my eyes, his gaze burned with passion and strength, and yet he was always the first to look away. "Ddraig Astar is tired and should be given the chance to rest, but he would never accept that if his haeraig told him that was the case. But if his haeraig was young and unproven, then perhaps he might see this as an opportunity."

I pawed at the ground. A fine layer of dust and ash coated the stone, with small fragments of charred wood. I idly picked at one small fragment as I tried to think on what Vinzent suggested. Could I really fly out at the head of the army? Like all Laxtal dragons, I had trained as a warrior. I had fought under the tutelage of Carlee, one of the finest warriors the clan had ever produced. I knew I was capable in training, but I had never been tested out there, in the world with all its threats and dangers. I had never commanded an army.

My focus slowly shifted towards the gathering warriors, already starting to decorate themselves in ceremonial chalk. Though I was far from the smallest dragon in the clan, I was also not amongst the largest. Many of the warriors were bigger than me. Could I really demand the respect needed from them to command them in battle?

I thumped my forepaw against the stone. I lifted my head and looked to the gathering warriors. Of course I could. I was Ellian, niece of the ddraig. Respect flowed through my veins. They would listen to me. I would prove myself to Ddraig Astar. All I needed was his permission to lead Laxtal into war.

The moment Ddraig Astar swooped to the floor, I scampered after him. The ddraig had no eyes for me, though. He took strong strides towards the Nixans. Any dragon in his path quickly moved out of the way.

"Ddraig Krateos, what have you learned?" Ddraig Astar asked. His wings remained partially unfurled.

Ddraig Krateos looked over his Laxtal counterpart's shoulder. Wings rustled, and all attention quickly turned towards the brown-scaled dragon who returned from the surface. The Nixan almost stumbled on her landing, bowing her head to the two ddraigs.

I hurried to Ddraig Astar's side, Vinzent pausing just behind my tail. Neither my ddraig nor Ddraig Krateos demanded I leave. Neither of them even noticed my presence.

"Tell us what you learned, Mawele," Ddraig Krateos said, prompting the bowing ness.

Mawele kept her eyes fixed on some scraps of charred wood between her paws. "I saw humans, my ddraigs. Hundreds of them. Perhaps six hundred, though I could not see them all clearly. They camp in a forest, obscuring their numbers. Behind them was a tall but narrow waterfall. There were rainbows in the mist, and a protruding rock that looks like a dragon's claw ripping out of the water."

Ddraig Astar bowed his head. "I know the place. It is as the beacons suggested, though their numbers are good to know. I thank you for this assistance, Ddraig Krateos."

"You must share knowledge of these beacons someday," Ddraig Krateos replied. His head did not move. "It is a magic most unlike our own. I must know these secrets."

Ddraig Astar curled the tip of his tail, but he smiled to the Nixan. "Fly safe, Ddraig Krateos. I must apologise for this intrusion. I trust we will negotiate again once my son has returned."

I stepped back as Ddraig Krateos flared his wings. Without another word, the Nixan leader kicked off the ground. The wind from his wings swirled up some ash from the floor. I almost sneezed as the remainder of the Nixan delegation launched after their ddraig, leaving just the Laxtals on the ground. As I watched them fly away, I realised I had not heard Ddraig Astar mention anything about me. Negotiations would wait until Anzig returned.

Perhaps Vinzent was right. I did need to prove myself to the ddraig. Not to replace Anzig when he returned, but to be seen as a viable and trustworthy option when my cousin was unable to fulfil his duties.

I spoke before any cowardice could rob me of my voice. "Ddraig Astar?"

The ddraig spun around to face me, his tail cracking through the ashen air. "Make it quick," he growled.

I lifted my head as high as I could, pushing out my chest. My claws gripped at the stony floor. "Let me go in your stead," I said, doing my best to project my voice. "Let me lead Laxtal to glory, in your honour."

A low growl rumbled from the ddraig's throat. His piercing amber eyes narrowed as he met my gaze. "You forget yourself, Ellian."

"I'm not, Ddraig. I promise," I replied quickly. All around us, there was a hush. Even the warriors paused in their preparations to look towards us. The eyes of the entire clan had fallen on us. "I can prove myself to you. Just give me this chance."

Ddraig Astar took a step forward. His lips pulled back, baring his teeth. He spoke with that snarl etched onto his muzzle. "You will stay here and hold the clan in my absence. I will say nothing more of it, and you will not think of anything more. You are not my son."

My hindleg moved back, but I held my ground. "Please, uncle. I can do more. I can help you."

The ddraig moved faster than I could react. His paw smashed against my muzzle. Pain exploded through my head as I crashed to the ground, felled in an instant. I did not whimper or cry out. I couldn't. All the breath had been robbed from my lungs.

Ddraig Astar's paw pressed heavily down on my shoulder, his weight pinning me in place. The hot air of his breath washed over my face. "You are too young for this. Too inexperienced. I would not trust you with such an important task," he hissed. He did not yell, though I could feel his anger in the tension of his paw, in the quiver of his voice. "You will do as you are commanded."

"Yes, Ddraig," I whispered. I squeezed my eyes closed. I wanted to sink into the stone, but it remained hard and unyielding. The ddraig's claws dug into my scales. I was sure they drew blood, but I made no movement beneath him.

Ddraig Astar snarled and snapped his teeth, before he kicked me away. He stalked away to his warriors, his movement sharp and twitching, like he still struggled to contain his anger.

No one came to help me up. I didn't want to move. I wanted to simply disappear, but I did not have that choice.

I hauled myself up to my paws, ignoring the pain in my shoulder. I turned away from the ddraig and limped a few paces. No matter how hard I tried, I could not keep my head high. Shame wanted to bring it down, to keep my tail tucked between my legs. I had been rebuked by the ddraig. Publicly. My leadership questioned.

I met the eyes of Saya. She held my gaze for a long time before she looked away, a smirk on her muzzle. She bowed her head more than was necessary and stepped out of my way. Behind her, Marin and Yalle both dipped their heads and moved aside, but their movements were no longer so assured, so instinctive. There was hesitancy there.

Vinzent did not move out of my way. My mate didn't look at me, his eyes still on the band of warriors. Ddraig Astar's voice echoed as he bellowed out commands, preparing the dragons to take flight. How could I ever have thought I could take his place? He had a confidence and power of voice that I could not match. He was a commander of war, and I was just a ness who thought she had more power than reality dictated.

"Huh," Vinzent said, almost a dismissive scoff. "I really thought he would let you."

I did not turn around until I heard the first wings take to the air. Only then did I look back and watch the hundreds of dragons depart Laxtal, an impressive force to muster against any other draconic army. They flew to war in the shadow of the Sxinix Mountains, leaving me behind to fight my own war in Laxtal.

My attempt to win the ddraig's approval had gone horribly wrong. The air was full of turbulence now. I would have to act quickly and decisively to restore the broken trust in me. If that was even possible. No one would forget Ddraig Astar's rebuke.

I knew in my heart that I had made a terrible mistake.

# CHAPTER TEN

**Azlak**

The farmhouse was a fast-fading memory. We had put three full days of flight and three nights of uninterrupted rest between us and those terrors. I was sure there were still some who put the blame for Keita's capture on me and my magic, and I probably deserved that. I knew there had been some trepidation when I had led the group to a disused barn to sleep in the next night, but it had passed without incident. So had the crumbling stone castle and the thicket of trees barely sheltered from the wind and rain. We were beginning to relax. Even the spectre of Nightwings could be ignored, though I still feared that it might be following us.

I tried to focus my mind on the image of our next destination; a network of caves overlooking a sheltered beach. It was several miles from the nearest human village, so I hoped for another night without any humans. This time I even hoped for the chance to light a fire that could protect us from the bitterly cold ocean wind.

My mood was lifted further by the knowledge that I had Seen a welcome day of rest once we reached the caves. We would be able to stay by the shore for a full day before we would need to move on again. There were enough weary wings beyond my own that the rest would be well needed. The flight from Xital had been long, and we had not flown the quickest route, following the path laid out by my visions to avoid large human settlements.

I had never seen the ocean before, save in my visions. I knew it was a sight few of the others had witnessed either. I doubted any of the Laxtal or Nixan dragons would have seen it. Our clans were hundreds of miles from the coast, and dragons rarely flew this side of the Sxinix now.

Our first glimpse of the ocean came shortly after the middle of the day. We were flying close to the small wisps of clouds to lessen the risk of any skyward-gazing humans chancing a sight of us. The air was chill at this height, despite the warming rays of sunlight bathing our wings.

I thought the glittering strip of blue in the distance was just another river, like the many we had already crossed that morning. But as we got closer, its size became apparent. I recognised it for what it was.

The structured and orderly green fields far below gradually gave way to wild, rugged moorland, not too dissimilar to the landscape of Laxtal. The heath and fern here was largely undisturbed by humans, so at Haeraig Anzig's orders, we descended to the warmer air nearer the ground. We quickly lost sight of the ocean but were close enough now that we could smell it. I had never known the scent of water to be so strong before. Mixed with the exotic aromas of salt and fish, the result was a strangely alluring smell that I had to follow.

Excitement amongst my fellow fliers was steadily growing too, as was their restraint in not racing past me. Even so, Haeraig Anzig asked me to pick up the pace, which I did with some reluctance. These long flights were starting to take their toll on my tired body. I dared not show it, but my wings were aching and crying for rest.

I was not the only one suffering with fatigue. I knew that Haeraig Anzig and Okazuni would also be feeling the strain of these distance flights, and probably the two Nixans as well. We were not built for feats of endurance; our smaller bodies were best suited to quick bursts of speed. Of course, they would never show their fatigue either. We would fly on until we collapsed from exhaustion. Only Keita, Carlee, and Nataik were built to endure long flights, but the veteran had her own problems to contend with.

Closing in on the mighty ocean, the heathlands gave way to sand dunes, and the haeraig called for a brief respite. It was not for his sake. I noticed that he had been glancing back at Carlee quite a lot. Unlike the rest of us, the veteran could no longer make any effort in disguising her weakness; it was clear she was struggling. Badly. She flew with her head below the level of her wings, and she lagged some distance behind the rest of the group.

I thought back to my most recent vision of Carlee's death. This journey was draining her of all her strength. I feared she would never return to Laxtal again. What did that mean for my visions? What effects might her death have on the future?

For a moment I was conflicted.

As I landed on the sandy ground, I wondered if I should inform Haeraig Anzig about my concerns for Carlee. The haeraig wasn't blind to Carlee's suffering, but perhaps he wasn't aware of the full extent of her troubles. However, I decided against it. I knew the respect the haeraig had for his aging mentor. He wouldn't want to know that she was heading slowly and inexorably towards her death.

"What's troubling you?" Isikian had landed next to me with his brother in close attention, though Inilta took just one look at me before walking away.

I pawed at the sand, wondering how much I should tell the Nixan. I had already revealed my innermost secrets to him, but somehow I saw my visions of others more private still. I rarely even informed the subjects what I saw. So often, when trying to avoid what I had told them, they set in motion the events I had warned them about. The future was changeable; there was no doubt about that. However, without the ability to constantly check the consequences of your actions it was not an easy thing to keep altered. It was like trying to divert the flow of a river from its natural path. It would always seek out a way to return to the way it had always travelled.

"It's nothing," I said evasively, knowing that Isikian wouldn't believe me. This time he didn't question me. He lingered for a moment, as though hoping I might crack and divulge something. I held fast, my mind feeling like it broke into shards on the inside, but I kept impassive outwardly. I turned my head away from him lest the fear in my eyes betray me. He left, but I sensed I may not be alone.

Someone touched my tail. I started, suppressing a yelp with some difficultly, and spun around to face Keita. I was somewhat surprised to see her there; Haeraig Anzig's near-constant companion frequently made a point of avoiding me in Laxtal. We hadn't exchanged words since leaving Xital, and for quite some time before that.

Unlike the haeraig, Keita had no respect for me. She had made it quite clear that were it her decision to make, I would be banished from Clan Laxtal, forced to live as a nomad in the wilderness between the clans. Thankfully that was unlikely to be my fate. Keita held little power within the clan, despite her close friendship with Haeraig Anzig. It would be a grave set of circumstances indeed that would result in my expulsion from the clan. I had Seen such an event, of course, but that had involved Ellian taking control of Laxtal. With my guidance, Ellian would never need to lead the clan. Haeraig Anzig would return to Laxtal in safety, hailed as a hero not just in our clan, but in Clan Nixa too. The successful recovery of precious Axinstone would ensure this. As for Ddraig Astar...

*Loud blasts reverberated through the forest. There was chaos amongst the dragons as they launched themselves skywards, not realising they were making themselves easier targets to the humans stationed in the trees. Many dragons thudded back down to the ground, still and silent, staining the mud red with their blood. The few dragons that escaped the crossfire to fly above the trees were soon shot down by more humans positioned at the borders of the forest. Every single dragon was gunned down, leaving none to fly into the sunrise.*

*There were no more blasts. Silence returned to the forest, only broken by the sounds of the humans retreating, though this soon faded into nothingness too. With the danger gone, the dawn birdsong returned to the forest.*

*One of the stricken dragons started moving, crawling to the centre of the carnage. His cobalt scales were stained crimson from a jagged wound below his wing, but in his eyes was a fierce determination to survive, no matter the injury.*

*"Ddraig Astar, are you hurt?" he whispered, weakly at first. "Ddraig Astar? Ddraig Astar, are you hurt?" Every time he repeated his litany his voice grew stronger, but there was no returning answer. No voice called out, no movement indicated anyone else still lived. Not even as he pawed at the red-scaled dragon lying motionless on his side...*

I choked back a cry of despair. That was the attack Haeraig Anzig would die in had I not sent him on this quest to retrieve the Axinstone. The last thing I had expected was that Ddraig Astar would take his son's place, both on the battlefield, and now in death.

I had saved the haeraig's life at the price of his father's.

My intervention was going to kill my clan's ddraig. If anyone ever learnt of this, I would be expelled from Laxtal, whether Anzig or Ellian were ddraig, it didn't matter. It was the excuse the clan had been waiting for.

"If you have something to say, I suggest you spit it out."

Startled, I jumped, spreading my wings in fright. Lost in the future, I had forgotten about Keita's presence. I could not mask the guilt on my face as Keita glared down at me, her one good eye blazing in fury, the other milky white and blind. Every inch of her extra height over me amplified. She towered tall as I shrank down as close to the sand as I could. I knew she could barely see, but that would be no disadvantage to her should she decide to fight me. She could overpower me in mere moments.

"I saved Haeraig Anzig's life by bringing him out here. I fear I've only sent someone else to their death instead," I said, knowing that Keita would not tolerate me remaining silent.

"Who?" she demanded. A snarl formed on her lips as she closed the already small distance between us to almost nothing. Her muzzle was nearly touching mine, not even giving me the opportunity to look away from her hostile glare.

I longed for the ability to sink beneath the sand and out of her sight, but knew it wouldn't happen. I couldn't be that lucky. I was forced to answer her question as best I could. "I can't say. Not until I know what I Saw is true or not. There's nothing any of us can do about it anyway."

Keita growled, but for once I held firm. I could not reveal to Keita that I had witnessed the death of our clan's beloved ddraig. She would go straight to Haeraig Anzig and the tenuous trust between us would snap as easily as a dry twig underpaw. She started to turn away, before freezing and slowly swinging her head around to glare back at me.

"When you know it to be true?" she snarled. Worryingly for me, her paws dug deeply into the sandy soil. I imagined how easily they could sink into my soft underbelly, if she so chose to attack. I let off an involuntary shudder at the thought, but the ness still had more to spit at me. "You mean to say you really don't know what's going to happen?"

"The future's always changing. Knowing about it can cause it to change."

"What you're telling me is that, despite your promises that we would be safe, you really have no idea what's actually going to happen?" Keita said, her voice shaking in rage. Her wings were partially unfurled, her entire body quivering, her claws ripping deeper into the sand.

"If I'm careful, I can keep us safe," I said quietly, trying to defuse Keita's anger, but it wasn't working. My belly rubbed against the sand as she loomed over me.

For a moment Keita couldn't even speak before she managed to splutter out, "If you're careful?" She laughed mirthlessly, which attracted the attention of Isikian, who wisely held his distance. "Since when have you ever been able to control your magic?"

"Haeraig Anzig trusts me," I whispered.

Keita didn't have a retort for that. She knew it to be true, even if she had no trust for me herself. Instead, she growled, "If any of us is hurt, you'll pay for it in your blood."

I didn't doubt her threat and was relieved when she walked away to join Haeraig Anzig and Carlee. They spoke briefly, but I was too far away to hear what they had to say. Judging by their lack of reactions, my visions were not discussed. I knew Haeraig Anzig would be eager to know the identity of any dragon whose death I had Seen, especially one within our clan. Despite any apparent impracticality, he would endeavour to find a way to save them. That was just the way he was; he would always do his best to help others, regardless of their status within the clan. He would make a good ddraig, but he was too inexperienced at leading. His father's death was coming too soon.

I stared forlornly down at the disturbed ground, where Keita's obvious rage left its scars. Drawing upon strength I did not know I had, I walked on unsteady and quivering legs away to a lone tree. Here I curled up in its welcoming shade, spreading a wing over my head, hiding from gazes, friendly or otherwise. I was sick of this. My weakness sickened me. I hated every moment of this life, of being Laxtal's omega, the least dragon in the clan. More than ever before, I wanted the mysterious dragon of my visions to reveal themselves. I wanted that dragon, who knew and understood my pain to share it. To carry some of my burden.

"Azlak?"

I hesitated, groaned inwardly at being ripped from my enforced hiding. I drew on my depleting reserves of mental fortitude once more, and slowly drew my wing back, squinting out from the dark shade and into the light. The silhouette of a dragon stood before me, black as coal, black as the darkest, moonless night but haloed by the sun. For one glorious moment my mind tricked me into believing this was the dragon I had longed for, but then, as my eyes adjusted to the gloom of the shadows, the familiar features of the haeraig appeared.

"I think we're ready to leave again," he said.

His voice was soft and gentle. Was it because he cared? Or was I only noticing that because it lacked the venom and anger of Keita's words?

I groaned again as I stood up, dreading the flight ahead. As much as I loathed being at the bottom of the clan's hierarchy, I hated leading even more.

I waited for Haeraig Anzig to gather everyone together, but he didn't. He placed his paw on my tail and looked into my eyes for as long as I could bear, searching for something in their depths.

"You know you can tell me if something is bothering you?" he said.

I couldn't bring myself to respond. There was no way I would be able to share my worries with Haeraig Anzig, least of all that which bothered me the most: my vision of his father's death.

He grunted. "I just want you to know that you don't have to do this alone."

The words were out of my mouth before I could stop them. "I'll always be alone, no matter where I call home and whatever company I keep. You won't be able to change that, Haeraig." My eyes did not leave his chest. I would not, could not, look into his eyes, for fear of my resolve shattering into pieces, just like the sunlight that began to splinter through the leaves of my sanctuary.

"You know that for certain?"

I sighed. "I do. I'm still waiting to find the one drake who'll truly make me happy."

Haeraig Anzig didn't question me further. Maybe he already believed I had no idea who it was. He made to move away before half turning back with sorrow in his words.

"I've always looked after you, Azlak. I see a lot of me in you. Neither of us have any siblings. We've both lost our mothers, and our fathers have had little time for us." I looked up towards his face. He bared his teeth in wry mirth. "And neither of us are physically strong. If it wasn't for your magic... I think you could have been like a brother to me."

He walked away, leaving me feeling pretty dejected.

I didn't know why Haeraig Anzig cared about me so much. By all rights he should want to have nothing to do with me, like Keita. Perhaps it was just pity; a rare trait amongst dragons, especially towards me. The weak were never pitied, not in Laxtal. They were scorned and shunned, as I had been my entire life. But maybe it was more than just pity. Could Haeraig Anzig be feeling some sort of kinship towards me? He was right though, our situations were similar, despite the massive gulf in our statuses.

Perhaps that's all it was, a similarity. Haeraig Anzig appreciated how flimsy his power within the clan really was. In some ways I was his double, his older brother by three days. I was what he would have become had he hatched with the anomaly of magic. And I could have been one of the most powerful dragons in the clan, thanks to the authority of my father, Marin. He may not be ddraig, but with a powerful son to provide support, perhaps he could have been. Especially if it had been Anzig who had become the omega.

Such mind-wanderings didn't warrant lingering on though. No matter how similar our situations, I was the one who hatched with the curse of magic, not the haeraig. Nothing would ever change that.

Even so, as we took flight and I led the group up the coast, I just couldn't shake the haeraig's words from my mind. Partly for selfish reasons, I had always wanted a sibling. I had hoped that any dragonet my parents had would share my pain, ease my burden, in possessing some form of magic, but it was not to be. Most unusually for nesses, my mother laid just one egg before she died. I was my mother's legacy. In the last few years, there had been just one other ness to lay a single egg; Zhara, the mate of Ddraig Astar and Haeraig Anzig's mother. Both Zhara and my mother were killed in the same human raid that had begun the western clans' war against the humans.

Just another meaningless connection between the two of us.

Nightfall was fast approaching when I began banking lower towards the caves where we would spend the next two nights. I didn't know why, but I knew that we had to spend a day resting at the beach or else we were doomed to fail. There were a couple of members of the group who could use the break.

Carefully skirting the small village a little further down the coast, we landed on the small beach. The cliffs pressed close to the cove in a semi-circular shape, providing shelter from the wind and any rain that might blow through. A large rocky outcrop jutted out into the ocean from the nearest headland, an arch cut into its base through which the waves could crash. The only way to access the beach from the shore was down a narrow path that wound down the steep cliffs. I knew from my visions that this path led to the nearest village, so I took care to avoid that end of the beach.

One thing I had not Seen of the caves was the flat stone structure that ran over the sand. It was cobbled and reminded me of the roads the humans built to run their travelling machines. This was certainly human made. It ran from the path in the cliffs to the water's edge, where it abruptly ended. No one else was paying it any heed, and my attention to it quickly dwindled.

At Haeraig Anzig's orders, Inilta and Isikian went to collect some firewood from the cliff tops, whilst some of the others tentatively explored the foaming water's edge. Keita was especially curious about the ocean and waded deeper than the others, but was caught out by an onrushing wave. Shrieking in indignation, she tried to fly out of the reach of the waves, but her sodden wings were too heavy and unable to give her lift. She was bowled over by the next wave that came crashing into the shore, muting any further cries as she inhaled a mouthful of water, tumbling with the other debris. She vanished into the water's turmoil for a few long seconds. Finally she emerged, ungracefully and bedraggled from the foam a few moments later, coughing and spluttering.

She silenced any laughs with a stern, withering glare, though she never looked in my direction to quell my smug smirk.

There were many caves in the white stone of the cliffs backing the beaches around here, many clustered around the horizontal fault lines that ran through the rock. Some were barely large enough to fit a single dragon, but others ran so deep they were mostly shrouded in darkness. There was just one that I had Seen that would be suitable for us. Its entrance was open to the beach and would let in plenty of moonlight, should the sky remain clear. From within escaped a meandering trickle of water, absorbed by the sand before it could reach the ocean. Its source was a large pool of water in the centre of the cave, fed in turn by an underground vent that bubbled in through a crack at the back of the cave.

Away to one side of the cave was a deep alcove with a smooth floor, perfect to light a fire on, and smoothed ledges hewn into the rough walls that looked like they had been created specifically for dragons to sleep on.

The Nixan brothers brought their gathered firewood to the centre of the alcove, before Inilta used his magic to light them. As the branches burned with pale blue flames dancing over their blackening twigs, a still-sodden Keita curled up as close to them as she could. She put her wing over her head and seemed to fall asleep almost straight away.

Haeraig Anzig remained on the beach with Carlee, leaving me with the two Nixans, Okazuni, and Nataik. For a moment I thought Isikian was going to come over to me, but then Inilta called his name and the healer settled down by his brother instead.

We were all tired from the long flight, so there was very little conversation as one-by-one everyone drifted off to sleep. My last conscious thought, before succumbing to the downward pressure of my heavy eyelids, was to see Carlee return to the sanctuary of the warm cave, alone. Briefly I wondered where the haeraig had gone, but my eyelids won a very one-sided battle, and I thought no more of the haeraig as sleep took hold of me and dragged me into its warm depths.

*The darkness was absolute. The air was cold, and the ground was hard and smooth. I believed I was outside. There was the faintest breath of wind, but there were no stars or moon to illuminate my surroundings. My breath was heavy as I tried to work out where I was, and more to the point, why I was there.*

*It took a few moments to realise it was not just my breath I could hear.*

*A pair of piercing red eyes opened in the dark, just a few feet in front of me.*

*"Hello, Little One," a gentle and feminine voice said. It seemed to belong to the pair of eyes.*

*"Who... who are you?" I asked, trying to back away but it didn't feel like I was moving anywhere.*

*The eyes laughed. "My name is Maznar. I doubt that will tell you much, but it is all I am going to say. And to forestall your next question: technically you are within your own mind. This is all a dream, but that doesn't make it any less real. I reached out to you because I am curious to learn about other dragons, especially ones as unique as you."*

*The darkness began to recede as Maznar spoke, but a fragment of it remained. The scrap of shadow coalesced into the shape of a ness with coal black scales and eyes that burned as red as any flame. I noticed with some intrigue that she had the same short, blunt muzzle that I had; even her stubby horns above her eyes were similar.*

*"Who are you?" was all I could say.*

*Maznar snickered. "I've already told you I won't say any more about myself. I just wanted to meet you."*

*"But why? Why me?"*

*Again, Maznar laughed, a light tinkering sound that was both calming and mocking. "I told you that too. You are unique. A Laxtal with magic! I would like to know all there is about you, and soon enough I will. Your dreams will reveal everything I could ever want."*

*"You're a Nixan?"*

*"Not as such. I have learned much about the clan of magic, but I do not live there. Or indeed in any other clan. I am without a clan and live away from other dragons. And no, I am not Laxtal either. I am not the dragon you seek," Maznar said, interrupting my next question before I could even begin to vocalise it. Though shocked that this stranger knew my most precious secret and desire, I chose not to query it. I doubted she would tell me the answer anyway.*

*"So why the sudden interest in me?"*

*I could see every one of Maznar's ivory teeth as she grinned widely. "Because your quest has the potential to change the world. The lives of dragons, humans, and other species you can only imagine will be changed. If you claim the Dragon's Head Rune – the Axinstone – then you will alter the lives of all. I can help or hinder you. I want to know which I would prefer," she said. Her burning eyes looked into mine, and within them I saw an incredible power and a determination unlike that of any dragon I had ever seen before. She then surprised me by looking away to examine her claws.*

*"I think I shall help you. But only a little to begin with," she said, still nonchalantly inspecting her claws as though she had no other cares in the world. "Once you wake you should go for a walk on the beach. Don't be afraid of anything you see out there, for you will be rewarded."*

*"What do you mean?"*

*"That'll ruin the surprise, Little One. It will be worth your while," Maznar said as her outline began to blur, and the shadows started to overtake her body once more. Soon she was a chuckling spectre in the darkness, with just her red eyes betraying her presence. Then they, too, were gone, and all was dark.*

Moonlight glimmered off the still water of the pool as my eyes snapped open.

Dawn still seemed to be some way off and Inilta's fire was starting to fade.

It was bitterly cold. A strong wind was blowing into the cave from the sea, stealing away the heat the spluttering fire gave.

I didn't know what had woken me, whether it was Maznar's dream or something else entirely, but either way, despite the chill and dark, sleep would not return to me. Though my body protested the movement, I jumped down from my ledge and negotiated my way around Haeraig Anzig and Keita, who lay sprawled across the floor, their tails intertwined.

I ventured out of the cave and onto the exposed beach, beneath the pale light of the moon, trying to seek what Maznar had hinted at. I didn't fear any humans spotting me. The closest village was many miles away and there would be no purpose for any human coming this far from their home.

No movement greeted my eyes, and the only sounds were that of the ocean crashing against the shore. I could hear both the ferocious churning of the waves against the cliff faces, and the gentler rush of the water on the beach. The soft sand was warm beneath my paws. It felt so strange. It got in between my scales more than dirt did, and the tiny grains were mixed in with bits of shell and the occasional long strand of seaweed.

I had no destination in mind; I didn't even really know why I had come outside in the first place. Maznar's instructions had been vague at best. Was I meant to be seeking something in particular? It was colder on the beach than it had been in the cave, more exposed to the wind, but I did not turn back.

There was a cluster of rocks not far from where the path to the dunes joined the beach. Unlike the barnacle and limpet-coated rocks closer to the water's edge, they were barren apart from a little red lichen and moss. I clambered up them to get a better view of the moonlit ocean.

Far over my head a few bats shot by, chittering away amongst themselves. They were followed by the silent and graceful form of an owl. Even higher still, a pinprick of light that was not a star gradually moved across the sky. I followed its progress against the backdrop of the few constellations I could recognise until it had vanished over the horizon beyond the sea.

There was a noise behind me: a gentle rustling followed by a soft crunch in the sand.

"Isikian?" I asked without turning. I didn't anticipate anyone else would come and seek me out.

I waited for a response, but none came. That was most unlike the healer, who was usually keen to talk to me. I turned around and froze.

Humans.

There were two humans standing mere feet from me. Staring.

I couldn't flee. My wings wouldn't respond. No point anyway. The humans would catch me in a few of their massive strides. I was completely at their mercy, and yet... Surely they could already have taken me by now. The humans at the farm had shown no hesitation in taking Keita, but these... They seemed as scared of me as I was of them.

"What are you doing here?" I somehow found the confidence to ask the humans. I had never interacted with humans before. Occasionally I had observed them from a distance on the rare instances they had come to Laxtal, before the war, but I had never been so close to them.

The humans looked at each other in astonishment. They both appeared fairly young, only just on the verge of adulthood. One was female and the other male, and it was him who spoke first, throwing his arm in front of his companion.

"Be careful, Jess," he said, before taking a step forward. The female pushed the other's arm away and stepped up to stand by his side.

"We could ask you the same, dragon," she said. There was no hostility in her voice, which surprised me so much I almost answered her straight away.

"I... Nothing. I'm a little lost," I said, knowing full well that the humans didn't believe me in the slightest.

"Why would a dragon be anywhere near here to begin with? It's not like you can just not notice which side of the mountains you're on," the male asked.

"Which must mean you're out here for a reason," the female added. The two had been slowly closing in on me until they could reach out and grab me if they wanted, but both kept their arms down by their side. For the moment.

"Give us one good reason why we shouldn't take you now and turn you into the council," the female said.

Her words carried no threat. As surely as they had known I wasn't lost, I knew that they had no intention of passing me over to the dragon hunters who had chased us away from the farm. This knowledge allowed me to frame my answer perfectly.

"If you'd have wanted to take me, you'd have done so already. You came to me because you were curious, not because you wanted to harm me," I said, clenching my paws against the rock, hoping that my intuition was correct. I was relieved when the female took a step back, with the male following her lead, but still wary that this was just a ruse to make me complacent.

"Alright, you have us. We saw you alone and, well, neither of us have ever properly met a dragon before. Ever since Erik Brightwell and Rico took control, dragons have become a bit of a rare sight around these parts," the female said. She took a seat on one of the rocks facing me.

I was very confused by her behaviour. Since the start of the war, all clans had been warned that every human was a threat to dragonkind. Clan Xital had made this abundantly clear. Ddraig Tsona had strictly forbidden dragons to approach any human, to matter the circumstance. He reasoned that they were not to be trusted. The events at the farm had only sought to confirm these warning, but now I was caught quite off guard.

"Well you've seen me now. I'm here, I'm real. Are you going to leave me alone?"

"But you haven't told us why you're here," the male said, sounding quite shocked.

"How could I possibly trust you enough to tell you that?" I asked of them.

The male was lost for words, and he turned to look out over the beach and towards the ocean. He tapped his paw, his foot, restlessly against the sand in a show of energy that far exceeded my nightly sluggishness.

"You said it yourself though, dragon," the female said as she stood up, an odd smile on her face. She took a step back towards me, and then recoiled as I bared my teeth at her. "If we wanted to hurt you, we would have done so already."

"So that means I should trust you?" I said with some degree of scorn. This was not human logic at its finest, I could tell.

"It means you don't have to be scared of us."

"I'm not scared," I said automatically. At first, I thought it was a lie to the humans, so that they could not capitalise on my weakness, but then I realised that it was the truth. I wasn't afraid of their presence. I didn't know why; everything I had been told about humans was that they were merciless and cruel to dragons, like those at the farm. But these two, they were somehow different.

I didn't know if I was making a huge mistake or not. I doubted Haeraig Anzig would have done the same, but he lacked the same knowledge I knew. Perhaps this was what Maznar had been talking about. Maybe she had wanted me to meet these humans. I sensed no danger from them, and though my magic was wild and uncontrollable, it very rarely failed to warn me of forthcoming danger. Though they had done nothing to earn it, I felt the two humans could be trusted.

"We're here looking for something. An artefact that was stolen from us by a human. We call it the Axinstone, but I think you have a different name for it. I believe you call it the Dragon's Head Rune," I said, watching the humans' reactions intently. I was no expert in human emotions, but they were temporarily stunned, and seemed quite horrified, mouths hanging open as they looked to each other.

"The Dragon's Head Rune? Isn't that the... You're trying to steal from George Symons?" the female said, leaping up from the boulder and pacing across the sand. She held her hands over her mouth. I didn't know if that man was the same as in my visions, but before I could question her, the male cut in with a question of his own.

"We? There are more of you here?" he said, glancing across at his partner. Unlike her, the male still seemed quite calm.

The female recovered her composure in time to answer her companion before I was able. "Of course. Dragons always travel in groups, never alone. You should know that, Jim."

"You are right. We rarely travel alone, and my companions aren't far from here," I said slowly. I was slightly surprised by the human's knowledge about our ways. I had always thought humans knew little about us, treating us like beasts of little consequence. I didn't understand. Why were these two humans so different to everything I had ever known about their kind; why were they so different to the humans on the farm? Maybe the humans had clans too, and one of these clans at least was not hostile to dragons. There had to be some way to turn this into our advantage.

"Can you trust us, dragon?" the female human said. Her hands twitched as she looked across at her partner. They seemed to be having a wordless conversation that I had no access to.

"Yes," I said, unsure of whether I was being truthful or not. I tried to edge back, but there was not much room to move on my rock. Did they intend on capturing me after all? Perhaps I had been wrong in telling the humans what we were here for. I was already starting to doubt my idea of human clans. It was a ridiculous notion; humans didn't act and behave like we do, and the chance that there were humans out there to help us was beyond hope. I had Seen nothing to indicate we would receive human help on our quest, but I found it so hard to find lies in their words.

I was torn, unsure if I could trust them or not.

"Then... Come with us."

It felt like I was under a spell. My legs started moving and my wings followed soon after. Before I knew it, I was keeping pace with the humans, following them away from the beach and back towards their village.

A vague sense of unease still lurked in the back of my mind, but for the time being I paid it no heed. I had nothing to fear.

# CHAPTER ELEVEN

**Anzig**

"Haeraig... Haeraig..."

I stirred into reluctant wakefulness as someone gently nudged me. Whispers and shadows lingered over my mind, a remnant of an already forgotten dream.

As I opened my eyes I could see nothing but a dark shadow looming over me. Vaguely I recognised the indistinct outline of Isikian's horns. It was still dark with only faint starlight illuminating the cave; the fire reduced to smouldering embers.

"Haeraig, there's something I need to talk to you about. Outside if you can stand," Isikian whispered. The healer's outline trembled and quivered in the biting chill of the pre-dawn air.

Though no one else was awake, Keita murmured softly by my side, her tail entwined in mine. Taking care not to wake her, I forced myself up to unsteady paws and gently untangled from our embrace. After shooting a dirty glare at the healer I followed him out onto the beach.

Dawn was little more than a suggestion of pink light above the eastern horizon, long since absent of mountains. It was still bitterly cold with a strong wind blowing from across the vast expanse of ocean. I shrank to the sand to try and recover a little heat but to no avail.

A strange smell hung in the air; familiar, yet I was not able to place it. I knew it should have made me uneasy, but I was too weary to care. It was faint and old, torn away by the wind. It offered no immediate danger.

The Nixan led me towards the rough surf as it pounded against the shore. He stepped over slippery rocks still slick with water. My paw splashed into rockpools, slimy with seaweed and yet rough with shells of small creatures that clung to the wet rock.

Isikian did not stop until he reached the underside of the great rock arch that stretched from the cliffs and plummeted into the surf a dozen feet away. The moonlight shone off the sea spray thrown up by the rocks, glistening in the gentle light.

The Nixan turned and glanced down at me. He hesitated for a moment before crouching down to my height. His tail thrashed in a rockpool in a clear display of concern, splashing up cold water.

"We're being held up, that's clear for me to see. You say we follow Azlak's visions, but that isn't the only reason, is it?" the Nixan said. In the dark it was hard to tell exactly where the healer was looking, but it was obvious his eyes were focused anywhere but at me.

I remained silent and glanced back at the cave, already knowing who Isikian was referring to. Carlee hadn't taken her customary place by my left wing for some time now. Instead, she laboured towards the rear of the group from almost the moment we took to the air.

"I know what you think of her, Haeraig. Even in Nixa we have heard tales of the magnificent feats of Carlee, but she is no longer that dragon. This must be torture for her," Isikian continued.

"What do you expect me to do, Isikian? I can't send her back," I asked the healer, knowing he could have no answer.

He was right of course. This was a painful end to the legend of Carlee, but what more could we do? She would never survive the lone journey home by herself, so we couldn't send her back. I could only hope she could prove useful to the group in some way, for it was clear she could offer no support in a physical capacity.

The Nixan shook his head. "I wasn't offering solutions, Haeraig. I just don't want you blinded by your admiration for an aging hero. I know you respect her immensely, which she deserves for what she has done, but you're mistaken if you believe she is still capable of those deeds."

"I understand. Maybe I was wrong to bring her, but I still feel she has something to offer. Her mind is still sharp and strong. Once we get to this human's lair she'll still be able to help," I said. I had to believe there was still something Carlee could do for us, or else I knew I was torturing her needlessly.

"I only hope you're right, Haeraig," Isikian said, bowing his head.

A noise further along the beach caught our attention.

Without hesitation, Isikian leapt up positioned himself defensively, between me and where the sound had come from. As it grew louder, we realised the sounds were pawsteps, crunching through the sand. They didn't sound heavy enough to be human, but the Nixan was taking no chances.

I peered around the healer to try and make out some movement in the gloom.

"By the waterline," Isikian murmured. His wings were partially unfurled, whether for flight or as sign of aggression, I wasn't sure.

I followed Isikian's gaze and could just make out an indistinct hazy silhouette against the moonlit rocks, a shadow against the sand close to where the beach met the exposed rockpools. It was far too small to be a human. A wildcat? No, definitely a dragon. In fact, it looked like...

"Azlak?"

Isikian recognised the silhouette at the same moment.

Sure enough, as the silhouette came closer, the faint pre-dawn light illuminated the dark shape, revealing the seer. His golden scales almost shone in the pale starlight. Azlak moved slowly, mere inches from where the wet sand glistened. He showed no fear to the waves, even as the water rushed up the pebbled sand, almost wetting his paws.

The seer dawdled with his head turned to the ocean. His paws scuffed against the sand. Then he seemed to realise he was being watched. He started in surprise and lowered his head, his chin almost to the sand. He cautiously approached, stepping carefully around the uneven rocks, looking more like a scolded dragonet than usual.

"Haeraig Anzig?" the seer whispered, once he was close enough to speak. "I didn't expect you to be awake already."

"Nor I of you," I said, swinging my head around to look back towards the cave. I had not even checked to see which dragons were still there. A dragon leaving the safety and warmth of the fire had not even gone through my mind. I looked back to the seer and tilted my head. "What brings you out here?"

Azlak didn't just fail to meet my eyes. He couldn't even manage to look anywhere close to me, his eyes instead drawn towards the white-tipped waves as they crashed to the beach. "I… heard something, Haeraig," he stammered. I got the feeling he had more to say, so I kept my silence and waited for him to continue. Several long seconds passed before he let out a quiet whimper. "You're going to think me a fool. They're all going to hate me even more."

"No one hates you, Azlak," I said, but I immediately regretted my words for I knew them to be a lie. Even the seer seemed to recognise that, as his withering gaze briefly touched on mine, before he stared to the horizon again.

Another short silence fell. Azlak opened his mouth a few times, but then closed it again. By my side, Isikian shuffled nervously. The healer's gaze kept moving towards the far headland, little more than a dark shadow protruding against the velvet black sky.

"Why would they hate you more?" Isikian said softly, when it became clear no one else was going to speak.

Azlak shot Isikian an anguished look as he tucked his tail in tight. His voice came out as a tiny squeak. "They're not like the others, I promise. They don't want to hurt us," he said, gradually getting louder with each word. "They want to meet you. They can help us."

I took a step forward. The tip of my tail quivered. "Who are you talking about?"

Azlak swallowed. His claws dug deep into the sand, moisture welling up from beneath the surface. "Humans," he said, his voice strangled. "There are two humans who want to meet you, Haeraig."

My wings flared from instinct. Humans. That had been the strange scent on the air. There were humans close by. My mind was filled with terrifying images. Of Keita being captured again. Of Carlee dying to their weapons. Of our mission failing, and the shame that would bring to my father.

"They aren't a threat, Haeraig," Azlak said. He pressed his belly into the sand, just as a wave rushed up the beach and wetted his paws. The seer didn't react to the water, though Isikian did jump to the side to avoid getting wet as well.

"Did you tell them where we are?" I asked, ignoring what Azlak had said. I turned my eyes to the sky. Our bodies were cold and our wings would be weary, but perhaps we could fly to safety before the humans came to the beach. How many would there be? I doubted we could fight them, not with how tired we would all be. This would not be like at the farmhouse.

Isikian gently placed a paw against my side. "It might be worth seeing what they have to say, Haeraig," he said quietly. He kept his gaze on the headland, making sure never to make eye contact with me. "If Azlak is right and they are friendly, then it might give us an insight as to why the humans are in our territory."

"Or they might kill us all," I muttered. It wasn't just the wind and night air that made me cold. Fear bubbled up inside my chest, threatening to burst forth and force myself into flight.

"Please, Haeraig," Azlak said. He tried to lower his head further, only to bump his chin against the wet sand. "I'm asking for you to trust me on this."

I hesitated. Could I trust Azlak on this? I had taken his word and trusted his visions so far. Putting my faith in those visions seemed easier to do when the danger was distant, across the mountains. Taking his word that humans were safe was much tougher. Realising that both dragons were still waiting for an answer, I forced myself to nod once. I tried to speak, but my mouth was dry. I tried again. "Take me to them."

Azlak lifted his head, his eyes bright in the shadows. He almost bounced on his paws, a smile coming to his muzzle. "Of course, Haeraig. Come with me, they aren't far."

Though every instinct screamed at me to flee, to fly back to the cave, I folded my wings to my back. I did not know what to expect from these humans, but if Azlak said I could trust them, then I would do my best to believe him. But I didn't want to go with just the seer. I looked to the Nixan. "Isikian, would you come with us?"

The healer sucked in his breath. He looked to the cave for a moment, as though attempting to think of a reason to decline my request. His shoulders slumped. "I'll come with you, Haeraig," he said. Truthfully, I doubted he thought he had a choice. I had not demanded his presence as an order, but I was still a haeraig.

Azlak was an entirely new dragon. He leaped forward, not even waiting for my permission to lead. He scampered across the sand without looking back to make sure we followed. For a brief moment I envied his confidence, before realising what that meant. I suppressed a shudder and decided to envy his energy instead. I felt like returning to the fire and sleeping until the sun rose, but the seer acted as though he didn't feel the cold.

With the seer's guidance, we made our way from the beach, away from the water and towards the dunes. I walked up the concrete protrusion that ran down the centre of the beach, finding the surface easier to walk on compared to the soft sand. Granules still stuck to my scales, irritating me with every step. I tried shaking them off, but some were annoyingly stubborn.

Doing my best to ignore thoughts of the warm fire, I squinted and tried to peer into the darkness ahead.

The concrete surface ended at the dunes, but it connected to one of the black ribbons that wound between the human lairs. I could see none of the mechanical beasts the humans used to travel, but there were many unusual scents about the place. The black surface itself smelled bitter, and an acrid scent of oil lingered on the air.

Isikian hissed. I lifted my head, and a moment later I recognised what he had sensed. Hidden beneath the oils was the scent of human. Then I saw the shadows moving in the darkness. A bright light winked into existence, almost blinding me as the beam fell across my body.

"This is your haeraig?" a deep voice asked, barely managing the correct pronunciation. The bright light lingered on me. I resisted the urge to throw my wing in front of my face. My eyes were barely open, barely able to see.

I should have answered, but the light pierced into my head. I could barely think, let alone speak.

"This is Haeraig Anzig of Laxtal," Isikian said, filling in the silence.

"It is a pleasure to meet you, Haeraig Anzig," a second human said.

I was sure there were only two humans, but I couldn't see to know for certain. I twisted my head, trying to escape the beam of light, but it continued to blind and burn at my eyes. "Will you switch that off?" I snapped. It was like the human wielded the brightness of the sun.

The beam of light dropped away, but the humans did not switch it off. Nor did they apologise. I blinked a few times, struggling to rid my vision of the dazzling after-images.

"Haeraig, this is Jim and Jess," Azlak said, gesturing with his wing to the two shapeless voids of darkness beyond the light. "They aren't like the humans who want to kill dragons. They said most humans don't want that."

"Then why are there humans raiding our land?" I growled. The confidence in my voice surprised me, especially in the presence of two humans. Perhaps because they were so indistinct in my vision, and even my scent of them was muted, that I could convince myself they weren't really there. I could have no such thoughts when they spoke.

"That is the mission of just one man," the human male said.

"George," I said with a snarl.

"No," Jess said, to my surprise. Given the twitch of Isikian's tail, I was sure he was surprised as well. "George is happy to follow orders, and I'm sure he agrees with much of what he's doing east of the mountains, but this is not his idea. This is not his war."

"Then who?" Isikian asked. The healer quickly fell into silence, ducking his head and taking a step back from the humans.

The bright beam of light swept across the ground and got lower. At least one of the humans sat down, bringing their head almost down to our level. I warily placed a paw back, but I did not retreat like Isikian.

"That is a man called Erik Brightwell," Jim answered. It was his voice that had lowered. He spoke in a hushed whisper, as though fearful that the man he talked about could overhear him. "He became prime minister ten years ago, and ever since then he's gradually increased his campaign against dragons. It started small at first, with restricted trade and passage across the mountains, but in the last couple of years, it's become this war."

I tilted my head. Ever since the first humans had come across the mountains in aggression towards my clan, we had believed this human called George had been the one leading their army. Clan Xital's intelligence had confirmed that belief. I pawed at the ground. "Why are they doing this?"

Through the darkness, I thought I saw Jess shake her head. I could barely see her, little more than a shadow against the black sky. The bright light in Jim's hand didn't help me see.

"Perhaps George is the only one who's sure," Jess said. Her heavy steps crunched across the sandy dirt, but she didn't move forward into the light. She remained in the darkness, just out of sight. "All we know is that Brightwell hates dragons, especially since Rico started whispering in his ear. I don't think he'll stop until you're all gone."

I snarled and turned away, pacing restlessly. Anger gave me some energy, but I could feel my strength waning as the cold air enveloped me. This conversation had brought with it anxiety and fear, but little else. "What can we do to fight them?"

"You need the Dragon's Head Rune," Jim said. His light swung towards me. I instinctively twisted my head away as the light passed over my back. It settled on the edge of the black tarmac. Far behind the two humans, I saw a pair of lights switch on. There were buildings back there, far enough away that they weren't an immediate threat, but I kept my senses alert.

"I don't know what George is using it for, but it's nothing good," Jess added. "Take it from him and you take a lot of his power. Beyond that, I don't know what you can do. Brightwell is in a strong position. He'll be prime minister for a long time to come."

"You need to make sure you show enough strength that people like George will reconsider supporting his plans," Jim said, but there was no conviction in his voice.

I suppressed a growl. This was not good advice. It was what we planned on doing anyway, but I feared for those chances anyway. Uniting the clans had proven more difficult than I or my father had realised. With the Axinstone and Nixa's support, we might have a chance. But I feared what might already be happening in Laxtal. The longer we took, the more danger my home was in.

Jess kept on talking, the humans seemingly unwilling to let silence last for long. "If it means anything to you, not all of Kernow supports Brightwell in this. If you can show him that dragons are stronger than he thinks, then there might be enough pressure over here to force him to stop these plans."

"That doesn't sound convincing," I muttered. I flicked my wings. These humans had nothing interesting to give, despite Azlak's excited introduction. It helped to ease my fear around them, but that was all.

"I wish we had better answers for you," Jim said. He sighed.

Jess stepped forward, into the light. I got my first good look at her. Her skin was pale, with long brown hair falling over her shoulders. Much of her body was clad in the humans' strange clothing, though as my body started to feel ever more cold and sluggish in the chill air, I wondered if perhaps they had the better idea.

"You should have this," the human said, extending her hand. She held a small black disk, attached to a strap that hung loosely between her fingers.

I leaned forward, almost touching the strange device with the tip of my muzzle. The black disk had no scent, though the straps around it were made of some kind of rubber. I could not determine any immediate purpose for the device, but before either human had chance to explain themselves, a deep and distant bellow caught everyone's attention. A roar reverberated through the air, coming from high towards the stars.

Jess's face paled. Before I could react, her hands closed around my forepaw tightly. Her flesh was hot against my scales. She tightened the strap around my ankle, securing the little device in place.

"Go! Run!" Jess said, releasing me again. She gave me a push as I stumbled away, tripping over my dragging tail.

"Don't fly. Stay on the ground," Jim urged. He finally switched off that infernal light, plunging everything into almost total darkness.

"What is it?" I asked, unmoving. I looked up to the sky. Individual stars returned to the darkness as my eyes adjusted again.

"Nightwings. Go. You can't be seen out here," Jess said. She took a few steps away, melting into the night.

I kept still, my tail curled close to my hind legs. The other human hurried away, their pawsteps soon fading into silence. On the air I heard another sound, a deep concussive beat coming from some distant height.

"Haeraig," Azlak hissed. His voice quivered with fear. "We must go."

I tore my gaze away from the sky. Though I was tempted to flare my wings and take to the air, I heeded the humans' warning. I hurried after Isikian and the seer, my paws sinking into the sand as we fled. The cave and the fire within would be our sanctuary. The eerie sound of Nightwings followed us all the way, but I never once looked back to see if the spectre was there.

My courage completely failed me.

The threat of Nightwings passed. I did not hear the bellowing roar again, and I even managed to get back to sleep before dawn truly arrived.

I was the last to wake. The cave was empty when I stirred, the fire almost completely burned out. The charcoal kindling barely glowed, small sparks drifting with the wind. I let out a satisfied groan as I stretched my legs and wings, feeling some of the tension in my joints pop and drain away.

The promise of warm sunlight and food drew me outside, though I could have comfortably stayed inside the cave for as long as I could. In the shelter of the cave, I could ignore the threat of humans and the fear of Nightwings. But inside that cave I would come no closer to reclaiming the Axinstone. I would shame my clan and my father, so I forced my paws to move and soon I emerged blinking into the late morning sunlight.

There was no scent of humans in the air, and my companions showed no fear as they lay sprawled across the beach. Isikian and his brother were close to the waves, though everyone else gave the water more distance.

Carlee stood nearby, keeping guard close to the cave entrance. The veteran dipped her head to me when she noticed my presence. "I heard about your adventure last night, Haeraig," she said, forgoing any formal greeting.

I struggled to resist the urge to lower my head, to sink towards the sand. "Azlak told you already?"

"Isikian, actually. He was eager to share what you learned, but he wanted to wait until you woke. It is good that we had no intention of flying today. It is almost midday," Carlee said. Though she worked hard to keep it out of her voice, I could still hear disapproval in her tone. Her body was tense, like she quivered on the verge of a pounce. But she stayed unmoving by my side, sat guard over a now empty cave.

"We all needed the rest. You especially," I said softly. I squinted as I looked up. Sure enough, the sun was high in the sky, close to its zenith. Morning had almost passed by entirely.

"Me?" Carlee asked, rustling her wings. "Do not insult me so, Haeraig."

I pawed at the sand. "I've seen how much you struggle each day, Carlee."

The old veteran scoffed. "I would do better each night if I got to sleep, Haeraig. I have kept watch every night. I failed to warn you in the farmhouse. I failed to stop you last night. It is too much for an old ness like me to stay awake every night."

I lifted my head sharply. Her rebuke cut deep, but I also felt a stab of relief. Carlee's struggles weren't because she lacked the stamina. It was because I had been foolish. "I should have assigned someone to keep watch," I said quietly. I felt like bowing my head in shame. It took all my strength to keep it up.

"Yes, you should have," Carlee growled. "If you are to be a strong haeraig, then you must think of things like this."

"I will. I promise."

Carlee rumbled to herself, then nodded once. "Good. You will make a powerful ddraig one day, but you must work for it. Now, you should tell me what this nightly escapade was all about. Why were you risking yourself in such a way?"

"Azlak seemed to think that these humans had something important to share with us," I said. I stretched out my foreleg, showing off the small strap and black device the human had tied against my ankle.

"How do we know we can trust them?" Carlee said. Her eyes narrowed as she looked to the strange little device.

"I suppose we don't," I replied. I shrugged my wings. "They could betray us to George or Nightwings, but I don't think they will. There was something about them, some feeling I got being around them. It was like they told me I didn't need to be afraid of them, without ever saying that. I don't know if I can explain it."

"Is that so?" Carlee said sharply. I was surprised to see a look of fear momentarily pass across her face. She turned away to stare at the ocean. Her voice cracked. "Anzig… I need to…"

Carlee quickly fell into silence. Pawsteps bounded across the sand towards us. I hissed in frustration as Isikian approached.

"Haeraig, I'm so glad to see you're awake," the healer said, seemingly oblivious of what he had interrupted. He swung his head around to gesture to those gathered close to the water. "Nataik thinks she knows what the humans gave us. She thinks it could help us."

"Then let us find out," Carlee said gruffly. She shoved past Isikian and trudged through the sand. The ghosts of her unspoken words echoed inside my mind. Unknowable and indistinct.

I flicked my tail to let out a little frustration. I knew I could trust Carlee. She would not lie or keep secrets from me, and yet I could not shake the feeling that there was something she was not telling me. Something important. If I were to become a strong haeraig, then I could not have dragons I trusted keeping information from me, no matter how petty or minor.

I sighed. That would be something to deal with later. I didn't want to keep anyone waiting, so I did my best to ignore my worries, putting them to the back of my mind with my other fears.

Nataik looked up as I approached. The serpentine Xigax dragon tucked her tail around her hindlegs. Her scales were golden brown, almost sandy in colour.

Inilta and Azlak came towards us, leaving just Keita and Okazuni basking by themselves in the dunes as far from the water as they could get. My tail twitched again as I thought of them both, tempted to call them down to the surf, but I stayed quiet.

"May I see this thing, Haeraig?" Nataik asked. She tilted her head as she looked towards my foreleg.

With the Xigax dragon's help, I was able to unhook the small strap. For the first time, I had a proper look at the small device. It was a deep black in colour, swirling with strange reflections. A rainbow band of colour ran around the circular edge. The whole thing was a little larger than my paw, but almost weightless.

"Have you seen anything like this before?" I asked, as she poked the tip of her muzzle against the shimmering surface.

Isikian crowded around Nataik, his wings fluttering with excitement. "Is this magic? I know the humans have their own type of it," the Nixan said.

Nataik nudged him away. "There is some magic to it, yes, but there is more to it than that. I had thought this to be a simple watch, like many humans wear. But that is not the case. You see these markings here?" the Xigax dragon said, gesturing with a claw to the rainbow band around the edge of the watch. "They are unique to what humans call a slate."

I furrowed my brow. I had never heard of such a thing before. Judging from the lingering silence, I didn't think anyone else had either.

"What is that?" I asked, the first to question Nataik. "What can it do?"

Nataik grinned widely, showing off the needle-sharp points of her teeth. "This, Haeraig, can do almost anything you can imagine. What might be most useful for us is that we can use it as a map. It can show us the way to go."

She placed the device on the ground and, with careful precision, pressed a single claw on the edge of the slate.

I leapt back as a harsh green light emerged, arced out, and created an odd pattern I could not identify. The organised lines of light slowly rotated on the spot, all joined to the little device on the ground. I waved a paw through the patterns and felt nothing but air.

"What does this all mean?" Isikian asked, looking as perplexed by the strange shapes as I.

Nataik indicated a flashing red light I had failed to notice before. "That shows where we are at the moment," she said, before waving her paw at a different section of the map. "And that..."

"That must be where we can find the Axinstone," Azlak whispered, interrupting the Xigax ness. "We can use this to find a way into the island lair."

Nataik glanced across to Azlak, who backed away and lowered his head in response to the sudden attention. "We could, yes," the ness said slowly. She studied the map; her eyes flicking rapidly to track and follow the many different lines. After a few seconds, she slowly extended a forepaw, pointing with a claw to a second red light, not too far from the one she had said represented our position. "This one is interesting. It seems to be moving away from us."

"It's Nightwings," Azlak said. He shivered, despite the warm sunlight that bathed on our scales.

I tried to find meaning in the map, but I could not see what seemed so clear for Azlak and Nataik. I was willing to believe them, though. They spoke the truth, and we could use this information. "If Nightwings is close, then perhaps we should fly now," I suggested.

"No, Haeraig," Azlak said sharply. He hissed and looked away. His claws sunk into the soft sand. "We must not fly today. My visions warn me. We have to stay here."

"You're scared of it, aren't you?" Carlee demanded. She stepped in front of me, looming over the cowering seer. Gone was the confident dragon of the previous night, who had led me and Isikian to the humans.

Azlak's wings twitched. He clenched his forepaw in the sand. "We should all be scared of Nightwings, Carlee. Every last one of us should be terrified. It is darkness and death."

"Death again, Azlak?" Carlee said. She sucked in her breath, before spinning around to face me. Her tail whipped against Azlak's muzzle as she moved, but the seer didn't make a sound. "We should be alert for danger."

Despite Azlak's assurances that we would be safe for another day, I glanced up to the clear sky, half expecting to see the shadow of Nightwings, whatever it was. Not even a cloud threatened to dim the sunshine. There was no danger there, and yet a chill settled on my wings.

"Rest while you can," I said, addressing everyone who had gathered around me. I put my paw over the map made of light. "We fly tomorrow at dawn. Stay on the beach and don't do anything to attract attention."

Carlee growled softly, but she said nothing to argue. I knew she would never speak against my orders, not in the presence of any other dragon. I did not doubt that she would complain privately when she could have me alone. For now, she scuffed her paws and wandered back towards the cave. Isikian and his brother followed her, the two Nixans quiet in conversation with each other.

Nataik switched off the map with a swipe of her paw. She nudged the slate towards me. "Look after this, Haeraig. It is a mighty gift those humans gave you. We should not waste it."

Before I could answer her, she slipped away. Her chameleonic scales quickly obscured her from sight as she melted into the sand. I was alone with Azlak.

"Darkness and death?" I asked the seer. I had not intended for there to be so much fear in my voice.

Azlak looked up to me for a brief moment. "Malice twisted by human magic. We cannot let Nightwings find us, or else we will fail."

I quelled the fear that threatened to rise in my belly. Instead, I slowly strapped the slate to my foreleg again. Azlak made no move to help me. When I was sure the gift from the humans was secure, I looked down on the seer. "Get some rest, Azlak. We had a long night, and we will need all the energy we can get tomorrow."

I turned from the seer, casting my gaze across the ocean. Birds wheeled just offshore, but otherwise I could see no sign of life towards the unnaturally flat horizon.

"Rest isn't all we'll need," Azlak muttered, so quietly that I didn't think the words were intended for me. When I turned my head to look back to him, the seer had wrapped his wing around his head.

I got the sudden feeling the seer wasn't telling me everything. I opened my mouth to question him, before realising that I didn't want to know what hidden truth the seer kept to himself. I fled before I could say a word.

# CHAPTER TWELVE

**Ellian**

Discontent was beginning to spread through Clan Laxtal. Confidence in my ability to lead had been badly shaken by Ddraig Astar's public dismissal of my competence, and in the three days since he had been gone, pockets of rebellion had begun to form in the shadows. None had yet come forward to actively challenge my rule, the support of Yalle and Marin was enough to prevent that, but I knew it was only a matter of time. Even the two veteran dragons were beginning to doubt me for no other reason than because the ddraig didn't fully trust me.

Vinzent had also become distant. Whereas before he had always kept me company at night, now he had taken to sleeping in his own chambers. He gave me no reasons for this new behaviour, and he always denied that there was a problem whenever I tried to bring it up. I knew he wasn't being truthful and it hurt too deeply to dwell on it. I forced myself to think that nothing was amiss, even in the cold and lonely nights when I had no one to drape their wing over me.

I longed to be able to spread my wings and fly wherever the wind took me. Better yet, with Anzig on the far side of the mountains, sharing in his excitement and danger, but my duties required me to stay close to the central lair. I couldn't leave the caves unannounced should some urgent matter require my attention, but I never felt safe within the caves. I constantly feared a challenge to spring from the shadows, but for the time being I was still afforded, albeit grudgingly, the respect a haeraig deserved.

On the few times I felt like I could escape my duties, I took to lying down just beyond the chasm that bisected the hill atop our lair. Despite the almost constant coming and going of dragons, I was left reasonably undisturbed out here, and I used this time to work out how to win back the favour of my clan. Like flying into a powerful headwind, I was battling to win the absent ddraig's approval. Without that, it would be almost impossible to win that of the clan.

The skies had clouded over, and most of the other dragons who had been resting outside awakened their rested wings with slow gentle stretches, before taking to the air, gliding lazily to the shelter of the caves; the prospect of rain outweighing the last few minutes of warmth in the air. Two dozen dragonets shrieked as they flew back to the lair, their game of one claw ten wing cut short by the oncoming weather. I couldn't help but smile as I watched them. I wondered which of them had taken on my crown as the finest one claw flyer. None had been able to touch me when I was their age, but those days were over now.

I chose to remain, half-hidden from my retreating clan, lying beneath a cluster of ferns. I had no desire to go inside yet. It would take the darkening clouds to unleash their burden, so desperately craved for, onto the parched ground, dusty and hard beneath my claws.

For a few minutes I revelled in the quiet that had descended on the land; the only sounds were the occasional screech of a bird, high overhead as it hunted for prey. I tracked its movements for a while. It must have been young, barely an adult, for its movements were unskilled and obvious as it circled beneath the clouds. Too noisy, too high, too fast; it wasn't going to catch its prey like that.

I soon became aware of another noise, one I didn't particularly want to hear: the questing pawsteps of a dragon gradually getting closer. I knew my short time of isolation was over; they would be searching for me. I sighed and crawled out from beneath the ferns and walked muzzle-first into a silver-scaled leg. Glancing up, I met Vinzent's eyes, and he sheepishly looked away.

"What do you want?" I demanded of him. I didn't even attempt to keep the irritation out of my voice. This was the first time in two days he had approached me while I was alone. I considered turning back and losing myself amongst the ferns again.

"I came to see if you were alright," Vinzent said in a small voice.

I snorted and barged past him, walking up to the crest of the hill, where the land suddenly gave way to the great chasm, whose length stretched as far as the eye could see in either direction. It was wide enough that even a human, lacking our wings, would have difficulty jumping it. I though, effortlessly glided to the other side, hoping that the physical barrier would deter Vinzent, but the dragonet was oblivious, thudding to his paws just a couple of feet from me.

"Ellian, why are you so angry with me?" he asked meekly.

I turned on the silver dragon and snarled. "Why are you so distant with me?" I retorted. "You promised to be my mate, Vinzent, yet ever since we returned to Laxtal you've kept your distance from me. You promised you would support me while Haeraig Anzig is away, but you've not helped me at all. You've barely spoken to me in the past few days, and you wonder why I'm angry with you? It's almost as though... it's like you regret saying you'll be my mate."

Vinzent's eyes were wide as he shook his head. "No, it's not at all like that, Ellian."

"Then what is it like? Because it looks like you don't care much for me after all," I said after Vinzent hesitated, squirming under my furious glare.

"Of course I care for you," Vinzent spluttered. "It's just... Mother told me I shouldn't interfere with your leadership. She said you wouldn't fully trust me or trust her. She wants to see you fly without my help."

"No ddraig flies alone," I growled. I whipped my tail against the ground, flicking up some dust. "If you want to be my mate, then you must be the wind in my wings. You need to support me, no matter what."

Vinzent bowed his head. "I know. Mother said I should wait until I know what's going to happen with the clan." He pawed the dry soil as he spoke, this simple task requiring his full attention. "She said it's a very big decision to make for a dragon so young, and with everything being so uncertain with Haeraig Anzig being away, that I needed to be sure. I was just scared of telling you. I didn't know what you'd say, so I hid away."

"Oh Vinzent, you can be so stupid at times," I said, exasperated with the silver dragon. I gently hit him on the shoulder. "Don't you see what Saya is trying to do? She wants me to fail. She also wants to keep you away from me so no one in the clan will think you had anything to do with my failure."

Vinzent sharply looked up, his eyes wide. His head arched back on his neck. "What do you mean?"

"If I fail before Ddraig Astar or Haeraig Anzig gets back, then your mother wants you to appear a strong contender to take control of the clan," I said with a sigh. "The failure of leadership must be mine alone for that to happen, so Saya asked you to stay away from me under the pretence that you're actually helping me."

"She's not… that's not what she's doing," Vinzent pleaded. He shook his head in denial of my accusations.

I struggled to hold back a growl of irritation. I didn't understand how Vinzent couldn't see what his mother was doing. It was so clear to me, so obvious. And yet the dragon who desired to be my mate failed to recognise it. I opened my mouth to speak, but before I could say anything, my eyes caught movement in the sky.

A dragon faltered and fell.

Fear gripped me. What if it was Anzig, returning to Laxtal injured and in failure?

I ran and took to wing, soaring out over the cliffs towards the open plains below. Vinzent's wings beat just behind me as he followed.

I could no longer see the fallen dragon. They had crashed into a thicket of trees, close to where the dragonets had been playing one claw. I pushed my wings hard, as though I were playing too, as though Vinzent was the claw hunting me down. The dragonets had scuffed out a safe zone for their game at the edge of the thicket. That was my target too, and I streaked towards the ground with my wings trimmed tight to my side.

I landed into a galloping run, closing my wings to my sides just in time so they didn't snag on grasping branches. The air chilled in the shade. The scent of rain was on the wind. We didn't have much time before the weather turned. Already the clouds were dark and black through the canopy.

There was movement up ahead. Branches cracked beneath the weight of a dragon, and tiny whimpers of pain reached my ears. I wrinkled my nose at the scent of blood, but there was more on the wind. More than just dragon. I paused for a moment to breathe in deep, Vinzent barging past me as I did so. Fur. Scavengers. Foxes.

A fierce yowling erupted. A draconic shriek of pain followed. Vinzent snarled in anger and leaped ahead, pushing through the trees and branches. I hurried right behind him.

We burst into a small clearing littered with debris, a hole punched into the canopy of branches above. An azure dragon limped and backed away from three foxes. It took me a moment to recognise the dragon. He was Adran, the guard who had not been at his post when we had returned from Xital. I knew he had flown with Ddraig Astar to battle, but why would he have returned if the rest of the army had not? There had been no messengers, no warnings. The beacons had not been lit; there was no word of the ddraig's activity.

Adran was in a bad way. His wings were badly torn, probably from his descent through the trees, and he seemed unable to put any weight on his right foreleg. His scales were bloody and dull; he teetered on the brink of exhaustion.

Vinzent did not hesitate. He lunged forward, catching one of the foxes by surprise. They both howled and screeched as they rolled, Vinzent's claws digging into the fox's fur.

A second fox jumped for them, but I reacted quickly. My shoulder smashed into the fox mid-air, sending the scavenger sprawling with a pained yelp. I whipped my tail against the third, but my reactions were too slow. The fox's teeth gripped close to the base of my tail, digging into the scales and threatening to puncture through.

I kicked hard, but the fox didn't release me. I growled in anger and pain, struggling to move while it had hold of me. One fox was easy, but two threatened to overwhelm me. Claw and tooth scraped against my scales, moving so quickly that I could barely lay a claw on them. Orange fur snagged in my claws, but I could not draw blood.

A kick finally landed. I smashed the fox across the face, claws ripping into its cheek. The scavenger shrieked and backed away, releasing my tail at last. My movement freed, I grappled with the second fox, my teeth snapping close to its throat. My claws found its underbelly. I slashed across, slicing through skin but only landed a shallow strike.

The fox yammered and hissed as it stumbled away. It then turned and fled into the undergrowth, the long bushy tail soon melting into the shadows. Its companion fled with it, before the third wrestled itself away from Vinzent's savagery.

The silver dragon snapped at the fleeing fox, teeth tearing a chunk of tail out. Blood dripped from his jaws, and the wild light in his eyes did not fade as he turned to face me. "Disgusting creatures," he growled.

I ignored Vinzent. Adran needed my attention more than the silver dragon. Now that the danger had passed, Adran slumped to the ground, his exhaustion finally overtaking him. Concerned, I looked over his wounds, but I was pleased to note that they weren't as bad as I first feared. Though his tattered wings would keep him grounded for quite some time, they would heal quickly enough. There also didn't appear to be any significant damage to his leg either; the bone certainly wasn't broken.

"It's alright, you're safe now," I said as I helped Adran back up to his paws, supporting most of his weight as he leant heavily on me, ignoring the stinging pain from my own wounds. I bit back the multitude of questions that burned the back of my throat. I wanted to know why the azure dragon was here and not with Ddraig Astar, but this was not the time to ask. First we needed to get him to safety, and then I could ask him all I needed to know.

It was slow moving as Adran was barely able to walk, but with Vinzent's help we were able to make it to the mouth of the ravine and the ancient scree that sealed away the gorge from the ground. Adran had been muttering under his breath the entire way, too quietly for me to make out the words, but he sounded distressed by something. My heart was sick with worry for my ddraig; I feared that something terrible had happened.

I waited with Adran while Vinzent flew into the lair to get further assistance. The two of us wouldn't be able to carry Adran across the pile of boulders that protected the lair, and nor would he be able to take to wing. Nervously, I pawed at the ground, still forcing myself to bite down on my tongue to prevent my fears and worries from bursting forth.

Five dragons came to our assistance, and between us all we were able to carry Adran into the depths of the lair and gently place him down safely inside, away from the oncoming rain and scavengers. A ripple of concern passed amongst the clan as I walked through the caves by Adran's side. Already, word had spread that a member of Ddraig Astar's attack force had returned to Laxtal, alone and injured. Many dragons asked questions as I walked on by, but I had no answers for them yet. I had nothing to say. Nothing to ease worries or soothe concerns, for I was as scared about Adran's news as any.

Adran was eventually bedded down in one of a series of small caves just off the main chamber. These were our healing halls, where a small group of dragons tended to the sick and injured with a combination of herbs and medicines, as well as the occasional human techniques learnt in times of peace.

I longed for a Nixan healer, for their magic was far superior to anything any Laxtal dragon could achieve. Usually this didn't bother me, but in a matter of healing, some magic could be the difference between life and death. Though Adran was in no danger of dying, I was impatient to question him, but I could not do so until he was strong enough to answer me. The healers informed me that it could be a few hours at least, and it wasn't long before they grew sick of my constant enquiries, and they politely, but firmly, shooed me away.

"We'll tell you when he's strong enough," one of them impatiently told me as they led me away from the halls. I knew they wouldn't have spoken to Ddraig Astar or his son in such a tone. Reluctantly, I listened to their advice, and went off in search of Vinzent. I had more to say to him, but to my frustration the silver dragon remained elusive.

Instead, I waited, alone, by the great firepit in the main chamber. Rain echoed through the caves. Thunder rumbled through the ground. My own thoughts were as dark as the weather. I could only hope that Adran brought good news, but I knew in my heart that he did not.

"The ddraig has fallen. We were ambushed at first light yesterday. We didn't stand a chance. I don't think anyone else survived," Adran said.

I sat, stunned, with Marin and Yalle by my sides. Saya and Vinzent were also present, a few feet away, and not a word was being spoken by anyone. I had momentarily stopped breathing.

"Ddraig Astar... dead?" Marin was eventually able to say.

Adran could only nod his head and turn away. He knew the magnitude of his words – his news threatened to tear Laxtal apart.

Yalle gestured me to one side. "What do we do?" he whispered, holding his wing above my body to shield our conversation from the other dragons present. Out of the corner of my eye I noticed Saya doing the same with Vinzent.

"I don't know. Will Laxtal support me until Haeraig Anzig returns?" I asked nervously. This news changed everything. Ddraig Astar was the foundation around which Clan Laxtal had thrived over the last few years. Every dragon in Laxtal respected and liked him, and he held prodigious influence amongst the surrounding clans. His loss was to the detriment of all dragonkind, not just our clan. His successor would be expected to continue his great work. Could I really hope to achieve anything that would come close to matching those expectations?

"You were his chosen representative in his absence," Yalle said softly. He hesitated, pawing at the stone. "But his absence was only meant to be short. We do not know when Anzig is meant to return. We do not know if he has already failed. It is one thing to lead the clan on behalf of another. It is something entirely different to rule by your own wings."

"I understand that," I said with a growl. "But I was still chosen by Ddraig Astar. That has to mean something."

Yalle's wing touched to my side, leading me a few paces further away from the distraught Adran and Marin. "It means something, yes. But you were not haeraig. Anzig is, and he is not here. Your right to rule is not established. Once Ddraig Astar's death is known, there will be those who will seek to claim it by force. There will be those already plotting it."

I resisted the urge to look at the one I knew who would be plotting just that. Saya and Vinzent's voices were inaudible, but I knew exactly what they said. This was the moment Saya would have longed for.

I scraped my claws against the stone. There would be many in the clan who would wish to cast me aside like a pretender, but that was not who I was. I may not have been haeraig, but both Ddraig Astar and Haeraig Anzig had trusted me to rule in their stead. I would not let Clan Laxtal fall into chaos. That would not be my legacy.

I forced myself to bury my grief and my fear as I pushed aside Yalle's wing. The albino dragon turned with me, facing the other four. I lifted my head and puffed out my chest.

"I was chosen to rule Laxtal until the ddraig returned," I said loudly. "Though we expected that to still be Ddraig Astar, we must now wait for Haeraig Anzig. He will return. I will pass on control of Laxtal to him and him alone. We must begin preparations for the wylax, so that we can declare him the true ddraig when he returns."

"A wise decision," Yalle said, sweeping his head low.

The wylax was the traditional ceremony that formally declared a new ddraig, passing on the leadership to a new dragon after the death – or defeat – of the former incumbent. I knew we would need to prepare for the wylax immediately, and to make it clear that Anzig was the intended ddraig upon his return. There could be no chance for a usurper to get ideas.

I looked to Saya and knew that thought was already too late. The ness sneered as she approached me, with Vinzent hovering by his mother's side. Though her tail dragged on the floor with her head held low in an expression of sorrow, I didn't like the triumphant gleam I saw in her eyes.

"Choose your words carefully, Saya," I growled, flaring my wings in an attempt to intimidate the older dragon. She didn't even give me the courtesy of pretending to be perturbed. She just smiled smugly and continued her saunter towards me.

"This clan needs a powerful leader, a dragon who is respected by all. We need this ddraig to step up and lead without fear or doubt," Saya said, mostly focussing her attention on Yalle and Marin, and ignoring me completely. "Our haeraig has flown to lands beyond the mountains, and we don't know when, or even if, he will return. We cannot risk the fate of our clan by waiting for what may never happen.

A decision needs to be made now on who will lead Clan Laxtal. We cannot wait to hold a wylax in some unknown future, when only the gods know."

Saya nosed her son forwards in a manner that could only be interpreted as nominating the young dragon for the role of ddraig. I stood across from Vinzent – the dragon who wished to become my mate – and waited for him to stand down or rebuke his mother's words. He would reject his mother's plots and stand by my side and support my claim to leadership of our clan.

He did not.

He remained with Saya, and stared at the ground beneath my paws, not even willing to look me and face the consequences of his choice. A furious growl rumbled from the back of my throat as I clawed at the rocks, not knowing if the splintering was the rock or my claws. My hind legs tensed and settled in preparation to spring. If Saya intended for Vinzent to fight me for leadership of this clan, then I would be ready. I would not back down. If this was what Vinzent truly wanted, then I would not stand aside simply because he had once told me he wished to be my mate. I owed it to Anzig. He had trusted me to look after the clan in his absence, and though he could never have foreseen his father's death, I would not fail him so easily.

At the silent encouragement of his mother's lazy glance, Vinzent took a couple of uncertain steps forward. "Look, Ellian," he said, hesitating. His wings were pressed tight against his back, keeping his stature as small as possible. I could tell he lacked the desire to challenge me, but my resolve remained firm. He had not pledged his support for me, and until he did so, I had no choice but to view him as a potential contender.

"I don't want to fight you Ellian," Vinzent whimpered, but still he made no moves to back away and rescind his challenge.

"Then what do you want?" I snarled, and this time it looked like the silver dragon intended to step back, but his mother only nudged him forward once more.

"I... I..." Vinzent stammered, looking back at his mother and then towards me, his head ducked down in shame.

Whatever it was he had to say remained trapped in his throat as a young dragon burst into the cave, tearing the veil off the archway in his haste. The newcomer was in some distress, violently kicking and twisting his way from his unexpected shroud. Barely had he released himself, pausing only to take a deep breath, before he was babbling his words at a rate that merged them all into one long cacophony of sound. I doubted anyone in the room would understand. It sounded like he kept on repeating 'Clan Xital', but I couldn't be sure.

"Easy, dragonet, slow down so I can understand you," I admonished the youngster, who fell into contrite silence. My ears rang in the abrupt absence of babbled words.

Saya pushed past her son and stood just in front of me, blocking the young dragonet from my sight. Though I growled at Saya, she simply ignored me as she puffed out her chest, standing as tall as her body could allow, just taller than me. "Who are you and why have you interrupted us?" the ness demanded of the youngling.

"My name is Altra. Forgive me, but I must speak with Ellian. It is urgent she hears my message," the dragonet said. Saya remained passive.

"If it's urgent, then you can tell me too. I will not be ignored and pushed aside in such a manner," the ness growled at the dragonet. Though I couldn't see him, I could hear his whimpers as Saya's confrontation was too great for him to resist. I pitied the dragonet, for I knew full well that Saya could be an intimidating foe, but I was also frustrated by the ness's machinations. She was putting personal pride and ambition ahead of the needs of the clan. Not only was she attempting to manipulate Vinzent against me, but she was trying to force her way into matters that did not concern her. A quick glance across to Yalle told me the experienced dragon was thinking much the same. He seemed troubled, his tail thrashing back and forth, caught between two minds of stepping forward, or holding his ground.

"Let Altra speak." An unlikely voice spoke up. Adran had quietly moved around to face Saya. Though his scales were still bloody and his stance unsteady, he stood before the ness without fear. "Until a challenge has been made, Ellian is the chosen leader of Laxtal. We must be the wind beneath her wings."

Saya spluttered for a moment and spread her wings out wide, but Adran stood firm and did not back away. I was worried the two would come to a confrontation. Given Adran's recent injuries, I was fearful for his safety. It quickly became apparent that my fears were unjust. Saya wilted like a flower at the onset of winter, as she lowered her head and folded her wings against her back.

"You're right. Ellian, I apologise. I spoke out of place," Saya said, finally stepping aside and allowing a terrified Altra to hesitantly step forward; his head twitching from side-to-side, eyes seeking out any hint of danger. I knew this would not be the last of Saya's attempts on my leadership, but I was content that for the time being at least, she had been cowed. The ness slunk into the shadows in the far side of the chamber. With a brief, wistful look towards me, Vinzent followed his mother away.

"I'm sorry you had to witness that – Altra is it? Please, relax, and deliver your message, only much slower this time," I told the frightened dragonet, trying to inject some false mirth into my voice. He looked like he wished he was anywhere else but in this place. The poor thing was pressed almost completely into the ground, and he never looked any higher than my paws.

The dragonet whimpered as a spasm passed through his body; his paws clawed at the rock beneath him as he summoned all his courage to speak up again. "We... we have received word from the southern beacons. A dozen dragons fly from Xital and the signals are quite clear. The ddraig is amongst them. Ddraig Tsona is coming. He is flying here as we speak. They might have sheltered from the rain, but they should be here by tomorrow," the dragonet yelped.

"Ddraig Tsona? Why? Why would he be coming here?" I asked of the dragonet, but he had no answer for me, and he remained silent, shaking his head vigorously.

"He can't have heard of... of this news already, could he?" Yalle asked, hiding the truth of Ddraig Astar's death from the messenger. The albino's voice wavered in fear.

I flared my wings uneasily, thinking back to Haeraig Zeena's words, that she suspected that Clan Xital was secretly plotting against some of the other eastern clans. Was this a sign of such treachery? Could Clan Xital really be behind the death of Ddraig Astar? I couldn't voice these concerns; I definitely did not want rumours of a Clan Xital betrayal starting to spread through the clan. That would sow the seeds of panic and mayhem when I had to try and keep control over a wary clan who would soon be mourning the death of their talismanic leader. Right now, Clan Laxtal needed to have faith in the leaders of all dragons, even if those very same leaders were responsible for the death of Ddraig Astar.

Some of my worry must have translated to my posture somehow, as Marin asked, "Ellian, what bothers you? Surely Ddraig Tsona's arrival must be coincidence?"

"It must be, yes," I replied, but I really wasn't sure whether I believed myself or not. As much as I wanted Haeraig Zeena's suspicions to be false, I couldn't shake the feeling that Ddraig Tsona's arrival and Ddraig Astar's death were somehow connected. My uncertain response didn't seem to convince any of the four dragons present, though none spoke of their concerns.

"You said Ddraig Tsona will arrive tomorrow morning, Altra?" I asked the dragonet.

Altra jumped at being at being addressed suddenly, almost taking to wing. "That's... that's what I was told, yes," he managed to squeak.

I glanced around the chamber, briefly meeting the eyes of Adran, Yalle, and Marin before they shielded their eyes from my gaze. Of Vinzent and Saya there was no sign; they had probably snuck out while we weren't paying attention to them. I was more terrified than I had ever been before about the prospect of coming face to face with the absolute leader of dragonkind, but I could not let that fear show. I was representing Clan Laxtal, and with that responsibility came a weight of expectations. I vowed not to fail my clan. I would soar despite the pressure placed on my wings. Whatever it was that Ddraig Tsona had come to Laxtal about, I would uphold the reputation and dignity Ddraig Astar had lived by.

"We had better prepare ourselves to greet his arrival," I said. My voice was strong, and seemed to carry confidence to the dragons around me. Yalle and Marin stood that little bit taller, and even Adran allowed his wounded wings a brief flutter of confident excitement.

The leaders of Clan Laxtal were ready for Ddraig Tsona.

# CHAPTER THIRTEEN

**Azlak**

We were almost at the great human city of Trevena. We had been following a route chosen by Nataik, from her studies of the map given to us by the two humans at the beach. It had been three days since we had left them, and so far there had been no indication that they had betrayed us. Thanks to the map, we had found shelter each night, in a ruined stone building, on a small island just offshore, where spray misted the air, and then in another cave overlooking the ocean from a more comfortable distance.

We made good time, despite our circuitous route around the settlements below. We had to. Since leaving the first beach, every time I closed my eyes, I had been plagued by visions of Nightwings. I constantly worried that we were not flying fast enough, that the spectre somehow knew where we were. But every time we looked at the map of magical light, the flashing red icon was always a safe distance from us. All I had ever seen of it was darkness and blood red eyes, but that was all I wanted to see. If it caught us, we would all be killed without mercy. It hunted us, and it was angry.

That fear gave urgency to my wings, and I pressed on with a pace far greater than any other day since leaving Xital. I knew some of the others would struggle. The pace burned at my wings. Okazuni and

Haeraig Anzig would likewise feel the pain, as would Carlee. I hoped that once we had safely reached George's lair, we would have a few more days of rest and recovery. We would not be safe; far from it. Sleeping so close to such a major human dwelling was fraught with danger, but such a risk could not be avoided.

Once more we flew as high as I dared. Close to the coast was densely populated; there were small villages edging almost every cove, beach, and bay. I vaguely recognised the shape of the land from the map, though Nataik surpassed my ability and was even able to recall some of the names of the settlements.

For the first time it was the Xigax dragon who had sought Haeraig Anzig's permission to fly at my wing. She seemed eager to impress me with her knowledge of humans and their strange ways, and I soon found myself learning quite a bit about them.

As it happened, Nataik had actually visited human territories quite frequently before the latest skirmishes had broken out. Though she had never been to this part of the coast before, I knew Haeraig Anzig would find her experience invaluable. She was the only one of us who really knew humans and what their habits were.

Behind us, the two Nixan dragons were in conversation with Haeraig Anzig. Now that we were getting so close to the human lair and the Axinstone, the two magic users were getting particularly edgy. They wanted to know from the haeraig what our plan of action was, but I knew that Haeraig Anzig was relying on me for that, and I didn't know how we could break into the human's lair. Keita was flying close behind the haeraig's tail, but not involved in the conversation.

Further back still was Okazuni, flying alongside Carlee. The veteran only had to make it through this one final day before she would be able to rest. She had flown better since our rest at the beach, but her wings were ailing again. Once again, I was reminded of my vision of her death; I hoped I was not soon to witness the real event. We needed her. Haeraig Anzig needed her.

Somehow though, Okazuni was able to provide the support she needed to fly throughout the day, and Carlee was able to match our pace. Far below us the human countryside passed us by. The small, isolated villages were getting larger and more frequent, and the network of roads the humans built to travel on were getting more common.

And there, in the distance, was the massive city of Trevena that Nataik had warned us about. First appearing as a dirty smudge of the horizon, it soon expanded to a sprawling grid of stone, brick, and metal structures. The coastal city was built around two shallow bays, with a tall headland jutting out between them. A wide golden beach stretched from one side of the city to the other, diminished to just a few feet wide at the tip of the central headland.

On either side of the city was another headland, whose tall cliffs allowed a perfect vantage point of the entire bay below. We settled down on the southern headland, behind a low rise that hid us from direct view of the city. It was almost evening. We had until nightfall to find somewhere safe to rest for the night. Nightwings was getting closer, I didn't need to see the map to know that. I felt like I could just turn my head and see it in the distance. The spectre was always on my mind; its shadow lingering in the corner of my eye. I had warned the haeraig of the dangers we faced if we didn't find shelter. He had been concerned, but he hadn't yet admonished me for our inability to escape the mysterious spectre.

Carlee collapsed to the ground the moment she landed, her quivering wing held over her head. Okazuni, who was also worn out from the days of flying, lay down next to her with a protective wing held out over the veteran's body.

"Azlak, if you will," Haeraig Anzig said, drawing my attention to the ferns at the summit of the headland, where he was crouched with Keita and Nataik. I moved to join them and looked out at the vista below.

Almost in the very centre of the bay rose an island. Perched on the summit of the island was a towering white stone building – a castle, as Nataik called it. This was George's lair.

Even from this distance I could see activity around the place. The water was alive with movement as humans flitted back and forth across the water on their hulking boats. On the island itself was a small harbour which was the focal point of much of the aquatic activity. It was impossible to be accurate, but there must have been over a hundred humans at the least.

There was something more though. It was hard to place, but there was an unnatural thrum of energy about the area. It toyed with my senses, like something in the corner of my eye, or a smell I couldn't quite identify; a noise just outside the register of my hearing. Haeraig

Anzig also seemed affected as his head periodically twitched, like he was trying to rid himself of an obstinate insect. Neither Nataik nor Keita seemed disturbed by anything whatsoever.

"So how do we get in?" Keita asked me, for once her voice not laced with anger. If anything she sounded awed; perhaps surprised that we had even reached this far under my guidance.

"I don't know. There's something about this place that interferes with my magic. I haven't yet been able to See anything inside that place," I said apologetically, drawing a slight growl from Keita, but not the usual explosive snarl I had come to expect from her.

"We'll think of something," Nataik said as she edged down to the very edge of the cliffs, peering down to the water below. "With that little map of yours, Haeraig, we don't even have to risk ourselves over on the island to find a way in. We can be as safe as we want to be here on the cliffs."

"Except..." I said, before hesitating. I didn't want to alarm the others, but I had already alerted their attention to it. Hiding the truth was no longer possible. Before I could continue the haeraig had stepped in front of me.

"We should find shelter before Nightwings returns. It tends to come back to Trevena every evening, so we can't be exposed when that happens," he said, somehow managing to warn everyone of the very danger I had dithered over explaining.

The Xigax ness tensed, her paw moving to the watch strapped to her foreleg. "Should we check the map?"

Haeraig Anzig nodded. "Work with Azlak and his map to keep track of Nightwings and to find us shelter." He stood as tall as his slight stature would allow him and looked across at his companion. "Keita, you can come with me and hunt. I think we can give Okazuni and Carlee a rest this time."

As Keita flew off with the haeraig to hunt, Nataik and I poured over the map the humans had given me, trying to ignore the flashing red dot that marked Nightwings. There were many caves in the area, so we focussed our attention on those. We had to find one that humans couldn't easily reach, one that couldn't be seen from the city or the island, but also allowed us to easily keep watch on both locations.

There was also an old human building further along the headland Nataik had seen on our descent. She had thought it worthwhile investigating. It would not be easy to find somewhere suitable, but it was imperative that we succeed.

We searched the ancient building shortly before sunset. Nataik called it Tin Mine, a place where the humans had once dug into the ground to extract the precious metal from the earth. All activity in this spot had long since ceased. In places the stonework was beginning to crumble, but it would still suit our needs well enough. We didn't have time to search anywhere else regardless; we had been unsuccessful in locating a suitable cave to dwell in. The old mine was our only option. At least I was confident there wouldn't be a repeat of the farmhouse. This headland appeared completely devoid of human activity, the abandoned tin mine aside. There wasn't even one of the black roads they used to operate their travelling machines on.

Inside was sparse, with no furnishings surviving the mine's abandonment. There was just the one chamber with smooth stone walls, blackened by age and soot – a single alcove on one which appeared to have been used as a fireplace. On the back wall were two archways, where once there had been passages leading down to the mines themselves. In their place now was rubble and broken stonework, the passages having long since collapsed.

It was cold, though with Inilta's magic there would at least be a warm corner for us to lie in. We were out of direct sight of the human city, and George's island. I knew we could safely have a fire without the risk of detection, so long as we waited until Nightwings passed.

Carlee had been reluctant to move from where she had sunk to the ground after landing. It took the coaxing of Haeraig Anzig, Keita, and Okazuni to get her inside the mine. My attempts to warn her of the approaching Nightwings was met with tired derision. The veteran was not normally the sort to treat me with such disdain, and the sharp words she had for me hurt deep. I retreated away from the others, who had gathered around the kindling waiting to be lit. Instead, I lay alone on the threshold of the doorway, long since missing its door.

I looked out to the north, searching the darkening sky for any sign of the spectre of Nightwings. Whatever it was, I knew the shadow was coming.

The darkness was total when I first heard it; a deep concussive thrum that caused the ground to shake. Silence fell behind me from the first beat and I shrank back inside, making sure I stayed out of sight from Nightwings as it passed by.

No one dared move. Even Carlee, who had already been asleep, was cowering with Haeraig Anzig and Keita, close to the cold fireplace.

Nightwings was getting closer, but still I could not see it. There was no moon to provide light, hidden behind a bank of clouds, and I could see barely three feet outside. I knew nothing of its whereabouts until I heard an almighty crunch from the top of the tin mine; like a great weight had just settled there. Claws scrabbled against the stone, and for a moment there was silence.

Then a voice called out from high above us. Almost masked by the stone, the voice was still recognisable as a human female. "Have you found them, Nightwings?"

Another short silence was interrupted by a low growl that reverberated through the building. "I thought I had one of them," a deep, melodious voice grumbled. "I've lost them now, but it matters not. They won't travel any more tonight."

"On your head if you're wrong," the first speaker said.

"You know George won't allow me to come to harm. Not by your hand or anyone else's," the second voice retorted in smug tones. I believed this speaker to be the spectre of Nightwings.

"I can clip those wings of yours without George ever knowing," the first voice said. The threat seemed to hit home, as Nightwings only snarled in response. Then the building shook once more, and the concussive beats of wings marked the spectre's departure.

We remained in silence, not even daring to move, fearing that Nightwings would return. The only sounds that reached us from outside was the wind rustling through the heather that grew right up to the mine's outer walls. It seemed the immediate danger had passed, for tonight at least.

"We should light the fire." Haeraig Anzig's voice finally broke the silence. There was no responding noise from outside, no roar from Nightwings. It had returned to the island in the middle of the bay with its human companions.

Inilta soon obliged, and the fire from his magic warmed the old building. For a short while, the haeraig stared into the flames, lost in deep thought. Carlee nudged against his side and whispered something in his ear, drawing the haeraig back from his reverie.

"Okazuni, take watch first," the haeraig said. Ever since departing the beach, he had ordered one dragon to remain awake, watching over the others while they slept. I had not dared question him about it, but I wondered if he feared more humans to stumble upon us in the night, ones who were not as friendly as Jim and Jess.

"I'll stay awake too, Haeraig." I blinked in surprise as Keita spoke up. The haeraig seemed surprised too, as he stared at Keita, mouth slightly open.

"Two pairs of eyes are better than one," Okazuni said, already turning his head towards the darkness outside the entrance. "Especially this close to that city."

Haeraig Anzig hesitated. He scratched the ground. Then he nodded. "Very well. You shall share first watch. Then wake Inilta and Isikian for second watch until morning."

Though I was sure the Nixans were both unhappy at being chosen for watch, we had all shared it since leaving the beach. Even Anzig had taken his turn.

Despite the security of two dragons keeping watch, I found it very hard to sleep. A violent storm raged outside; thunder shook the mine as rain drummed against the stonework, creating a cacophony of noise that I couldn't block out. Even that was the least of my concerns though. Images flashed before my eyes, too quick to register what was truly happening in each.

*A dragon I didn't know flew against the setting sun, a dark shadow just behind...*

*Haeraig Anzig cried out in pain, lying in the grass with a bleeding gash across his face. Another dragon stood over him, ready to strike...*

*A human stood on the top of a stone tower, holding a splintered shard of rock out to the storm as lightning flashed around him. A large gold-scaled Xital dragon was perched on the battlements at the human's side...*

*Fire tore through the forests of Laxtal. Dragons scattered, panicked, as they flew from the flames...*

*Ddraig Krateos of Nixa, a wound in his chest, bowed before Haeraig Anzig. Ddraig Krateos's daughter, Haeraig Zeena, sorrowful, looks away...*

*The spectre of Nightwings, diminished in size somehow, stood in a cave; only its red eyes clearly visible. It leaned forward and whispered something to a golden dragon – me. "I'm not Laxtal, like the one you seek, but I can help you find him..."*

*A dark-skinned human with blazing tattoos of golden light stepped off a great ship and breathed in the coastal air.*

*Two pure white eggs; Haeraig Anzig stood over them protectively, hissing at an unknown attacker...*

Nightwings somehow knew about the other Laxtal dragon with magic. How it knew, I couldn't even begin to fathom, but... If that vision was to come to pass, I would need to speak to the great spectre. How could I approach death and darkness without fear? And why was it no longer the massive spectre I had heard and witnessed?

I tried to work my mind through some of the other visions, hoping there was some clue in them, but I didn't even know which ones were to come to pass first. I only succeeded in giving myself a headache, and I eventually quelled my mind into an uneasy state of rest.

As my eyes closed and darkness took me, I heard a voice in my mind. *"There you are Little One. So, you have reached Trevena at last. Sleep well, while the night is safe. Maznar is watching out for you all." I saw a brief glimpse of the black-scaled ness smiling at me as she curled up in a dungeon.*

# CHAPTER FOURTEEN

**Ellian**

Clan Laxtal gathered once more, but this time there was a strong sense of unease. Knowledge of the beloved ddraig's death had not spread, but Adran's unexpected return fuelled rumours. The presence of Ddraig Tsona had attributed to a significant amount of unrest in the shadows. No one dared to speak out against the Xital dragon and there were few indeed who were not intimidated by his presence.

I had barely exchanged any words with Ddraig Tsona since his arrival earlier in the day. Though I had wanted to, I had been unable to muster the courage to ask him why he had come to Laxtal. Neither the ddraig nor the entourage of Xital dragons he had brought with him had volunteered that information. They had remained silent, sheltering in the guest chambers and enjoying the feast Laxtal's hunters had provided them. I tried not to read too much into Ddraig Tsona's unexpected arrival, but my mind kept on playing over the conspiracies that had been seeded by Haeraig Zeena's words.

It had not been my decision to summon the clan to the main chamber. That had been Ddraig Tsona, once he had eaten. He demanded that the clan gather so that he could share the reason for his arrival with everyone, and not just me. I knew that I also needed to share my news, though Laxtal would not like it.

The Xital ddraig stood to my right as I faced my clan, the great firepit right in front of, but below me. Vinzent was also by my side. Saya would not be parted from her son's company, so she too, appeared along with Yalle and Marin on the raised podium that allowed us to gaze out over the heads of those gathered before us.

I knew that the next few moments would define my leadership of the clan. I would either be treated with respect, or with utter disdain. The clan would be devastated by the loss of Ddraig Astar, but the real unknown was whether or not they would consider me their leader until Anzig returned.

"Will you speak to your clan first, or shall I?" the royal Xital dragon asked quietly, so that no one else could hear his words.

"I will speak to them, Ddraig Tsona," I replied, almost offended that the Xital dragon did not believe I was capable. I was afraid of the reaction I would receive, but knew it was my duty to give my clan this news; that alone gave me the motivation to step forward to face the horde of impatient dragons.

Starting at the front of the chamber, a sudden hush rippled backwards through the clan, until I was faced with absolute silence. I had the attention of every dragon present, so eager were they for information. Ddraig Astar had been a wonderful speaker. Now it turned to me to inspire a reaction amongst my clan.

"For countless generations, Clan Laxtal has been at the forefront of dragonkind. Our clan has been strong, and it has been united against any threat. There have been times when our resolve has been shaken, but we have stood firm. I will not lie to you now. Your resolve is about to be shaken to your very core, but we must stand as one. Ddraig Astar was ambushed at dawn three nights ago. With great regret, I must tell you now that he did not survive."

I had to raise my voice to speak out over the wave of anguish that spread through the clan. "Please, I beg of you, stand strong with me until his son returns home to stand before the wylax. Support me as haeraig and Ddraig Anzig will uphold his father's memory and lead us to greater things. This I swear."

Many of the dragons were open in their anguish as a cacophony of wails echoed around the great chamber. Caught up in their grief I almost lowered my head and turned away, but I forced myself to stay strong and hold my head up high. I could not show weakness now. This was my only chance to win over my clan.

"Fly with me now, and this loss will only hurt for a short while. I will not let Clan Laxtal fall into disarray waiting for Ddraig Anzig to return. He shall come home to find his clan as strong as it has ever been, with the wylax prepared to declare him as the true ddraig of this clan," I shouted, feeling confidence coursing through my blood for the first time. I looked down at the gathered dragons, and in the brief moments they were able to hold my gaze, I could see respect and loyalty there. They were willing to put their faith in me as their leader.

One dragon stepped forward from the gathered throng. He lowered his head. "I am willing to accept you as haeraig," he said.

A second dragon came forward and repeated the words of the first, followed by a third, and then a fourth. Dozens soon followed until a deafening roar of approval washed over me. Before long almost every dragon in the clan had bowed their head to me and declared their support.

I turned to the dragons behind me. "And will you accept me as haeraig?"

Vinzent was the first to answer. "Of course, Haeraig Ellian," he said.

Yalle and Marin were also quick to answer to the affirmative, and though Saya paused and delayed her answer, she also agreed to support me as haeraig.

Then Ddraig Tsona stepped forward and quite calmly addressed the clan. "Anzig will not be returning."

The wind was taken from beneath my wings. "What? What do you mean, Ddraig Tsona?" I asked, perhaps a little harsher in tone than was proper to address the Xital dragon.

"He failed his mission. He barely made it over the mountains before he was captured by humans and killed," the Xital said, as calmly as though he had described an oncoming rain shower.

I tried to articulate words but found it impossible. I didn't want to believe the Xital's words. They couldn't be true. Anzig could not have fallen.

The chamber had fallen to silence. Like me, the rest of the clan were struggling to deal with the shock of losing ddraig and haeraig at the same time. The silence wasn't broken until Vinzent stared down the Xital ddraig.

"How do you know this?" the silver dragon demanded of Ddraig Tsona. He spoke in a tone rarely used against a Xital dragon, let alone their ddraig. Vinzent's insolence seemed to snap the clan out of a collective trance, and here and there other calls came demanding to know how Ddraig Tsona knew of Anzig's death. It was the most open display of rebellion against a Xital that I had seen, and I was filled with pride that the clan refused to accept Ddraig Tsona's word as truth without demanding any explanation or proof.

The royal dragon did not appear too perturbed by Vinzent's outburst, and his smug glower threatened to physically sicken me. "What does it matter where I get my information?" He flicked a few grains of dirt off his claws, scattering them around Vinzent's paws. "Do you doubt me?"

"I do not simply doubt you, Ddraig Tsona," I said, standing by Vinzent's side. "I don't believe you."

"You insolent little brat," the Xital spat. He slammed his paw down and approached me. He did not stop until the tip of his muzzle touched mine. "You have no place..."

"I am haeraig of this clan, and leader in the absence of our ddraig. I have every right to question this information," I said, pushing back at the golden dragon. A growl of anger came to my voice. "You have no right to speak such a way to me."

Ddraig Tsona snarled and pulled away. "If you must know, one of his companions made his way back to Xital a few nights ago. The little one, Okazuni I believe his name was, told me how they had been captured at a farm just the other side of the mountains. The Nyrian succumbed to his wounds that night," he explained. He showed no effort in trying to conceal the harshness of his words.

A shiver of fear ran through my spine. I did not know if the Xital dragon spoke the truth. I suspected more lies. It was all a Xital could do, sometimes. They lied for power. They lied for control. They lied because they liked lying. Ddraig Tsona's given evidence was by no means conclusive proof to my mind, but judging by the distraught cries emanating from the rest of the chamber, there were many dragons who now believed the Xital.

But Ddraig Tsona was not done yet. He pushed Vinzent away, sending the silver dragon sprawling on the dusty rock, before turning to face me once more. I held my ground and didn't give the older, larger, and more experienced dragon the satisfaction of forcing me back. I would not let myself feel intimidated by the royal. If what he had said was true then that made me the clan ddraig, and that meant I would not be bullied by any dragon – royal or otherwise.

"I can make it so you can be the most respected leader this clan has ever seen, if you pledge to support me without hesitation or doubt. I will allow you to stand for the wylax and rule Laxtal, should you swear fealty and loyalty to me. You must pledge that your clan will forget all about this alliance with Nixa," the Xital growled, dropping his voice so that only I could hear him. "But if you should refuse this, then I will ensure that you will be a dragon forgotten by all. You shall be alone: clanless, friendless, and homeless. Choose wisely, Ellian, for I will not give you another opportunity."

"Ddraig Astar was always adamant that our clan will never be ruled or controlled by anyone but a Laxtal dragon. You will find that we are not so easily swayed from this," I said, eliciting a nervous shuffle from Yalle and Marin. Saya made a small noise in the back of her throat. She was quelled by a fierce glare from Ddraig Tsona, who then turned his obstinate gaze back on me.

"Then you are a fool, Ellian. If you think I will let Clan Laxtal be led by such an inexperienced dragon without any support from Clan Xital, then you are sorely mistaken. In times like these experience and reason must lead us, not the brash innocence of youth," the Xital dragon snarled.

"What do you mean, in times like these?"

Ddraig Tsona was so close to me now his muzzle practically touched mine. I could feel his hot breath against my scales and I forced myself to hold ground.

"War has come to our borders, Ellian, as your cousin so rightly warned us," he hissed. He then raised his voice so the rest of the chamber could hear him. "Clan Laxtal needs a leader with strength and knowledge in times of war or else it risks defeat. Would you see your clan fall? Would you see your home destroyed by the invading humans? Without experience to guide you, I can guarantee that this will happen."

I could see the Xital's goal now. He sought to undermine my authority as ddraig before I had a chance to consolidate it, though his ultimate motive remained unclear. Why would he seek to weaken one of dragonkind's most powerful clans when we were on the verge of outright war with the humans? Unless, of course, Haeraig Zeena's suspicions had been correct and Clan Xital had their own hidden agendas for this war. As it was, I could only watch on in horror as more and more dragons seemed taken in by the royal dragon's words.

"We have strong leaders. I have advisors who can guide me better than any interloper from outside our clan," I told the Xital, but he charged into me with his shoulder and pushed me to the ground before I could even react. His claws raked across my face, drawing lines of sharp, searing pain that just missed my eyes.

I staggered back, but I did not concede. Nor did I retaliate to his assault. "You dare?" I hissed. I wiped away the blood on my face, staining the lilac scales of my paw. I knew fresh blood welled into its place. "You attack me here? If you seek to usurp Laxtal then challenge me and see how my clan accepts unjust rule."

"You use inflammatory language, Ellian," Ddraig Tsona snarled. "You accuse me of usurping. Of scheming to be an unjust ruler. I see it as the immaturity of youth, as proof that you are not fit to rule."

'I did not hear a challenge, Ddraig Tsona."

The drake's eyes burned bright and hot enough to kindle flame. "Do you really wish to throw away the respect and honour you have flown so hard to build?"

I snarled. "I did not hear a challenge." I braced my hindpaws against the stone. My senses closed around me. I had eyes and ears only for the golden Xital dragon.

"And so ends the shortest reign of any ddraig in Laxtal's history," Ddraig Tsona said with a sigh. He then raised his voice to a bellow. "I challenge you, Ellian of Laxtal. For rulership of this clan."

Ddraig Tsona moved quicker than I expected.

His shoulder smashed into me, knocking me from my paws. I struggled to push back against him, my claws swiping empty air. I had no chance to recover. His heavy paws bashed against my head. One, then the other. My vision burst into white light. It cleared in time to see golden scales above me.

A paw pressed to my throat, claws pinching my scales.

I flared my wings in concession of defeat, and I knew in that moment I had lost control of the clan.

Ddraig Tsona cuffed me once more, a ferocious blow to the side of my head that left me dazed. He stepped over me, his tail also catching me as he passed.

"It pains me to do this, but this clan needs a strong leader to recover from the loss of Ddraig Astar. I know it goes against the normal order of things, but I believe it best that I take control of Laxtal until a suitable replacement is found," the royal dragon roared to the clan. "As a show of my commitment to this promise, I do not demand a wylax to fortify my rule. Clan Laxtal shall hold one once a suitable ddraig emerges."

Silence met his words. Their earlier bravado was gone. No one dared to speak up against the ddraig of Xital anymore.

I slowly rolled to my belly and squeezed my eyes shut. Shame burned hot through my blood.

Someone touched my back. I looked up to see Vinzent standing over me. His entire body was quivering in ill-suppressed rage. "He has no right..." he said through clenched teeth. He glared at the royal dragon with a fury I had never witnessed before.

"Vinzent, don't," I warned the silver dragonet, but I knew he had not heard me as he started to advance on the Xital. I cringed, looking back across at Yalle and Marin, who both refused to meet my eye. Not far from those two was Saya. The ness looked fearful as her son approached the royal dragon.

Ddraig Tsona turned before Vinzent addressed him, as though he already knew the dragonet was coming. He leered at Vinzent, a horrid look of utter superiority etched into his poise. He didn't even consider the silver dragon as a threat.

Vinzent didn't appear to notice this. "You cannot do this, Ddraig Tsona. You have no right to challenge Ddraig Ellian for control of this clan."

"No right? I have every right, dragonet. Any dragon may challenge for the leadership of any clan. I am simply doing what I know is right for the good of dragonkind. The rest of your clan can see that for they do not dispute my challenge. They know that I will lead this clan, no matter what a whelp like you may believe," Ddraig Tsona said, never once looking towards his adversary.

The dragonet did not back down. "There are dragons here who will do anything in their power to keep Clan Laxtal out of the paws of Clan Xital."

Ddraig Tsona didn't even look at his challenger, instead showing more interest in cleaning his claws. "Will those dragons step forward?"

I stood by Vinzent's side, but I was the only dragon who moved. None dared to go against the Xital drake.

Vinzent turned to face Saya, who cowered back towards Yalle and Marin. "Mother, will you not stand strong for Laxtal?"

Saya continued to back away, wide-eyed as all the colour seemed to fade from her scales. "I'm sorry my son. I will not go against the wishes of Clan Xital," she said.

"Nor will I," Marin added, bowing his head towards the royal dragon.

For just a moment, Yalle seemed to step forward, but under the harsh gaze of Ddraig Tsona, he backed down. "I do not agree with it, but nor will I challenge it," he said. The albino did not bow towards Ddraig Tsona. "Sometimes we must stand back and think what is best for the clan. Surely you can see that Laxtal would be better suited having a leader with experience? We need a dragon who can defeat the humans, and if that means we must accept Xital rule for now, then so be it."

"And why do you doubt that Ellian can be that leader?" Vinzent snarled. His claws gouged into the rock beneath his paws as he spoke, leaving three shallow lines in the stone.

None of the three senior Laxtal dragons answered. They all looked away and refused to meet either of our eyes.

"Your clan's silence has spoken louder than their words," Ddraig Tsona crowed. He flared his wings and pushed himself up onto his hind paws so that he towered high above us. "You have tried to challenge me, and you have failed. As a consequence, I feel your continued stay in this clan is untenable. I hereby banish both of you from Clan Laxtal. You are to leave this territory and never return."

"No, you can't do that," I cried, backing away from the Xital ddraig. Vinzent did not move as he uttered a low growl from the base of his throat.

No dragon could even look towards me. "Don't listen to this, please," I pleaded with them. "You don't need to bow to the whims of Clan Xital and let them take control of you. Stand strong for Laxtal."

I may not have said anything, for I received no reaction other than awkward guilt. I had failed my clan, and they had failed me.

"Clan Laxtal needs a strong leader. With the threat of humanity closing in on your borders, dragonkind needs to band together and act as one. You have shown aversion to this idea, Ellian, and that is why I have no choice but to expel you from this clan. You have brought this judgement down upon yourself," Ddraig Tsona said sternly.

Such was the conviction in his words that I almost doubted my beliefs. Had we misjudged him and allowed ourselves to fall into conspiracy, fuelled by Haeraig Zeena's warnings? The Xital drake spoke of unity and fighting together, yet he cautioned against our alliance with Nixa. Heart and mind conflicted with each other. I didn't know what to believe, but I knew one thing to be true.

No matter Ddraig Tsona's intentions, he had me exactly where he wanted. The clan saw me in the light he intended. Inexperienced and petty. Incapable of rule.

Vinzent snarled, but still he made no move for the Xital ddraig. I glanced across at the young dragonet, and I could see doubt in his eyes too. I was sure he was thinking he had made the same mistake as me.

I lowered my head in ultimate submission to the Xital. "If this is what must be," I whispered in sorrow. I looked around the massive chamber, at each of the dragons who silently stood on and watched.

"Fly now, Ellian and Vinzent. Don't look back until you leave this clan, and never think of returning here," Ddraig Tsona said. His voice rung out through the cave, leaving no dragon in doubt that we were no longer welcome within these lands.

"You will pay for this. I will make you suffer," Vinzent spat, but before the Xital could even react, the dragonet was already in the air, powering his way towards the tunnels that led to the surface. I considered leaving the Xital with a similar retort, but the thunderous look on his face wilted my brief surge of courage caused by Vinzent's words. I took to wing and left behind almost every dragon I had ever known, abandoning the one place I had called home.

I flew through the network of tunnels for the last time, keeping close to the silver tail of my fellow outcast. No one followed us. I doubted anyone would want to be seen going against the wishes of Clan Laxtal's new ddraig. It was just going to be the two of us. Not all that long ago my heart would have sung at the prospect of spending so much time alone with Vinzent, but now all I felt was utter devastation. I still didn't know if I could trust Vinzent's commitment towards me, and now that we were both exiled from the clan, everything changed again. We could fall no lower. We were both dragons without power, prospects, or a home. Getting a mate would soon become the last thing on our minds.

Vinzent pulled up and landed when we emerged into the outermost chamber of the lair. He seemed reluctant to go out into the light that streamed in from outside. I took to the ground by his side, but he scampered away when I tried to place my wing over him.

"What are we going to do, Ellian?" he asked, not once looking in my direction. His wingtips trailed along the ground as he paced around the cave walls.

I looked out into the light. My eyes were blinded to any sort of detail, but I could hear the wind in the trees. The sound was soothing, and it calmed down my racing mind. It gave me chance to think – not of the long term, but of where the next beat of my wings would take us.

"I know there's a cave the nomads use on our western borders. We should easily make it there before nightfall." My voice was dull and listless even to my own ears. Had I really been reduced to this so soon?

In the uncontested lands between the clans, nomadic dragons roamed the plains and the forests, always searching for the richest hunting grounds. Most clans were open to these nomads crossing into their territory, though some, like Clan Xital, opposed this. Dotted throughout the landscape were the temporary lairs they used. That I knew of, there were four within a day's flight of the central lair. Three were little more than simple warrens dug out from the soil, but the one to the west was a small cave on the banks of a river. There were always dragons present there, gorging off the fish they caught.

"But what then, Ellian? What do we do once we get there? I won't just stand aside and let that monster lead our clan into ruin," Vinzent snarled, smashing his paw against the rock. He fell silent and still after that; his only movement was his heaving chest as he exhaled heavily.

"We must though. You don't think it pains me, leaving our clan behind?" I said, finally able to place a wing over him as I stood by his side.

He glanced across at me from the corner of his eye and sighed. "Why not go to Nixa? Surely they'd help us reclaim our clan if we asked them."

I shook my head as he pulled away from me and snarled again. "They wouldn't help us," I said, chasing after the silver dragon. "They said they wouldn't help us until Anzig returned with the Axinstone. If... If Anzig has failed, then Ddraig Krateos will not offer us aid."

"But we could try, at least," Vinzent cried, turning around to face me. He tried to stare me down, but I refused to look away.

"We will not fly to Nixa," I said, intentionally keeping my voice quiet. "We will fly to the nomads' cave and that is the last I will hear of it. Now get moving, because I do not want to think of the consequences if Ddraig Tsona finds us here."

"But..." Vinzent started to protest, but I cuffed him over the muzzle, catching him completely unawares.

"But nothing, Vinzent," I roared at him. I advanced with my wings flared, but he backed away until he pushed up against the rock wall and could retreat no further. "We have lost the clan, and there is nothing more to it."

I cuffed him once more before turning my back on him and flying out of the cave. My eyes hadn't even adjusted to the light before I banked up sharply to avoid the ravine walls. I could hear Vinzent's wingbeats not far behind, but I didn't look back to make sure he was keeping close. I flew hard and fast. I wanted to put as much distance between myself and Ddraig Tsona and my clan, lest my heartache at being banished force me to turn around and disgrace myself further by returning and failing all over again. There was a part of me that wanted Vinzent to fail to keep up with me, but I also knew that his wings were bigger and stronger than mine and I would not be able to outpace him over any distance.

I turned to the west, where in the far distance the Sxinix Mountains rose from the horizon as little more than a tiny smudge. My cousin had crossed those peaks not long ago and met his death on the other side. I glared at the mountains, as though they were themselves responsible for Anzig's failure. For a moment I had a mad urge to follow in his wingbeats and cross the mountains. I could pick up his quest where he had failed and return home with the Axinstone. Surely if I did that, I could reclaim my clan? Then I realised the folly of what I had been thinking. Anzig had travelled with seven other dragons and had failed. I would be traveling alone into human territory, with no knowledge of where to go. I would be killed within an hour of crossing into the western lands. I had to put such ridiculous thoughts aside. My future now lay with the nomadic dragons, and that was all there was to it.

So great was my haste that I ignored all the game down on the plains we flew over. Hunger was starting to grip my stomach, but I didn't want to stop and hunt. I believed Ddraig Tsona's threats, and I didn't want him to fly out and find us. I knew he would have some way of punishing us for killing prey on what the Xital now considered to be his hunting grounds.

The only sound that accompanied me was the rhythmic beats of Vinzent's wings as he kept pace close to my tail, always staying a few feet away and never once coming up to my wingtip like he usually would. He didn't attempt to talk to me, and I didn't once glance back at him. I refused to acknowledge his presence, and he seemed content to return the favour.

The sun was approaching the horizon by the time the great river started winding through the plains beneath me. Here it ran from north to south. Upstream it found its way to Nixa, before delving deep into the mountains where its source emerged from an underground pool. I had been there once before, on an expedition with Anzig and Zhara, his mother, many years ago. Zhara always liked showing her only son the beauty of nature, and often took him on trips out to explore Laxtal and the surrounding lands. Zhara would always invite me to join them, as she was the closest thing to a mother I could really remember. I was too young to understand death when my parents passed, but I had grieved as strongly as Anzig had when Zhara was killed by the humans at the start of this war.

A large, rocky promontory jutted out into the river at a point where the waters churned over an uneven bed. It was here where the nomadic dragons often stayed, in a cave that opened out near the base of the outcrop. The top of the outcrop was flat and covered in heather. It was almost sunset, and there were about a dozen dragons basking in the last of the sunlight before retreating into the cave for the night. None of them paid us any attention as we descended, and only one dragon lazily opened an eye when we landed right by her side. My wings quivered and trembled as I folded them against my back.

"Well now what? Any great plan in mind, Ellian?" Vinzent said grumpily – the first words he had spoken since leaving the central lair.

I growled at him in answer, an act which got the attention of another of the dragons.

"Ellian?"

I looked around in shock. I recognised that voice, though I had not heard it in many years. A dragon with dark blue scales and piercing yellow eyes stared at me, mouth slightly open in shock – a feeling that I reciprocated. I could barely believe what I was seeing.

"Mulner," I cried. My tiredness was forgotten as I crossed the distance between us and placed my head upon his shoulder. He was hesitant at first, but he placed his wing around me and pressed his head against my neck. "Oh it has been too long. Why have you stayed away?"

I felt a touch on my tail.

"Who is this?" Vinzent growled. The silver dragonet glared at his blue-scaled rival.

Mulner laughed. "I remember you. You're Saya's son. Good to see you haven't changed since you were a tiny dragonet. I'm Mulner, though I doubt you remember me at all. I'm Ellian's brother," he said.

"Brother?" Vinzent spluttered. "I thought you'd died."

Mulner laughed again. "No, of course not. I just couldn't stay in Laxtal once our parents had gone. There was nothing left for me there but for my sister. I wanted to bring Ellian with me too, but Ddraig Astar refused. He said I was too young to raise a dragon by myself."

"You could have come back any time you wanted," I said. There were so many things I wanted to say, but they all stuck in my throat.

"I know. I once got as far as the gorge, but I couldn't bring myself to go any further. I watched as our father died in those caves. Even then, I had considered leaving, and then mother was killed hunting. There were too many memories haunting those caves for me ever to go back," Mulner said. His wings tightened their grip around my body.

"I still care for the clan though," my brother continued. "I have a group of dragons here who patrol the borders with me. We have been concerned over the last few months of the amount of humans we've seen around this area. In fact, we have four dragons out at the moment keeping track of the movement of a band of humans we spotted just a few days ago. I don't know why they're here, but we have heard of conflicts between Laxtal and the humans already."

Mulner paused and looked me in the eye, briefly. "We heard rumour that Ddraig Astar had been killed. Please say this isn't true."

I shook my head. "It is true. But that's not the worst of it. We've been told Anzig has been killed by humans too," I said.

Mulner pulled away. "What?" he exclaimed. "Then who is leading Clan Laxtal if you are not? We were Ddraig Astar's only other living relatives. Surely leadership would have fallen to you?"

"It did," Vinzent snarled. "And it would have stayed with her had she let me challenge him for it."

"We both know that's not true, Vinzent," I whispered.

His eyes were wild as he turned to face me, wings flared and claws scratching at the ground. "You doubted me?" he snarled.

"Challenge who?" Mulner asked before I had chance to answer Vinzent.

"Ddraig Tsona of Xital. He has taken control of Laxtal," I said, not looking at Vinzent or his crazed glare.

"What? And the clan just let him?" Mulner asked, incredulously. He too had flared his wings, but his reaction was of shock, not of aggression.

Vinzent snarled at my brother, but we both ignored the silver dragonet.

I looked out over the undulating plains, back towards the clan I had left behind. The other dragons were starting to return to the cave as the sun touched the horizon. "They were too scared to do anything else," I said, holding my head low as the shame of submitting to the Xital washed over me once more.

"And do you plan on reclaiming leadership, because I'm sure you'll find some dragons here willing to help. We have our reasons to stay away from the clans, but they will not let Laxtal fall into the paws of a Xital," Mulner said. Vinzent emitted a low grumble from the back of his throat, no doubt agreeing with my brother, but not willing to vocalise his support. I shook my head, and Vinzent's grumble turned to another snarl.

"Ddraig Tsona took leadership fairly, I can see that now. I think we were deluded by conspiracy and rumour against him," I paused and sighed, lying down in the grass. Mulner sat down by my side, while Vinzent stalked away to the cave entrance. The silver dragonet paused for a moment before going inside. "I think he does have the wellbeing of dragonkind at heart, though I didn't believe it at the time."

"Then why did you doubt him?" Mulner asked quietly.

"Haeraig Zeena of Nixa warned me that she believed a Xital dragon was assisting the humans. I was convinced that it was Ddraig Tsona, but now I don't believe that's true. If there is a dragon helping the humans, then it comes from someone else within the clan," I said.

Mulner didn't say anything as he looked out to the horizon. He was watching a couple of dragons as they flew back to the cave. Only once they had landed and disappeared into the dark of the shelter did he turn to face me.

"I don't like that rumour because it would help explain some unusual behaviour we have noticed in the humans. They have already forced us out of some of our regular lairs as they seem to find them with great accuracy. We haven't been able to work out how they've been finding them so well, but it would make sense if a Xital has been feeding them information on where some of our most hidden shelters are," he said. His tail thrashed against the ground, kicking up a small cloud of dust.

"Ddraig Tsona is trying to unite the clans to better fight off the humans. I don't think he's the one helping the humans," I said, but the words were bitter in my mouth. If he cared so much about uniting us, then why had he urged me to ignore the alliance with Nixa?

I stretched my aching wings out and a very satisfying pop relieved a little of the tension in my muscles.

"I wouldn't discount him just yet, Ellian," my brother warned. His mouth hung upon, revealing his teeth as he thought. "I think you'd be right to distrust everyone from that clan until we can reveal the truth."

"But what's the purpose of it all?" I asked.

"I don't know."

The two of us sat in silence for a few minutes, neither of us wanting to go inside just yet, even though the night chill was already starting to set in as the last of the sun's light faded away. It would soon be too dark to see anything, yet we still sat and just watched for movement in the gloom.

"We might have some answers tomorrow," Mulner said eventually. "I'm expecting some dragons back here who have been tracking that group of humans. Maybe they've heard something that could explain what is going on. It's unlikely, but it's about time we started to understand something about why the humans have crossed the mountains."

"I doubt it will be that easy," I said, wishing all the while that it could be. I hoped that Ddraig Tsona could be trusted; that he truly was unifying the clans and not attempting to sabotage them. I had wasted my chance to help dictate the shape of this war and my only solace was that it had reunited me with my long-lost brother.

Mulner got up to his paws. By now he was little more than a shadow in the corner of my vision. "Come on Ellian. You've had a long flight. Lie by the fire tonight and we can worry about all this tomorrow," he said. His teeth gleamed in the soft glow of the firelight that emanated from inside the cave as he grinned. "I still can't believe I have my little baby sister back, and that she was ddraig of Laxtal, even if it was for such a short time."

I smiled, despite the bitterness that welled up once again over losing control of the clan. "I'm glad to have you around again too," I said. I nuzzled up against his shoulder again before following him into the lair of the nomads.

My new home.

# CHAPTER FIFTEEN

**Anzig**

*I stood my ground, my head refusing to bow.*

*My father stood before me. It was easy for him to look down on me, the diminutive son who was an embarrassment to him. Even when I tried to be confident, he spurned me. This was no different, and the snarl in his voice spoke of his anger and shame.*

*"I will not let you go to Xital in my name. You are not ready for this."*

*My claws dug deep gouges into the rock. "How will you know that unless you give me the chance?" I replied, more confidence in my voice than I could have expected. "Let me represent Laxtal. I will bring you and our clan honour."*

*Ddraig Astar raised a paw. I was sure he was about to strike me. I did not cringe or recoil. That would give him the victory he thought he deserved. His eyes burned bright, fire amongst the amber irises. "You will only bring shame to this clan."*

*"How do you know that?" I demanded, my wings flaring to give some meagre increase to my size. I had never felt so small before my*

*father. He seemed to grow in stature, practically every scale straining with muscle and bulk.*

*"How could you not?" my father spat. His neck snaked out, bringing the tip of his muzzle into contact with mine. His hot breath washed over my face, the reek of brimstone and dead flesh sickening me. "You have never been anything but an embarrassment to me, Anzig."*

*"That's not true," I snarled, rage burning hot in my blood. I stomped hard, cracking the stone beneath my forepaw.*

*My father tilted his head. The amber in his eyes was gone, replaced solely by flame and rage. "Is it not?" he hissed. His terrifying visage took up my vision. I could see nothing else but him. "Name one thing you have achieved, son. Name one thing you have done."*

*My bravado faded, the wind beneath my wings extinguished. I floundered for an answer, but neither tongue nor mind worked. "I... I..."*

*"I can think of one thing," Astar growled. His muzzle pressed against mine. "Your mother died because of your incompetence. You lead her to her death."*

*The unjust accusations flattened me to the ground. I shrank away, while my father grew ever larger. "Please, Ddraig. Give me this chance in Xital to prove you wrong."*

*Ddraig Astar's forepaw smashed against the ground, splintering rock and throwing me off balance. He raised his paw again, ready to strike, but his head lifted in distraction. He squinted his eyes and peered into the vague darkness that surrounded us. I thought I could hear faint movement and whispers, but I did not dare turn my head to see.*

*My father shrank to his usual size. He looked down at me and sneered. Then he faded into darkness, leaving me alone in a strange place. Shadows swirled around me, cold and dark. I slowly turned on the spot, the stone floor of Laxtal soft underpaw. I couldn't see where my father had gone. What had distracted him? Had he decided to fly to Xital after all, leaving me alone as a shamed haeraig?*

*Then I saw them. Red eyes gleaming from the shadow. I stepped back.*

*The eyes lunged. A gigantic dragon head grew from the shadows, mouth wide with shadowy saliva dripping from very solid looking teeth. I screamed and threw my wing up as the jaw snapped down around me.*

I jerked awake, tail slapping against the ground. My heart raced, drumming a frantic beat that could surely be heard across the water, on George's island. Unlike most dreams, the details of this one stuck to my mind, refusing to fade away. I could still see the anger in my father's eyes, the disappointment and shame hiding just beneath it.

I held my paws to my head, claws hooked against my short, stubby horns. Then I flicked my tail. I would get no more sleep tonight.

A quick look up confirmed that it was still before dawn. Sunlight didn't touch the horizon, which meant Nightwings would be safely inside George's castle in the middle of the bay. It was our second night in the old mine, having found no way across the water the previous day. A dark silhouette shrouded the doorway. One dragon stood watch, the firelight on their back to stay warm.

Slowly, so I didn't wake anyone else, I rose to my paws. If I wasn't able to sleep, I knew I might as well volunteer to keep watch instead.

I was surprised to see Carlee. I had expected Okazuni. The Nyrian had been the dragon I had asked take second watch, but as I looked back into the mine, I could see him curled up close to the fire by Keita's side.

The veteran glanced back as I approached. "Can't sleep?"

I shook my head. "Nightmare."

"Did you want to talk about it?" Carlee asked. She lifted her right wing, giving me a place to huddle against her. Despite the juvenile appearance, I eagerly rested by her side, her wing draped over my back.

The words choked in my throat. Shame burned at my eyes, and I needed to turn my head quickly so that I could hide the tears that threatened to well up there. Tears that no dragon were allowed to shed. I took a few deep breaths, trying to control my emotions. I was not afraid of being vulnerable in front of her, but she would tell Ddraig Astar if she knew I had been crying. He was already ashamed of me. I didn't need to give him another reason to despise me.

"It was about my father," I said, my voice thick as I struggled to speak around those hated tears.

"Tell me about it."

If Carlee heard the tears in my voice, she mentioned nothing of it. She was calm and gentle, her wing a comfort over me. "I was in Laxtal, before leaving for Xital," I said. I cleared my throat. The words came easier than I expected. "I dreamed about our last conversation. The things he said to me."

"And he meant every word of it," Carlee said.

The air stole from my lungs. I couldn't breathe. Shrieks of anguish deafened me so much that I barely heard that the veteran continued speaking.

"But what has made you so upset? I was there when you spoke to your father. What else happened in this dream?"

I spluttered as I pushed myself away from Carlee, leaving the embrace of her wing. I stared at her, though I avoided her eye. "What? But he said… he said he was ashamed of me. That he hated me."

Carlee furrowed her brow, staying silent. Then her gaze softened and she crept closer to me, lightly touching the tip of her muzzle against the side of mine. "Oh, Anzig. It was a dream, nothing more than that. Your father would never say such terrible things to you. He would never even think them."

"But he said it. I remember him saying it," I said, my voice rising into a shrill shriek, before I remembered the dragons sleeping close by. I forced my voice down into a low hiss again. "He told me he hated me, and that if I went to Xital I would bring shame to my clan. And after that he… he said…"

I frowned, my tongue stilled. I could not remember what came after that. How had that conversation led me to arriving in Xital anyway?

Carlee lightly touched a paw to my cheek. "Anzig, it was just a dream. Your father was proud of you when you left for Xital, as he has been every day since your egg hatched. This I know to be true."

My memories of Ddraig Astar's anger began to crack and the truth emerged. He had never shouted his anger at me, never told me of his shame. He had wished me luck, and that he looked forward to hearing about my success on our return to Laxtal.

I let out a dry sob, glad that the tears did not threaten to return, for I did not think I would be able to hold them back again. The worry and fear clamped around my heart started to fade. It had been just a dream, nothing more.

Carlee leaned into me, her wing again extending to drape over my back. "Dreams always feel more real beneath the starlight, both the good and the bad. Come the daylight, you'll wonder why you ever let such a dream worry you."

I hung my head. Already I could feel the shame of my overreaction, letting myself get fooled by a mere dream. I knew now that my father had not been disgusted with me, but I still feared that he might feel that should he know everything that I thought. He believed me to be the strong leader Laxtal needed, but would a strong leader really be so scared be a dream?

"I'll take watch until dawn," I said, stepping away from Carlee's wing for a second time. I didn't deserve her comfort, and being left alone was all I wanted after my shameful display. My dreamed father was probably right about me, even if my real one didn't know it yet.

"Are you sure?" Carlee asked, seemingly more aware of my thoughts than I expected. I kept my face turned away from her.

"Yeah, I'll be fine," I lied. I didn't look back, even as I heard the veteran trudge back inside the mine, leaving me alone with the stars and my thoughts. It wasn't until I knew she was asleep before I finally allowed the tears to streak down my scales.

Morning came with a pink sky and a moment of terror. Barely had the sunlight crept above the horizon before gigantic wingbeats came from across the bay. I fled inside the mine. My movement woke

Isikian and Carlee, who both quickly jerked upright to their paws as they heard the approaching wingbeats.

"Stay back," I hissed, trying to put some confidence into my voice.

As it had done the previous morning, Nightwings roared overhead without stopping. Those of us already awake cowered as far from the entrance as we could, lest the unknowable spectre somehow see any of us. That also meant we could not see it either, but I was glad for that. I wanted nothing to do with Nightwings.

A shaky voice breached the silence that followed. "It won't be back until sunset," Azlak said, the seer's eyes white with visions of the future.

I flicked my tail. "Can you See a way across the bay?"

Azlak shook his head, just like he had done so the previous day. "No, still nothing. There is something over there that is interfering with my magic. I can't focus it."

"Like you could before," Keita muttered, only loud enough for me and Okazuni to hear. The little Nyrian let out a quiet snicker of amusement.

If Azlak heard either the snide comment or the laugh, he didn't react. His belly was already low to the ground as he blinked, his eyes reverting back to pale gold. He remained quiet, saying nothing more.

"Then we should go to the port like I suggested yesterday," Nataik said. She uncurled her long, sinuous body and fluttered her wings before the fire, taking in some of the flame's warmth.

I pawed at the ground. We had not been idle the previous day, exploring the headland and trying to find the caves that ran below the bay, which were indicated on the map the humans had given us. We had not found them. Keeping hidden from the city and the island in the middle of the bay limited what we could do during the daylight hours, and the threat of Nightwings kept us grounded at night. Nataik had suggested that, if we could not fly across the water for fear of being discovered, then we should stow on one of the many boats that crossed to the island.

"We have no other choice, Haeraig," Inilta said, recognising my hesitation.

Reluctantly, I agreed. This was the cumulation of my mad decision in Xital, of my choice to come deep into human lands and reclaim the

Axinstone. It was also the end result of flying so far with no thought given to a plan to break into George's castle. My reliance on Azlak's visions could only get me so far, and he had Seen no way to safely cross the water. Only ways where we were killed in our attempt.

"We will not cross the water today," I said, looking around the group. No one met my eyes, all dropping their gaze as mine met theirs. "We do not all need to explore this port. Keita, I would like you to stay up here and hunt for the caves. Keep Okazuni, Isikian, and Inilta with you."

The two Nixans made no attempt to protest my decision, simply nodding their heads at my words. Keita opened her mouth, her forepaw clenched, but she snapped her jaw closed at a touch of Okazuni's tail.

"We'll do what we can, Haeraig," the little Nyrian said.

I nodded once, then turned to look outside. The sun had fully breached the horizon, and while the night chill still lingered on the coast, the air was beginning to warm. "Take a short while to bask, then get ready to leave," I said, knowing that many of us would still be too cold to properly fly, even with the fire.

My companions gratefully took the time to warm up. Though I was also chilled from the night, I didn't lie down on the grass and spread my wings like the others. Instead, I kept alert and watchful. The city of Trevena was hidden behind the headland, but the sounds of the city were clear. It was like a constant, low rumble of activity, a constant irritation to my ears that matched the annoying itch on my scales. Ever since we had arrived at the mine, it had felt like my scales were coated in a fine layer of irritating mud, but nothing I had been able to do had soothed the annoyance.

The knowledge of what we had to do did not help ease that irritation. Worry chewed at my gut. My instincts screamed to take to wing and fly towards the mountains, far beyond the eastern horizon. To return home to safe territory, where there were no humans. But I couldn't. To do that would be to prove myself the failure my dream father had believed me to be. I would lead my dragons into the port in the hope we could discover a way across the bay.

The time soon came to depart. Truthfully, I doubted I could delay it any longer without looking weak and afraid. I called Azlak, Nataik, and Carlee to me. They were the dragons who had the most knowledge about humans. Their help would be invaluable in learning how to best find our way across the water.

Before I had chance to delay any further, I took the first step. We would not take to wing and risk being seen by humans. There had been few of them in our days on the headland, kept away from the old mine by fencing a short distance away. We slipped through a gap in the metal wire fence and quickly scampered through the long grass. I wanted to look back, to perhaps see Keita and the other dragons behind, but I knew that if I did so, my resolve to go into the human port would waver. I could not show that weakness.

The discomfort on my scales grew as I walked through the long, wiry grass. My head was drawn towards the island, my attention unable to focus on anything else. It was like something called to me from across the water, luring me towards it. My paws stumbled, and I had to focus hard on moving forward.

"Are you alright, Anzig?"

Carlee came to my side. She must have seen my stumble. I opened my mouth to speak, but the words didn't come. The itching at my scales flared to a full heat. Somewhere behind me, I heard a gasp of shock that could have mirrored my own. Carlee's form wavered in my eyes.

White light burst across my vision as pain exploded inside my head. Sheer agony rolled through me, and before I even had chance to scream, everything flicked to black.

*Shadows swirled all around me. They were formless and vague, not in any shape that I could recognise. Colours flashed deep inside them, many colours that were beyond my recognition, that I had never before seen. Amongst them were colours that were familiar. Deep brown. Burnished gold. The display dazzled me, but I could not understand its purpose, nor see pattern in the swirls of shadow.*

*I stretched towards them, though I could not sense a body that I could call my own. This realisation did not disturb me, though somewhere deep inside my thoughts I recognised that it probably should.*

*My awareness touched the closest shadow, the one tinged with gold. Whispers filled my mind. Whispers in a voice that was not my own. I struggled to hear, the words indistinct, but the closer my awareness grew, the harder it was to listen.*

*Warmth tickled at the corners of my mind. I withdrew from the shadows and shifted my focus. Away to what I perceived as my left was the source of heat. My thoughts filled with awe. I stared upon a vortex of fiery light, embers of red and orange dancing around a central core of pure light and scalding heat. The force of that heat stripped away my thoughts until all I could do was gaze upon the hot strength, feeling it both renew and destroy me. I could not look away. I couldn't even think of looking away. That golden light was my entire world. I...*

Someone shook me, their paws on my shoulders. My mind snapped back to my body with a painful jolt. Breath filled my lungs, my body convulsing as though it had not taken in air for many minutes. Even as my eyes opened, the image of the burning golden light lingered in my vision, imposed over the view of the island as I overlooked the bay.

"He's waking up," Carlee said, her voice hoarse. "What about him?"

"I think he's coming to as well," Nataik replied.

A short pause followed. My mind struggled to understand. "Go and fetch the healer," Carlee said. "We're not going anywhere today."

Wings rustled, but they didn't come from the ground. A dragon swooped down from the sky, a shadow briefly passing over my prone body. Carlee hissed at the newcomer.

"Sorry, Carlee, I had to," Okazuni said, the moment his paws touched the ground. "The two Nixans, they've collapsed. I didn't know what else to do. I... is the haeraig alright? Has it happened to him too?"

"The Nixans as well?" Carlee said, a low hiss coming into her voice. "Something strange is at work here."

"It is strange that it didn't touch us at all," Nataik said quietly. "Is Keita unharmed?"

"She is, yes." Okazuni stuttered. His paws dragged across the ground as his shadow approached me.

"Go back to her and look after the Nixans. Let us deal with the haeraig and Azlak," Carlee commanded. She stood over me, as though expecting an attack from the Nyrian.

Sensation slowly trickled back into my body. My paws and legs tingled, and my heart rampaged inside my chest. My head throbbed in pain in time with that beat, a sickly sense of nausea welling from deep within my gut. I had never felt so wretched before, and I was at a loss to explain what had happened.

I struggled to move. My paws clenched first, and then I was able to groan and slowly lift my head. Everything was blurred, and I struggled to focus clearly on anything. Even Carlee, standing directly above me, was indistinct.

"How are you feeling, Haeraig?" Carlee asked. Her muzzle touched against my shoulder. "What happened? Are you hurt in any way?"

I squeezed my eyes closed. Still, that vortex of fiery light imprinted against the darkness behind my eyelids, though the heat had faded to almost nothing. "I don't know what happened," I said, surprised at how weak my voice sounded to my ears.

When I managed to open my eyes again, I caught the eye of another dragon. It was not Carlee or Nataik, who both still stood unharmed by whatever had befallen me. Instead, I looked into the pained eyes of Azlak. Like me, the seer was prone on his side, paws tense and wings slightly unfurled. He had felt the same pain I had. The same pain that had seemingly hurt the Nixans back at the mine.

"Do you think you can walk?"

I struggled to answer. Partly because my mouth failed to respond to what my mind wanted, but also because I didn't really know. My body tingled, and my tail twitched with nervous energy. The pain hadn't fully receded from behind my eyes.

I struggled up to my paws. Disorientation took hold of me, but I shrugged off Carlee's attempts to support my weight. After a few seconds, I began to feel more confident, though I still didn't move too quickly.

"We should keep going," I said, not wanting to retreat to the mine. I could not accept that weakness. Whatever had laid me down had passed. I would overcome the uneasiness in my body.

I had barely taken a step before I almost fell over. Thankfully, I was saved by a pitiful voice calling to me. Azlak spoke, barely in a harsh whisper.

"We must go back, Haeraig. I Saw things. Whatever happened to us then, it guided my magic and showed us what we must do," the seer said. He scraped at the ground with his claws. "We were resting on the answer this whole time."

"What are you talking about?" Carlee snapped. She turned away from me, glaring at the small seer.

"Let me show you," Azlak replied. He ducked his head. "Haeraig, would you lead us back to the mine? I feel strong enough to walk again."

I wasn't sure how strong I was, but given Azlak's admission, I knew I could not refuse to return to the mine. The hill up to the crest of the headland suddenly looked much steeper and taller, with the stone chimney of the mine barely visible. All the same, I knew I had to make it back. My head pounded with every step, but I just focused on one paw ahead of another. I ignored the lingering heat from that golden vortex and the irritation that still settled on my scales.

The journey back to the mine felt so much longer. It was full of stumbled steps and irritating whispers, of voices that I couldn't properly hear. No matter how much I growled or shook my head, I was unable to fully clear my thoughts.

Okazuni scampered out from the mine as we approached. His eyes were wide as he looked towards me, and then to Azlak. I couldn't decide whether he was scared we were about to collapse again, or if he was upset that we had returned so much sooner than expected. I then wondered why he might have been upset about that, or why I had thought that. I shook my head again. I wasn't thinking properly. There was something about the air here, possibly the smoke drifting from Trevena, faint enough to barely smell, but present all the same.

"Are the Nixans awake?" I asked the Nyrian.

"Yes, Haeraig. They're just inside with Keita," Okazuni said. He took a step back and then aside, letting me into the old building.

Inilta lay close to the corner, his head resting in his paws with his wings partially unfurled. He barely moved, but for a twitch of his tail. His brother was more alert. The healer sat upright, his muzzle drawn back in a pained expression.

"Let me take a look at you both," Isikian said. He carefully rose to all four paws and took a step towards me but came no closer than that until I had dipped my head to give him permission. He reached out with one paw, lightly touching it against the scales of my muzzle. I closed my eyes. His touch was surprisingly cold, and I felt as his magic extended out from his paw to soothe some of the pain that lingered.

I breathed slowly in response to the healer's magic. It flowed easily through me, piecing together the wrongs caused by the blackout. Then his paw was gone, and with it went the relaxing calmness radiating from my muzzle. I opened my eyes to see the healer tilt his head inquisitively, before moving away to place his paw on Azlak's muzzle.

The healer's paw touched Azlak for only a few seconds, far shorter a time than it had felt for me. Isikian dropped back to his haunches and lowered his head, deep in thought for a few seconds further.

"That was a pulse of corrupted magic that came from George's island," Isikian explained slowly. "I can offer no explanation as to why you were so badly affected, Haeraig. All I can say is that magic is unpredictable and wild. You do not need to be Nixan to feel it so strongly."

"But what caused it?" I asked. Without the healing touch of the Nixan, my headache was already starting to return. I carefully sat down, making sure not to make any sudden movements to jar my aching skull.

"It means they are experimenting on the Axinstone," Inilta said tersely. He tightened his wings to his body and shakily stood, his paws splayed wide.

Isikian scratched his claws against the stone ground. "Human-Nixans are using the power of the Axinstone, but human magic is different from our own. Fuelled by the Axinstone their magic becomes immensely powerful, but this magic is not natural to them. It is dangerous. I don't know what they're doing down there, but we have to retrieve the Axinstone before they create some sort of monstrosity, or worse, spark a great disaster."

A monstrosity created by magic? My mind was drawn to Nightwings, and by the uncertain look in Isikian's eye, he had just made the same connection too. It seemed the humans' monster had already been created.

"This proves we have to do all we can to get to the island quickly," Azlak said, his shaky voice interrupting whatever Isikian was about to say.

"You said you Saw where we needed to go," I said, turning to face the seer.

Azlak bowed his head. "We were searching for the caves that run beneath the bay, but they do not open onto the cliffs. They are deeper than that," the seer said, before he paused and shivered. "They connect to the old mine shafts. We get to them through there." Azlak pointed with his muzzle, gesturing towards the collapsed archway at the far end of the room. Heavy rocks blocked the passage beyond.

"Through those rocks?" Inilta asked dryly, putting to voice what my immediate thoughts had turned to.

"We will lift them," Azlak said quietly. His voice dropped to a whisper so faint that I could barely hear him. I wished I hadn't. "We must."

I recovered slowly, my headache taking most of the day to fade. Stone by stone, we had been working hard on clearing out the broken archways. It was a difficult challenge. Many of the chunks of shattered stone were larger than us, and it took a lot of effort just to dislodge any of them. Isikian remained ready to jump in to heal any scrapes and injuries caused by the falling rubble.

Any hope we may have had of getting into the caves before sunset were quelled as the sun crept towards the horizon. We were tired and sore, despite the healing efforts of Isikian.

The piercing pain from the island had not returned, but the memory of that bright light and the fierce warmth inside my mind did not leave me. I feared it would return, and not even the effort of dragging heavy masonry was able to relieve me of that.

Finally, with golden sunlight shining into the old mine, we had cleared a gap large enough for us all to wriggle through. The impenetrable darkness beyond filled me with apprehension. Surely, that could not be the only way, but Azlak had Seen nothing else. We would have little choice, for every night spent so close to the human city increased our risk of being caught. Either by Nightwings, or any wandering human.

Our work done, I dropped back onto my haunches, doing my best to ignore the gap made in the rubble. Some small part of my mind feared what was in there, deep horrors long sealed away from the light that could now crawl out. If I didn't look, then they wouldn't come.

Though I wanted little more to do than curl up and put my wing over my head, Carlee's voice pulled me back to my duties. "Haeraig, we should hunt and eat, before we are too exhausted."

Only then did I truly appreciate the hunger gnawing at my gut. I flicked the tip of my tail and looked around the small group of dragons, eyeing them up to see who still looked most capable of hunting. I immediately discounted Azlak and Nataik. I would need them to stay behind, and I wasn't going to risk Carlee's strength, not after the work she had put in during the long day. The Nixans, too, would need to stay in the mine. I needed their advice, and I also needed to know they were both well after the morning's magical attack. That didn't leave many dragons to hunt.

"Keita, would you find some food for us. Take Okazuni with you," I said, looking towards my oldest friend. The Nyrian drake was already by her side. "Stay safe and out of sight from humans. Don't take any unnecessary risks."

Okazuni's eyes flicked across to the ness, a slight smile on his muzzle. "Don't worry, Haeraig. We'll come back with some rabbits, and the humans won't ever see us."

"Hunt safe," I said, turning away from them before they scampered out into the bright light of the sunset.

I looked back to the other dragons. Inilta already prepared to light a fire using his magic, his brother sat close by. Neither of the Nixans showed any signs of wanting a conversation, and nor did they show any lingering effects of the magical pulse from the island. Instead of trying to open a conversation with them, I turned to Azlak. The seer dropped lower to the ground as my gaze fell over his golden body.

"How long will it take us to cross the bay through the caves?" I asked him.

"I have not Seen precisely," Azlak said, shaking his head. "But I have Seen us standing on the island at sunset. If we were to leave at first light, then we will make it there in less than a full day."

"That is a long time to be away from sunlight," Carlee growled.

"We will have Inilta's fire," I replied.

The Nixan looked up at the mention of his name, but he said nothing. He merely narrowed his eyes and focused his magic on building the fire, using the stockpile of dried wood we had already collected. I looked forward to the warmth his magic would bring almost as much as I longed for something to fill my belly.

"Let us hope that is enough," Nataik added. She flicked her tail as she looked towards the gap we had cleared. "Caverns like this can become waterlogged, especially with the changing tide. I would hate to be trapped down there for too long."

I suppressed a shudder as thoughts immediately turned to that scenario, of being trapped in the darkness with the sound of rushing water getting ever closer. I looked to the bright sunlight to strip those thoughts from my mind.

"We should rest well tonight so we can use our energy in the morning," I said. I continued to peer out into the light, my tail dragging across the dusty ground as it lashed from side to side. "Keita and Okazuni will bring us plenty to eat, but we all need to know what is waiting for us on the far side of those caves. Nataik, you know the most about these humans. What would you suggest?"

Nataik clicked her tongue. "If I knew something about where the Axinstone was located, Haeraig…" she said, before trailing off to a slight growl from Carlee.

"Get us inside the castle," Isikian said, interrupting even as I opened my mouth to speak. "We will find the Axinstone once we're close enough to it."

"It's as much a plan as any we've had so far," Nataik muttered. I was sure she deliberately spoke just loud enough so I could hear her, but quiet enough to feign ignorance should I question her on it. I chose to keep my tongue and stay quiet.

"Getting to the island is the next step. We can worry about the rest then," Carlee said. She fluttered her wings and stepped back from the other ness. She then turned her head to me. "Haeraig, if I might have a private word with you outside?"

I nodded, though I was sure I knew what was coming. She had already warned me about the lack of a plan. This close to our destination, I should have come up with something more reliable and secure than simply following Azlak's visions. I had no knowledge of what to expect on the island. No thoughts on how we could break into the castle and steal the Axinstone, nor even any plan on how to escape afterwards.

Carlee remained silent as we moved away from the mine. The sun wasn't far above the eastern horizon, with golden light shimmering off the ocean to the west. There were hardly any clouds above, though the wind was cold with the promise of a changing season. Winter was not far away, but there was little chance of us being stranded in human lands until spring. If we could escape the castle, at least.

"What are your intentions with Keita?" Carlee said, surprising me so much that I forgot all that I had been thinking about.

I stared at Carlee, mouth hanging open. I stood completely still, one paw still raised in the air. "What?"

"Tch," Carlee said, scratching aside a tuft of thick grass to get a more comfortable place to sit. "Do not try to hide your thoughts from me, Haeraig. I have seen my share of young dragons wondering whether to follow their hearts or not. You have loved Keita as a friend for most of your life. Is that all she is to you, or is there more?"

My breath stuck in my throat. I shrank down, physically and mentally, as I turned away from the old veteran. She knew my thoughts as easily as if I'd spoken them aloud.

Carlee did not release me from her fierce gaze. She did not look at me as a dragon and her haeraig. There was no respect or deference there. This was a mentor and a teacher educating her ward. A small part of my mind was relieved she had done this away from the others. The rest of my mind knew she would not relent until I gave her an answer.

"There is more," I whispered.

"Then you should make it clear to Keita what your intentions are," Carlee warned. Her gaze did not soften at all. "You risk losing her if she does not know how you feel."

That startled me out of my reverie. "Lose her? To who?"

Carlee shook her head in wry amusement. "Are you really so blind to it, Anzig? If anything, I would have thought you were helping push them together. Keita seems quite enamoured with Okazuni."

"She wouldn't dream of it," I said nervously. The little red dragon couldn't be making a move on Keita, the only ness I had ever considered to become my mate.

"She's been of age and without a mate for quite some time, Haeraig. She can't wait forever," Carlee said. She paused, her eyes flicking across to me. "To him, she would be a very fine mate. A ness of significant power within Laxtal would help his stature at home."

"I shouldn't have given them time alone," I growled, tempted to chase after them.

"Don't be ridiculous, Anzig," Carlee replied. She lightly put her paw on my tail to stop me going anywhere. "You wouldn't even have noticed if I hadn't told you. And besides, they've gone hunting. They wouldn't risk annoying everyone by failing to bring back some food to do anything so rash."

I ducked my head in apology. "She means everything to me," I said quietly. It was the closest I had ever come to admitting my love for Keita to another dragon.

Carlee sighed and stretched her wings. "Then you should tell her that. She can't know your thoughts unless you speak them."

I looked away, knowing that Carlee was right. I had never told Keita the true depths of my feelings, and because of this I risked losing her. "I'll speak to Okazuni. I'll demand that he back off from her," I said, speaking down to the sandy ground.

"Don't speak to Okazuni, Haeraig," Carlee said. She didn't release the pressure on my tail. "You need to speak to Keita. She must know how you feel, or else she will see no reason to wait for you."

I took in a deep breath, then let it out slowly. "I'll speak to her. Once we have the Axinstone and we're on our way home, I'll tell her how I feel."

Finally, Carlee released my tail. She extended her wings for a moment, lightly brushing one against my back. "One day you will be ddraig of Laxtal. I will not always be around to guide you. A strong and intelligent mate will be crucial for you to succeed. Ketia can be that mate for you, but only if you give her the opportunity."

I curled my tail around my hindlegs as I looked out over the ocean. "I don't want to lose her."

Carlee settled by my side. "Then do something to keep her."

I bowed my head. Though the words were harsh, I knew them to be true. I could not risk losing the only ness I had ever wanted to be with. No one else in Laxtal had ever caught my eye. It could only ever be Keita. If she would not fly by my side, then I wanted no one. For my own future and that of any potential family I might have, I needed to confess my true feelings. I could only hope I had not left it too late already.

Dusk was starting to settle before Keita and Okazuni finally returned with the spoils of their hunt. They arrived with several rabbits, and even a couple of seabirds they had been fortunate to catch close to the cliffs. My joy at Keita returning, especially with a feast, was tempered by the growing twilight. My thoughts turned to the spectre of Nightwings.

I was not the only one. Azlak looked to the sky, ignoring the food the hunters had brought. The seer fluttered his wings. "Quickly," he whispered, stepping back with one paw to huddle in the doorway of the mine. His concerns were fully justified, for we had barely passed the threshold of the mine before I felt the terrifying concussion that heralded the approach of the spectre.

Keita dragged the last of her kill into safety and quickly scampered down the dark corridor and into the room we had taken up shelter, into Inilta's light. I did not follow her. For a single, suicidal moment I paused and turned around, wishing at last to discover what manner of creature Nightwings was. A shadow passed across the sun, just a sliver

226

above the horizon. I edged forward, then a sharp pain in my tail caused me to gasp and realise the stupidity of such an act. I turned to see Azlak digging his claws into my tail, his wings flared in terror.

I scarpered back into the shadows just in time, for with a deafening roar Nightwings swooped down onto the mine. The stonework crunched under the spectre's immense weight. Azlak cowered beside me as the sounds of two human voices drifted to us.

"Where are they Nightwings?" one was saying. The human already sounded quite irate, and the low growl that emanated from Nightwings suggested the spectre was feeling none too pleased either.

"They're not resting. I can't track them down just yet," the spectre grumbled.

"George grows uneasy with these dragons so close to his castle, Nightwings. Need I remind you he tasked you to hunt them down," the second human warned.

That the humans knew we were somewhere around here was disconcerting. I knew we hadn't been seen by any since those on the beach over a week ago. Had the seer been wrong to trust those two? I glanced across to the golden seer, but he had his wing drawn across his face.

"I can do nothing now," Nightwings growled. A stream of powdered stone trickled to the ground just outside the open archway.

"Then perhaps this will give you the motivation you need," the first human said. Its words were followed by an agonised shriek so loud the crumbling stonework shuddered a little. Even though I knew it was the abominable spectre that made the noise, I still felt sickened. No creature should be subject to so much pain, and unyielding suffering was etched into every syllable of the spectre's scream.

The awful sound gradually quietened until it faded completely; never getting further away, but somehow simply diminishing, until all that remained were the two humans squabbling amongst themselves. They argued about how to return to the island and showed no concern for the plight of the spectre.

Two soft thuds startled us, and for a moment the humans seemed so close; just a stone wall separating us from them. Then I heard the distinctive sounds of their pawsteps on the sandy dunes as they walked away.

Before the seer could stop me, I scampered outside in time to see the humans' shadows vanishing into the darkness. They appeared to be wearing a strange suit and a rigid wrapping that enclosed their heads. I looked up at the roof of the mine. There were deep gouges into the stonework where Nightwings had landed, but of the spectre itself there was no trace.

A presence by my side warned me of the company of Azlak. The seer's eyes were white.

"She longs for freedom," he said mournfully.

"She?" I asked. So the spectre was a she, not an it. Curious. I then latched onto the rest of the seer's declaration. "How do you know that?" The seer's magic was in foresight, in seeing the actual events that were to happen. He had never been able to judge reasons or motives before.

"She tells you so," was the seer's reply.

"I speak with Nightwings? When?" I asked, utterly shocked. I didn't know how I could bear to be in the presence of such a fearful creature, though I was loathe to admit such a weakness even to myself.

"I don't know. I couldn't See properly. There was water, lots of it. But we should go inside, Haeraig. I cannot be sure if the humans will come back again," Azlak said. He ducked his head in subservience, acknowledging that his words had been a suggestion, and not an order.

With one last glance up to confirm Nightwings had indeed gone, I returned into the mine. Azlak followed at my tail.

I was glad to return to the warmth of the fire. Inilta tended to the blaze, the pale blue flames burning like they fed of the finest coal from the northern mines. The Nixan was alone as he worked. His brother helped share out the food hunted by Keita and Okazuni. Before I had the opportunity to come forward and take my rightful first claim of the food, Nataik stepped across me and Azlak.

"My apologies, Haeraig," she said, dipping her head in respect. "I wished to see the map of Azlak's. They might reveal something about these caves and the route we need to take beneath the bay. I am sure none of us wish to get lost under there. It would be good to know the route first."

With a reluctant look towards the freshly killed rabbit, I turned aside and allowed Azlak to unclip the map strapped around his foreleg.

Before long, the strange lights of the map lit up the room, conflicting with the flickering luminescence of the fire and threw ever changing shadows against the wall. I struggled to understand what I saw, but Nataik scanned through the lines with clear purpose and intent, using a paw to sift through the map.

"There is nothing here that indicates the natural caves connect to the mines," the Xigax dragon said, after studying the map in silence for a short while. I tried not to listen too much to the sound of crunching bones and tearing flesh and Keita and Okazuni began to eat.

"I am confident in my visions," Azlak said. The seer peered over Nataik's shoulder. "I know that we will find a way through. I have not Seen the entire route, but we need to go down and take the first left fork. The tunnel descends sharply, and after two hundred paces there is a crack in the wall wide enough for us all to fit through. That cuts through into the natural caves. It wasn't meant to be there. That's why it doesn't show on the maps, I think."

Nataik sniffed. "Your visions have proven inconsistent at times. How can we know for sure?"

"I know," Azlak said, the growl in his voice seeming to surprise Nataik. It certainly surprised me. "The magic that came from the island this morning was stronger than anything I've ever known. It also showed me more than one future. I know this is the right one. I've spent all day following what I have Seen. I have never been more sure of a vision before."

"That's enough for me," I said, speaking before Nataik could offer any further protests or arguments. "We shall take the tunnels tomorrow. Do you think you can guide us through to the island, Nataik?"

The Xigax dragon bowed her head. "Yes, I can. If I am interpreting these marks correctly, then the tunnels should emerge somewhere amongst the foundations of the castle. We should be able to get inside without risk of detection."

"Then we shall leave at first light tomorrow. Eat while you can," I instructed. I turned away, hoping to get to the rabbit and seabird. As haeraig, I should have the choice cuts, after the hunters had taken their fill. But once more, I was intercepted.

"Haeraig, one last word before we rest?" Carlee asked me.

I looked across to the food, trying to ignore the growl of my stomach. I sighed and dipped my head towards the veteran. "Eat what you can. We will need our energy tomorrow. I shall be back shortly," I said, giving my companions permission to take their share of the kills before me.

Though I wanted to join them, I turned to follow Carlee out onto the dunes, overlooking the bright lights of the human city on the other side of the bay. The threat of Nightwings had faded once more. We had not known her to fly back out from George's castle during the night.

Despite the darkness, there was still a significant amount of movement on the water as boats crossed from the mainland to the island. Even from this distance, I could still hear noises from the human city. Most of it was incomprehensible to my ears; just random sounds the source of which I couldn't even begin to fathom. I longed to get back to the relative peace of Laxtal, where I could revel in the silence of the plains, with only the sounds of other dragons and the occasional prey to bother me.

I turned to Carlee, who was also looking out over the bay. "What did you have to say?" I asked the veteran.

"Haeraig, I know we've come too far to turn back, but I feel like we shouldn't keep pushing on without any plan in mind," Carlee said, still keeping her eyes trained on the distant lights of the human city. Here it was. The conversation I had expected earlier. "I don't think I've ever been on a campaign with so little organisation, and certainly not one without any form of advance strategy. I fear that if we continue like this, we'll all end up dead."

Had any other dragon uttered those words, I would have bristled at the thinly veiled criticism at my leadership abilities, but this was Carlee. She had guided and advised me almost since the day I had hatched, and I remained silent in thought as I pondered over her counsel. She was right, of course. We didn't have any real plan, other than to follow the visions Azlak Saw along the way. To the most part, that strategy had served us well so far, but I knew it was too much to ask for to rely on them inside the humans' castle.

Carlee seemed to know exactly what thoughts were running through my mind. "I know you put faith in the seer, but I don't think that will be enough once we get over there," she said.

I stared across at the island, visible in the darkness thanks to the lights around its perimeter. The castle itself was also well lit, and every now and then I could see the flickers of movement that gave away the presence of humans. It certainly was an imposing sight, and I had to suppress a shiver of fear that threatened to run down my spine.

"I suppose we'll just get through the mines and see what opportunities present themselves on the other side," I said eventually. I hoped that we would at least be able to find some safe shelter on the island while we were able to locate the Axinstone. Once we had done that, I knew then at least we would be able to form a solid plan of action, but until then we had to rely upon lucky chance and Azlak's visions to stay safe.

"I don't like this, Haeraig," Carlee said, matching my thoughts exactly.

I remembered back to when we were in Xital, what felt like so long ago now. Azlak had convinced me to come for the Axinstone, telling me I was destined to succeed. That seemed like far from the truth now, and I couldn't help but wonder if the seer had got it wrong, for I could see very little chance of success.

It seemed more likely now that I was destined to die.

Carlee sighed and flexed her wings. "I guess I just don't see how this can help us against the humans. Even if we return home safely with the Axinstone, who are we really benefiting? I doubt the humans would be massively weakened by its loss, and only Clan Nixa would gain any sort of use out of its power. This entire quest seems to be based on confusion and hidden agendas. I don't know who will benefit most from retrieving the Axinstone, but I doubt it will be us."

"But what other chance is there for us, Carlee? One clan can't stand up against the humans, not without aid, and that is what Clan Nixa has promised to provide," I said. I turned my head to face the veteran. Her face was a mask of shadow against the lights of the city.

"I can recount many times before when Clan Nixa has promised aid to another clan," Carlee said grimly. "Not once have they actually followed through with their pledge."

"I know that, but this time even they could be under threat. If the clans can't work together then we'll be defeated one by one. I think Haeraig Zeena understands that, and if she does, then hopefully Ddraig Krateos is like of mind," I said. This kept Carlee silent for a few minutes as she pondered my words, and we both looked back out over the water.

A sudden flurry of movement on the island caught my attention. Pinpricks of light that had previously been roaming back and forth with no real pattern began to converge on one point, near where one of the water-bound lights had come to shore. Even from this great distance, I could hear another piercing shriek caused by utter agony. The harrowing sound was accompanied by an unsettling wave of magic that caused my vision to blur and spin for a few moments. I widened my stance to prevent myself from the indignity of falling over, before vigorously shaking my head to rid myself of the magic's ill effects, while Carlee seemed quite untouched by it all.

That cry had sounded much like Nightwings, but why the humans were harming the spectre was quite beyond me. If it truly was a creature of their creation, then why did they see the need to cause it such great pain?

"You trust easily, Haeraig. That is a rare trait indeed amongst dragons, but it means that you could be the best leader Laxtal has ever seen. I just don't want to see your trust taken advantage of," Carlee said as though nothing had happened on the island.

"What do you mean?"

Carlee sighed. "No other dragon would have taken on this mission on the advice of Azlak. You are one of the only dragons to trust the seer, and to be honest I still don't know if it was the right choice. You are also quick to trust Clan Nixa when few other Laxtals would. If your trust is well placed then you will be hailed a hero, Haeraig. But if not then I fear there will be no chance for you to recover."

"I know that I am not wrong in placing my trust in Azlak. I don't know why exactly, but I feel like he's one of the few dragons who would never tell me a lie," I said.

"Then I don't want to be there when you discover he has told you an untruth," Carlee said gravely.

I said nothing in reply, knowing in my heart that Azlak would never do that to me. Along with the seer, only Ellian, Keita, and Carlee I knew I could trust implicitly. All other dragons I had to convince myself to assume there was some hidden scheme or plot to further their own ambitions to my detriment, but I usually found this a difficult mindset to enter. Carlee was right: I trusted too easily for a dragon, but that wasn't something I could change.

"You should get some rest, Haeraig. I don't think any of us have any doubts that tomorrow will not be pleasant. I am not happy going through the mines, but if Azlak says it's the only way..." the veteran said.

"We've been here for too long already, Carlee. If there was another way across the bay, we would have found it by now. There's too much risk of being caught if we fly over, and I have no wish to run into Nightwings," I said.

"Again though, we just have Azlak's word that the spectre is something to be feared. What if he's mistaken?" Carlee asked, but then she shook her head and settled down in the sand, flaring her wings and spreading them across the ground, as she would if the sun was beating down on her back. "No. Don't answer that. Maybe I'm just being old and worrisome. You get your rest, Haeraig. I shall take the first watch tonight."

I paused for a moment, concerned about Carlee. I had never heard her speak in such a way before, and never had I thought her as old. Yes, she was a veteran of many fights and she had lived many years, but she was not old. I thought about saying something to console her, but the look of melancholy on her face and in her posture was harrowing. I couldn't bear to be near her as I feared that this sad and old dragon would be how I remembered Carlee, not the feisty and proud warrior she used to be.

I retreated into the mine and the food within without a backwards glance. I could only hope that Carlee was more positive in the morning. With a trip into the mines ahead of us, we needed her guidance and support more than ever.

# CHAPTER SIXTEEN

**Azlak**

*"You are heading right towards danger, Little One. You really should turn back. I said last time that I would help you, and that I would look out for you, but I fear that will no longer be enough. Every wingbeat that takes you closer to George's castle leaves me less able to assist you."*

*Once again, I found myself in the presence of the black-scaled dragon of mystery. She seemed to be suffering somewhat this time; she didn't seem capable of holding her wings tight against her back, and she kept her left foreleg off the ground. Her eyes, burning with strength and passion, showed no weakness.*

*"We will do what we must," I replied.*

*"Then what you must do is die," Maznar said in sorrow. "I cannot save you if you come into danger on the island, no matter how much I wish I could."*

*"Why are you so sure we'll fail? I've Seen the future and I know that we can succeed, if I follow my visions correctly," I replied. I didn't know why I had to try and convince Maznar that we weren't embarking on a hopeless suicide mission; maybe I hoped she would help us further if she knew there was a chance of success.*

*The mysterious dragon limped away, and for the first time I took stock of our location. We were on top of a great stone structure with nothing but the open sky above us. I could hear the ocean too, and the sounds of waves upon the shore seemed to come from all around. I put my paws up on the wall that surrounded us and was surprised to see the same bay I was sleeping beside, only now I found myself looking out from the centre of the island. I was perched atop George's castle.*

*"Trevena. It looks beautiful from here, doesn't it?" Maznar asked as she hobbled to my side. She was looking out over the human city, and I had to agree with her. There definitely was an eerie beauty about the mass of lights across the bay, and its mirrored reflection in the rippling water. Locked inside my dream, there was no movement or noise coming from the city. In fact, apart from the gentle rush of the waves against the sand, there was nothing to be heard.*

*"Why have you brought me here, Maznar?"*

*"To show you." The ness edged closer towards me until her slightly trailing wingtip was touching mine.*

*"Show me what?"*

*Before I could react, Maznar shoved her body against mine. I was unbalanced against the wall, and with a second firm shove I was sent tumbling from the precipice, the ebony dragon following right behind. I didn't even have time to flare my wings, but the expected impact against the ground never came. Instead, I seemed to have plummeted into a dark mist and the sensation of falling had been arrested. It felt like I was floating, suspended in nothingness.*

*Above me, Maznar looked quite sheepish. "Sorry. I still haven't worked out how to change the dream's location with considerable trauma for the dreamer. I think I'm getting closer though," she said, before twisting around in the mist to look at something beyond my shoulder.*

*As I looked, a scene materialised in front of me. There was a group of humans dressed in a strange sort of green patchwork clothing. They were gathered around a cluster of canvas tents. I could only see the face of one of them; the others were all obscured from view and blurred out of perspective.*

*"This is a memory taken from a dream last night, so this took place the day before. That's George there, in the middle," Maznar told me, referring to the only human I could see clearly. "He was a soldier*

*once, and an excellent one at that. He won many medals for bravery and honour before retiring from service about ten years ago. From there, he turned to science and business."*

*The sight of the group of humans faded into dark mist again, though this time George remained in focus. Maznar squawked in surprise as austere white walls started to form around us. George was now dressed in a white and black outfit that made him look quite angular. It was a strange look, but one I knew a lot of humans chose if they wanted to look impressive towards their rivals. It was a tactic that would never work amongst dragons. We relied on physical intimidation or subtle tactical manoeuvring to belittle our rivals. Vanity wasn't impressive to a dragon.*

*"Oh, I don't know how I did that, I thought I'd have to get George to attack you. Everything is so much easier with you," Maznar said, obviously delighted by her improved control over my dreaming state.*

*"You were telling me about George?" I prompted, as it looked like Maznar had completely lost her focus. The image of the human had started to fade away into the dark smoke that had begun to seep into the room.*

*"Right, yes," Maznar said, and the room regained almost perfect clarity, though there was still a strange blurring around the edges of my vision. "After leaving the military, George decided to go into business. He teamed up with a man who calls himself Rico, but I believe that is not his true name. Along with a group of old friends – a scientist, a magician, and a few former army allies amongst them – George started designing, inventing, and building weapons unlike any humanity has ever seen before. His company sells most of their inventions, but the best are kept for the company's personal use."*

*"And why are you telling me all of this?"*

*"So that you know the type of human you're up against. This is a man who has plans and schemes above anything you could have ever imagined. He does not deal with inconsequential dragons like you. He walks amongst gods. There is no weakness to exploit in his castle or in his plans, and George is not a man who can be negotiated with. If he wants to keep the Dragon's Head Rune – and I am confident that he does, for it is important to his plans – then he will not let it go.*

*"I don't know what visions you have had, Little One, but I can't see any way in which you can succeed. Please, this is the last time I shall say this; go home and be safe."*

*Without any transition, we were once again standing on the roof of George's castle, overlooking the bay as though nothing had happened. "We're not leaving, Maznar. Without the Axinstone, our clan will be overrun by the human armies. We have no choice but to continue."*

*Maznar bowed her head. "I have tried to dissuade you, but you are the most stubborn dragon I have ever known. Very well. If you must travel on, then may I recommend the kitchens?"*

*"What do you mean?" I asked, but there was no answer from the ness. In fact, she was fading from view as light bleached everything white until soon I could see nothing at all. I panicked, unsure what was happening.*

*Somewhere a voice was calling out.*

*Calling my name.*

*"Azlak... Azlak!"*

"Azlak for Dirus's sake, wake up. We're waiting on you."

A sharp pain across my muzzle brought me to my senses. I blearily opened my eyes to see the red scales of Keita's legs and paws right in front of me. Despite the flickering firelight I could see out of the corner of my eyes, it was still dark.

"Just give me a moment," I murmured as I struggled to keep my eyes open. I heard Keita huff, but she didn't say anything further and left me alone. My mind raced with all the information Maznar had given me, but I was reluctant to approach the haeraig with this knowledge. The mysterious dragon had not told me if she had contacted any of the others, and I doubted if the haeraig would approve of me taking advice from this unknown entity.

I could hear some mutterings of discontent around the chamber, and as I opened my eyes fully I could see that Keita had been right, everyone else was waiting on me. They were all on their paws, if some being a little unsteady, like Okazuni. With a supreme effort, I lifted myself up off the ground, cast a wistful glance towards the warm fire, and then went over to join the other dragons.

I avoided the gaze of my companions, knowing that a few harsh glares were being shot in my direction. They blamed me for having to get up so early, and to go without an early morning bask in the dawn sunlight. It was our only option though, if we were to get across to the island.

"Azlak, will you lead us down?" Haeraig Anzig asked me.

I shook my head. I had absolutely no desire to lead the group, not with hate-filled eyes boring into the back of my skull. "I told you the route yesterday. I will not be needed to guide us, Haeraig. I recommend Nataik and Inilta, so that we may have some light," I said, looking right down into the ground. "I can give Nataik the map should we lose our way."

"In other words, you don't know where we're going," Keita said harshly. Strictly speaking, her words were true as I hadn't Seen our full path through the mines. I had only Seen the beginning of that journey. Had I been feeling more confident, or more awake, I may have protested this, but as it was I stayed silent and let Nataik take the map from my foreleg. I heard the haeraig mutter something to Keita, but I couldn't make out whether it was something in my defence or not.

"No point putting this off then," the haeraig said in a louder voice. Even he was tentative as he approached the stairwell to the mines proper. We were used to travelling underground, especially given the central lair of Laxtal being a complicated network of caves, but there we knew we had the option of coming to the surface whenever we pleased. What lay ahead of us was a different proposition altogether. There would be no opportunity to resurface until we reached the island. Above us would lie the bay, and all around us would be the tidal caves of the abandoned mine shaft. I could only hope I had Seen everything. The last I wanted was to be trapped in the caves with ocean water rushing in.

I was the last to descend into the dark, following Carlee down at the back of the group. Beside Haeraig Anzig at the front of the pack was Inilta, a ball of magical light bobbing by the Nixan's head to show us the way. Nataik followed right behind them, having hurried forward the moment she had taken the map from me.

The shaft delved down in a steep slope, the flight of steps an awkward affair for us. More than once I almost slipped on the damp stone, nearly stepping on Carlee's tail in the process. It was with some relief that we reached the bottom of the stairs and into the mine proper. It was a rough chamber hewn out of solid rock, with three passageways leading out of it, one to the right, one to the left, and one directly in front of us.

Water dripped down from the ceiling, and pools of seawater covered the floor. But for Inilta's light, the cavern would have been utterly black. We took the left path, following what I had Seen in my visions. Not far beyond that was the crack in the wall, exactly where I said it would be. Relief flooded through me. If I had gotten this right, then perhaps the rest was too.

I could hear the pounding of the waves above us, a dull roar that unnerved me to no end. It sounded like the water was about to come crashing down into the caverns and trap us all. However, no surge of seawater assaulted us, and the further we walked, the quieter the waves became, until it became a calmer, rhythmic rushing as we moved deeper into the bay and away from the shore.

No one spoke as we cautiously picked our way through the uneven tunnel. We were all too tired and nervous to engage in any meaningful conversation. Even Isikian, who was usually happy to drop back and share a few words with me, walked in complete silence near the front of the group. Progress was slow, but I knew that if we were in danger of being caught out by the changing tide, my visions would warn me. I hoped.

I kept on thinking about what Maznar had told me about George. Until now, we hadn't really known much about him, other than what the two humans on the beach had told me. How Maznar got her information, I didn't know, but I was willing to put a little faith in her and assume that what she said was true. It meant that a difficult task was going to become even harder. I knew little of human culture, but I did know that their fighters were determined, dedicated, and thorough, especially the ones that received the small metal amulets they prized so highly. We would have to take Maznar's word for it that George would not give up the Axinstone easily.

One piece of information continued to intrigue and confuse me. The kitchens. I didn't know what relevance the area humans prepared their food would have to retrieving the Axinstone, but I knew we would have to explore every possibility. I didn't know how I could suggest getting into the kitchens without bringing up the topic of Maznar, but I would have to think of a way quickly.

I soon had to focus more on the path ahead as the rocks became wetter, the deeper we went. Once or twice one of the dragons ahead almost fell, only to regain their composure at the last moment. The cave seemed to groan under the weight of the water above it, with every sound amplified by the empty passageway, with each drip of water sounding like a ferocious torrent; each pawstep like a rampaging army of dragons.

Up ahead, a brief commotion broke out as a few of the dragons jostled for position. I couldn't make out the identity of all the dragons involved through the shadows cast by Inilta's light, but after it ended, Keita had fallen to the back. She was treading very carefully and pausing every time she went to place her paw on the uneven ground. She had difficulty seeing at the best of times, and in the near darkness she would be almost completely blind.

Keita growled as I walked by her side, but she did not try and push me away like I knew she would normally have done. Instead, she let me stay beside her, though she was careful to keep her eyes averted away from me, but in doing so her gaze was away from the dangers that lurked on the ground along the path.

"Careful," I advised her, but she did not react to my words. She kept her head held high as she looked directly ahead. It didn't take long for the inevitable fall, and she wasn't quite able to suppress a gasp of pain as she fell sideways into the damp rock wall. I walked on past her. She had not heeded my concern, so she could walk as the omega if that's what she craved. Not once had she shown a scrap of respect towards me, and I wasn't...

*Seven dragons gathered in a dark stone room, huddled around the top of a flight of stairs descending further down. A green dragon turned to a gold one. "Where is she?" The green dragon's voice trembled in ill-concealed accusation. "She was right with you. How did she get lost?"*

I had to.

I couldn't leave her behind and face the haeraig's accusations that I had willingly left her alone in the dark. My actions had already killed his father. I wouldn't take his lifelong friend too.

I looked back at Keita, barely visible in the darkness and already struggling a few feet behind me as she tried to find even ground to place her paws.

I stopped walking.

"Keita, take hold of my tail," I said.

"What?" she replied. Her tone was sharp, but I knew it wasn't just my imagination that detected a bit of hopelessness there. I felt that she already knew she needed my help, but she wasn't yet ready to admit that to herself, least of all to me.

"Take hold of my tail," I repeated. "I'll guide you along, at least until we're out of here."

"Why...?" Keita asked. Gone was her usual condescending manner she reserved for me. She wasn't demanding why she should accept my help. She was asking why I was offering.

"Because..." I paused, wondering whether to tell Keita what I had just Seen. I didn't want to alarm her, and she had reacted poorly to my previous visions that implied death or failure. "I just don't want you to get left behind. I worry about what would happen if you got lost down here."

"Who said I'd get lost?" Keita argued, a touch of her old venom back in her voice as her pride resurfaced.

I sighed. She left me with little choice. "Because I Saw it. I saw the haeraig's devastation at losing you in here. I will not allow that. I have already caused him enough pain." The words were out of my mouth before I could curtail them, and it was beyond all hope that Keita would miss it.

"What do you mean, caused him enough pain?" she demanded.

I couldn't tell her. This was not the right time to reveal the death of Ddraig Astar, especially not to Keita, but now that I had mentioned Haeraig Anzig's hardship at my paw, I knew I could not avoid the matter for too much longer. I could only hope that I could resist until after we had reclaimed the Axinstone. That was imperative, but Keita was waiting for an answer now.

"I can't tell you yet. Please, just this once, trust me, Keita. It's best for all of us if this knowledge stays with me. I must carry this burden alone. I wouldn't trouble your mind with my worries," I said. Though Keita didn't appear to be convinced, she remained silent. For now though, we had bigger problems to worry about, as Inilta's light was rapidly fading ahead, and they didn't seem to have noticed our absence. They were also well beyond earshot now. We were alone.

Keita growled softly as she too noticed that we had been left behind. "I won't press you for now, Azlak, but you will tell me everything once we get back to the surface," she hissed. I did not doubt that she would try and eke the information out of me the moment we got out of these dark and gloomy caves, but for now she took hold of my tail in her jaws, biting perhaps a little harder than she needed to, and let me lead her onwards. I tried to keep to the flattest part of the ground, warning Keita whenever I had to step over a small crevasse or stalagmite growing from the floor, but there were several occasions still when she stumbled. Her teeth tore at the tip of my tail. I had to resist the urge to shake her off.

Together we gradually made our way forward, using the diminishing light from Inilta's magic to make out a safe path for Keita's weak vision. Even I could barely see anything now; I dreaded to think how little she could see. All I could rely on was my shaky memory of my visions of the route through the caves. If what I had Seen was correct, all we needed to do was keep going straight, but that was hard to do when I could barely see the end of my own muzzle.

Keita grunted and squeezed a little tighter on my tail. I could feel her shaking. She was scared. I wanted to reassure her, to tell her that I would lead us both out of the dark, but I could make no such promise. For once I found myself in a situation I had failed to predict and that scared me. I had no idea what was about to happen and the implications of that worried me. Did it mean there was no future for me? Was I doomed to wander the dark caves until I died?

I forced that thought to the back of my mind. I had to remain confident that I could get us out of the caves, or else I risked taking another dragon from Haeraig Anzig's life. I couldn't do that to him; I couldn't do that to my clan. I had to keep on putting one paw in front of the other and hope that I maintained a straight path. Eventually one of the other dragons would notice we were missing, and they would come back and fetch us.

Keita tugged hard on my tail, forcing me to stop.

"Are we going up?" she asked, taking her jaws away from my tail. I could hear her moving by my side, her wingtip brushing against mine.

I frowned. The ground beneath my paws did feel like it was sloping up ever so slightly. That wasn't the only thing that caught my attention though.

"Do you hear that?"

Keita shuffled around next to me, always staying in contact, whether by the tip of her wing or the end of her tail. "I don't hear anything," she said.

"It sounds like waves against a beach. I think we're close to the surface."

"Either that or the caves are flooding," Ketia added in a dry tone. I could tell she still didn't trust me to guide us out, but she still had no real choice in the matter. She had to follow me.

"Come on. Keep your wing on mine," I said, pushing on again, but keeping my wing outstretched so Keita could stay in contact without having to bite down on my tail again. I didn't know if it was my imagination, but I thought there was a little bit of grey ahead, a welcome change from the constricting blackness that surrounded us.

There was a new sound now, one that was definitely not water against the shore. This was different, a harsher sound, less rhythmic than the waves. It echoed back and forth across the rock so I couldn't work out exactly what it was. Thudding. Jarring noises.

It was not my imagination. The darkness was receding as I could just about make out Keita's silhouette beside me, but the noises were getting closer, coming down the tunnel towards us as we made our way up. They were accompanied by a scent, one that was both unfamiliar, yet at the same time one that I would never forget.

Human.

I barged Keita aside into a small alcove as a bright, piercing white light shone directly ahead of us, sweeping back and forth across the cave. Just behind it I could make out a dark shape that was vaguely human in appearance, but I couldn't look for too long. The light hurt my eyes and I was forced to bring my wing in front of my face.

Keita placed her wing around me. Her span was able to cover my entire body, shielding my bright gold scales from reflecting the humans' light. Neither of us dared make a noise as the human searched for something. Was it us he sought? Had the humans already captured the others? Keita trembled beside me. There was nothing we could do but wait...

*A human ran down a dark tunnel, a bright light in his hand. He talked to another human, not present, through the use of something small and black in his hand. He stopped at a metal ladder and started climbing. Sunlight shone down from a hole in the roof of the cave. As the human disappeared into the light, two dragons emerged out of the darkness: one gold, the other red. Without hesitating, the dragons took to the air and silently followed the human up and out of the cave...*

...for the human to leave, so we could follow him. That was our path; though I dreaded the moment I would have to tell Keita that.

I peered around Keita's wings to look at the human. I could barely see him, but I believed him to be the same one that I had seen in my vision. This was the one we had to follow.

The human turned away. If he had been searching for us, then he had given up as he began to walk back the way he had come from. I could see him reach for something and hold it against his head – the black object I had seen him use before. This was our chance.

I pushed Keita's wing aside and silently stalked down the cave, towards the human.

"What are you doing?" Keita hissed, reluctantly following me.

"Just come with me, and keep quiet," I replied, hoping that she would do so. She wouldn't like it, but surely it would be preferable to staying alone in the dark. I didn't look back to see if she followed, but I could hear her keep just behind my tail. It was brighter now, and she was able to find her own path safely.

I kept the human just within sight whilst trying my hardest to reduce the noise we were making. Our claws made mercifully little noise against the damp stone and the human appeared to be oblivious to our presence, only a few dozen feet away.

We turned past a bend in the tunnel and there before us was the shaft of light coming down from the distant roof, the sunlight glinting off the wet rocks, with the metal ladder gleaming in the sudden burst of radiance. The human had already climbed halfway up the shining ladder and was fast disappearing into the light until I could see him no longer. I still didn't know where we would emerge once we reached the surface, but I spread my wings in preparation for flight. By my side, Keita did the same, though with a little reluctance. I felt a surge of fearful pride that she had taken to following my lead, but I couldn't think about that for the moment. We were about to surface in the middle of an island dominated by a human castle; we had to be on our guard at all times.

As we reached the top of the cave, I clung on to the ladder and slowly climbed up the rest of the way. The air was thick with the scent of humans, it pervaded everything around me. It made me nervous, and I could tell Keita felt the same way.

"Are you sure about this, Azlak?" the ness whispered from where she had perched on to the ladder below me.

"Not in the slightest," I replied, and launched up and out of the caves, into the light.

# chapter seventeen

**Ellian**

It took me a few moments to realise where I was when I woke. A strange low ceiling greeted me, and a dozen dragons I didn't recognise lay scattered throughout the cave. The glowing remnants of the fire in the centre of the cave still smoked and sparked, filming everything with a grey haze. It was only when I saw my brother lying a few wingspans away did the events of the previous day come back to me. I looked around the chamber for Vinzent, but the dragonet was nowhere to be seen.

Quietly, I got to my paws and more thoroughly examined my new home. The cave was almost a perfect sphere and was lit from the wide entry that overlooked the river. A few ledges lined the walls, and these seemed to be used to store trinkets the nomads had found on their travels. There were a few pieces of human-crafted items, including some metallic dishes I had seen before, but had never quite worked out their exact purpose. I could also see a collection of rugs that were no doubt used when a simple fire was not enough to keep away the worst of the winter night's chill. It was a small lair, but I doubted there was ever more than a couple of dozen dragons present.

Hunger compelled me to leave the cave and head down to the river. The morning sky was clear, but there was a threat of clouds in the east.

Any hunting would have to be done soon, as I had no desire to be out in the rain. It had been a long time since I had hunted for fish, and it took me a while before I was able to strike any of the slippery fiends and drive them out of the water. Eventually I got my fill, by which time a few of the other dragons had woken and were resting at the top of the promontory. I considered going up and joining them, but I thought I saw a flash of silver scales, so I settled down on the riverbank instead.

It wasn't long before Mulner came down to join me. He lay on the bank with his tail drifting lazily in the water; one sleepy eye looking up to the sky with the other drooping closed. He didn't respond to any of my questions about the daily routines of the nomads, instead he just grunted and mumbled something incomprehensible. Of course, I remembered now that Mulner had never been lively in the mornings. One of my few memories of him had been when I had teased and tormented him as he struggled to wake up. It had taken our mother's intervention to protect him that time. I smiled at the memory, though I didn't mention it to Mulner.

My wings were grateful for the rest as they were still aching from the exertions of the previous day. All I had to do was lie down and wait for the dragons who had been tracking the humans to return. It gave me the chance to think back on the last few days. Yes, I had lost control of Clan Laxtal to Ddraig Tsona, but the more I thought about it, the better I felt. Mulner had advised me not to rule out the Xital ddraig of being the humans' informant, but I now believed that to be unlikely. I trusted that Laxtal was in safe paws for the time being, at least until the war was over. I doubted I would ever be able to return, even after the Xital drake had passed the leadership back to the clan, but strangely I didn't feel too disheartened. For the moment I was quite content to stay with the nomads: Mulner had briefly introduced me to the small group last night, and they had already made me feel welcome.

Vinzent was my only concern. He had not spoken to me since we had arrived, but he had glared at me from the shadows before we had slept. I knew he was still annoyed that I had refused to go straight to Nixa, but I feared that there was something more behind his frustration.

I had no time to dwell upon it though, as a thunderclap disturbed the peace of the morning. I squawked and leaped back as a dragon materialised almost right on top of me.

"Airil?" I cried, instantly recognising the bright blue scales of the Nixan dragon.

The Nixan shrieked with laughter as he saw me. "Ellian! I wasn't expecting to be blessed with your company today," he said, before noticing that I had flung myself on my back in an attempt to avoid him. "Oh, I am so sorry, I did it again didn't I?" He hung his head in shame.

"You've met before?" Mulner growled from the water's edge. He had barely even flinched at Airil's teleportation.

"He was with Ddraig Krateos when he came to Laxtal a short while ago," I explained as I struggled up to my paws. I nosed against Airil, lifting his chin so he looked up from the ground. "But what are you doing here?"

"He's been helping scout the surrounding area. I must say it's been very helpful having a Nixan around, especially one with his particular talents," Mulner answered. My brother seemed to have woken up a bit now as he sat up, though he left his tail floating in the river. He looked up at the sky, tracking something I was unable to see.

"Ddraig Krateos didn't want anyone coming out to assist any of the surrounding clans," Airil added timidly. "Strictly speaking he didn't give me permission to come and help the nomads either, but I wasn't doing anything sitting around in the lair. Kaz was pretty bored too, but it was harder for him to get out here. I couldn't carry him this far south."

"Assistance is pretty rare from Clan Nixa, so naturally we were delighted to have him," Mulner said, glancing down from his vigil for just a moment. The Nixan perked up a little, but he still couldn't meet my eye as he looked away every time I caught him glancing in my direction. My brother then directly addressed the Nixan, still looking up to the sky. "Were you able to track the humans?"

Airil grinned. "We were. They travelled without any particular direction, which is most unusual given their recent patterns. However, Cinson was able to get quite close, and he overheard a lot of what they said. I'll leave it to him to tell you what though, if you can wait until they return. They shouldn't be long now," he said, joining Mulner in looking up to the skies, but the Nixan soon lost interest in the pale blue expanse.

Mulner stood up and shook his wings and tail. "Come fetch me when they arrive would you? I have some things to organise," my brother said. Airil nodded, and Mulner took to wing and soared back up to the cave.

The Nixan turned back to me and looked down at my forepaws. "I'm so sorry. I didn't mean to appear on top of you," he said bashfully.

"Don't worry about it. I'm sure it must happen a lot," I said with a smile.

Airil shook his head. "That doesn't make it any better. I don't know what happened; I was aiming for the top of the outcrop there. I should be better than that," he said. He slumped down on to the ground, and I joined him in looking out over the river. A small rat scurried through the undergrowth on the far side of the water, fleeing into the tall grass when it noticed us. Even if I had wanted to chase after it, the rat was already too far away for me to catch up and find again, but Airil... Distance was no bother to him. It must be wonderful, just to be able to appear where you wanted to be. I couldn't even imagine how it must feel.

"How does it work?" I asked before realising the words were being formed in my mouth.

"What do you mean?"

"Your magic. How do you make yourself appear somewhere else?"

Airil pawed at the ground, batting at a small pebble and knocking it back and forth. "I can't explain it really. To me it's as simple as flying. I just...do it," he said hesitantly. He growled softly as he flung the pebble into the river.

"It must feel incredible," I said wistfully. There were times I was a little jealous of Clan Nixa. They alone possessed magic and I often wondered what it must feel like to control such amazing powers and abilities. At other times, I was annoyed by their show of superiority, much like Clan Xital's overbearing smugness. I did not get that impression from Airil. He seemed different to the other dragons from his clan.

Airil grinned. It was a smile that revealed all his teeth and lit up his eyes, resulting in an image that was both unsettling and infectious. "Take my paw," he said, offering it out for me to grasp.

"Why?" I asked, a little apprehensive to say the least. I wasn't sure I liked the way the Nixan was twitching with anticipation.

"Because I can show you what it's like," he said, extending his paw further. I looked down at the offered limb, and then back up to Airil's beaming face. I still felt a flutter of nerves in my heart, but I decided I could trust the Nixan. I placed my paw in his.

The world exploded in a burst of colour and light. Heat prickled at my scales as I heard a great wind but could feel nothing but stillness. In the smallest fraction of a second, I could see everything: trees, mountains, rivers, lakes, giant constructs of glass and metal. I saw it all. Everything there was to see in the world, lined up in one great montage of images.

Then it was gone. I was back on the grass, my lungs and heart racing as my mind tried to catch up with what my eyes had just seen. Airil was still stood in front of me, his yellow eyes staring into mine.

I looked away, embarrassed by the close attention the Nixan was giving me, and it was only then that I realised we were not on the riverbank anymore.

"We've moved," I yelped in shock. I didn't recognise this place. Gone were the river and the cave. Instead, I found myself on the edge of a dense forest that backed on to the Sxinix Mountains. I scented the air: there was no smell of any dragons or humans anywhere near here. We were completely alone.

"Of course we moved. I wasn't going to go through all that and leave us in the same place," Airil said with a laugh. He sounded tired as he flopped down onto his side and closed his eyes. He breathed in deeply.

"Are you alright?" I asked, suddenly full of concern for the Nixan as he flexed his wings tentatively.

"I'll be fine," he said. "It just takes a lot more energy to move someone who isn't Nixan. Just give me a few minutes and I'll be alright."

I lay down by his side and looked around again, trying to find some familiar landmark. I could see nothing. Not even the mountains were similar to those close to the nomad lair.

"How far did we travel?" I asked in awe.

"About an hour's flight to the north," Airil said. He smiled as he stretched his wings out – the tip just brushing against my side. I almost flinched away from the contact, but I was able to remain still. The Nixan didn't seem to notice my momentary discomfort. "It was something special, wasn't it?"

"It was absolutely wonderful, I can only imagine what it must feel like for you. Thank you for showing me," I said.

"The pleasure was all mine," Airil replied. Again, his wingtip brushed against me as he stretched out on the grass. "But tell me Ellian, why are you out here? Shouldn't you be with your clan?"

I turned away from the Nixan and growled softly.

"I'm sorry, I didn't mean to pry," Airil said hastily.

"No, it's alright. It's not you. It's just... well, it's a long story really," I said. I don't know why I then told the Nixan everything that had happened over the last few days. He wasn't a dragon of any sort of power within his clan; there was nothing he could do to help me, but it was soothing just being able to talk openly to another dragon about all of it.

Airil listened in silence as I told him about Astar's death, and of Ddraig Tsona's arrival in Laxtal. I even told him of Vinzent's promise to become my mate once we were ready. He growled when I mentioned the news of Anzig's death, but he didn't interrupt me until I had finished. I hurried through the retelling of my doomed challenge against the Xital ddraig as I didn't want to face my failures so soon after they had overwhelmed me.

"I think Ddraig Tsona is mistaken in saying Anzig is dead," Airil said after I had concluded my tale of being banished from Laxtal.

"What do you mean? You think he's still alive?" I asked, barely daring to hope. If my cousin was still alive...

"I came straight here from Laxtal, so I never went back to Nixa, but I know Ddraig Krateos had a number of telepaths tracking Isikian and Inilta. They're too far away to be contacted, but our telepaths are at least able to pinpoint where they are. The last I heard was that they had reached the ocean. They did that before we came to arrange that alliance. Didn't Ddraig Tsona say they only made it to the mountains? That can't be right," Airil said. His words filled my chest with hope. Maybe the Xital dragon had been wrong, and that my cousin hadn't been killed. There was still a chance he could return.

"Of course, that raises further issues with Ddraig Tsona. Haeraig Zeena was already suspicious of him. If he's been brazenly lying to you that Laxtal's haeraig was killed... I don't like that at all," the Nixan said with a frown. He growled again as he slowly lifted himself up to his paws. "I really should return to Nixa and inform Ddraig Krateos, but I have duties here first. I won't abandon your brother, not when he still needs me. Speaking of which, we should probably get back before Cinson and the others return."

"Mulner will probably be wondering where we are," I added.

"And Vinzent too. He'll think I'm trying to steal you away or something," Airil said with a laugh. His eyes were bright as he offered his paw out to me. This time I took it without hesitation and my entire world was torn to shreds.

We returned to the lair just in time. After we materialised by the river and I had regained my bearings, I noticed three dragons flying towards us. Airil collapsed in exhaustion, and I stood guard over him as the newcomers came to land close by. Two were Laxtal dragons, but the third seemed to be from the east. His green-scaled body was longer and more slender than the others. His tail was also long and thin, tapering to a very fine point that was a distinguishing feature of Clan Xigax. They often used their tails to restrain their enemies in battle while they attacked with their claws and teeth.

They asked for Mulner, and though I was reluctant to leave Airil, I flew up to the cave to fetch my brother. I found him in a heated discussion with Vinzent. I had missed the start of the argument, but it didn't take me long to pick up that the silver dragonet believed the nomads weren't doing enough to help the clans against the humans. Mulner vociferously disagreed.

"I'm telling you again, I am not ordering these dragons back to their clans," my brother snarled. He stared the youngster down. "They all have their own reasons for leaving the lairs. I will not force them to go back."

"But you're doing nothing in this war. Dragonkind will be ruined, and you stand back and do nothing," Vinzent retorted. He extended his wings and puffed out his chest.

Mulner replied by slashing Vinzent across the face. His claws drew blood and the silver dragonet reeled back in shock.

"Never accuse me of that again. We have done more than you know, dragonet," Mulner said in a low growl.

Vinzent whimpered and turned away from my brother, only to face me. He cowered even lower to the ground. I pushed past him and ignored his muted protests.

"Cinson and the others are back," I told my brother. He grunted in acknowledgement before stalking outside.

Vinzent whimpered again. "Ellian, we can't stay here. We have to help Laxtal fight," he said quietly. He held a paw to his wounded face and stared down into the ground.

"We'll see what the nomads have learned before we make any judgements on whether they're helping. And remember this is my brother you're talking to. I would recommend thinking before speaking next time," I growled. I didn't give Vinzent any opportunity to respond as I followed my brother outside. I was more interested to hear what Cinson had to say than listen to Vinzent's complaints. The silver dragonet slinked out behind me.

I was glad to see Airil had sat back up and looked like he was already starting to recover from the return to the cave. He smiled at me as I approached.

"We tracked a group of humans for a few days," Cinson, the Xigax dragon, was saying. "It seems like they've broken away from the larger human force we saw last week. If I had to judge what they were planning, I'd say they were trying to get home. I don't think they want to be here, but they're lost and can't find the mountain passes."

"Why would they want to go home?" I asked, surprised by this news. We had been told quite clearly by Clan Xital that all humans sought the end of dragonkind. They wanted to destroy each and every clan and populate our lands with their cities of machines and metal.

Cinson shrugged. "I wouldn't know. If they've been discussing the reasons for their desertion then we didn't hear them."

"Do you think we could use this to our advantage?" I asked. A lot of possibilities raced through my mind at this piece of news. It would be dangerous, but already I was thinking of approaching these humans and trying to get some information off them. If we could work out the purpose of the main human forces, then that would assist the clans greatly.

"I know what you're thinking Ellian, and no, I'm not letting you do that," Mulner said.

Vinzent growled, but if he had any objections he didn't voice them as he was quelled by a sharp glance from both Mulner and me.

"Just think of what we could learn," I said, but my brother wasn't having anything to do with it.

"No, it's too dangerous. What if they're not friendly, and this is just a ruse to lure some dragons in," he said.

I shook my head and kicked the ground with my paw but could think of no response to that. Airil however, had.

"I could keep watch," the Nixan said with a smile. "If Ellian goes to meet these humans, I can stand guard nearby. If ever it looks like she's in trouble, I can get her out of there in an instant."

Mulner threw a filthy look at the Nixan, but as I had been just moments earlier, my brother was now stuck without an answer. With a savage snarl, he took a swipe at the air between us. He glared at me. "If you really want to do this, I won't stop you. But Ellian, please, don't do this if you're only trying to redeem yourself from losing Laxtal. There's no point taking stupid risks over something like that," he said.

"I know," I said, bowing my head. This wasn't about proving myself. Not entirely, anyway. I knew that doing this had the potential to help all of dragonkind.

"Ellian..." Vinzent whispered. He was practically lying down in the grass now and seemed completely incapable of adding anything further. I had never seen him so bereft of confidence before, and I had no idea what had caused it. He had still seemed so sure of himself after fleeing from Laxtal. Something here had upset him greatly, and I doubted it was just his argument with my brother.

"If I'm to watch over you we should fly there so I don't tire myself out," Airil said, completely ignoring Vinzent's muted protests. The Nixan paused and looked up to the sky and sniffed at the air. "Though I will admit I'm a little unsure of the direction."

"I can guide you back to where we last saw them," Cinson offered. Airil gladly accepted the Xigax dragon's assistance, but no one else seemed keen on joining us.

For a moment I wondered if this must have been what Anzig had felt like, gathering his group of dragons to fly over the mountains. Of course, while my brother thought I was flying into danger, it was nothing compared to what Anzig faced, if he still lived. He had set himself against the entire human nation. There was nothing I could do to help him directly, but, if by some miracle he succeeded, I could at least try to have dragonkind ready to retaliate with the Axinstone in Clan Nixa's possession.

"No point delaying," I said. I looked around at the small group. Mulner and the two other Laxtal nomads stared down into the ground and remained silent. Vinzent had slunk back so far he was almost in the river. No one else was ready to speak up against me so I flared my wings. Airil and Cinson followed suit, and before any of the nomads had further opportunity to protest, we took to the air and flew away to the west.

Cinson took up the lead position, leaving me to fly alongside Airil. The Nixan was pleasant company, a relief to be around after the constant nagging and whining from Vinzent. It was not long before conversation inevitably turned towards the humans we tracked.

"How many of them are there?" I asked, after about half an hour of flight. The land beneath us was largely empty and bare, with few signs of dragons. I imagined most had already fled back to the larger lairs, seeking safety in the numbers of the major clans. Mulner and his small band of nomads appeared to be in the minority.

"In the larger group, we estimate several thousand, but in the group we tracked there's maybe fifty at most," Airil replied. He gestured with his head towards the north, whereas we flew more west, towards the Sxinix Mountains. "The big group is that way, but we can't be sure what their plans are. We fear they might be targeting Nixa, but there's no way of knowing at the moment."

Cinson drifted back from his lead position to fly alongside my other wing. I always marvelled at how Xigax dragons were able to fly. Their long, sinuous bodies looked like they should be clumsy while they stood on the ground, with their ratio of torso to wing looking wrong. But Cinson flew with a grace and ease that surprised me, though I doubted he would be able to match me for outright speed.

"The large force is led by a human called General Arnold Summers," the Xigax dragon explained. "We have heard him talk a lot of a man called George Symons, who we believe to be the same one your cousin hopes to steal the Axinstone from."

"And we know nothing about their plans?" I asked. No matter how much I searched the horizon, I could see no trace of the several thousand humans. Either they hid themselves well, or they were too far to see even from our flying height.

"Nothing," Cinson growled. "They don't even seem to be preparing an attack. They are behaving nothing like an army should. Airil is right in one thing. It seems like they're searching for something, but I'm not convinced it's the Nixan lair."

"What else could it be?" Airil challenged, but with no aggression in his tone.

"I don't know," Cinson admitted. He drifted a little further away from me, his focus on the horizon directly to our west, where the mountains rose tall. "But we need to find out."

"That's what we're planning on doing," I said. I wrenched my eyes away from the north, instead focusing west. The smaller band of humans was our immediate concern. The larger group could wait until we knew what their intentions were, and for that we needed to speak to one.

Cinson made a strange noise from the back of his throat. It wasn't quite a growl, but nor did it seem like he fully agreed with what I said. "Have you ever spoken with a human before?" the Xigax dragon said, after a short pause.

I shook my head, careful that I didn't disrupt my flight. "Never, no."

Again, Cinson made that odd, guttural noise. "I'm starting to think your brother may have been right." He gave me no chance to respond, putting forth a burst of speed that surprised me.

I thought to chase after the Xigax dragon, to argue with him further, but I had no desire to feel like I flew with Vinzent again. I growled and glared at the fleeing dragon, but I stayed by Airil's side.

"I think you've got this," Airil said brightly. He looked away too slowly. I saw the fear in his eyes. We all fell into silence after that, too nervous to speak any further. There was nothing more we could learn, not until we stood face to face with the humans.

After about an hour of flight, Cinson descended to the ground. He landed under the shelter of a few trees and pointed out the signs of humans as we fluttered down after him. There was an expansive area that had been cleared of fallen debris from the trees, and a pile of blackened wood still gently smoked. Airil also unearthed a long metal hook we were unable to determine the purpose of.

"They camped here last night," Cinson said. He bounded across the clearing, looking for something to indicate where the humans had gone. It wasn't hard to find. Fifty humans left tracks and the soil was still a little damp from a downpour a few days ago, forming a trail that led away to the west. I placed a paw in one of the prints they had left behind, marvelling at just how big it was. I could fit three of my paws in just the one of theirs.

"Having second thoughts?" Airil asked me quietly. He had come up to my side and was watching me compare my paw with the human prints. Further down the trail Cinson glanced back at us, but I doubted he had heard the Nixan's words.

"Of course not," I retorted with a playful swipe at Airil. "I just... I just forgot how big they really are."

"I know," Airil said sombrely. He placed his paw next to mine in the human's print. "It gets to me too. I look at them and wonder how we'd ever be able to defeat them. But Ddraig Krateos believes that with the Axinstone, we can do it. If he says we can then I know it's possible. We're just relying on your cousin to come back safely with it."

"You really believe he's still alive?"

"I only know that he didn't die where Ddraig Tsona claimed. He got further than that so I'm hopeful they're all still alive. Maybe even returning as we speak," the Nixan said.

"Then we should find out what's going on here," I said, leaping after Cinson and following the Xigax dragon down the track. The humans were travelling closer to the mountains and slightly north. If they were indeed trying to reach the closest pass across the Sxinix, then they were going entirely in the wrong direction. The Gota-Sxinix to the south was the only pass large enough for a human to cross within hundreds of miles.

We continued on paw for about forty minutes. Nerves and excitement had caused us to fall into silence as we chased after the humans.

Finally, just after midday, we found them. We could smell them before we heard them, and then heard them before we could see them – a great free-for-all of smells and noise as they tramped onwards. They weren't even trying to be quiet as they talked loudly amongst themselves, with each of their great paws crunching the ground as they walked.

Cinson shivered as he came to a halt. "This is as far as I go," he said quietly, bowing his head to the ground. "I will wait for you here, but I cannot go any further."

I didn't attempt to encourage the Xigax dragon to continue. This was my choice to approach the humans, not his. I wouldn't ask him to go on when he was clearly uncomfortable about doing so. From now on it would just be the Nixan and me.

A call of halt from the humans caused me to freeze. I was afraid they already knew we were here, but none came back down the trail. I breathed a sigh of relief, and then wondered why I had been so terrified. I was about to reveal myself to them anyway. What difference did it make how the humans discovered I was following them? We continued on, but I couldn't stop my body from shaking ever so slightly as we neared the human group. I could just about see them now: they appeared to have paused for a break as most were sat down in the shade of a few trees. All were dressed in similar green clothing and each carried a large, bulging pack of some sorts.

"This is it..." I said nervously.

Airil unfurled one wing and for a moment he looked like he was about to place it over my body, before changing his mind. Instead, he settled with saying, "I'll be watching. I'll get you the moment I think you're in danger."

"I'm sure I'll be fine," I said, trying to inject a little belief into my voice. I tried to think back to how I felt when I had the entire clan beneath my wings, just before Ddraig Tsona had so comprehensively crushed me. I needed that confidence now.

"All the same, you be careful," Airil said. I got the feeling he had something else to say, but he looked away and remained silent.

Before I had any chance to reconsider the potential folly of my actions, I took to wing and left Airil behind. A multitude of thoughts raced through my mind as I wondered what I was going to say and what the humans' reactions would be. There hadn't been any peaceful negotiations between our species for a number of years now. First they had ceased trading with us, and that eventually led to outright hostility against our clans. Now I, a banished dragon, would attempt to rebuild the connection between us.

I was almost amongst them before they even noticed my presence. I cry of warning broke out as I landed in the grass, a short distance away from the closest human who turned around to face me, scrambling back as he tried in vain to find the weapon holstered at his hip.

"Please, I don't mean to harm you," I said, looking away from the human and sitting down. I tucked my wings against my side, trying to make myself appear small and harmless. I trusted that Airil would notice if anyone showed aggression towards me, as I was not in a position to defend myself against the superior strength of the humans.

No attack came. The humans all seemed to have frozen, each unsure what to do or how to react. Finally, one came forward.

"You know we should just kill you," the human said. He placed his hand on the weapon at his side but he made no movement to draw it.

"I know. But you're not here to kill dragons are you, human?" I asked. I looked around at the group of humans. There was movement amongst them, but still they seemed a little unsure of what they should be doing. None were going for their weapons. "If you wanted me dead, you wouldn't have given me the chance to talk. The thing is, I knew you wouldn't harm me, or else I'd have stayed away."

"And how did you know that?" the human asked, folding his arms across his chest.

"We don't allow humans to roam our lands and not track them. We've been following you for some time. You don't want to fight, you want to get back home but you can't find the mountain pass," I said. I glanced up at the human's face, but he was looking at something over my left shoulder.

The human frowned and rubbed his jaw. "I won't deny that we don't believe in the slaughter of dragons. That's why we've turned back. But you're wrong in thinking we want to return home. We deserted the army, so we gave up our right to return to Kernow. We don't have a home anymore," he said.

I bowed my head. "Then we are more alike than you can realise. I am Ellian. I was the ddraig of Clan Laxtal until I was thrown out of the clan by a dragon about whom I have suspicions of being a traitor. I know how it feels to be without a home."

"And I am James McArthur. These men have chosen to follow and are loyal to me. They will follow me to the end, whatever end Dirus may have for us. I don't know what we can do, but Ellian of Laxtal, we are willing to offer you aid in return for assistance from you. We're weary of wandering the land and want somewhere to settle, somewhere to feel safe once more. Our food supplies are low, so any help dragonkind can offer us would be greatly accepted. We are desperate," the human said. He sat down on the grass in front of me, putting his hands upon his knees.

Behind him, the other humans were all listening, engrossed in this development. It only took a quick glance at their faces to tell me that James McArthur was telling the truth. They all had a pinched, haggard look I hadn't noticed before.

I pawed at the grass. This group of humans only numbered fifty, but I knew they would be a great ally to have. Of course, I knew Mulner and Vinzent would protest that we couldn't trust them. But I didn't believe that was the human way. They wouldn't take our help and then betray us. Some dragons argued that humans had no honour, but that was not what I had seen. I had already made my decision. I didn't care what Mulner thought.

"My brother knows these lands better than I do. I'm sure he'll be able to recommend a place for you as our cave won't fit fifty dragons, let alone fifty humans," I said, thinking of where the humans could possibly reside. They were probably used to more elaborate dwellings than simple caves, but there was little else we could offer.

"And your brother will tolerate our presence?" James McArthur asked.

I laughed. "He probably won't like it to begin with, but if I say you can be trusted, Mulner will listen to me. I can guarantee there will be dissent, but I know I can convince them to let you settle nearby."

"Then we must thank you, Ellian. I promise you that I will offer any assistance you require in repayment for this." He offered out his hand. I was vaguely familiar with this human concept, and I reached up and grasped his hand in my paw.

Had any Nixan seer been around to witness this, I was sure they would have seen that I had just changed the course of the future.

Now I just had to break the news to my brother that fifty humans would be joining his band of nomads. Of all my challenges of the day, that was likely to be the most testing.

# CHAPTER EIGHTEEN

**Anzig**

The humans had been waiting for us. We hadn't even made it out of the caves before they had seized us. We had struggled, but there had been far too many of them. To my surprise, we had not been harmed in any way. Instead, they had locked us away in a damp stone room far below the surface. For two days, they had left us abandoned. No one had come to see us in all that time.

A small shaft of sunlight that emerged from a barred window slowly tracked across the dusty floor. The thick wooden door prevented our escape, despite Nataik's best efforts in trying to open it. The Xigax dragon had spent many hours trying to break the locking mechanism, but had achieved nothing for all her efforts.

Carlee and Okazuni were curled up together in one corner of the room, huddled up against the cold wind that whistled through the small cracks in the walls and door. Inilta lay in the small square of sunshine in the middle of the room, his wings spread out in exhaustion. He had tried to keep us warm by lighting a fire, but his magic had wavered and flickered out some time ago. Isikian was lying at his brother's side. The healer held his paws over his eyes; he had been complaining about a headache he was unable to cure himself of.

I then looked across to the other corner of the room and bowed my head in sorrow. That corner was empty. It was only once we had been thrown into the dungeon that we realised our number was two short. Azlak and Keita were missing. I could only hope they had not been killed in the ambush. My heart longed for them to have survived, but I could not be certain.

I had thrown myself repeatedly at the door in an attempt to force my way out of our prison, but had only succeeded in giving myself a bruised shoulder. Carlee had eventually calmed me out of my rage, and ever since I had been wallowing in depression. We had failed. Humans had captured us, and in the process we had lost Keita, as well as the only dragon who would have been able to help us. Azlak would have been able to See our way out, but without him we were lost.

I pressed my forehead against the cold stone wall, trying to soothe the pain that was building behind my eyes. The growing headache managed to distract from the gnawing hunger in my gut, but that was small consolation. A small trickle of dust fell on the back of my head as my blunt horns scraped against the stone.

Nataik thumped at the door with her clenched paw, drawing a slight reaction from Inilta and Isikian, who both hissed at the unwanted noise. The two Nixans were suffering considerably. I figured it was a result of the massive amounts of raw magic emitted from somewhere within the castle. Even I could feel it. Normally it was a warm, gentle feeling that invigorated me, but at other times my mind was wracked with pluses of blinding white light followed by a period of unsettling disorientation. Every time it got worse, but Carlee, Okazuni, and Nataik never seemed to be affected by the pulses of magic.

The Xigax ness admitted defeat. She slunk away from the door and slumped down by my side. "It's hopeless, Haeraig. They've got that door firmly locked from the other side," she said wearily.

"Then we've failed," I said, bowing my head and turning away from Nataik. I collapsed on to my side.

A low growl emanated from the corner of the room as Carlee struggled to her paws. "Never say that. We made it to the castle. We are in the same building as the Axinstone. We have not failed. Not yet," she said. Her wings were slightly flared for balance as she fought to stay upright. We were all feeling the ill-effects of being out of the sun for so long, our bodies were cold and weary. We hadn't eaten in that time either. There hadn't even been a rat scurrying through the dark and gloomy depths of the castle. Most of us had barely slept.

"But where can we go from here? There's no way out," I said. I felt like curling up and pulling my wing over my face, but Carlee towered over me and stared me in the eye. I couldn't turn away. Not without submitting to my mentor.

"One thing I've learnt, Haeraig Anzig, is that there is always a way out," she growled, before finally releasing me from her gaze. She sat down and faced away from me, wrapping her tail tightly around her legs. "I was once trapped and alone in Clan Duma. Every dragon I met wanted to kill me – there was a bitter dispute over territory between our clans at the time. It's all mostly been forgotten now, but at the time the battles were fierce, and it resulted in Duma losing a lot of power. The point is, I was alone and without hope. I couldn't see any way to survive that day but I didn't give up. I fought to stay alive for long enough that reinforcements came. I will not let you give up when we're so close."

"We have no reinforcements," I said bitterly. "We are alone here."

"Not if Keita and Azlak still live."

I sighed. I couldn't follow my pessimism without admitting they were dead. I was not yet ready to do that. "So what do we do now?"

"We wait. An opportunity will present itself to escape, and when it comes, we must be ready." Carlee looked up to the distant window and sighed. "The humans had plenty of opportunity to kill us if that was their motive. We are being kept alive for a reason."

"She's right, Haeraig," Nataik said. The Xigax dragon tentatively sidled closer to us. Even this close it was still hard to keep track of her. Her scales blended so seamlessly into the dull grey stones behind her. "The humans were only ever trying to capture us. They want us here for a reason, but I don't know what that could be. I don't think I want to know."

I nodded. Waiting frustrated me, but I understood that it was all we could do. We had no hope of escape without human intervention, for good or for ill. I very much agreed with Nataik in that I didn't want to know why the humans had kept us alive. Whatever it was could not bode well for us.

I struggled to rise to my paws, but stumbled and fell sideways into the wall. I tried a second time, but met with the same results, so I gave up and remained lying. Even that pitiful attempt had left me exhausted.

"When was the last time you slept, Haeraig?" Carlee asked. She stood over me again and looked me in the eye.

I was reluctant to say, but I knew I would not be able to deny Carlee. She would force me to answer if I didn't do so willingly. "Before the mines," I said quietly.

I had been too afraid to sleep since then. I was worried that if I closed my eyes for just a moment then humans would come bursting through the door and slay us in my moment of weakness. I had to remain alert to help my companions. My negligence had already lost two of our number, and two dragons I very much cared about. I couldn't let that happen again, but Carlee didn't share my concern.

"Get some sleep, Haeraig. When we get out of here you need to be well rested," she said.

"But..."

"I'll wake you if anything happens, Haeraig," Carlee said, curtailing my brief protest.

My growl became a whimper as I quickly relented. She was right. She always was. There was no use trying to remain awake when I was already barely able to stand. I would be useless were any humans to come in. My aging mentor had safely kept watch almost every night since we had left Xital. I knew I could trust her once more to keep us safe while I slept.

For a moment I considered telling Inilta to move from the sunlit patch in the middle of the room. As haeraig I had the right to do so, but I knew that wouldn't be fair on the Nixan. He had exhausted himself trying to keep us warm as long as possible. He deserved uninterrupted rest in what little sunlight we had.

I curled up on my own, wishing that Keita could lie by my side. I longed for her tail entwined with mine, my wing stretched over her body. I wondered if she was still alive, if she was on the island, lost and scared. I clenched my paws, claws scraping along the cold and hard stone floor. Closing my eyes, I tried to force myself into sleep, but my mind raced as I tried to work out how I could save Keita, if she still lived. It was my fault she was missing so I would do anything to get her back.

*I opened my eyes and she was there. Keita sat just a short distance away. She was looking the other way with a small golden dragon by her side: Azlak. I couldn't really make out where they were as there was nothing but vague silhouettes and shadows beyond them. They remained still, but as I tried to approach them my steps brought me no closer to the two dragons.*

*"She is alive still." An unknown voice stopped me in my tracks.*

*I spun around. This way, then that, franticly searching for the source of the voice, but could not find it. When I looked back towards my friends, they were gone. Keita and Azlak had vanished without a trace, swallowed by the shadows.*

*"Where are you?" I called out. My voice reverberated off unseen walls back to me. Each echo sounded more fearful than the last. The voice had been oddly familiar, but just couldn't think where I had heard it before.*

*"Here," the voice said, and a form began to emerge out of the gloom. A ness crouched there. Her wings were outstretched. She looked ready to pounce at a moment's notice. "My name is Maznar. I have spoken with your companion Azlak several times since you began your journey. I have guided him to the island when he refused my advice to turn around and go home. I have come into your dream to ask that you trust me now like he trusted me."*

*"You're Nixan?" I asked. My head pounded. That much remained constant from my waking self.*

*"I do not come from Nixa," the stranger replied, shaking her head. "I ask if you can trust me. I will say nothing else if you decide you cannot."*

*The stranger waited for my acceptance. I was hesitant. There was something about her black scales and red eyes I found familiar, but at the same time I knew that I had never seen her before. I thought about Carlee's words of a few days ago, that I was too quick to trust. I knew she would advise against placing my faith in this mysterious dragon. At the same time though, I could see no reason why I should doubt her. Almost without my will, I bowed my head and agreed to trust Maznar.*

*"Good. I had hoped as much. I will not linger on convincing you to abandon your quest. I tried that with Azlak, and your clan seem such a stubborn group. I cannot help you directly, but I shall do what I can to free you from your cell. I told Azlak to go straight for the*

*kitchens, but he ignored my words, and that chance has now passed. You would have avoided the ambush that way, but that can't be helped now," she said. For a moment the dark shadows behind the ness cleared enough for me to glimpse a stone wall that looked similar, but not quite the same, as the ones that formed our cell. Maznar looked a little uncomfortable as the shadows enveloped the walls once more.*

*"How do you plan on helping us?" I asked, choosing not to mention the sight of the dungeon cell behind Maznar. It wasn't our prison – was the stranger a prisoner of the humans as well?*

*The black-scaled dragon smiled nervously. "I can control dreams and, in turn the thoughts and intentions through them. There is a human here who I shall convince to set you free. It won't be easy, and once free you'll still face an island teeming with humans."*

*"And what do we do once we're out? How do we get the Axinstone?"*

*Maznar laughed. "Find your seer. He'll be able to tell you what to do, not me. Listen to the human, she might have advice for you. Beyond that, I have no guidance to offer you other than to remain cautious. You do not know the full ferocity of George. If you knew what I know, you would likely turn away from your quest and return home."*

*The stranger leered at me. Her unfurled wings merged with the shadows, blurring the edge of her body. She became the darkness. "The spectre of Nightwings is death. You should wish you never encounter her, but I fear that would be a wasted task. Meeting her is inevitable."*

*"But what is she?"*

*"Death," Maznar repeated with a snarl. "There is nothing else you need to know about Nightwings. She is death."*

*Such was her anger I did not dare try and press her for more knowledge. She had at least confirmed Azlak's original description of the spectre. We had been right to fear Nightwings.*

*Maznar faded further into the shadows. All I could see was her piercing eyes; red gems before a dark void. "Be careful Anzig. You are stuck here with no allies, so take advantage of any help where you can. Just... do not attack the human I send to free you," she said. Her voice grew distant as the shadows finally dimmed her eyes and reclaimed her completely. "I shall let you sleep peacefully now. We shall meet again. Of that, I am sure."*

I remembered nothing else from my dreams. Maznar was the only thing on my mind when I woke, but I knew some time had passed since I had fallen into slumber. I could hear some movement around the small cell, as well as the quiet voices of the two Nixans. Carlee was sat facing the door, her back to the rest of the room. The others were all huddled together, with Nataik's slender body almost wrapping around the three dragons.

I was a little unsure as to whether I should believe the dream. I didn't want to put any false hope into thinking Azlak and Keita were still alive if Maznar had simply been a figment of my imagination. The power to control dreams? Did any such magic even exist? I certainly hadn't heard of any dragon with such an ability before, but then, my knowledge of Clan Nixa wasn't particularly strong.

Thankfully I could call upon the knowledge of another. I called Isikian to my side. The healer reluctantly got up from where he lay and stepped over Nataik's tail to approach me. "Haeraig?" he sleepily murmured.

"Are there any dragons with the ability to enter and control dreams?" I asked.

Isikian's wings flared in momentary shock. That woke him up. His brow creased in thought. "It is a very rare ability, Haeraig. I don't believe there are any living dragons with that particular magic. In fact, in recent history the only dragon I can think of to possess that magic was Ddraig Krateos's mother," he said.

"And is the name Maznar familiar to you?"

The Nixan shook his head. "I can't say it is, Haeraig. Why do you ask?"

"Because I was contacted by a ness of that name through my dreams. She said she wasn't Nixan, but it definitely felt like magic to me. I wasn't sure if such a thing could happen," I replied.

"A ness? Are you sure? Not a drake?" Isikian asked frantically, suddenly quite awake.

I nodded, confused. I didn't know why it mattered whether Maznar was a drake or ness, but it was something that disturbed Isikian greatly.

"That's impossible," the Nixan hissed. The healer's distress was obvious as his wings flared and closed intermittently. "There cannot be another one. This has to be some sort of mistake, Haeraig. This dragon can't exist."

"I know it seems unlikely, but it was different to any other dream I've ever had before. I can't explain it really, but it felt like it was real, even though I knew I was asleep," I said, trying to explain what I had felt when talking to Maznar. I wished Azlak were around, so he could confirm that he had spoken to the mysterious stranger, as she had claimed.

"And what did she tell you?" Isikian asked nervously.

"She said she's sending a human to help free us. If one turns up, then you have to admit that Maznar is real," I said. I glanced towards the door. Isikian tracked my movement, but no sound emanated from the corridors beyond.

"This troubles me, Haeraig. Magic is something only Nixans can possess. This ness is not part of our clan, but if you are right, then her existence is worrying for Nixa." Isikian sighed and turned away. "Please excuse me, Haeraig, I must discuss these matters with my brother."

I allowed the Nixan to leave with a slight nod, and he went and nudged his brother to follow him to the far corner of the cell, where they quietly discussed the revelation of Maznar. I couldn't hear what was being said, but at one point Isikian had to restrain his brother who had made a dash for the door. What he had been attempting to achieve, I wasn't sure, but Inilta had seemed very adamant in escaping from this prison by any means necessary.

Once Inilta had calmed down again, a lull descended on the cell. Though there was a possibility that rescue could be coming, I didn't inform the others of it. I didn't want to raise any false hope. There was the possibility I was wrong, and that I had dreamt the whole thing. I could tell that Isikian hoped for such a thing, even if it did mean we had no chance of escape.

As the minutes and the hours passed by, I began to doubt myself further. Others were getting restless. Nataik had been pacing around for some time now, shooting the occasional glare at the door as though attempting to open it through force of will alone.

A dull thud scared everyone to attention.

A second knock at the door followed, before a quiet clink of metal scraping against another metallic surface.

"Do not attack unless provoked," I hissed, seeing that Nataik was fading from sight, her haunches poised for pouncing.

The Xigax dragon growled, but I knew she would not disobey a direct order. Her scales continued to blend in with the dirty stonework, but her tightened muscles relaxed slightly. She was still prepared to attack, but like the rest of us she would wait to see if indeed there was a threat on the other side of the door.

Another knock, and this time a voice followed. Human. "Hello? Are you there?"

"Your name, human?" I asked boldly. I tried to inject as much confidence as I could into my voice, partly to intimidate the human, but also to instil some respect into my companions. I knew that their trust in my ability to lead them had waned ever since our first night in human lands. I needed to win that back.

"My name is Marianne. You must be Anzig of Clan Laxtal?" She stumbled over the pronunciation of my name and that of the clan.

The human continued to fumble with something on the other side of the door as the metallic clinks continued. I resisted throwing a smug look towards Isikian despite knowing that this was the human Maznar had sent us. I was sure the Nixan wouldn't appreciate being reminded of the existence of the mysterious black ness.

I did not question how the human already knew who I was. Our presence must have been revealed to her through a dream induced by Maznar, and the dragon had instructed the human to free us. The human knowing my name was one of the least bizarre things about the whole exchange. I confirmed with the human that I was who she believed me to be. A loud snick then preceded the door slowly creaking open.

A human woman was framed in the doorway. She was dressed in an odd white material that gave her very angular edges. She carried a heavy bag over one shoulder, pulling her posture off-centre. There was no one else with her, and she looked terrified about facing six dragons by herself. "Hurry. I don't think we have much time," she said, waving us out. She cast a nervous glance to the side, down the corridor.

I was the only one to move, and I paused and looked back from the doorway, at the human's side. "Follow me," I encouraged the others. I knew they would be feeling uncomfortable about following a human; I would have been too, had it not been for Maznar's warning that this was going to happen.

Carlee was the first. Following her lead, the rest hesitantly followed, falling into line behind me and Marianne. Our human guide led us through the dark corridors of the castle. There were no other humans anywhere to be seen; the place was utterly deserted. Vibrating softly through the stone walls were the muffled sounds of activity throughout the great castle, but the human leading us never once seemed concerned that we were about to be discovered.

It was an effort to keep up with the human's long strides as she ran, exhausted and weak as we all were, but we managed to keep pace. I did my best to stay by her side.

"Where are you taking us?" I asked her, craning my head up at a sharp angle. She just motioned for me to keep quiet. I suppressed a growl. I wouldn't take such attitude from a fellow dragon, but I had to remind myself that human culture was completely different to ours. Amongst their kind it was completely acceptable to tell others to keep silent, even their superiors. I believed it not to be an intentional display of insolence from the human.

I could hear some of the others start to grumble at the high pace we were forced to keep. I understood their pain; we had been inactive in the dark for a couple of days. We were not in any sort of condition for sprinting through the depths of a human castle. I did not allow myself to show such a weakness.

"What are these all used for?" I asked, trying a different approach to get the human to talk. There were so many old stone rooms down here, and none of them were occupied, or indeed showed any signs of use whatsoever. The human again didn't answer me.

She paused at the bottom of some stairs. At the top was a closed door with daylight streaming through the cracks at its sides. Shadows moved through the light. There were humans there, not very far away.

Marianne knelt down so she could look me in the eye. I tried to hold her gaze, but her eyes kept twitching away, looking at numerous things almost at once.

"There aren't any cameras down here, so as long as you stay quiet, it should be some time before you're noticed," the human whispered. We all froze as some of the shadows seemed to pause beyond the door. Nothing happened, but it was a while before the human started to talk again.

"If you want the Dragon's Head Rune you'll need to go down to the laboratory. Now, I work down there, so I can tell you now that it's heavily guarded during the day. There's another twelve staff down there, and there's always at least six wizards for security. Not everyone here will be as accommodating as me. In fact, everyone else will just throw you straight back into the cell or just flat-out kill you. During the night it's no better. Security never sleeps here and Nightwings is on hand after dark. Trust me on this; you do not want to run in to her."

She held out a piece of paper with some odd markings on it and placed a little mark on it. "Still, you need to get in somehow, so I drew up a quick map so you can... You can read maps right?" she asked as I took the paper in my paw. I looked at the markings and was unable to understand anything I was supposed to be seeing. It was all just lines and squiggles.

"Nataik, can you make sense of it?" I asked the Xigax dragon, passing her the scrap of paper.

Nataik only needed a moment before she nodded her head. "I should be able to get us there, Haeraig," she said, before looking up to the human. "Is this the only way into the laboratory?"

The human shook her head. "It's the only doorway, but there's also all the ventilation systems. If you're able to find a way into that, it should be large enough to fit some of you. I'm not saying that's the best way, but it's a possibility."

Carlee took the map from Nataik and frowned over it.

I felt a surge of fear and excitement, knowing that we were now one step closer to our goal. We were free from our cell and on our way to where the Axinstone was being kept. If we could evade human security, I saw no reason why we couldn't be flying back to Laxtal within the day.

"It won't be easy, Haeraig, but I think I have an idea," Carlee said. There was a gleam in her eye as she glanced across at Inilta.

"Take this as well. I was told you might be hungry," Marianne said, drawing my attention back to her as she placed her heavy bag on the floor. I put my nose over it and caught the scent of meat. It wasn't fresh, but it smelled alright to eat. I thanked the human, for my stomach was aching with hunger. There wouldn't be enough to satisfy us all, but it would be enough to give us that little energy we needed.

"And one last thing," the human said, holding out a strange slender carving of metal. She placed it in my paw. "The key to get out of the dungeons. Please, once you get out, throw it away, somewhere it can never be found. If they catch you with this, they could trace it back to me."

I assured the human that we would do just that. I didn't want her to suffer for helping us. There was only one other thing I wanted to know from the human.

"Have you heard of any other dragons being seen on the island? Two of our company have gone missing, and we'd like to find them again," I asked, hoping for any news of Azlak and Keita.

"I've heard rumours of two more dragons around, but no one really wants to talk about it. It's bad luck to talk about dragons in these parts. It's all the prime minister, you see. He's got it in for your kind and will stop at nothing to see your entire species crushed beneath the boot of humanity. He has enough supporters to carry through his threats too, especially as he has people like George and Rico helping him.

"If I see your friends I'll try and help them however I can, but I can't promise anything," Marianne said. She held out her paw and seemed to wait for me to do something, but I didn't know what she was expecting. She withdrew her arm and coughed.

"Thank you for your help, Marianne," I said. I bowed my head as she turned away to look up the stairs. She smiled and stood up.

"Stay in the shadows and you'll do fine. Now go and find your way down to the lab. You can't be here when I open that door," she said.

With Nataik leading the way, we heeded the human's advice and fled without hesitation. Together with Isikian's help, we dragged the heavy bag along with us. The smell of meat, even cooked and dry, was enough to get my mouth watering.

I trusted Nataik to know where she was going, for every corridor looked exactly the same. It was all dank and dreary stonework lit by a harsh white light emanating from a series of long tubes on the ceiling. Behind us I could hear the quiet sound of a door opening and then being firmly shut again. I hoped Marianne would remain safe. I understood that she had risked a lot in helping us. There were no sounds of pursuit, so for the moment it seemed we were all safe.

We paused to regroup and organise in one of the many cells. Dust motes sparkled in the sunlight that streamed in from a large window near the ceiling. We couldn't go any further without eating, or without having some sort of plan in mind, or else we would just get ourselves captured again. Okazuni was the last to come in, and with Nataik's help he pushed the door closed behind him.

Once I was sure we were safe again, I ripped open the bag. Inside were several large cuts of cooked meat. Enough for a normal meal for us all, but we were all ravenous. It was everything I could do not to growl at the others and gorge myself.

The meat was salted and cooked dry. It was not particularly enjoyable to eat, but it was satisfying to my belly. Soon, not a single scrap remained, no matter how much Okazuni tried to nibble and lick and the small folds in the empty bag.

I felt a little better for the food, but our situation wasn't much improved. We had broken free of the cell, but I didn't know where we were in the castle. My head still ached from the magical assault. One beat of our wings was not enough to succeed. We needed a thermal to lift us higher.

"You said you had a plan, Carlee," I asked the veteran once she had finished eating. She had sat down at the back of the group, who had formed into a semi-circle facing me. Once I had addressed her though, Carlee came to the front. All eyes were on her.

"The human was right. We can't get into the laboratory when the humans guard it so tightly. We need to get the humans out before we even have a chance," she said. "I think I have a way. All human buildings have a device – an 'alarm' I think - that makes a loud noise when it smells fire. When this alarm goes, humans all have to go outside and wait for wailing giant machines, carrying masked humans. These masked humans take charge, and don't allow people back in for a long time. We could make that our opportunity." She looked at Inilta, whose eyes widened as he met her gaze.

"If I can get close enough to the Axinstone, I will have enough power to create an inferno," the Nixan said. Small flames danced over the tips of his claws and his eyes burned with anticipation.

Nataik fluttered her wings to get everyone's attention. "I could take him through the ventilation shafts to get close to the lab. If he'll fit, that is," she said, casting an uncertain eye over the Nixan. I understood her concern. He was not as large as Carlee, but he was certainly thicker built than the slender, serpentine form of the Xigax dragon. We would be relying on him squeezing through the shafts if we wanted this plan to succeed. We had no time to come up with anything else. This was our only chance, and if Inilta was unable to get into the ventilation shafts, then we would have to react accordingly.

"Go," I said, thrilled to finally have a plan that could be actioned. I flicked my tail and pawed at the ground, holding back the nervous excitement. "Okazuni, go with them to the dungeon door, then come back with the key."

The three dragons bowed their heads, then fled the safety of the room. I paced with nervous energy, waiting. For now, it was all I could do. I had to wait until Inilta was able to summon his inferno. Only then could I act, hurrying through the castle towards this laboratory the human had told us about. Once there, we could steal the Axinstone and flee in the chaos Carlee promised.

More than anything, I longed to stretch my wings and fly. I wanted to feel sunlight on my scales. But even that had to wait.

Okazuni soon returned, key in mouth, and curled up in the corner with Carlee. Still I prowled, waiting, hoping. We would have no way of knowing if Nataik and Inilta had been captured. We all had known the risks from the start, but that was little comfort now.

Hours seemed to pass by.

Carlee had spread her wing out over Okazuni. Her span almost completely engulfed the Nyrian dragon as he lay, idly batting the key between his paws until he seemed to grow annoyed with the metallic tinkle as it bounced across the stone.

Isikian was also restless. The Nixan was pacing back and forth beneath the window. His pristine emerald scales shone in the sunlight, producing a radiance my faded green scales could never match. The healer stopped to look out the window, his wings fluttering for balance as he rose onto his hind legs. It took me a few moments, but then I could hear it too: an all-too-familiar concussive beat that was gradually getting louder.

Nightwings was back. Even trapped inside, I could feel the compression of air as the spectre passed overhead. A loud roar followed, and then silence again.

Isikian's reaction was instant. He pushed himself away from the wall and fled straight for the door.

I only just got between Isikian and the door in time to stop him running out on his own. The Nixan tried to claw and scratch at me, but I held firm and didn't allow the larger dragon to push me aside. I put all my weight down on his forepaw and butted upwards with my head, catching the Nixan on the underside of his jaw. His attack immediately ceased.

"I'm sorry, Haeraig. Please, I must warn my brother," he said quietly, turning his head and looking into the ground.

"You won't find him in time, Isikian. Our best chance is to stick to the plan and hope that Nightwings doesn't find us. There's nothing more we can do," I replied. Though the healer hissed, he didn't vocalise his arguments.

In the corner, Carlee rose to her paws and furled her wings, drawing an annoyed whine from the Nyrian curled by her side.

"Anzig is right, young one. We have committed to a course of action. It would be wrong to alter that now," the veteran said. She closed the gap between us and placed a comforting paw on Isikian's forehead. "Nataik and your brother are both smart dragons. They know they're in danger, but they also know how to keep themselves safe."

"But Nightwings is here," Isikian said, before Carlee cut him off.

"If we heard the spectre, then I have no doubt they did too. They'll know she's back. They will keep out of her sight," she said.

Isikian pawed at the ground. "I guess you're right," he said quietly.

"I know I'm right. The best thing we can do now is stick to the plan. A creature as big as Nightwings won't be hard to avoid," Carlee said with a mirthless chuckle. "If she can't see us, she can't hurt us. The human was right. If we stick to the shadows then we stand every chance of succeeding. Your brother and Nataik included."

Isikian sighed and turned away from both of us. He sat down in the sunlit patch in the middle of the room and looked out the window. "I can feel the Axinstone. Can you feel it too, Haeraig? The warmth of raw magic? It's so close now."

I sat down by Isikian's side. "I can feel it. I know I shouldn't, but I can."

Carlee growled as she sat at my other side. She opened her mouth to say something, but was interrupted by a wailing noise that erupted from somewhere above us.

"They've done it!" Isikian cried, leaping to his paws. He was restrained by Carlee, who had placed a paw on the Nixan's tail.

"Give the humans five minutes to evacuate. Then we fly," the veteran said.

I could hear the commotion upstairs; the pounding of human paws, and the anguished cries in their voices. The harsh notes of the alarm prevailed over everything else. From somewhere, I could just make out the roar of Nightwings. Shadows passed by the window above us as the humans escaped outside.

The smell of smoke began to permeate the room. That was what Carlee had been waiting for. She spread her wings and waited for the rest of us to do the same.

"Stay close to my tail. It won't do to get lost now," she said.

"Lead on Carlee. We'll be right behind you," I replied. I had no issue letting Carlee lead now. This was when she would be strongest.

This was it. The culmination of my hastily-spoken plan back in Xital four weeks ago. It was still every bit the dangerous mission it had sounded then, but what felt like a lifetime had passed since that moment. We were deep in human territory. In the depths of a castle. We had no allies and very little prospect of surviving our quest. Nightwings would haunt our every wingbeat. And yet, still we flew on, chasing Carlee's tail as she led us through the dungeons of the castle. We carried the hopes of dragonkind on our backs.

We would not give up.

# CHAPTER NINETEEN

**Azlak**

For two days we had kept out of sight of the humans, as we searched for Haeraig Anzig and his companions. I had tried to follow Maznar's advice and break into the kitchens, but my nerve failed me at the last moment. Though it had been night, and the kitchens appeared deserted, I couldn't bring myself to squeeze through the open window I had found. I had slunk back to Keita, defeated.

We had found a refuge just by the water's edge. On the ocean side of the island, away from the glare of the massive human city of Trevena, was a small beach. Just behind the beach, near where the sand gave way to heather and lavender, was an ancient stone structure. It was a simple thing, consisting of a stone slab held aloft by four vertical support stones. I had no idea what the original purpose was, but it had obviously been placed down by humans long ago. Scratched markings on the stone spoke of gods and firebirds, but I understood little more than that.

The ground beneath our paws was soft and grainy, but it held warmth well, even during the cold nights. Better still, it shielded us from prying human eyes as they crossed the bay, as well as Nightwings as she flew over at dawn and dusk. I had still not caught a proper glimpse of her. She remained an enigmatic spectre of darkness and death.

There was a strange power on the island. Most of the time I felt it as a gentle heat that was both relaxing and energising. Other times it became an agonising burst of white light that disorientated me. Given that Keita didn't seem to feel it, I assumed it was the Axinstone, and what I experienced was its magic as the humans experimented on it.

I knew we were achieving nothing by hiding away in this ancient megalith, but I couldn't muster the courage to go back to the human castle. Keita was no help. She had barely spoken a word since we had come from the caves. Completely ignoring me, she had built a nest of heather to lie on.

Evening was approaching quickly once more. I looked out over the expansive ocean as the shadows from the castle started to creep along the beach. I knew we couldn't stay here forever. There was enough food, thanks to the vast number of seabirds that descended on the island every day, but it would only be a matter of time before we were discovered. I didn't want to know what fate met us then, and thankfully my visions hadn't shown me. The fate of Haeraig Anzig too, remained a mystery. I was sure we would know if he'd been successful in seizing the Axinstone; I imagined the commotion the humans would make. But, apart from the occasional outburst of magic, the island had remained at peace, gently resting. The haeraig was still on the island, but whether or not he remained free was another matter entirely.

I placed my paw on the white lichen-coated support stone and closed my eyes. I felt lost. I wanted to know what course to take. As much as my magic excluded me from my clan, I didn't know how I would be able to cope without it. Not knowing what may happen was a terrifying thought. Of course, I had no control over...

*A shadow descended on the castle. Nightwings disappeared into a great chamber on the side of the island and down into its depths. Silence and a sense of normality swept over the island. Then came a loud explosion and fire erupted from the lower levels of the castle. A great wailing emanated around the island, as smoke and humans billowed out of whatever exit lay close. By the water, two dragons darted out from the shadow of a stone megalith and flew towards the mayhem. They evaded capture and flew into the fiery depths of the burning castle.*

I gasped as a pulse of magic emanated out from the castle. Keita looked up for just a moment, before dipping her head back under her wing. I smiled. That was our signal to act. Was that explosion caused by human or dragon? I didn't know yet, but that didn't matter.

*The same megalith by the ocean. An agonised roar scared a group of seven dragons. A great shadow fell from the sky and impacted the ground behind the smouldering castle. The worst of the fire had been extinguished, but thick black smoke obscured the twilit sky and the first stars of the young night.*

*The dragons looked anxiously amongst themselves. Something wasn't right. Someone was missing...*

I collapsed to the ground, feeling the anguish I was going to feel in the future overwhelm me. Who was it who was missing? The vision had been hazy. I couldn't be sure, but I saw that the two Nixans were there. They were very clear, but the others had been nothing but a blur. I couldn't be certain who was who.

*The mine overlooking the ocean. Seven dragons flew out from the burning island in the distance. One clutched the Axinstone in his paws.*

Seven. Why was it only ever seven dragons? Who was left behind? Which escape was real? Who was destined to remain on the island?

"Azlak..." Keita said uncertainly, the first noise she had made all day. At first I thought it was out of concern for me, but then I heard what I had missed. A deep roar from the mainland. The loud thrum of Nightwings's flight. She was coming back, much earlier than her normal routine.

This was it. I knew it.

"We have to go in," I said, scrambling to my paws. "I've Seen us escaping with the Axinstone. This is our chance." I chose not to say that I had failed to See all eight of us. Keita didn't need to know that.

Keita backed away, shaking her head. "We can't go in, not with Nightwings there." Her tail hit the support stones of our shelter.

"What if Haeraig Anzig starts that explosion? What if he needs our help? I know that we need to be inside that castle. I don't know why, and I don't yet know what we need to do once we get in there, but I do know that we can't just lie out here and do nothing," I said. I flared my wings, making myself look larger, all the while knowing Keita was considerably bigger than me. She was not going to be intimidated by me physically, but to my surprise she did relent.

"I won't stay out here alone," she said, turning her head away. "If you lead, I'll follow."

I nodded, and then slunk out of the megalith to look towards the castle. There was a lot of movement. I had learned that in the evening a lot of the humans would take the short trip across the water back to Trevena. None had any reason to come to the ocean side of the island, so I knew I was safe from observation, at least until the human security completed their once-nightly patrol of the island. That was when we had to hide ourselves in the heather, but that wouldn't be for a few more hours yet. I was sure we'd be long gone by the time they came.

Slowly, Keita emerged from the shelter to wait by my side. She flinched at every movement from across the island and crouched low so that she was barely visible amongst the heather.

Time was hard to judge in some of my visions. I didn't know how long we had to wait before the explosion that marked our signal to fly. I stayed on my paws the whole time, not even daring to take my eyes away from the shadowy castle for a moment, should I miss some crucial detail.

Then it happened.

An eruption of orange flames tinged with flashes of pale blue erupted out of the mainland-side of the castle. I recognised the colour of Inilta's magic and with it, hope coursed through my veins. The others were still alive. This had been dragon-made.

"Come on," I called out to Keita, launching myself into the air. Keita followed just behind, keeping close to my tail as I powered towards the castle. Humans spilled from within, running in all directions. I paid them no heed, and to the most part, they all ignored me. The humans, fearing for their own lives, scattered this way and that, but the calmer ones seemed to head towards the small harbour on the bay side of the island. There weren't many boats there, but already some of the humans were starting to board them.

A few humans yelled out as I flew over them. One or two even tried to reach up and grab us, hands flailing in the air, but none came close. Their lunges seemed more from instinct, than real conviction. I hadn't Seen where in the castle we were supposed to enter, so I used my judgement and angled down towards the lowest level above ground, where I could see an open window. The smoke was strongest here. Surely this could not be far from where the dragons were?

Whereas the outside of the castle looked old, inside seemed much more modern. I was no expert in human technology or architecture, but I could tell that the austere white walls and smooth, reflective floors were much newer than the stonework that formed the outside.

"Where to now?" Keita asked as she landed by my side. Our claws clacked on the smooth floor as we walked. It was difficult to remain standing as the floor was so slippery underpaw.

I looked around, trying to find some sign as to where we should go. Everything all looked the same; vast expanses of white corridors with featureless brown doors hiding small, square rooms. There were few windows, but the building was kept well-lit by a series of bright tubes that were fixed along the ceilings.

*Two dragons crept down a corridor. One red, one gold. They looked at each other, then quickly behind them, startled by something. A door leading off the corridor was almost thrown off its hinges as it crashed open and a human emerged. The human dived down on the gold dragon and snapped his wings before he had chance to react...*

"Fly!" I yelled, leaping into the air just as a door smashed open not far behind us. The human threw himself to the floor. His fingers brushed against my tail as I dived out of his reach.

Keita shrieked as she took to the air, swiping at the human as she flew over him. Her claws drew lines of red on the human's face, just above his eye.

The human took a few moments to stand back up, but in that time we had already flown up and around a corner. He chased not far behind us, but I didn't dare slow to look back. Without any knowledge of where we were going, we flew blindly, twisting and turning down empty corridor after empty corridor. Some turns we made cleanly, others, we scraped along the smooth white surface of the walls. Though we were fortunate not to fly into the path of any other humans, we could not lose our pursuer. The pounding pawsteps of the one chasing us never diminished.

*The gold dragon banked left and dived through an open door. The red ness on his tail just managed to correct her flight to follow him. A heartbeat later, the human giving pursuit ran past, missing the open doorway, but nearly falling from the open window set into the corridor's end wall.*

I almost missed it, but I saw the door just in time to bank to my left. Keita almost crashed into me, but she too was able to make the turn. The room was furnished with a long, thin table in the centre of the room, which we dived under to shelter from the human. Just like in my vision, he did not follow us, but ran on ahead. His pawsteps stopped, and I heard him start muttering, but was unable to make out what he was saying. He stayed there for a few minutes, before slamming a window shut and stalking away. It was only after a few more deep breaths that I had the courage to emerge from beneath the table.

I couldn't stop shaking. If I'd have been a fraction slower, the human would have broken my wings and crippled me. If the loss of my magic frightened me, a dragon without wings was a fate much worse.

"We shouldn't stay here," Keita said in a wavering voice. Slowly she approached the door and looked out into the corridor.

I took a deep breath and shook my wings. She was right. We had no idea if the human was coming back, or if there were any more still inside the building. Despite the alarm that was still going off, I doubted all humans would have abandoned the castle. More than just the one must have stayed behind.

We followed the scent of smoke. Where there was fire, there would be Inilta. I knew that to be true without having to See it. This time Keita led the way, though I would guide her if I caught another brief glimpse of the future. We came across no further humans until we reached a closed metallic door. Smoke poured out through the cracks between the door and the frame. We paused, wondering how we could get past this barrier when, with a loud beep, the door slid open.

There was no time to react before a human female, gasping and wheezing, emerged from the haze. She was joined by two others. For a few moments we all just stood and stared at each other. Finally the first female bent down on one knee. She reached out for me, her hand stopping just before my muzzle.

"Marianne, what are you doing, come on," one of her companions said, pulling her by the hand as she and the third human started running down the corridor.

"Your friends. They're down in the lab. Quickly though, they'll need your help. I think Nightwings is being released again. Good luck, little dragon," the human said, before she finally allowed herself to be pulled along by her insistent companion. She looked back at me and smiled. They were soon out of sight.

"What was that about?" Keita asked. I shook my head. I had no idea, but the confirmation that the others were still alive, and not far ahead, lifted us both.

The smoke was starting to clear as a loud whirring emanated from the walls. Every few feet near the ceiling were a series of small spinning circles sucking the smoke out of the corridors. Though my eyes stung as we scurried down the flight of stairs behind the metallic door, it wasn't long before I could almost see perfectly again.

Strange sounds were coming from where we were running to. I could hear the crackle of the fire as well as feel its heat, though that could also have been the magic emanating from the Axinstone. There were also noises I couldn't identify; loud cracks and pops interspersed with deafening crashes. Above all of that was the sporadic, menacing roar of the great spectre.

Nightwings was down there too.

Keita trod on my tail after hearing the spectre's voice. "What can we do against her?" she squeaked.

Then I heard the voice I had been waiting to hear.

"Cover me Inilta!"

Haeraig Anzig's voice drifted up the stairs, somehow heard over the cacophony of noises that threatened to drown him out. He then yelled out in frustration. Keita had heard him too, and all reservations she had held about Nightwings's presence must have evaporated in the heat of the moment. She bounded down the stairs before I could react. With a frustrated snarl I chased after her, but she was too quick for me.

We emerged into a massive room lit by windows that stretched from floor to high ceiling on one wall. The room was filled with many different bizarre machines and contraptions, the usage for which I couldn't even begin, or care to imagine. The largest machine was topped by a container the size of a dragon. Inside was a shard of rock that pulsed with light and magic. On its surface burned the image of a dragon's head, vivid and alive with flame.

The Axinstone. It was there. So close it would take just a couple of wingbeats to reach it.

But we were not alone. There were six humans, all wearing similar sharp white clothes. One of them held a small firearm, whereas the other five wielded raw magic from their fingers. Arcs of coloured light moved from hand-to-hand as the humans prowled around the room.

The legend was true. Human-Nixans existed.

Inilta was the only defence against them. Fuelled by the Axinstone, his flames intercepted and annulled the humans' magic. The Nixan stood on a table in the middle of the room, while the others cowered beneath. No human was able to get close, but at the same time none of the dragons could break cover to attack the humans. They were caught in a magical standoff, but Inilta was outnumbered.

I could not see Nightwings, but her occasional roars sounded close by, though muffled through the wall on the opposite side of the expansive room. She sounded frustrated, like she was trapped and unable to reach us. I quivered at the sheer volume of her voice. She was out of sight, but I was terrified at her closeness to us all.

The humans had not yet noticed our arrival. We had the chance to surprise them and give the haeraig and Inilta the chance to attack, but I knew we could not proceed without any plan in mind. I put my paw on Keita's tail as she prepared to dive into the room. Wisely, she didn't make any noise of protest, but I could tell from the look of her face that she didn't appreciate being held back.

I quickly looked around, trying to find some vantage point from which to attack the humans, but nothing was close enough without being seen. There didn't seem to be anything for it, other than to blindly leap into the fray. Keita tugged at her tail and tried to free herself of my grip. Reluctantly, I lifted my paw and released her.

She roared, a pitiful imitation of the ferocious snarls Nightwings was making, but it was enough to gain the attention of the humans. A pulse of purple lightning exploded where Keita had been standing moments earlier, the ness having taken to wing just in time.

Inilta quickly reacted to the distraction as an eruption of flames engulfed the human with the firearm. A few bangs emitted from it, seemingly in panic, but no harm came to any dragon. The human started to scream as the flames took hold. The sound was harrowing, but Inilta did not waver as the other humans tried in vain to extinguish the fire.

Haeraig Anzig burst out from his shelter with the other dragons on his tail. They dragged one of the humans to the ground and Nataik quickly choked the life out of it, by squeezing with all her strength around the human's throat. The Human-Nixans were too slow to react to save their colleagues, as the dragons had scattered again before human magic scorched the lifeless bodies they left behind.

Keita joined the fray. She and Okazuni flew amongst the humans, slashing out with tooth and claw. They aimed for the humans' faces, while staying well clear of their magic tipped fingers. Arcs of lightning seared the air. They sizzled and crackled, but never reached their targets as Inilta's fire dampened it every time. The Nixan's power was terrifying.

Carlee and Nataik had also taken to wing. The two nesses hurled any small item they could find at the humans, trying to distract them from effectively attacking the other dragons.

I crept around the edges of the conflict, trying to reach the machines on the far side of the room. In the confusion of the fight, I hoped to reach the Axinstone first.

"Haeraig, no!" Isikian yelled.

Haeraig Anzig had also broken away from the fight, but he was much further ahead than me. He was clinging to the side of the contraption that held the Axinstone and already struggling to open it. He had almost forced it open when the healer's shout distracted him. With a cry, he slipped and fell, only just righting himself in time to swoop away from the hard cold floor.

Nightwings roared again and the entire building shuddered.

"Azlak, get it out of there," Isikian called out as he dodged a bolt of human magic. They were all closing in on the humans now, forcing them to slowly retreat towards the doorway.

I could feel the Axinstone's power. It was like a great heat against my scales as intense as Inilta's flames, but never burning me. There was a voice whispering in my head. It urged me on, willing me to claim the Axinstone for all of dragonkind. The voice was achingly familiar. It was the voice of my saviour: the Laxtal drake with magic.

It took me just a moment to smash the glass that protected the Axinstone. A ringing alarm added its harsh voice to the cacophony of noise. I put it all to the back of my mind as I reached out to the thrumming shard of power and grasped it in my paws. An explosion of white light threw me back into the air, but somehow I clung on to the precious stone as I fell.

The power in my paws was immense. I could feel magic coursing through every scale, swelling up from some deep location within me. Through the white light that enveloped my sight, I Saw images of the future. Eternity expanded within my mind, a golden tree with an infinite number of branches. In that instant I knew everything, every path to take, every action to choose, and every eventuality that could ever be.

My wings had flared to arrest the fall I didn't even realise I was in. I saw nothing of the present, but I knew to react because of the future I Saw. I landed, feeling the cold floor beneath my paws. I was safe here, but as I looked around the room, I could See the dangers that faced the others.

*The four humans were still standing. Spears of flame jabbed at them, but they remained untouched. Three of them held up their hands. A wall of purple and red light surrounded them, shielding them from Inilta's flames. The fourth had conjured a ball of pure magic in her hands.*

*The human threw the roiling sphere at Inilta. The Nixan was too slow to react, and the magic engulfed him. Isikian shrieked in agony as his brother was torn apart by the ball of lightning.*

*The great inferno was extinguished.*

"Inilta, fly!" I yelled. My mind snapped back to the present as my vision played out anew.

The four humans were still standing. Spears of flame jabbed at them, but they remained untouched. Three of them held up their hands. A wall of purple and red light surrounded them, shielding them from Inilta's flames. The fourth had conjured a ball of pure magic in her hands.

The human threw the sphere of magic at Inilta. This time the Nixan was already reacting to my cry and flew into the air just before the crackling ball of lightning struck him.

With a deafening explosion, the magic tore a hole in the side of the room. The building shook as chunks of debris were incinerated in a purple flame that grew in ferocity as it merged with Inilta's blue-tinged conflagration. One of the humans was crushed by the falling debris, and his companions backed away from the flames and crumbling wall.

The allure of the future pulled at my mind again. Infinite possibilities teased my thoughts. I struggled to block them out and focus on the present.

Nightwings roared again, but this time the sound was not muffled. She was not hidden behind any wall. Flashes of her future danced across my vision. Battles she would fight. Betrayals she would initiate and suffer. Deaths she might face and cause. An ever-increasing tally of pain. But also love. I had not expected that.

The spectre snickered – an awful sound that chilled my spine. A shadow moved in the flames as future and present mingled. Fire burned through the future, twisting everything into an inferno none could survive. We needed to leave, and quickly. Or else we would all be destroyed.

Haeraig Anzig called to fly. An unnecessary call as Keita and Okazuni had already fled into the stairwell, with Nataik and Carlee close on their tails. The two Nixans paused momentarily to take the Axinstone from my paws. The twisting conflagration of the future faded. My magic still burned with the proximity of the Axinstone, but I no longer Saw everything.

"Hurry," Isikian whispered to me as he fled, but I glanced back to see the haeraig wasn't moving. He was staring at the fire and the three humans who were battling to extinguish the flames.

"Haeraig, come on," I urged, but he shook his head.

"I have to see her. We must know what she is," he said, batting away my paw as I tried to drag his tail back. He seemed entranced, whether by magic or not, I wasn't sure. We couldn't stay, not even for the few seconds it would take before Nightwings came through the smoke and haze. I didn't need to recognise every possible future to know that.

I struck the haeraig across the face.

He snarled, but we both cowered in fear as a shadow loomed over us. Nightwings chuckled again.

"Hello, Little Ones," she said.

My paws couldn't move. My wings were paralysed.

I forced my head to look up.

Standing in the ruins of the laboratory, sneering down at us, was an ebony dragon that was far bigger than the tallest human, towering over even them. A creature twisted by magic.

"What's the matter, Little Ones? Don't you recognise me?" Nightwings asked. Her red eyes flashed in mirth. She lowered her head, bigger than my body, down to our height. Her hot breath washed over us.

Haeraig Anzig squeaked in utter fear.

There was no mistaking her identity.

"Maznar," I whispered.

Nightwings – Maznar – laughed again. "Fly away Little Ones. Give me the thrill of the hunt. You will not escape this island," she growled.

We needed no other opportunity. With the delirious laughter of Nightwings ringing in our ears, we took to wing and fled before the great spectre changed her mind.

Glass shattered as Nightwings smashed through the great windows of the laboratory. I shared a fearful glance with the haeraig. On our own we were vulnerable, both to the threat of the spectre and humans.

We had lost sight of the others, but I could still hear them in the distance. Keita shouted for us to hurry. Pawsteps of humans were closing in on us. They had joined the chase too.

"Get back to the mine!" I yelled ahead, hoping the others could still hear me. I had Seen them returning to the mainland with the Axinstone. I could only hope that we were living that eventuality. We had to get off this island before Nightwings hunted us all down, but even then, I could not be sure how we could escape her.

Everything was a blur of white walls and floors. I didn't know where we were flying. The others had gone. It was just me and the haeraig. We must have taken a wrong turn somewhere, but the sounds of human pursuit were relentless. They were not giving up on finding us.

"Not that way," I said sharply as Haeraig Anzig had gone to bank to the right. I hadn't Seen anything specific, but I knew that flying down that corridor would lead to death. As if to confirm my fears, I caught sight of a sickly flash of purple magic as we shot past.

The humans were getting closer. A weapon fired with a deafening blast. Something ricocheted off the wall to my right. I had felt the heat as it had passed my wing.

I banked left into yet another corridor, the haeraig following my lead. Orange sunlight almost blinded us. I squinted. The sun was starting to sink below the horizon. If we survived that long, I hoped we could hide under the cover of darkness, but my vision of seven dragons returning had been before sunset. We had to push on and catch up to the others.

The shadow came quickly.

We had no warning before Nightwings's monstrous tail crashed through the windows, sending fragments of glass and stone everywhere. A shard of glass pierced my wing, but I didn't dare pause even for a moment. The spectre-made-flesh roared again, flying just outside the windows. Her wingbeats seemed to be retreating.

Ahead was an open door. Beyond that I could see the shimmering ocean, and further still was a headland upon which stood the mine. Every wingbeat was agony, but still I flew on. I could see my destination, and the other six dragons not too far ahead.

It was only once I flew out into the evening sky that I realised I was no longer being pursued. I was completely alone.

Haeraig Anzig hadn't made it.

# CHAPTER TWENTY

**Anzig**

I had never been more terrified.

Azlak was flying just in front of me. I knew I should have been leading the way, but I had become disorientated in the confusion. I had no idea where we were, or where we were going.

The seer had already corrected my course several times, warning me of danger only his prophetic abilities could know of. But even he seemed unable to find a safe route out of here, and it felt like we were flying in endless loops.

Humans were never far behind. Nightwings – Maznar – the ness Azlak had trusted – was surely nearby.

With an almighty crash, the ceiling collapsed as Nightwings smashed against the window with her tail. The falling debris cut me off from the seer. In panic I flew in the only direction I could: up and out through the tear the spectre had created in the side of the building.

Nightwings's teeth snapped down a muzzle's length from my face.

Instinctively I banked hard to the left, my claws scraping along the tough scales on Nightwings's neck to no effect other than to enrage the great spectre. Her massive jaws followed my every movement. I left my thoughts somewhere behind me as I darted vainly in any direction, trying to evade her ivory teeth. She tracked my every move and was right behind me as I flew back over the castle.

I folded my right wing and spun down between two parapets, hoping the move would shake off the monstrous ness, but she just crashed straight through the stone. She wasn't hindered in the slightest.

"That's not going to work, Little One," Nightwings snickered. She was enjoying this. She toyed with me.

I flashed open both wings and veered away to the right as I plummeted. The move caught the spectre off guard as she flew past me. I heard her shriek out to herself, but I wasn't staying to listen. I had already banked back on myself and was flying as fast as I possibly could in the direction of the mainland. As soon as I was past the castle, I dived low to the ground, hoping I would blend in against the rapidly darkening ground.

Fear brought great speed to my wings, and I quickly covered the short distance between the castle and the beach that ringed the island. There weren't many humans out at the moment. Most had already fled back to the mainland, or were attempting to control the fire that was still raging away inside the laboratory. It was easy to avoid those guarding the shoreline.

A cold shadow passed over me. Almost too late, I looked up and saw Nightwings descending towards me. I had nowhere to go.

She bellowed out a triumphant roar as I desperately tried to gain altitude and change direction at the last moment. I had made it to the top of the trees that grew from the sandy dunes when Nightwings lunged for me.

I flared my wings. Her teeth grazed my side as she overshot me. I cried out in pain, but terror overcame the agony for the moment. The great spectre was in front of me now. She wouldn't be able to surprise me again, but she was also blocking my escape over the water.

Nightwings laughed as she hovered in the air, just out over the water. I was beginning to find it hard to power my left wing. It was reluctant to move at all, making my flight uneven.

"End of the road, Little One. You're going die now. Then I find the rest of your little party. I'll slaughter them all and take the Dragon's Head Rune back to my master," she leered.

I knew there was no hope. Nightwings covered the distance between us with terrifying speed. I reacted with pure instinct, and one beat of my agonised wings lifted me above Nightwings's muzzle as she bit down on the tip of my tail.

Again I shrieked in pain as her teeth mangled the muscles and bones in my tail. I slammed down along the length of her muzzle, as she clenched harder onto my tail.

Through the red fog of pain I saw an opportunity. I slashed out with my claws and raked Nightwings across the eyes. Left. Then Right. Blood poured from her eyes and leaked onto my scales.

The spectre released my tail, flinging me out across the water as she screamed in pain. I felt a momentary pang of sympathy for the Maznar that had helped us: I knew I had likely blinded her, but I could not pity her. This was not Maznar, not anymore. As Nightwings she would have killed us all.

I corrected my flight as best I could, watching on numbly as the spectre fell into the crashing waves. I had been launched high, out over the water. The spectre had thrown me closer to the mainland.

"Little One. Please. Help me. You have to free me," Nightwings cried out, as she surfaced amid the pounding swell. The venom from her voice was gone, but I didn't look back.

Every faltering wingbeat threatened to plunge me into unconsciousness. I could feel a pressure in my skull as my mind tried to fade into darkness. It took all of my focus to just fly in a straight line. I kept veering to the left as my wing failed to function and my tail hung limply behind me, making it difficult to maintain height or direction.

The spectre of Nightwings shrieked one last time. I no longer had any capacity to fear her.

I...

Thought eluded me. Nothing processed.

Was this what dying was like?

I could feel life draining from my body.

My wings collapsed beneath my weight and I fell... much less than I anticipated.

Grass. I could feel grass.

I started laughing. Hysterical despite the agony every breath caused in my chest.

Shadows approached me. Voices spoke to me.

Darkness took me.

# END OF BOOK 1

*The Destiny of Dragons* continues in book 2: Impossible Magic.

# ABOUT THE AUTHOR

J.F.R. Coates was born and raised in picturesque Somerset, England, but she moved to Brisbane, Australia as a teenager. She grew up reading from a young age, starting with Enid Blyton's *The Famous Five* and *Secret Seven*, before finding her calling with J.R.R. Tolkien's *The Hobbit*. Speculative Fiction has gripped her ever since, and now she calls amongst her favourite authors Maggie Furey, Robin Hobb, and Neil Gaiman.

She still lives in Brisbane, where she lives with her husband and – as seems ubiquitous for authors –two cats.

You can follow her on your social media of choice: Twitter, Facebook, Mastodon, Instagram, and Bluesky. Just search for jfrcoates.

She also has a Patreon, which allows for sneak-previews of what's to come, as well as additional stories that fit in around her novels. All support is always gratefully received.

https://www.patreon.com/jfrcoates